A BARON OF BONDS

A CONDUIT OF LIGHT SERIES

BOOK TWO

CHELSEY ANN TOMPKINS

For Reed.
Thank you for responding to a
message about Star Wars.
Thank you for loving me.

AUTHOR'S NOTE

This book warrants a list of content warnings. Oftentimes, these lists also become heavy spoilers for the story ahead, so I have listed them in the back of the book if you would like to read them first. Take care of yourself.

PRONUNCIATION GUIDE

Characters:
    Ash'Arah— ASH-ARE-UH
    Geyrand— (HARD G) G-AIR-AND
    Heimlen— HIGH-M-LEN
    Karus— CAR-US
    Moira— MOY-RUH
    Revich— REV-ICK
    Clairannia— CLAIR-AWE-NEE-UH
    Figuerah— FIG-AIR-UH
    Pompeii— POM-PAY
    Saelyn— SAY-LIN
    Ilyenna— ILL-YEN-UH
    Philius— PHILL-E-US
    Mychael— MY-KAY-EL

Places:
    Arcaynen— ARE-CAY-NEN
    Hyrithia— HIGH-RIH-THEE-UH
    Viridis— VER-IH-DIS

Conduits/magic:
    Medicus— MEH-DIH-CUS
    Iumenta—EYE-YOU-MEN-TAH
    Agricola—AH-GRIH-COLA
    Lapis— LAP-IH-S
    Rhyzolm— R-EYE-ZOLM

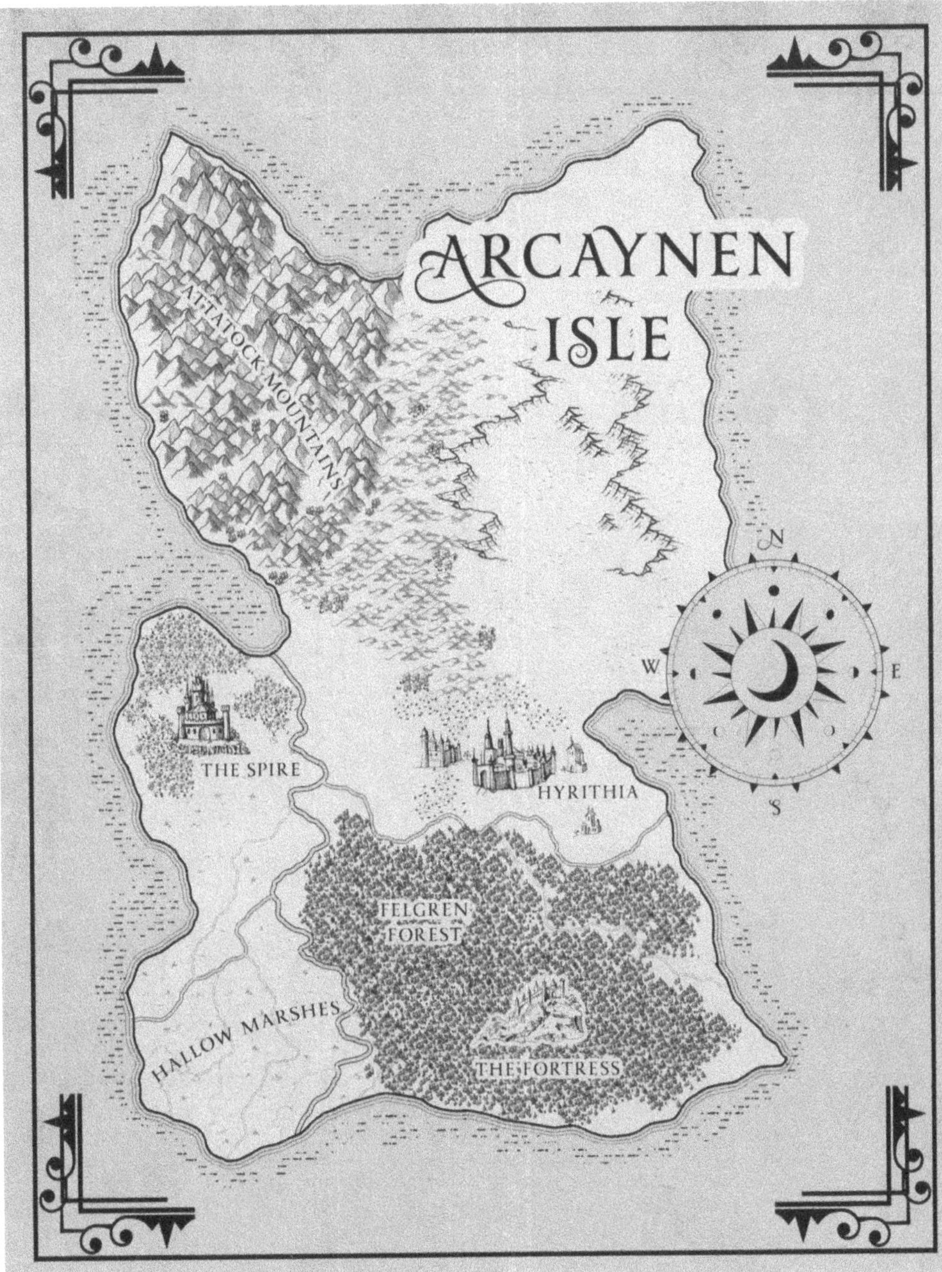

ARCAYNEN ISLE
CATTATOCK MOUNTAINS
THE SPIRE
HYRITHIA
FELGREN FOREST
HALLOW MARSHES
THE FORTRESS
N
W
E
S

PROLOGUE

REV

seven years before

"Eyes like emeralds, Karus, they came to me first."

I adjusted my grip, using my knee to help pull her further into my arms. My heart raced, unwilling to slow. Unwilling were my lungs to breathe without her pressed to my chest. Unwilling were my hands to ever let her go.

Karus did not respond as I shifted her again, one hand grasped around her thigh, her light skirts doing nothing to withhold the shape of it. My other hand was clasped around her arm, my fingers entwined over hers. The crook of my elbow cradled her head. I studied her newly white-streaked hair and the subtle burns on her cheeks and lips from the sun she had held to destroy the Blight.

It'd been nothing short of glorious. The strength and power it must have taken to hold the simulated sun for that long…I was sure it stretched miles.

But she was drained. She lost…something of herself.

I knew she wasn't going to wake and recognize me. I knew she wasn't going to make a miraculous recovery, even with the help of Clairannia's medicus magic. In the very depths of my soul, I knew.

I knew she was lost.

I adjusted her weight again and forced the lump in my throat to move, doing what I could to keep her with me in my arms as I shook.

I'd take forever to get back.

The Fortress with its bleak halls that had begun to seem more like home than anything I'd ever known, could wait.

The world could wait.

The immense power that constantly droned in my skull for the last twenty minutes, asking a question I must answer, could *fucking wait*.

I continued with my story, my words drifting in the night air with no one around to hear.

It was just us.

Only us.

"I remember holding the rhyzolm in my hand and closing my eyes. For the first time, I had been given a task only I could complete, and I took it very seriously. Even at only nineteen," I chuckled. "You were so hidden, Karus. If you'd have used your magic more often, I would have been able to get a better glimpse of who you were and where you were. It took months before I saw any other part of you.

"And I knew. I knew then that I was done for. I knew that those eyes would haunt me for the rest of my days. They'd stay and I'd be powerless against whatever it was that forced me to witness—forced me to see the shape of your face come to light."

I kissed her forehead, slowing even further, the question of power that needed a Baron became but a small sting in my mind.

I would not break. Not yet.

"You were the most beautiful thing I'd ever seen. You'll be glad to know, I was smitten by twenty. And if you would just hear me now, I'd be happy to bear your teasing about it for all of eternity, Karus. If you'd just open your eyes and listen to me now…"

She didn't wake. She didn't bat her eyes in recognition. I wanted her to. I wanted her to look at me with the purest green of life and smile my way. I wanted her to forgive me, yell at me, hate me.

I wanted her to know me.

But she didn't. And she wouldn't.

I continued. A man with little success, but a man with hope, is still alive.

I cleared my throat, tears still at bay. "And so, I followed the pull. That guiding light you shone even when you were not allowed to use it. When I found myself on the outskirts of Hyrithia, I panicked. I would never be able to get to you if you were there. I'd never be able to hold your hand or press my lips to yours if you were there."

The power of the Baron of Felgren *screamed*. It found its way into a place I could not ignore, and I finally addressed its presence.

"What do you want?" I asked aloud into the still snowfall of a winter night, desiring only to be rid of what interrupted me. I had more to say to my love in my arms and it was wasting my fucking time.

"Do you accept, Revich of the Hallow Marshes, the power of the Baron of Felgren?"

It was a living thing. Some ancient power of Felgren with a voice that sounded like the wind through the trees. I would not fear it. I would not dwell on its previous master. There were more important things to do.

"I accept on one condition," I voiced aloud, stopping where I stood in the light dusting of snow, unwilling to continue forward unless I was speaking to *her*. "I want to share this power. I want the ability to split it into two equal pieces upon the time of my choosing." I paused, thinking of how to clarify my demands, understanding how important it was to be precise. "When I give half of my power away to whomever I choose, that person will then accept or reject it. If they accept, half of the power will no longer be mine. It will be theirs to use at their will and I'll have no control over it any longer."

There was a pause. I gazed upon my love, waiting for the wind to reply, uncaring more than I should of its answer.

"You wish to share the power of the Baron of Felgren? This has never been done before and is irreparable should you wish to continue."

"I do. I don't care what has been done before. I will not become Baron of Felgren without the ability to create another while I still hold the title."

I gasped as Karus inhaled, parting her lips to breathe, her eyes still closed. I chose to believe she somehow knew what I would offer her someday.

"Your conditions are met. You will hold all of the power of the Baron of Felgren until you do or do not wish to share it with one other, as long as they pass the Baron trial."

I almost fell. I almost dropped my love.

The rush, the fuel that hit my veins was like a strike of lightning and I knew I could summon the earth to move should I wish it.

I knew I could carry the life of the forest farther than its current boundaries between the great rivers should I so much as speak a word.

This power was great. This power was mighty, all consuming, and yet, I still only desired to share it.

She'd make a great Baron. She'd use it for love, and life, and never for power for power's sake.

By the Blightress, I loved her.

I shifted her weight once more, continuing my steps forward toward the looming black towers of the Fortress, trying to ignore what now flowed through my veins, seeking a release from the cage of my body.

"But that was nothing compared to when I first saw you in front of me," I resumed. "I pretended to be a merchant, bringing mushrooms from Lia's kitchen and bits of things she gave me to sell at market. The guards let me pass on market day, and I was so smug, someday you'll laugh about it."

I grinned down at her serene face, so unlike the panicked features I had endured minutes before. "You were there, as I knew you would be. Don't ask how, love, I just knew. And I watched you. Followed you even. I could not get enough of your movements, your green eyes that lit in laughter as you bartered for your goods. I didn't care about anything but you. I wanted to know you. I wanted *you* to know *me.* I didn't care what Heimlen planned to get you here.

I just knew you needed to come, and for fuck's sake, Karus, I ignored any hint of malice. I ignored any trace of convenience that I should have seen and stopped. It's partly my fault they are dead. It is some blame I will take for the rest of my life that thousands of your people lay in graves and that you mourn them."

The stairs to the blackest fortress of night met the tips of my boots and I regretted not taking longer.

I *should* have taken longer.

They all were there, of course. Clairannia, Figuerah, Moira, Pompeii. My Overseer's forehead was lined with worry and pain as he watched me carry the woman I loved closer to the Fortress.

I did not want to give her up.

I did not want to hand her over even as Figuerah drew nearer, her arms outstretched, her smooth, dark cheeks streaked with tears. The obnoxious faerie fluttered behind her shoulder—a look of concern I didn't know she was capable of on her pointed face.

I kissed my beloved's lips one last time and placed her into Figuerah's arms. Clairannia swept in to squeeze my shoulders, whispering words meant to soothe me, but there was no softness in that moment.

My time was over.

Karus did not know me.

She did not love me.

She did not know the pain she caused, the deep tear on my very soul, and the gutted scrape of an invisible knife at my chest.

I loved her.

I'd loved her for longer than she knew.

But one day she would come back.

One day again, she'd love me, too.

And I held onto that truth in that moment.

I held onto that truth for years to come.

My knees hit the stones of the black staircase as they took her into the Fortress. And it was there, in the early hours of nightfall, that I allowed myself to weep.

PART ONE

CHAPTER 1

REV

"You cannot think of Felgren as just a forest. I'd guess by now, something in your very soul understands that it is not. Something ancient speaks to you. Don't ignore it. Don't ever dismiss it. It is what makes you a channeler. It is what makes you whole."

I cupped my hands into the clear waters of the stream. Tadpoles had hatched a few weeks prior, and I scooped a few of them into my hands, careful to not harm their budding legs.

I had all four of my channelers hanging on my every word. They crept closer, gaining a glimpse at the small creatures I held.

I loved each of my pupils already. Perhaps that was one of my greatest faults—loving so easily. It had caused great pain to many, myself included, when I loved and trusted the man who I thought of as my father. Baron Heimlen, the Baron before me, had murdered thousands of channelers in Hyrithia in order to train the one woman who could save it.

Regardless of my past, these four young channelers had found their way into my heart, and I wanted nothing more than to teach them and protect them from themselves—from the world in which we lived where heartbreak and suffering had once been my only companions.

I knew these wounds, and I knew their purpose, but I would not see these four make my mistakes. I would see them thrive and prosper, finding themselves useful in society outside of this forest and living to their fullest potential. I would teach them to always listen to the people they would serve out of the goodness of their hearts. I would teach them to use their gifts to make the isle a better place to live, and grow, and love.

Those were things I had always had an inkling of, even as a child. And those were the very things Karus had brought out through loving me. I recalled those seven years without her here— just a shell of the woman she was—and I remembered planning our future as Barons. Even if she did not accept, even if she could not bear to take the role of the man who betrayed us both, she would still inspire me to do better. Because of her, I would be a *better* Baron.

I eyed Ilyenna, watching her carefully as she swept her hands through the river rocks. Debris from the bottom swirled and encircled her spread fingers, winding up her wrists. Her conduit ring was a tangle of silver and gold, wrapping around her forefinger in a littering of aquamarine stones which shone in the midday light of the sun. I'd been looking for a lapis conduit for years. I was fairly sure I had found one.

"Do you know, Baron Revich, what happened to that tree?" Talon, the first male channeler in decades, stood sure-footed on top of two large river rocks. His light brown skin looked warm in the sun. His two black braids fell in thick bands down his back as he pointed across the stream to the wall of boulders that rose high before us.

Water trickled through the forest from the Vitra River to the north of Felgren. Years past, this wall of rock and river water fed life into the largest maple tree I had ever discovered in Felgren. Its blackened bark and wood now shone smooth atop the outcropping. Fine shoots of green, new life of the tree, swayed slightly in the afternoon breeze.

"I will tell you a story, Talon, if you'd care to listen." I smirked, jumping over the stream to lean against a nearby tree, hands deep in my pockets, ready to lose myself in one of my favorite stories. Karus had agreed to telling the world about what had lead to our present, saying there was too much to learn from our past to keep any of it hidden.

Talon hopped off the rocks with a swiftness and agility I admired. He and I had been training together in physical strength these past few weeks. Building the muscle back into my body felt right. It helped with the nightmares, too, as by the end of the day, I was exhausted from the energy of a man five years younger who could outrun, out climb, and out balance me.

I had him in arm wrestling, though. Where Talon was toned and lithe, I was building back the dense strength I used to hold. I had begun filling into my clothes again. The garments no longer hung from me in a representation of the disarray of the man I had become.

Ilyenna rose from the water and joined Talon. The redheaded twins, Rell and Renn, fixed their skirts around their knees and sat side by side as they always did. Their bright brown eyes glinted with mischief on their freckled faces as they whispered to one another.

"Once," I began, lowering my voice and relishing in their captivated attention, "a beautiful young channeler was brought to this very stream. She was led here by a strikingly handsome man who was young, foolish, and recklessly in love with her."

"*Karus.*"

The whisper came from Ilyenna and the sidelong look Talon gave her was hard to miss. I had wondered about those two for a while now.

"Yes, though, she had a different name then. Ash'Arah was the name she was born with, but not the name she chose." I cleared my throat, my chest tightening as the memories of that beautiful young woman seven years ago filled my head. "I brought her here to think. To rest. She had just made a discovery I will tell you about another time, and I could only think of this place to take her. I loved it here." I gestured around them. "The stream, the tree, towering as it once was, would glisten in the sunset. Its leaves were massive, bigger than my hand."

I held it up to show them. They waited for me to continue, and I tilted my head back against the tree, looking up at the dark clouds beginning to form in remembrance of that fateful day. "I asked her to show me. I asked her to let me in, to show me the power she held. I wanted to see what she could do. I wanted to know why my rhyzolm had led me to her in our greatest hour of need, revealing her to be the strongest channeler on the isle."

"She did *that*?" Rell pointed to the tree, mouth agape at the mere idea that a new channeler held enough power to burn it.

"Not to start. The first thing she did was tell the tree to bloom. Thousands of its winged seeds engulfed us, settling in on the shore, the rocks, her chestnut hair…it was unlike anything I had ever seen. And she did it without much thought at all."

"Then why did she burn it?" Talon asked, looking back over his shoulder. "Why would she have it bloom and then kill it?"

I chuckled. "It is not dead, Talon. Its shoots are strong and green with life. She burned it, yes, to show me the destruction she could inflict." I stepped forward to the edge of the stream, gazing up at the tree's blackened husk, the promise that it fought to live evident at its base. "But," I continued, looking back at my channelers, "even the most broken things can find their way back to a life worth living."

CHAPTER 2
KARUS

Rain slipped off the tip of my nose, falling far into the dark hole below me. My eyes flicked to the lumens, both frighteningly quiet after their plunge into the damp tunnel. The woman stood, draped in black—a stark contrast to her pale skin and white hair.

The Blightress stared up at me as if she'd always known this moment would come.

I, however, had not.

Seconds ticked by.

I knew I should move.

I knew I should run.

I knew that I had come to a fork of two paths. One led me back to the man I loved—the man I never wanted to hurt again.

The other led to answers. This ancient woman held the answers to the endless questions that rose within me, stinging like needles since the last time I had heard her voice.

I'd spent the last seven years in a mist, and now? Now, I wanted to know *why*. I wanted to know myself again and maybe—just maybe—the woman who could speak into my thoughts could help me.

Her iridescent eyes flickered and her smirk only grew, seeming to know what warred through me like the thunder that warred through the dark sky above us.

"Will you come with me, Little Sprout?"

I wasn't sure if she had spoken aloud or if she had once again spoken in my mind, just as she did months ago when my memories had returned.

"If I go with you, we heal the lumens first." I exhaled slowly, my heart at an erratic pulse as I pulled the rhyzolm from my pocket.

"Little Sprout, I would not leave these marvelous creatures to suffer. Do you think me capable of such a thing?"

I didn't know what she was capable of. I didn't know her other than the stories I'd heard in my childhood. We'd all been told stories of doom if you angered—tales of warning that called the Blightress powerful and menacing, willing to steal you if you fell to your own wrath.

But through some of my early research, the seeds of doubt had already been planted in my mind. Her role in our history held more beneath the surface of what we had been told.

I shook my head silently, thinking carefully of what I could bargain with. She wanted me to follow her into what looked like a tunnel of blighted walls. I knew I would be gone for more than a few minutes and Revich would come looking. If I left the rhyzolm for him to find, it would be alright. Surely, he wouldn't panic if he knew I was alive and that he could follow.

"And…" I added, sliding my legs over the hole, ripping off some of my already torn dress in the movement. "I want to be able to leave when I am ready. I will come with you of my own free will, and I will return of it as well. You will not harm me, the lumens, or anyone I love."

Her eyes ensnared me as they darkened to shades of deep blue, green, and purple. "You would do well, Little Sprout, not to assume you know my intentions. I agree to your terms and offer one of my own."

She lifted her long, pale finger toward the opening above her and dark vines entangled together to form a staircase that led down to where she stood. "You will listen, Karus of Felgren. I will answer the questions I can, but most of all, you will listen."

Nodding, I squeezed the rhyzolm tightly in my hand before subtly placing it on the ripped fabric from my dress, pouring all of my hopes into its green surface. Rev *must* find it. The stone that shared our story must find its way back to him so that he could find his way back to me.

With one final breath, the downpour of rain soaking me through, I pursed my lips and began my descent.

CHAPTER 3

REV

Standing inside Viridis, I reflected on the last time I saw its beauty. Years ago, the gilded halls had shone in the sunlight that would pour through the glass-domed ceiling. The courtyard of swaying tress at its center would softly rustle in an ever-flowing breeze that had no source. But that was Viridis. The magic it contained allowed the unexplainable.

My gaze lifted to the highest levels—fourteen in total—and I did my best to remember what they once were. The Blight now surrounded every surface, every crevice of stone and pocket of books. In those first few years, we had dared to steal books back from its dark grip. The more we did so, the more the Blight grew, until one day it pulled Clairannia into its center. It took all of us to get her out, scraped and bleeding.

I never could hold the *Simulair Solum* spell like Karus could.

I refused to let anyone in from that point forward. Figuerah tried to convince me on several occasions that as long as we all were there, we could save each other from the Blight's desire to consume.

I would not relent. I would not become a Baron who would risk lives at the cost of books. I began sending inquiries throughout

Arcaynen that day, requesting copies of the books in all the libraries of the great cities.

No one had gone back into Viridis until Karus had asked. I had been afraid to say no. *By the Blightress*, I never wanted to say no to her.

Shoving my hands in my pockets, I stepped forward to get a closer look at the trees that grew on the staircase landing. When Karus had cried out in anguish that day weeks ago, the Blight had grown into something I'd never seen before. When she had tried to use her magic to heal the courtyard, she had instead produced these monstrous trees.

There were thirteen of them. Their trunks pulsed still as if in slumbering breaths. Black fruit hung heavily on their branches, but no longer fell to grow new monstrosities.

Seven years after she had destroyed most of it, we still knew little about the Blight. Moira reported to me regularly on what the fae had learned, but with Karus's sun that pushed it back, the concern for the disease was not as forefront in anyone's thinking.

I studied it regularly. It gave me purpose, just as finding the rhyzolm had. All those years, I grasped the hand of hope, refusing to loosen my grip even slightly in fear that even a small slip would cause me to lose her forever.

I knew that when she came back to me, she would want to know more. I knew that when she returned to herself, she would ask what I'd been doing all this time.

I chuckled, kicking aside the pulp of a black fruit that had not rooted into the marble, its pit spilling inky sludge. No, Karus would never let me wallow in my pain. Even when she had been gone from me, I could hear her voice still, urging me to keep going, urging me to keep fighting because I had to. Because it's what she would have done.

I had been Baron of Felgren for seven years without her, but *still* her voice stayed within me. The day she had demanded to know what I was doing about the Blight, I refused to pretend I did not love her. Seeing her rage about what she thought I wasn't doing, I refused to go a single moment longer without telling her the words I was forced to silence for years.

I pulled the pocketknife from my vest and pried a sample of bark from the black tree in front of me. As it gave way, it tore in a sickening sound of flesh ripped from bone. I dropped the dark, sticky wood into a jar, taking a moment to pick up the pit of the black fruit and add it to another.

I corked each lid and wiped my hands and blade with a handkerchief before turning to leave through Viridis's green, glistening portal. As I stepped through, the eerie silence of the desecrated library followed me out into the massive stone hallway in the Fortress.

My gut wrenched at the sight of the enormous rhyzolm on the endless doors of Viridis. The stone marked the portal that would grow if one would say their true name aloud. Again, I wished I had the stone we shared. Karus insisted on taking it with her everywhere, saying it was helping with the return of her memories when she held it.

I didn't like it. I wanted to keep that rhyzolm myself in case…in case I needed it to find her. I feared losing her again every second of every day now that she had come back. There were times these past two months when I couldn't sleep and would take the rhyzolm from the music box at her bedside table, clutching it as I paced the dark halls of the Fortress. It would hum as I held it, pulling me back to where she was as it always had before I gave it to her. Anxieties aside, it was no longer mine to keep. Returning all of her memories, all of herself, was more important than this constant fear of losing her.

My magic shone blue on the way to the laboratorium. A dreary, desolate place, I used it to research the Blight.

"*Incendo*," I murmured, unbuttoning my vest to hang on the rack near the door, donning a black coat to keep the filth of the Blight off my clothes. I set the jars down on the long table and opened the journal I had not touched in weeks.

Karus did not yet know of this place, but I planned to bring her tonight. I had let her in on the details of the last seven years slowly, letting her absorb the events that had led up to her awakening little by little.

I knew she would appreciate this place. I knew she would be proud of the progress I had made, little as it was.

I wrote the date and time in the journal and opened the jars, spilling their contents onto a clean porcelain tray. Using a metal pick, I studied the bark and pit closely, writing notes about their appearance, texture, and smell.

The scent was awful. It always was with the Blight. Every specimen I had ever taken back to the laboratorium reeked of decay, warning the most primal part of me that it was dangerous. Using a small knife and the pick, I split the pit of the fruit. Black liquid seeped onto the tray, viscous and glistening in the bright glow of the flickering torches along the walls.

I let the ooze seep across the surface, watching the reaction of the bark from the deformed tree. As soon as the liquid touched the edges of the wood, it began to pulse as the tree itself had—just as I expected it might.

As with every sample of the Blight I had ever taken, it reacted to its own parts with life. It was as if the fuel it needed to survive was more of itself.

I slumped into the tall black chair beside the table and rubbed the side of my neck. I understood the reaction. I understood the smell, the appearance, the texture. I understood that there were different versions of the Blight—that there were parts of it we still had not seen. But I did not understand its origins. I did not know how it had come to be, why it grew in Karus's presence and magic. Through all these years and research later, I still knew little of what I considered essential to our future.

Once again, I thought of searching Heimlen's study for answers. When I had discovered what was hidden there after Karus had found it first, I refused to go back, disgusted and enraged at the man I thought I knew.

But it might be time. I was stronger now than I had been then, and I knew we needed answers. Karus had proven that the Blight wanted her, and if we were going to stop it from consuming Felgren once more, we were going to have to make the choices we did not want to.

It could wait, though. I would begin my search through Heimlen's study tomorrow, after sending the channelers off on their research in the library we used to store what books we had left. It was possible Karus would want to go with me this time.

No, it was likely. Once she learned of the research I had done, she would want to help me discover more about the Blight.

Lost in thought, I felt a tug on my legs that I knew well. Pompeii was calling me to come to him. Our connection was silent and strong. He had been a good friend to me as Overseer to the Fortress before Karus had fallen, and since then, we had grown into family.

I stood and stretched. I knew better than to leave the specimens out on the tray. I had made that mistake only once before, discovering hours later that two separate pieces of the Blight left out together had grown into something new and steadily pulsing across the long table.

I took a large jar from the shelf and scraped everything into it before wiping the tray clean with the towels I used in my research, tossing them into a bin by the door for Pompeii to wash later.

The tug on my legs was more insistent this time, so I quickly wrote down what I'd observed before closing the journal and sliding out of my black coat. I rinsed my hands in the basin and opened the door, heading to Pompeii who pulled me to the foyer.

CHAPTER 4
KARUS

I kneeled before the lumens, smoothing back Parvus's ear while carefully examining his leg. I had no doubt it was broken, and looking at Rauca's, I knew hers were, too.

I whispered, *"Sarchio"* and watched as my dark green magic swirled around Parvus's wound in an attempt to mend what bone had been broken when he had fallen into the tunnel.

Long, pale fingers, cold and soft, covered my hand as black wisps of the Blightress's power swirled with mine. Parvus whimpered, and I looked into those eerie, iridescent eyes in panic, thinking she was doing more harm and already betraying her word.

She grinned, her wide mouth red and lovely, as she murmured, "Look, Karus. Look at what we have done together."

I turned my head back to the lumen's broken leg and watched it straighten and grow stronger, the fur repairing itself before my eyes. Parvus stood slowly, then stretched with his front legs forward, yawning in a nervous way before walking to Rauca to inspect her.

I took the Blightress's hand and moved both of us to the lumen, whispering the healing word over her back legs, and again watching in disbelief as both of them healed quickly.

I had never mended anything so fast before. Clairannia had

recently taught me more of her medicus magic, and though I had seen some success with my words, nothing had been remotely close to mending bone.

I stood as Rauca did, the lumens giving each other licks and assurance that they were alright.

I turned to the Blightress. "You are still so powerful. After centuries…"

She stood as well, that wide grin gleaming across her face. "Yes, Little Sprout. I still hold power, for there is power in wrath, as you have recently discovered."

I shook my head and let loose a breath, reminding myself I needed this and that I'd only be gone for a short while.

"I am listening then. You have done as I've asked so far, so I will listen. Tell me your story."

She stroked the top of Parvus's head, her long black nails scratching behind his ears as he panted happily, his tongue lolling out of his mouth now that he was out of danger.

The opening above us began to close in a groaning portrayal of roots weaving together to shut us out from the surface.

In the last glimpse of light before we were flooded into pitch black, the Blightress pointed down the tunnel. "Use your light, Karus, to see. For I have something to show you."

CHAPTER 5

SAELYN

I was seven years old, and I only knew Felgren.

I knew it had existed forever, and I knew that it was more than a place.

Felgren lived.

It lived through the roots and earth. It lived through the giant wolves and even the smallest creatures that scuttled through the underbrush.

I laid on my back, my long hair sprawled out around me, the sun glistening through the trees, blinking hello as the breeze shifted the branches.

"Saelyn!"

I heard my name called again, but I did not wish to go. Why would I leave my bed of soft dirt and tickling grass? Why would I rise to hear a half-hearted scolding from Pah-Pah before he snuck me treats and sent me on my way?

I was seven, and I knew Felgren lived in me.

I knew that our fates were linked forever by its past and my future.

I sighed and giggled as roots of the trees twisted around my arms. Felgren wanted me to stay, too. So, I nestled more into my forest bed, closed my eyes, and ignored my name being called on the wind.

CHAPTER 6
REV

I walked into chaos.

Pompeii was shouting at Moira, who was desperately attempting to open the heavy doors to Felgren. Clairannia and Figuerah were speaking hurriedly to the channelers, and Lia, our resident cook, was pacing in front of the dining hall doors, wringing her hands on her apron.

"Where is she?"

At the tone of my voice that vibrated off the stone hall, everyone turned and one look from Pompeii had me riddled with fear.

He stepped forward and placed a hand on my shoulder. "We don't know. She has not returned since this morning."

"She was supposed to meet me and Lia to bake cinnamon buns before lunch." Moira stopped her attempt to open doors of wood and iron and flew in circles around our heads. "When I came to the kitchens, Lia had not seen her since breakfast."

"Fuck." It was all I could say as I brushed Pompeii's hand from my shoulder, throwing open the doors and doing my best to subdue utter panic.

"Parvus and Rauca are missing, too!" Figuerah shouted behind me as she and Clairannia followed while Moira raced ahead. "We were just at the den with the channelers—there was no sign of them." She placed two fingers in her mouth and a high-pitched whistle pierced through the downpour of rain.

Fuck, fuck, fuck.

Karus must be hurt. She must be unable to get back to the Fortress or send the lumens ahead of her. She wouldn't leave willingly—that I knew.

Figuerah's call and iumenta magic had three lumens racing toward us. We had no time for saddles. We had no time to waste.

I pulled myself onto a lumen, pure black, with eyes glinting silver in the gray light. "Moira, lead us to the field you and Karus explored yesterday. She mentioned a field of clover."

With the faerie ahead and two conduits behind, we raced through the trees, each of us fearing the worst.

CHAPTER 7
KARUS

Sitting on Parvus's back, the dim glow of my green light pulsed to my heartbeat. My orb of magic was steady, strong, and pounded eerily to the rhythm of the Blight's roots around us.

The tunnel I had entered an hour ago was lined with these roots, and I understood then just how deep the parasitic growth ran. The Blight had been gone from the field of clover above, but its roots had never receded.

The Blightress rode ahead of me on Rauca. Both lumens did not seem to fear her or where we were, which helped calm my nerves. She did not speak again for some time, and I tried to hold back all of the questions I desperately held.

I knew I was on borrowed time.

"How much further? I can't be away too long. They will be looking for me soon."

The Blightress turned her head, her golden crown reflecting in my green light. "Do you mean the Baron? Is that who will look for you, Karus?"

I swallowed. "Yes."

She tsked and sighed heavily in the stale air. "Have you forgotten his betrayal then?"

I inhaled deeply, attempting to steady myself. "How is it you know so much about my life?"

"How is it you know so little of mine?" She turned back to face the tunnel ahead which loomed well beyond my vision. "I have been listening, Little Sprout. You, however, have not."

I clenched my jaw. "Why do you call me that? You used that same term when you helped me wake weeks ago. What does it mean?"

"Precisely what you think. I see you as a little sprout. Just awakened to the surface, not yet everything you have the potential to be. You bask in rays and soak in the rain, yet you do not know what you will become."

My anger rose swiftly to the surface. I was growing tired of this charade as my guilt of Revich's reaction to discovering me gone began to overtake my need for answers.

"And you do? You think that because you can speak to me in my mind and help me heal the lumens that you know me? That you understand my power? Yes, Revich will look for me. He will search to the ends of the isle for me and when I return to him, he will be angry with me and love me still. How dare you question him," I warned. "You know nothing of us."

"I know Barons," she countered. "I know their power. I am intimately aware of their strength as the Barons of Felgren."

She slid off Rauca's back and patted her head, moving to her back legs to inspect their healing. "We are here, Karus."

I glanced around, finding that where we'd traveled in the blighted tunnel looked no different than where we had been moving the last hour. Behind us was a dark path and before us was utter abyss. The constant pulsing of the roots along the dirt walls was beginning to drive me mad.

"What is it you wanted to show me? And what do you mean you know the strength of Barons?"

"You'll rush my story, Little Sprout, with all these questions. A good story is told in many parts over much time."

"Stop toying with me!" My voice sunk into the dirt walls, barely traveling through the tunnel. I jumped off Parvus's back and seethed before her, done with her cryptic way of speaking.

Her head tilted. "Would you believe I never once stole a child when they showed their anger?" She grinned in cloying amusement, referring to the nursery rhymes parents told their children about the Blightress. "Since the days of old, my anger has been touted as something to fear, something to avoid, and yet,"—she gripped my arm firmly, her long black nails digging into my skin and pulling me closer to the walls of the tunnel—"anger has never been my downfall, Karus. Nor yours."

I squinted in my pulsing light. Black blooms formed along the blighted roots. More and more of them budded and bloomed down the dirt-clotted walls, and the pulsing of my orb quickened along with my heartbeat.

I reached out to touch the soft petals. My conduit ring, given back to me by my love, seemed to glisten brighter in the darkness.

Each bloom was small, no bigger than the tips of my fingers, and each held a glowing blue center. They nestled together, hundreds of them now, clustered and growing from each of the Blight's roots.

"I've never seen these before," I whispered in the stillness.

The Blightress bent down to inhale the blooms' scent. I smelled it too. A salty breeze mixed with decay overpowered my nose.

"As I said, you do not yet know what you will become, nor what your anger can do." She reached out to brush the white streaks of hair that fell to frame my face—the color matching her own. "I know how you got these, Karus. I know what it takes to be strong when you have no other choice. And I know what power is held in anger. Let me teach you. Let me show you what you can become when you embrace what lives inside."

She clicked her tongue and called the lumens to the dark shadows ahead of us. "Go on," she called to them both, and before I could move to stop them, they jumped into the dark, disappearing immediately.

"Is that a portal?" I stated in shock, realizing now that the darkness ahead of us appeared misty, yet flat, as if it held a surface.

"It is. I cannot produce them as I once could, but I keep this one here so that I may return to Felgren from my home when I wish."

I stepped closer, my curiosity reeling me forward. "Where is home for you?"

She moved beside me, silent, tall, and cold. "If you wish to know, you must follow your lumens and see." She placed a delicate hand into the portal, swirling the black mist and laughing to herself. "Our bargain still stands. You may leave when you are ready and no harm will come to you or anyone you love."

She took a step into the portal and I heard her last words before she left completely. "Curiosity is nothing to fear, Little Sprout."

CHAPTER 8

SAELYN

I was ten, and I understood why my mother struggled to look at me.

Pah-Pah smiled my way, remarking, "My, my, Sae, each day you look more and more like your father. It's as if I'm teaching *him* to whistle through the grass, not his daughter."

The man who I thought of as my grandfather was sitting cross-legged in front of me, Thevin to the side.

"Who do *I* look most like, would you say?" Thevin asked, and I rolled my eyes, pulling a thick blade of grass to use as a new whistle.

"You know perfectly well you look exactly like your mother." Pah-Pah raised a sharp brow, adjusting his hold on the grass.

"You just want to talk about *you* all the time, Thevin." I shoved him and his dimpled smile lit his face in mischief.

"Do not." He shook his head of golden curls and stuck his tongue out at me.

"Do, too!" I stuck mine right back out at him, making a face that I hoped he found disgusting.

"Children," Pah-Pah scolded, interrupting our usual argument, "we are not bickering or making faces. We are learning how to whistle through the grass, and if I must, I will send you back to your rooms where both of your mothers can reprimand you as they wish."

I sighed and settled back to my task, pulling the blade taught between my thumbs. "Tell me more about my father, Pah-Pah," I spoke sweetly, knowing full well everything there was to know about him already.

"Your mother named you after your father, as you know. You have your father's eyes and hair. His mannerisms, his humor. I miss him, but watching you grow up helps a little." He blew between his thumbs and a sharp trilling sound flew through the trees.

"My mother misses him, too." I looked down to my lap, recalling our last conversation at breakfast this morning. Her words had been short, her lips taut and thin. She hadn't even looked me in the eyes.

My mother was powerful. It seemed to run through my family as I knew my father had been too. With each day, my own power grew. Even at ten, I knew it would one day surpass her own. I wondered if it would surpass everyone's.

"Yes, my little one. Your mother misses your father, too." Pah-Pah grinned as a dull noise came from my hands. It was not a true whistle yet, but at least I had made more sound than Thevin had managed. I grinned smugly at him and he shoved me away.

Thevin and I had grown up in Felgren together, both born in the forest and only a few months apart. Though, in the past few years he was often gone, traveling with his parents to distant places that I longed to see. Every summer, he would return, just as annoying, but just as fun as the last.

I shoved him back, this time so hard he fell over, and I let out a yell of triumph before landing on top of him to pin him to the ground, giggling in our usual game.

Pah-Pah sighed and threw grass on top of us as we tumbled and rolled along the open field, both trying to pin the other.

It was good to be ten.

It was good to be loved.

And as we rolled, I heard my name as it was whispered on the wind.

CHAPTER 9
REV

The rain was relentless.

So was my heartbeat as it tore through my chest. I stood in a hardened calm, knowing I could snap at any moment.

Moira had led us to the field of clover and I recognized it as a place the Blight once grew.

I scanned the field's edge, looking for any sign of a fight. Figuerah encased her hands with her golden magic, whispering to the three lumens we'd brought with us. She would be able to use her iumenta power to guide them in their hunt for Karus.

Clairannia had already run to the middle of the field, yelling her name, though it was cut short by the downpour and barely audible across the field.

I tried to think like Karus.

She would not just leave me. She would know my panic, my torment when we discovered that she had not returned.

I refused to dwell on thoughts of her death.

I would not fucking *believe* that she had come back to me after seven years only to die two months later.

No.

If she was hurt, if she was conscious, she would have tried to leave a sign of herself.

"Figuerah," I called, "can you communicate to the lumens to look for a rhyzolm?"

I knew exactly what she would have done. She would have been clever, leaving behind what I could use to find her again.

"Karus's rhyzolm?" Figuerah thought for a moment and then continued to swirl her magic in front of the three lumens sitting in rapt attention.

I felt useless.

All I could provide was rage and panic. I could move mountains, rivers, and trees if I so desired. I could move the very earth we stood upon, but that would not bring us to Karus.

I began to walk the perimeter of the soggy field, rain pouring off my face, slipping from my hair, chilling my very soul. I called her name over and over just to hear it, announcing to the world I still needed her and would not let her go.

There must be something. Some sign of struggle, some reason she had left this place. Again, my thoughts turned to her in pain somewhere, dragged off by some creature, or fallen with a broken leg and bleeding.

Figuerah gave her last command and the lumens sprinted across the field, circling around one spot in the middle. The black lumen I rode looked at me before raising his massive head to howl through the rain.

I ran to him as he caught another trail, leading all of us in a straight line to the edge of the trees. Ahead, something white lay in the clover and the lumen picked it up in his mouth.

My knees hit the ground in a squelch, and I recognized a piece of Karus's torn dress. Some relief swept through me, though new questions arose.

I turned to the black lumen and he panted, spitting the rhyzolm onto my hand.

"Good boy," I muttered, patting his snout before he rose his head to howl once more.

I stood and closed my eyes, squeezing the stone tightly. Its cool surface hummed, and I almost cried out, thankful that my love was not dead.

"What is it?" Moira buzzed in my ear as Clairannia and Figuerah caught up to us.

"It's the rhyzolm. She left it here for me to find."

"Can you sense her? Can it lead you to her?" Moira flew to the top of the lumen's head, landing there and petting him softly.

"Yes. She is alive. I cannot tell if she is hurt, but I know she is alive."

I turned north, scanning the tree line, knowing I had quite the journey ahead.

"Well, where is she, Revich? What direction has she gone?" Figuerah asked in exasperation.

"She is north of here." I mounted my lumen, needing to get back to the Fortress for supplies. "She is nearing the boundaries of Hyrithia."

CHAPTER 10
KARUS

"*Karus!*"

My name from Revich's lips pierced the space of what was the absence of light.

In my first step through the Blightress's portal, his desperate call revealed my mistake. His anguished roar pierced my heart while the relentless chill of doubt settled into my skin.

"Revich?" I turned, not knowing which direction in the darkness that engulfed me.

He yelled my name again, and I screamed his.

I should not have done this.

"Revich!" I cried again, no longer hearing my own name in the abyssal black.

If this really was a portal, I had not transported to the other side.

I had been through two in my lifetime. Both had been green, both had transported me instantly across a span of distance I did not know.

I looked down to my hands. I could not see them. I closed my eyes and the place I stood looked no different. I felt the tears threaten to fall and took a breath. Opening my eyes again, I reproduced my orb of light, whispering, *"Illuminare"* and stepped in the direction I hoped was forward.

The cold of the void seeped through my skin, through my soaked dress that had hardly begun to dry in the blighted tunnel. I took what strength I had left and steadied my heart.

I felt pulled, yanked in many different directions since I'd entered the portal. I turned my head, unwilling to turn my feet, convinced that I needed to decide on a way that was forward.

It was all dark. It was all the blackest of space in the utter deprivation of light.

I walked on, nothing changing, no sign of anything but vacancy.

Was I supposed to do something? Say something? How had the lumens made it through this abyss, and what secret did the Blightress know and should have told me?

I continued walking, never knowing how long, unable to time the moments that had already passed. My green light pulsed, the only evidence that time moved at all.

Flare…dim.

Flare…dim.

Flare.

Nothingness surrounded me. Endless space of…nothing. Any hope I held dwindled rapidly like the last rays of light at deep dusk, and I caught myself slipping into madness.

I began to speak, my voice soft and stagnated in the dim light. "My name is Karus," I began, clearing my throat of its imperfections. "It means beloved."

I thought of what I might say to the Blightress's portal. I thought of what I could possibly confess to leave.

"I chose my name. I took it for my own. I have been loved so fiercely in the last seven years, that I do not recognize anything but beloved."

My light pulsed brighter, faster, evidence of my body's refusal to stay calm and quiet.

"I am loved by many, and I love them in return, but my heart belongs to one man."

Please let this be what the portal needed. If the doors to Viridis could request the soul who enters to know themselves at their truest name, it was possible this portal requested something of its inhabitant as well.

"Rev. His name is Rev. He loves me more than I can explain, more than words could ever weave to tell, and his heart is mine, and I—" I wiped the tears that fell down my cheeks, wanting to fall with them.

My feet pushed me forward, even in my stumble, my soul continually being pulled all over.

Minutes passed. An hour.

In my creeping insanity, I stiffened and promised myself that I would get out. I *must* get out. I didn't care anymore about the answers to my questions. No one who would trap me in a portal could possibly help me understand more of myself.

I didn't want to know her. I didn't want to leave the lumens, but I would. I would fight my way back to Revich and *never* leave his side again.

I wiped my nose with my sleeve and spoke into the dark. "I must get back to him. I cannot stay here. I *will not* stay here!"

A determined rage burned from the deepest part of me, and I seethed my next words. "I will leave. *Now.* I'm *done* with this place."

I turned around, no longer caring if I lost all sense of the direction I had gone.

Faster now—flare, dim, flare, dim.

"Do you hear me!" I screamed. "I will leave! Show me the way out! NOW!"

A light blinded me, and I fell forward, catching myself with my hands. My orb of light extinguished the moment they touched the rocky earth.

Hard, wet, solid earth. I muffled a cry of relief, shielding my eyes.

I'd tumbled into a massive cave, the light of the surface beaming through a small opening above.

I glanced behind to see the swirling mist of black—the portal had let me go, or I had forced myself from it. I didn't know which, and I was too relieved to care.

I stood and wiped my wet hands on my dried dress. The previously white fibers were now gray and dull.

How much time had passed? In my heart, I refused to believe it had been more than an hour or two, but based on the stiff, dry, and discolored fabric of my dress, I knew it had been longer.

I wiped my eyes, rubbing them as they adjusted to the light. I was standing in a cave at least double the size of Viridis. The sound of water trickled down the walls, leaving the air riddled with moisture.

I took in my surroundings. A structure hung in the middle of the cave, tree-like limbs sprouting from its top, tangled and black. They adhered to the cave ceiling, and I rubbed my eyes once more, unsure of what I had just seen.

Thump, thump.

Thump, thump.

A monstrous heart beat steadily, hanging heavily from the cave like a grotesque abscess born from wrath and ruin.

For that's what it exuded. The unmistakable feeling of anger, deep and destructive, seeped through each beat, as the heart cast a dull, crimson glow through the cavern.

I stood for a moment, staring at what hung enormous before me. Each pulse beat with me. Each echo of the throbbing mass of blood and flesh reflected inside my own chest.

I told myself I didn't care.

I convinced myself that I couldn't stop, couldn't process what this meant or whose heart this was.

I had somewhere to be, and it was not here. It was not in this cave, even with realization pouring through me and more questions forming at its presence.

It could wait. Everything could wait, and I refused to stay any longer.

I continued forward, stumbling over the jagged, rocky ground, slick with algae. I looked for an entrance to another tunnel or door of some kind, my resolute heart refusing to contemplate the constant beating I knew well.

I spied what looked like steps upward, and following the ridge, I saw their end at the entrance to the surface above. I ran to their base, taking a moment to breathe, reminding myself that I had a long way to go.

I took each step with care, whispering, *"I will get out. I will find him. I will get out. I will find my way back to him."*

I repeated the words over and over, never stumbling, never slipping on the endless stone steps. I would not falter and I would not fail.

As I neared the top, I looked down onto the growth still beating, still mocking me in its steady, unyielding pulse.

I shivered, my resolve releasing just a moment before I caught myself again, refusing to stop any longer. I took each step quicker, still careful, still cautious of my feet which tended to trip on the simplest of things.

The fresh air above me became a welcome wave of cool salvation. I gripped the edge of the hole above as I finally reached my destination and pulled myself up completely, ignoring the last few steps.

I curled my fingers around wet grass, pulling at their roots, a cry escaping my throat as I let myself sob. I pulled my legs to my chest, my face lying against the muddy ground.

It was there, in the first rays of dawn, that I let my body release its fear, its anger, and its repulsion for what I'd just seen and been through. My tears fell, unheard and unfaltering, as they soaked through the ground that fed the heart of the Blight beneath.

CHAPTER II

KARUS

I counted the minutes passing.

Five. Fifteen. Thirty-three.

I hated what I had done, and even more, I hated that I had chosen to do it. In all my years of living, I had made some terrible choices and this was one of them.

If the Blightress really wanted to speak with me, she could have done so from that hole. I could have gotten help for the lumens, and we all could've…

My head pounded with the choices I could have made. Revich's scream of my name replayed over and over as I flipped onto my back, shivering on the wet ground.

I closed my eyes and imagined his heat pressed to mine, his soft lips grazing my neck as he trailed his hands to my legs, lifting them to wrap around his waist.

I decided I didn't deserve him.

Our companion ceremony was only weeks away and I would be bound to a man I could not live without who deserved a woman with more sense than me.

I struck the palm of my hand into the soggy earth in anger and ripped the grass from its weak roots. What was the use of all my magic if I could not simply create my own portal and travel back into his arms?

I finally sat up and looked around. My memories of his warm breath on my skin forced blood to pump steadily through my stiff limbs.

I was in a murky forest. Tall trees loomed and puddles of still water, dark and foul-smelling, encompassed the landscape for as far as I could see. Rocks and jagged boulders sliced from the earth like bones exposed from skin.

I hated this place.

I hated the consequences of the decision I'd made, and as I dug the dirt out of my longer fingernails, I admitted that I hated the Blightress, too.

I WAS WEAK, STUMBLING THROUGH A FOREST THAT WAS NOT MINE. There were trees, and moss, and small creatures darting throughout, but it was not Felgren. This place had a dark aura, a desolate embodiment of what I assumed was the Blightress's presence.

I wondered in my haze, my stomach growling endlessly, where she was now, convinced if I saw her again, I'd do what I could to force her to send me back.

Realizing my stupidity and waste of time, I called for Parvus. If he and Rauca were still here, I could try to weave my power into the call as I had seen Figuerah do with her Iumenta magic before.

I brought my fingers to my mouth, disgusting as they were, and whistled. My power swirled and seemed to dissipate through the emaciated growth of trees.

At the sound that disturbed the deathly stillness of the wood, I heard the groan of roots and branches ahead. My blood chilled as an impossible creature of legs and limbs began to take shape. Its features formed from what was once a sickly-looking tree covered in moss and fungus.

It rose from bended limbs, its tangle of branches at the top of its canopy forming into eye sockets, a jaw, and then a long, ragged neck. The sound of its transformation stilled my body and I watched in the deepest fear as it lifted a leg from the roots of the earth and took a step in my direction.

I missed the pounding of heavy feet as Parvus bounded to my side and nudged under my legs to lift me onto his back, hardly slowing his gait. I barely caught his fur as the creature formed from the forest opened its jaws in a sickening snap of twigs and vines, revealing an imitation of sharp teeth that I knew could break bones. It roared in a thundering wave of ancient fury that resounded through the forest and was returned somewhere nearby.

Parvus ran faster than I had ever seen, darting over rocks and splashing through the rumbling puddles of clouded water. I clung to the fur at his neck, yelling all the spell enhancements I could remember in an attempt to stop the creature.

"*Fulgyren!*" I shouted, lightning striking its wood exterior, doing little more than angering it as the roar came again. More of the forest began to move in the same haunting way. More hideous limbs stretched out over the earth, and more snapping of jaws echoed through the trees as two more creatures began to take chase.

"Parvus! They're gaining!" His howl erupted as he picked up even more speed and I sent my power out in an attempt to set the monsters aflame.

A ragged branch swiped out, its rough bark slicing my cheek as fire crackled through the forest and the creatures roared again, this time in pain.

We raced toward a dark cliff, the other side an impossible leap.

"Parvus!" I screamed, my grip tightening on his gray fur, urging him to stop before we toppled into oblivion and a sure death.

He leapt without hesitation and we flew through the air with a raging river a few hundred feet below us. I pushed my face into his neck, bracing for an impact that did not come.

We pounded onto the other side of the ravine and Parvus turned to watch the creatures shrieking, their bark skin blackened from my fire, but no longer burning.

The leap was impossible. Parvus had jumped over fifty feet, and I did not understand how we still lived.

I slid off his back, hitting the ground hard, rolling my ankle in the sticky mud and looked up at the giant wolf. He panted with his usual grin, tongue lolling to one side. He closed his mouth and watched the creatures turn and leave on the other side of the ravine.

I had fallen quite far and immediately realized why. Parvus stood twice his usual height with long legs grown into muddy fur and dark branches which looked eerily like the thorny limbs of the Blight.

"Parvus?" I gasped, my lip trembling in fear of what had been done to my friend.

His legs began to sink into the ground, the black limbs fading to the shape and length of what was normal for a lumen.

I shook my head in disbelief.

It was wrong.

It was all wrong since I had lowered myself into that hole in the field of clover.

"What has she done to you?" I whispered, righting myself and pulling his face to my chest, holding onto the lumen who had been my partner since arriving in Felgren over seven years ago.

He licked my bleeding cheek and whined—his usual way of telling me he was concerned for me, as if I was the one who just sprouted black, woody legs and leapt an impossible distance.

"Parvus, where is Rauca? We need to leave. We need to get back to Felgren."

He licked me again and turned his body in a motion to hop back onto his back. I did so and scratched his ears, thanking him for saving me.

My ankle was sore, but I decided to save my strength and not heal it or the gash on my face. I was weaker now and knew I might need what magic I had left to make it through whatever came next.

CHAPTER 12

SAELYN

I was fourteen, and I was clever.

I had already devoured all of the books I could get my hands on about magic and had found scraps of writings and scrolls in places where I was not supposed to be.

My mother was busy with her duties and I didn't mind her absence so much now that I could practice magic on my own.

I missed Thevin that winter, partially because he had become more interesting in the last few years and partially because I couldn't wait to show him all the different magic I could perform.

I pulled my cloak closer to my cheeks and whispered to the frost-bitten leaves of a fern that had so stubbornly stayed green since winter's arrival. My magic swirled from my hands, melting the ice and righting the tips of the verdant blades. I giggled, delighted in my power.

"Saelyn, where did you learn to do that?"

I jumped at Pah-Pah's voice behind me. "I—"

"You know you are not to get ahead of your studies, child, and your mother will be very cross when she learns that you have defied her wishes yet *again*." He shook his head and held out a hand to help me up from the snowy ground.

I frowned, angry that he had discovered me practicing my power. I did not like how closely I was watched these days and resented that my mother felt it needed to be done.

She was right, though. I cared little for her rules and did not understand their necessity. I was growing into a young woman now, and I deserved to be treated with the proper amount of respect and space.

I sighed and kept my hands where they lie in my lap, muttering, "*Revertayden en tepiore.*"

I watched as the leaves of the fern reversed to ice again and Pah-Pah's steps flowed backward.

I did my best to look at him innocently as he smiled at me, approaching again, but for him, what would be the first time.

"Saelyn, I'm glad I found you. It's freezing out in the cold, child. Come, your mother is asking for you to join her for lunch."

Pah-Pah held out a hand encased in a warm, wool glove for me to take.

Yes, I was too clever and powerful by half, and my own mother didn't know the whole of it.

I turned back to look at the frost-bitten leaves of the fern, already plotting to come back and try again.

The sun was setting and the glow shone bright off the patches of snow. I grinned, but continued forward as my name filtered through the blistery wind.

KARUS

Parvus took me through more swampy forest, more desolate trees with limbs encased in various fungi I had not seen before. Some of them oozed black liquid that slid down the branches, leaving streaks of discolored bark in their wake.

I leaned forward on Parvus's back, too exhausted to sit up any longer, too angry with myself to do anything other than trust my lumen with leading me to safety.

I hoped beyond reason that Revich had found the rhyzolm. I wished more than anything that I would be reunited with him soon and that this would all be a nightmare settling into my past.

I could have warmed my skin with my power, but decided I deserved to freeze. I thought less of myself in those moments of hunger and exhaustion than I ever had before.

I wallowed in remorse for what felt like hours, fading into sleep a few times as I sunk into Parvus's fur.

We finally stopped at the edge of a gentle river and Parvus waded in, lapping water generously with his long tongue. I slid from his back, my boots splashing as I took in where we were.

A white cliff faced us, its sandstone edges a stark difference to the dark, dreary forest of trees that encased it. Carved into its face were ornate window ledges, stairwells and flowing tresses of vines, green as Felgren after a summer storm. A palace had been carved into this cliffside and I had no doubts of who ruled there.

A howl erupted in the afternoon haze and I couldn't help but grin as Rauca's black and white face emerged from the landing stairwell of an upper floor. Moments later, the black form of the Blightress gracefully stood beside the lumen, patting her head in reassurance and smirking down at me.

I could kill her.

I could maim her, disfigure her, destroy her.

Any anger I felt in my own decision making was a hundred times more wrathful towards her, and before I could subside my rage, the hanging vines below her landing edge creeped upward, tangling on her gown of black, winding up her arms and chest.

"Karus, my child, I see that you have not denied yourself what you are entitled to these past few weeks," she called down to me. Her voice filled the air and echoed over the water in an unnatural abundance. Before I could speak, the vines withered, drooping and falling to the stone at her feet.

Rauca left the landing and I saw the lumen's body wind its way down through the various stairwells that opened to the world outside the palace.

She found her way to the river and howled again, Parvus joining her this time. The soil-encrusted roots of the trees along the river's edge cut through the earth and wound together on each side, creating a bridge wide enough to cross.

I didn't know if it was the lumens or the Blightress who created it, and at that point, I didn't care.

"I want to leave," I called out from the river's edge, my voice a rasp and shaking. "I wish to return as you said I could when I was ready."

Parvus licked my hand and ran across the bridge to join his mother lumen on the other side. I stared up at the Blightress, waiting for my bargain to be fulfilled.

"I will allow you to go, Karus, when you have listened. Or did you forget that part of our agreement?"

I clenched my fists, my long nails cutting into my skin. "I have tried to listen! It is you who has not spoken!"

"I'll speak when you are ready to hear, and by the looks of it, that is now. Come, join me in my palace. You can bathe and eat if you wish. You must be hungry." She turned and followed the same path as Rauca, descending stairs and standing in the open doorway to her realm. "One hour. All I ask is one more hour of your time, and I will see to it that you are free of this place. During that time, you will wash and eat, drink and listen."

"How long was I in there?" I refused to step onto the bridge, forcing her to walk to the edge of it.

"In the portal? No more than two weeks' time."

I shook my head and bit my lips together. The pain kept me from falling as I stepped onto the rooted bridge. If I must spend one more hour with her to leave, I was going to get it over with. I was going to return to Revich.

She held a pale hand out for me to take as I neared the other side of the riverbank. I took it reluctantly, knowing I had little fight left, weak and confused at how I was still even alive.

Her grip was tight and cold as she led me silently into her white stone palace. It had been carved deep into the cliffside, the entrance expanding just as wide as the foyer of the Fortress. But as the fortress was all black stone and windowless, this palace was bright and airy. Openings to the outside graced the walls and the hazy sunlight filtered through them, warming the air.

"This way." She held my hand still and led me up one of the many staircases that filtered off through the entrance. We climbed a few levels, winding around and around, sometimes getting a glimpse of the outside world. I followed without hinderance or complaint, the two lumens' paws padding behind me.

We entered a beautifully furnished room with a large four-poster bed along one wall, the wood of which was peeling white birch. A massive fireplace was lit with a wooden rocking chair next to it.

A cauldron was boiling over the fire with something enticing bubbling on its surface.

"Your bath is drawn through there, and I've given you something else to wear." She pointed toward the only open door in the room and began stirring the pot with a wooden ladle.

"Does my bathing count toward the hour I have left?"

She laughed, the sound coming deep from her chest. "Oh, Karus, you are quite determined to go back to him, aren't you?" She tsked and shook her head. "I'm afraid I need the whole hour to tell you what you need to know. Surely, you can bathe quickly?"

I straightened my back and moved to the rocking chair by the fire. I refused to waste any time. Rev wouldn't care if I returned to him smelling foul and wearing a soiled dress.

Her face erupted in a knowing smirk and she snapped her fingers, black trails of her magic leaving the room. Moments later, I heard something dragging on the floor. She smoothed her trailing dress, never taking her eyes from mine as she waited for something.

A creature entered the room, pushing another rocking chair ahead of itself. It looked almost human in its formation of a head, arms, and legs, but it was entirely made from plant material. Its legs were branches wound together. Its torso a tangle of sprouts and moss. Its long arms were covered in leaves while its head was capped like the top of a giant mushroom.

It blinked at me in surprise as I open-mouthed stared back.

It pushed the chair under the Blightress and she sat. "Thank you, Grower. Please, give our guest some food and drink."

I stared stupidly as the creature bent down to the bubbling stew and ladled some of its contents into a carved wooden bowl. I took its offering, stumbling in my words of thanks before it nodded its capped head and poured water from the mantle into a glass for me to take as well.

Parvus and Rauca, who were stretched out on the floor, didn't bat an eye at the creature.

"That is all," she stated, and it left, closing the door behind it with a trailing branch from its arms.

"What..." I stared at the door in bewilderment, holding a steaming bowl of stew in one hand and a glass of water in the other.

"Have you never seen a Grower, Karus?" She tsked again and

sighed, placing her head onto her fist. "My, my, the things you still do not know."

I righted myself and closed my mouth. "I am listening and you have fifty minutes left." I watched her as I drank heavily from my cup, gulping the cool water without a sputter. I placed the empty cup on the floor and began my descent into the soup. The flavor was rich with beef and vegetable broth, its base thickened from starchy potatoes. I'd never eaten anything so wonderful in my life.

"I'll get to it then." She grinned and began to rock, turning her face to the fire.

"First, I will answer the question you have not asked, but are dying to know."

I swallowed a slice of soft, savory carrot whole, doing my best to both placate my rumbling stomach and focus on her words.

"I have always had a way with portal magic. The one you entered is of my own creation from centuries ago. In order to leave, you must be true to your innermost desires and emotions. I am not sure what you showed it to get out, but by your demeanor now, I can guess."

"You said it was two weeks I was in that portal. How is it that I am still alive?"

"Again, I was once adept at portal magic. Please listen, Karus, and trust your instincts here. Time slows almost to a standstill in that place. It took great effort from me to do so, but I have had many years to perfect it. It is the only way to enter this land unharmed."

I glanced to the lumens and furrowed my brows.

"It has no effect on such creatures. Lumens are not capable of withholding their innermost desires and so they left immediately, only seeking to explore."

The last few words of each of her sentences she spoke slowly, drawing out what could be said quicker. I found it infuriating and frowned into my soup.

"Alright. What are you hiding then, there in the cavern. What was that thing hanging and pulsing?"

"Do you not listen, child?" She pursed her lips. "You must trust what you assume. Indeed, that is the heart of the Blight. Indeed, it is my own."

I set my bowl on my lap, my meal half eaten, but remembering what I saw there in the cave, I could not take one bite more. "How—how did you end up like this?" I cleared my throat. "I mean, how is it possible that your heart has become…that?"

She began to rock again, leaning her white head of hair back on the chair, her golden crown still shining in the light. "What do we have left? Forty-five minutes?"

I nodded.

"I will stay to the important parts then, Karus." She crossed a leg at the knee, closed her eyes, and inhaled deeply. "I was born in Felgren and I was the most powerful thing it had ever seen."

CHAPTER 14

SAELYN

I was fifteen and worried I was in love.

Thevin lay next to me in a field of gold, his eyes closed to the summer sun, his light lashes long and pale. I studied his face and a look of disgust crossed mine.

Why did my heart beat quicker noticing the light splatter of freckles across his nose, and why did I assume his full lips must be soft, just like his hands and golden curls?

I wanted to gag, but actually, I didn't. That's what worried me.

I scoffed and fell back into the tall grass, angry with myself for getting worked up over a boy and *Thevin* no less.

"What should we do today, Pip?"

I rolled my eyes in irritation. He insisted on the nickname he had given me in our gangly youth, short for pipsqueak. I had been all lanky limbs and bony legs when we were younger, but I was filling out quite nicely in my opinion.

My face was beginning to shape into something of a woman and my breasts and hips were not far behind.

"Don't call me that. I'm not a pipsqueak anymore, if you haven't noticed."

He sat up and squinted down at me. His eyes were a piercing ice blue and my cheeks reddened at his gaze. He looked me up and down and grinned. "You know, I think you might be right. When did that happen?"

I threw grass at him like we did as children and he laughed, grabbing my hand before I could throw more. His smile lit his face, producing the one dimple on his left cheek that had my heart skipping a beat. He paused and tilted his head slightly as he looked at me, and I wanted to sink into the ground and live there forever and ever.

He cleared his throat. "Come on. Let's race the lumens and go explore. It's a beautiful day and we cannot waste it."

I smiled and took his hand to stand up, brushing the dirt from my backside before reaching up to run my hand through his curls to remove the grass.

He shook his head like a lumen, bits flying around us, and I laughed, ignoring my name being called on the summer wind.

CHAPTER 15

KARUS

"My heart had always belonged to Felgren. Even as a young child, I would ride bareback on a lumen through the trees and it was like they called to me."

The Blightress continued her rocking and spoke her story. I listened with rapt attention, yet counted down the minutes in the back of my mind.

"I was as much a daughter of the forest as I was to my own mother and father. It took care of me better than they ever could. It took some time before my people realized what I could do. Never before had they seen one who could channel magic and use it to heal wounds, call to animals, grow fruit, or dig up stones."

"You had all the magic of each kind of conduit?" I asked, placing the bowl of soup on the floor and folding my hands in my lap.

"Have. I have all the magic of each conduit. And more." She tilted her head again in that unsettling way, her iridescent eyes glinting in the firelight. "Have you not discovered this about yourself, Little Sprout?"

I clamped my mouth shut, determined not to interrupt her again. I'd dwell on that question later.

When I didn't respond, she sighed and continued. "After I had grown into womanhood, I became more of a leader to my people. We were only just discovering the uses of my power, and I was sought out for them. I acted as healer, speaker, grower, and finder of all things with glimmer on the isle, and I loved every moment of it. Using my gift to help others was everything I wanted in life except for one thing."

She stared at me, daring me to speak.

"And what was that?" I didn't have time to play her game.

"A family, Karus. I wanted to settle down with the man I had loved since childhood, and grow babies, and pour all of my love into what we could make together." Her gaze moved to the fire as it hardened. "That, however, was not what happened.

"You see, when you give some of yourself to another, you are no longer whole. Instead, a piece of you is gone and the more often you do this, the more parts of you that go missing. I am still missing those parts of me." She turned her gaze back to mine, fury in her eyes. "And I want them back."

"What does this have to do with me? I don't have these pieces you seek."

"You do, Karus, but I am not asking you to return the power I gave to you." She shook her head and a slow smile crossed her lips. "I am taking back the power of the Baron of Felgren."

I scoffed, laughing in disbelief. "You gave me nothing, and you will take nothing from Revich."

"Would you like to hear of your mother? Of how she and your father led one of the many expeditions into my realm, funded by your Queen?"

I shook my head in refusal. Too many answers to questions I had never asked were just spoken and in such a casual manner. I didn't believe a word of it. "You still speak in riddles and lies. Your time is almost up, so get on with your tale."

Her magic shuddered around her fingers as she gripped the arms of her chair. I smirked, playing with fire and ignoring any threat of the burn.

She leaned forward, her brows narrow, her red lips open wide to speak her next words slowly, "I discovered you in your mother's womb long before she knew you existed, but not before I tore out your father's heart in front of her."

I stood, knocking the bowl over, its contents spilling onto the white stone floor.

"Parvus, Rauca, we're leaving." I whistled through my teeth and moved to the door.

"Stop." Dark trails of her magic encased the door. I gripped its handle, pulling hard without success. "I still have a few minutes yet, Karus. If you will not sit and listen, you will stand and listen."

Her power gripped my arms taut to my side and her magic covered my mouth, silencing the retort I was about to speak.

Parvus rose and scratched at the door while Rauca nuzzled the side of my dress.

"You were hardly a sprout in your mother's womb when I found you there. Your spirit called to mine and instead of letting your mother perish as easily as all who try to steal my power, I fed you pieces of me instead. You reminded me of something I had lost long ago, and I wanted you to live for reasons you refuse to hear."

She moved toward me, the strings of her magic dangling from her fingers. She whispered in my ear, "You are ever much a part of me as you are to the woman who bore you or the woman who raised you, Karus, and one day, you will be ready to truly listen."

I pushed on my magic, willing it to untangle me from her inky mist. I was still weak, the fight something I struggled to find.

A black portal opened up in the doorway and I almost collapsed in fear of what was next.

"Do not fret, child, I will fulfill my end of the bargain. I have hurt none and will return you of your own free will."

Her black magic unfurled from my arms and mouth, and I almost fell in the freedom of it. Panting, I glared at her with unmistakable loathing.

"I hate you," I spat. "I never want to see you or this wretched place again. Do not call to me, do not find me."

"Oh, *Little Sprout*, I won't. You'll do that yourself."

I turned from her, fuming, and began my step into the portal, hoping with all I could muster that it would not trap me for weeks.

"And, Karus," she lilted as I pushed inside, "Next time, be more specific on *where* I should return you."

Darkness encased me, and I fell to my knees on soft ground. I heard Parvus and Rauca bound out of the portal behind me as it closed in a sucking *slurp*.

I took a moment to breathe, a small cry escaping my lips.

Please, please, please, please.

I needed to look up and see Felgren. I needed to look up and see Rev, angry as he might be.

I did not.

Before me was an endless horizon of grassland. The Attatok Mountains breathed to my right, looming with snowcapped peaks that winked at me in the distance.

I slammed my fists into the ground and screamed, the very earth below me rumbling in response as I closed my eyes and fell into oblivion.

CHAPTER 16
KARUS

"*Ash!*"

A distant yell rattled me from the dark sleep I had slipped into.

It had been two weeks since I had left with the lumens in that forsaken hole in the place I loved. Two weeks since I had made the choice to delve into a sickening semblance of all the Blightress was and had been for hundreds of years.

I loathed her.

I wanted to rip that crimson grin from her face and force her to see how much Revich loved me. I would find a way to someday return to her and show her that I was worth what I said I was worth. I was no sprout. I was a *fucking* tree of life just in my midst of blooming again after the winter, and I would find my way back to my love where I would never leave his side again.

"Ashton!"

The call flew across the tall grasses that swayed like waves in the fierce wind. A storm rumbled from the sky above me, and I opened my eyes to see the face of a child staring back at me.

"What are you doing down there?" he asked, tilting his head. His ginger curls bounced with the movement and I grinned.

Half a moment later, Parvus's face stared down at me too, another of his high whines piercing the air. He stuffed his snout under my back, nudging me to rise.

The little boy laughed in the pure delight that children do, and Parvus gave him a lick. I groaned and sat up, seeing that the child must be no more than four or five years old.

The boy reached up to pet Parvus's head, his hands barely able to graze the top.

"Ashton!" I heard the call again and spied a figure behind us, running closer across the grass.

"Hello," I greeted the boy and pet Rauca who came up to lick my arm. "Are you Ashton? Is that your father coming now?"

"That's my father and this is my lumen," he replied, squeezing Parvus whose enormous tongue continued to loll out of his mouth.

"Oh, really?" I laughed, rising and rubbing my aching back. "And when did you decide that?"

"When he fell out of the sky with you and I came to see who you were." He pointed to Rauca. "That one is yours. We can each have one or we…we can share them both."

"That is generous of you," I chuckled. "His name is Parvus, and I'm not sure your father will think it's a good idea."

I bent down to the boy whose nose was graced with freckles. "I'll put in a good word, though, with your father," I whispered and winked.

"Ashton!" His father panted behind me, running past and picking him up swiftly as if he were in danger.

I pulled my hair from my face and wiped my filthy hands on my filthy dress, embarrassed.

I caught his stare as he held his son to his chest and gasped. "Geyrand?"

At the same time, he shook his head and breathed, "Ash?"

He set his son on the ground and rushed forward, pulling me into his arms. I laughed at the warm embrace of the man I once knew very well.

He rocked us back and forth, his relief rumbling in his chest.

"We've been looking for you for weeks, Ash." He pulled my face back as I struggled to subside my tears.

Finally, I was embraced by someone who cared about me. Finally, I was cared for. I had not seen this man in over seven years, and yet, he loved me in some way still.

"I'm sorry—I mean, Karus." He grinned wide, ignoring my dirty face and dress, but eyeing my white-streaked hair. "It's going to take some time to get used to this new you."

"Geyrand…how are you here? Where are we?" I stepped back, still holding his arms. Ashton had ignored our reunion and was attempting to climb onto Parvus's back. The lumen bent his hind legs in an effort to aid the boy, but he slipped off again with giggles and an encouraging nudge from Rauca.

"The outskirts of Hyrithia to the north. I live nearby with my companion and son. Karus,"—he shook his head again in disbelief —"we've all been looking for you. What happened? The Baron—"

I shook his arms. "You've seen Revich?" my voice cracked.

"Yes, but he is not here. We have to get you to the castle. It's a day's ride from my home. We'll stop there." Geyrand's face held a concerned smile. "It's good to see you again. Whatever happened to you…you're safe now."

He let go of my arms and picked up his son who had managed to get his middle over Parvus's back. Holding him on his side by the waist, the boy laughed in delight, kicking his legs behind him.

I stroked Parvus and Rauca in reassurance for myself as much as them. Thunder rolled closer and the first drops of the promised storm fell. "We can ride the lumens. I promise they're safe."

Geyrand looked them over, one eyebrow raised.

"Please, Pa! That one is mine!" Ashton pointed to Parvus who turned in an offer of his back.

I held Ashton's hand as his father wearily climbed onto the massive wolf and then handed the boy to him. Both father and son's face lit up with matching delight and matching features, and I laughed seeing my first lover and his child together.

I climbed onto Rauca, patting her and whispering, "Don't worry, we'll see Revich soon."

"Faster, Pravis!" Ashton shouted, digging into the fur at his neck and leaning forward.

I chuckled at the name and asked, "How far are we from your home, Geyrand?"

The rain began to pick up as lightning flashed across the mountains.

He looked up at the tumultuous sky. Rain fell across his face and down the red curls pulled back from his shoulders. I recognized deep within my memories the young man I had once known intimately.

"It's a good half-hour walk. We were out this far because I was on patrol for any sign of you."

I nudged Rauca's side, signaling for her to pick up the pace and Parvus matched her. "Why did Revich think I'd be out here? Did he find the rhyzolm?"

"I don't understand how the stone works, but he has felt you all over the isle these past weeks."

"I don't understand. How could I have been all over the isle?"

Geyrand grunted in a unified agreement that he did not know. I remembered well this part of him, never saying more than what he deemed necessary.

Gritting my teeth, I swallowed my need for answers. They would come in time. What mattered now was that I was headed toward safety. I was headed toward clean clothes and a warm bath.

I was one step closer to reuniting with my love.

We reached a small stable next to a modest house with a generous garden. Rows of fruit trees grew with an abundance of apples and pears and my mouth watered.

"The lumens can sleep here for the night. It's not a lot, but it's warm and dry." Geyrand grabbed a pitchfork and pulled fresh hay from a nearby stall, tossing it to the open walkway. The occupants of two stalls huffed and neighed at the sight of the massive wolves, but neither Parvus nor Rauca paid them any mind. At their fresh bed, they settled down and began grooming their matted fur.

"Do you have something they could eat?" I asked, patting them both while Ashton tried to nestle down with them too.

Geyrand picked him up again, holding him to one side. "I'll ask Viv if we have something." He turned to the door and nodded toward the house.

Whispering to the lumens that I'd be back with food soon, I followed. Before Geyrand could even open the door, I heard singing.

Though it wasn't a song I knew, it filtered through the house like a welcoming beckon into a warm home with the promise of good food and good sleep.

"Vivianna? There's someone here I'd like you to meet."

Geyrand entered the doorway just as Ashton ran inside yelling, "Mama!" and tracking a good amount of mud through the stone hallway.

I pulled my dripping hair behind my neck and followed. The beautiful voice stopped and giggles erupted from the expansive kitchen I stepped into.

Vivianna held her son, her belly round with growing another child. She stopped her tickling and gasped, "Karus? It's you, isn't it?"

I grinned and nodded, dripping rainwater onto the stone floor. "I'm so sorry about the mess. Can I help clean this up?" I looked around for something to use when I found her in front of me.

She took my filthy hands in hers and shook her head. "I don't care a bit for it, love." She wiped a tear from her face and laughed. "Karus. It's good to meet you."

Her embrace was unexpected, but I leaned into it, bending down to meet her with my own. She smelled of flour and flaky pastries and all things kneaded and baked. I smiled and whispered, "It's good to meet you, too."

"Ashton, help me feed the lumens."

I heard Geyrand rustling around the kitchen before heading out the way we came.

"I have so many things to ask you." Vivianna pulled back and squeezed my hands. "I will not utter a single one until you are your-self again. And you will take your time doing it. Come, I'll show you where you can bathe and find something for you to wear. Then we'll fill your belly and you can talk. If you'd like."

She held one of my hands and I blindly followed her through the living room, past the roaring fire and into a modest washing room with a bath. It was nowhere near the size of mine and Revich's and I didn't care in the least.

She took a bucket and headed to the door. "Please. Let me," I interrupted. I took the standing water from the basin by the mirror and splashed its contents into the tub. "*Compleren.*" I gripped the side of the wooden tub and we watched as magic spun from the tips of my caked fingernails, the water expanding upon itself and filling almost to the edge.

She clapped her hands saying, "Lovely! I could put you to good use around here!" Helping me out of what was left of my dress, she busied herself with adding drops of oils to the water that smelled of lavender and rose.

"I use these on the days my back is aching and my legs are the most swollen. They'll perk you right up and you'll be feeling your-self again in no time." Her small face lit up as I stepped into the water and sunk under the surface, nodding, but assured that I would not feel myself again for a little while yet.

"*Caloren,*" I mumbled, the wisps of my green magic swirling around me to heat the water.

She handed me a worn bar of soap and left the room, taking my embarrassing clothing with her.

I was numb in the quiet stillness of the steaming water. It felt as if I had left for the field of clover in Felgren less than a day before, but somehow, weeks had passed. I filled my lungs and sank under the surface.

I thought of Rev. I thought of screaming to him across the land that I was alright—that I would be with him again soon. I thought of all I had learned and all I had seen.

I didn't want to think about any of it. I didn't want to start processing the secrets that were plain in the Blightress's words as she spoke of my parents…as she spoke of the Queen.

Rising to the surface, I inhaled sharply, refusing to cry any more tears at the choices I had made. Instead, I focused on what I could do.

I had water. I had soap. And I could scrub.

I TOOK MY TIME SCOURING AND SCRUBBING AWAY ANY REMNANTS OF the places I had been, and though it was too short and large on my frame, I was thankful for the clean, dry dress Vivianna had brought me. It was a rosy pink with long sleeves and a frilly collar. Brass buttons traveled up the front with a rose imprinted on each one. I was sure it complimented her pale complexion and strawberry ringlets well. I laughed at my reflection in the mirror and wondered what Revich would say when he saw me.

I padded back through the house to voices that drifted through the rooms. Curled up on a chair next to the fire was Ashton holding a carved wooden sword in his chubby fingers. His head lay against the armrest and his legs were tucked up to his chest as if he had been planning a battle and passed out before it could begin. I took the frayed blanket from the back of the chair and laid it across his small body smoothing his precious curls back from his face.

I loved him already, this child of the man I had grown up with. He looked so much like Geyrand. My heart filled with happiness knowing that the first man I had ever been intimate with had found love and companionship and made this beautiful little boy.

I wanted to introduce Revich to him. I wanted Rev to meet the people I had known as Ash'Arah. The people I had loved and lived with every day. The people who made me who I was. And though they had not given me in return what I needed to thrive, they were a part of my history and that was not something I was willing to forget.

I made my way back to the kitchen, which was warm and

smelled of a rich broth. Candles were lit along a wide table as the storm raged outside.

The companions who made this dwelling a home leaned into each other, speaking low as Geyrand wrote in a book and Vivianna strung a bit of thread through a needle. She looked up to me as I silently wandered in, not wanting to disturb their time together, but urged forward by my rumbling stomach.

"Karus! Please, come sit with us. I'll get you some food, love. You must be starving." She began to rise when Geyrand gently pushed her back down to her seat, planting a kiss on top of her head. He headed to the pot nestled into the brick stove.

I smiled at his gesture and sat across from her, hugging my arms, thankful I had found a safe place to land, but wishing I was somewhere else.

Vivianna pulled on her needle and began to sew. She hummed in the quiet, and I watched as silver thread nestled its way into a long strip of blush fabric. She pulled underneath before the needle poked back onto the other side once again. The movements were calming in some way. I had not picked up a needle and thread since I had left Hyrithia years ago, and realized then, I missed it.

"Is that your growth band?" I asked, thanking Geyrand for the bowl of stew and water he placed in front of me.

"Yes, it is. I admit I am a little behind, but I've found that with one child already, I am often behind on things." She continued her work, her needle threading in and out of the fabric with craft as the outline of a full moon took its shape.

"How far have you come?" I blew on a spoonful of brown broth and soft potatoes before eagerly shoving it into my mouth, chewing as slowly as I could convince myself to.

"This is my seventh moon, though I am actually already half-way to my eighth!" She chuckled and shook her head. "Time breezes by in the blink of an eye these days. We still keep Ashton's growth band woven through his bed even though his year of uncertainty is well past him."

Vivianna laid her work down on the table and I saw where six full moons were sewn into the fabric. She would continue to wear it around her waist until her birthing day came. Then, they would weave the band through the crib of the babe in hope that it would protect the child in its first and most dangerous year of life.

I nodded, taking another bite. "I am happy for you." I looked up to meet Geyrand's sharp amber gaze. "For both of you. If I could have wished anything for you, Geyrand, it would have been exactly this."

Something crossed his face and I tilted mine with a silent gesture to tell me what he was thinking.

"Ash—Karus," he corrected, taking a deep breath. "There are things you need to know. Things about your time away."

Vivianna smoothed her hand across his own and looked to him, nodding.

"I suppose I should start at the beginning."

I set my spoon down in my bowl and placed my hands in my lap, suddenly cold at the thought of what could disturb him so.

"When you were…taken seven years ago, Prince Philius and I did not sit idly by."

I took a deep breath and clenched my jaw, unsure if I was ready for this. I had just escaped news of my past and did not want to hear more of it.

"It took weeks for the Prince to recover fully from the Black Fever. When he had come to understand what the Queen had agreed to…he did not take it well. It didn't help that I urged him to do something. I was not like myself, Karus. I loved you, and I wanted you back home. It was easy enough to convince the Prince of the same."

I swallowed, hating hearing his words. I did not want to listen to this. I didn't know if I could get through more blows without Revich by my side.

"The Queen was resolute. The city was healing. But they didn't know you. They didn't know how much you'd resist your fate like we did. So, we traveled to Felgren."

"You came to find me in Felgren?" I had never heard about this. But knowing who was Baron at the time, it did not surprise me I had not been told.

"We left by night without telling anyone and traveled for two days to the edge of the forest. When we arrived at the border, we could not get in. A shield of magic protected it all the way around. We spent days traveling the outskirts trying to find a weakness and push our way inside."

Tears welled in my eyes and I shivered.

"Finally, the Queen found us. She sent half her guards to bring us back. I was reassigned to patrol the north and the Prince was followed at all times at the castle. We could not try again."

He looked down and shook his head in shame. "I'm so sorry. I thought that was it. I thought I'd never see you again and that it was time to let go. I put everything I had into building a life here, and a year later, I met Viv. She helped me heal."

Vivianna cupped his face and pressed her forehead to his.

"By then, we had received word that you were dead. The Queen was told that you had emitted a power so forceful, you could not control it and it killed you. We were all devastated. Myself, the Queen, but the Prince…"

He trailed off and placed his elbows on the table, covering his mouth with his sun-kissed hands. "Prince Philius is not the same. He is a different man now, Karus."

I took a shaky breath and pushed my bowl forward. "Thank you, Geyrand. For trying to fight for me. I don't know if Revich told you—"

"He did. He explained why he lied." Geyrand chuckled, a light settling back into his eyes. "He's a good man. And he loves you better than I ever could."

I could not bear to hear his words. The tears fell and I needed to sleep. I needed to fall into a place of dark where I could move closer to Revich's embrace.

"I am tired. I don't doubt that Revich will be here soon once he realizes I'm not far." I stood to find a place of rest, wherever that may be.

"There's one more thing, Karus." Geyrand rose with me, moving around the table. "Baron Revich has been arrested by the Queen."

I scoffed. "How? She has no authority over the Baron of Felgren. Besides, no cell could hold him. He is too powerful."

"She does not hold him in a cell. She keeps him under guard with her, and he wears a silver band of amethyst across his arm which holds his power within. He is to stand trial for crimes against Hyrithia and lying to Her Majesty. The Lady of the Spire and the Madame of the Mountains will arrive to weigh in on the trial in three days' time."

I shook my head profusely. "Crimes?" I huffed. "That's not possible. Revich didn't do anything wrong. He protected me when my mind was lost, and he protected all of you by lying." A silent rage stormed in my chest and my gaze darted to the window to observe the night.

If Revich was in danger, I would not stay here a moment longer, storm or no.

Vivianna rose as well. "Karus, you cannot leave now. The storm is strong and our old horses could not make the journey to the castle. Your lumens need rest. *You* need rest, love."

"I'm not going to just sit here and—"

"He is safe for now." Geyrand grasped my shoulders. "The Queen needs him to find you. I have already sent word across the plains and news of your safety will make its way to Hyrithia before dawn. He will know we are coming. He made me promise on your life that I would bring you to him if I found you out here."

Sobs shuddered through me and I slid to the floor on my knees, my hands over my face. I did this to him. Whatever he had faced since I had left with the Blightress, I was the reason. Geyrand sat in front of me and pulled me to his chest where he rocked me back and forth, saying nothing in the cries of a defeated woman.

CHAPTER 17

KARUS

The rain-soaked grass squelched under my boots as I watched the sun rise in the east. I inhaled the fresh morning air through my nose and held it, counting to ten before releasing the breath through my mouth.

Dark green slivers of my magic escaped my lungs as well, and I took another breath in a feeble attempt to stay calm.

I was bad at this.

Even at twenty-seven years old, I had not learned to control my anger. Images flashed in my mind of Revich being watched and his magic subdued in the Queen's custody. If I did not gain control of my rage, I would arrive at the castle and burn it to ashes.

"Are you ready?" Geyrand uttered softly in the cool dawn, his breath leaving his lungs in a gust of white.

I pulled my borrowed cloak around me tighter and nodded. Standing in front of Geyrand's home, I wanted to scream. I wanted to tear the very ground open at my feet and scar the earth so that it looked as I felt about myself. I wanted to storm into the Castle of Hyrithia and rip through every single room until I found Rev.

Today would be a day of reckoning for all I had put him through. I would have him see that I was sorry—that I would find a way to make up for our lost time, for his despair in my leaving him again, and I would beg for him to forgive me.

Then I would put the Queen in her place. I would force her mouth shut as I told her of my life these past seven years. There would be no trial for Revich of that, I was certain.

"Do not enter the castle like that." Geyrand looked me up and down, his brows raised and a grimace across his freckled face. "Be careful now. The Queen and the other rulers of Arcaynen have influence and power. You do not. Now, you play the game of politics. If you want to leave for Felgren with Revich, you need to stay calm. If the Queen sees you like this…you know how she gets when she sees your anger."

He was right, of course. The Queen had always thought of my anger as an annoyance—something I *should* be able to control easily but never could.

I was hardly able to think of her as the woman who raised me now. Replaced was the monarch who stood in my way.

I whistled in the chilled air and the lumens peaked their heads from the sable doors. I ignored the red of their eyes and the vines at their throats as their colors and textures turned back to the lumens I knew.

"How far are we from the castle gates?"

"A full day's ride. We should be there around dusk."

"How fitting," I mumbled, thinking of the last time I was within the city walls. I climbed on top of Parvus's back, giving him his favorite scratches behind his ears.

Geyrand settled himself on the back of Rauca and she whined at me.

"We're going to see Revich. You'll get to knock him over soon enough." She howled into the morning and we were off, the long ride ahead. It was one I would face over and over if it meant I would be back with the man I called home.

We stopped twice. Once at another sentry's cottage to give water to the lumens and eat quickly. Geyrand knew every one of the patrol guards in the grasslands to the north of Hyrithia and this one was in a state of shock at the sight of the lumens.

We stopped again at a small stream that cut through the hills so the lumens could drink and we could replenish our pouches with fresh water. We had been riding for close to nine hours and I knew Parvus and Rauca were reaching their limit. My own back ached and my arms were sore from holding onto Parvus's fur so tightly.

"We should arrive in another hour. Their stamina is impressive." Geyrand motioned to the lumens who had curled together on the bank of the creek. Parvus's head was tucked into Rauca's chest as she laid her snout on his.

"A lumen's strength is fueled by Felgren."

"How long do they live?"

"The oldest of the pack is seventy-one seasons. But time is different in Felgren. I'm not sure how old she is in years here."

He nodded, pursing his lips before asking, "How long have you been in Felgren, Karus? What has it felt like to you?"

I took a long drink from my pouch. The truth was, I had no idea how long it felt inside of Felgren after I lost my memories. Each day had been the same as the last and I could not count time in the state I was in. I made a mental note to ask Revich someday.

"I don't actually know. I was so lost for so long. The magic I used that night…" I shook my head and took another drink. "Revich was right. It was immensely powerful and it broke me in ways I cannot describe. I drifted each day in a haze of lost memories and time." I shook my head again and inhaled deeply. "Revich's love brought me back. One day, I'll tell you the full story and you can see how much I need him."

He took my hand and squeezed. "I believe it. You will be companions?"

"Yes. As soon as this mess is over, we are going to the ceremony right away. I won't wait any longer."

He nodded again and grinned. We sat along the grassy shore for a bit longer, giving the lumens their much deserved and needed rest before calling them to finish the journey.

We rode for another hour before reaching the peak of the tallest hill that rose before Hyrithia to the north. The same hill the Prince, Geyrand, and I would roll down on summer days, bruised and aching by evening.

The city expanded over a vast distance, the edges of its boundaries too far to see. Smoke rose from chimneys and the echo of voices and carriages and bustle from the largest city on the isle met us in a familiar wave of movement.

That's what Hyrithia had always felt like. Constantly moving, bargaining, trading. The cogs of the core of the city never stopped. Even the night markets kept people busy with new inventions and the selling of wares.

I loved this city, but I had grown to love Felgren more, and I missed the tall trees and lifting breeze that filled my heart with joy.

Autumn had cast its hold on Hyrithia. The tops of the trees surrounding the city were tipped with orange, yellow, and red. The sun was setting to the west and the air felt as if it would drop to chill the grass with dew at any moment.

Revich was there.

He was in that tall castle that shone in an orange haze with the goodbye of the sun. "Rev," I whispered to the wind, somehow hoping the sound of my voice would reach his ears.

"Remember, you have been gone for over seven years. The Queen suspects the Baron is malicious, and the Prince...well..." Geyrand pointed to the northern wall of the castle where the stone did not match the rest of the facade. "Do you see that discoloration?"

I nodded.

"When the Prince heard of your death, that wall of the castle collapsed, killing five servants and one guard. We'd never seen anything like that from him. No one knew he was a channeler."

I thought of the Black Fever that had torn its way through this city years ago. From what I knew now, it had been controlled by Baron Heimlen through channelers. That was how he was able to spread it from person to person, by feeling for their magic. The Prince had been the last one infected by the disease, and therefore, must be a channeler, even though I'd never seen him use his power.

"Has he used his magic since?"

"As far as I know, no."

I swallowed hard. All of these questions and problems could wait.

"Ready for this?" Geyrand asked, his eyes hardened, his body stiff.

"Yes. Yes, I'm ready."

~

"KARUS OF FELGREN!" THE GUARD WHO ADDRESSED US AS WE neared the city gates was one I did not recognize. She looked to be only a few years older than me with tawny skin and dark eyes. The sides of her head were shaved, resulting in one long, intricate braid that cascaded down her armor. There was no warmth or welcome in her call, and her instructions came with authority.

"You will be escorted to the Queen's throne room. There, you will receive further instructions and give your statement to her majesties regarding the trial of the Baron of—" She stumbled for a moment on her words, coughing and clearing her throat, the slightest hue of green left there. "Of the Baron of Felgren."

Geyrand's eyes shot in my direction, but I ignored him. I knew this woman had nothing to do with Revich's imprisonment or trial, but she was lucky she merely choked on her words.

"We will follow you then, Captain Yarah." Geyrand replied.

"You will dismount your beasts and walk to the castle from here."

Parvus growled and I stroked between his eyes replying, "The lumens come with us."

The captain inhaled deeply, her eyes narrowing at the sight of them. "My orders are to keep the beasts outside of the city gates. The Queen cannot risk her people's safety."

I looked to Geyrand for strength. The strength to hold back my simmering rage.

I closed my eyes and focused. If I was to get to Revich, I needed to control the urges I felt—the urge to tear through the guards, the castle, and anyone who stood in my way to get to him.

I had hurt him. *Me.* And I just needed to keep my magic, my anger, and my immense guilt under control until I could get him out of this situation—the one I had played a part in.

I nodded in agreement of the captain's orders and slid off Parvus's back. "You both must stay out here." He whined and I rubbed the top of his snout. "I will be safe. You can find a place to hunt and rest. I will call for you before the morning. I promise."

Geyrand dismounted Rauca and both lumens watched as we followed the captain over the stone bridge and up the dusty path that led to the gates of Hyrithia.

As I strode forward, the iron portcullis rose, the clicks of each gear pushing me forward to reuniting with Rev.

I wished this had gone differently. I wished I could have met my former family again with Rev at my side, holding my hand as he always did as if it were just an extension of himself.

But we were past that opportunity, so I kept moving forward. I could not change the past, but I could try to protect our future.

I noticed little of the place I had known. Everything around me was a blur of noise and movement, hurried people and commerce, evidence of a thriving city.

I kept my eyes on the captain's back, barely noticing how more guards surrounded us as we neared the castle doors.

I wondered if the Queen feared me now and what I could do.

I didn't care. I didn't care or process what was happening in real time like I should have. Rev would have played this out nicely. He would have seen the different outcomes and planned ahead in the back of his mind.

It seemed I was incapable of that.

The only thing I saw was red.

"The Queen will bring the Baron of Felgren forth and you will state your defense of his actions and lies against the crown. You will then be escorted to your own private chambers and the Queen will see you privately if she wishes it."

Geyrand reached out and squeezed my shoulder. "And the Prince? Is he to attend this meeting as well?"

Captain Yarah glanced to the guard beside her who shook her head once. "The Prince is occupied elsewhere."

Rev.

Rev.

Rev.

I repeated his name in my thoughts as the doors opened, and we entered the great foyer of the castle. The familiar scent of fresh-cut blooms, mint, and chalk met my nose.

Little had changed in seven years, and chills swept through my heated body as I picked up my pace, my breath desperate to escape my lungs, my legs beginning to overtake the captain's lead.

My feet knew the way, and as a surge of power radiated across my skin, I knew I could not—would not—be stopped.

"Wait!" the captain yelled, her hand reaching for my arm. Static met her fingers and she pulled back in a yelp as I picked up my rosy skirts and began to run.

I flew past the main staircase, careening left.

Rev.

I passed the halls that lead to the kitchens and the secret one that led to the guard's chambers.

Rev.

I heard the clank of running armor behind me and picked up speed, my boots pounding on the gray stone as I dodged servants and off-duty guards alike—my ravage through the castle upsetting more than one tray and bundle of linens.

Finally, the crimson doors to the throne room loomed ahead, and I could not even yell his name for fear of pausing even the slightest in my desperate pursuit of the man I loved.

I sent my magic out ahead of me in a sparking ball of power. The doors burst open, each slamming into the walls of the gilded hall, their hinges groaning at the violence.

I stormed inside without falter, a hurricane of great wind and strength, unyielding in my pursuit across the tiled floor. Green swirls of power radiated from my fingers unbidden and uncontrolled.

"WHERE IS HE?" I thundered, my eyes darting all around the massive room, unable to focus on any one face, unable to discern if I knew any of the people I had burst upon. A woman gone seven years and a woman changed stood before them all, uncaring about her past, looking only for her future.

The Queen was surrounded by her royal guards immediately. I recognized her at least. They drew their swords as if they could stop what I had started.

Rev.

He stepped down from the dais with ease as if he'd been patiently waiting.

He strode toward me as if we had all the time and means in the world to reunite and live—live for each other, live for what we believed in and believed we could do for this world.

I could no longer move, my boots were adhered to the floor, my legs pillars of iron.

I could no longer breathe as my lungs collapsed and I exhaled in anguish—a cry of relief, of absolute guilt. My magic spun from me to greet him first, tangling around his body like a tether, pulling him forward.

He moved swiftly with the gait he'd always used. I laughed thinking of all the times I'd been annoyed by his pace and now I could not get him to move any faster.

His eyes were black. The blackest I had ever seen and they stayed on me without heed of the guards moving to pull him back— without bothering to move from my own as one guard approached to pull him around.

Revich's azure strike of power sent the guard sliding across the floor on his backside while flames, the color of a dimly-lit sea, burst through the mosaic floor in straight lines toward me. They formed around my body to enclose me into a room of his making. The only space still open from his enclosure faced him as he continued forward, closing the gap between us that had been far too wide for far too long.

His cage of solid blue magic closed around his back and above us. I heard the shouts and screams from the throne room as the last of the noise and view was cut off completely, solidifying us in our room of his making.

"Rev!" My voice broke as he reached me, pulling me to his chest. I sobbed, my hands gripping the back of his shirt so tightly, my fingernails bent in the pressure.

I could do nothing else.

I thought I would die there in his arms as he gripped my body so tightly, it didn't matter that I could not breathe before. I could not now in his embrace either.

He pulled me back, both of his strong hands clasped around my face. "Do you know me?"

I sobbed again, a pathetic creature in truth—one without the strength left to answer him with words.

He shook my head in panic. "*Do you know me, Karus?*"

I cried out again and nodded, my lips reaching his just as he gritted his teeth and moved down to mine.

"I'm sorry," I managed to mumble between our mouths. "Forgive me." He gripped me harder. "*Please,*" I begged.

I heard nothing else in our glowing cage of the power of the Baron of Felgren. The colors swirled a solid black and blue all around us and we heard nothing but the sound of our hurried breaths and pressed lips. We kissed each other with force, our tongues ready to bruise, our teeth ready to bite, to maim, and mark what each of us thought of as our own.

He consumed me with his lips, his tongue and teeth, and I him, neither willing to let the other have more than what we ourselves wanted—what we each needed.

I tore through his shirt just as he pulled on my thighs, once again and for the hundredth time lifting me up onto his waist, my shaking legs wrapping around his hips in a possessive clutch.

His shirt ripped and I pulled at the sleeves in a wild fury, yanking the apparently useless amethyst band from his arm and throwing it to the ground. Either by the force of my magic or the strength of my throw, it shattered, bits of purple stone flying across our space and skittering along the mosaic floor.

Holding my back, he swept us down to the patterned tile, an expanse of purple and midnight thistle, each inlay a tiny part of what created a masterpiece in the castle.

He was the masterpiece. *He* was the part of me that created something so beautiful, I could not be without it. I had tried. For seven years I had breathed and my body had pumped blood through my veins, but I had not *lived.*

This. This was living.

I gripped his black hair in my hands, our mouths still harsh and furious, our chests finally touching as he yanked down the top of my dress, brass buttons flying to the barrier and bouncing off its swirling surface.

I fumbled my hands to his pants, unbuttoning them swiftly and using my boots to slide them down just as he cupped my breasts and squeezed, the pain fueling our lust further as I pulled up my skirts and ripped aside my undergarments, finding the thick of him and guiding it inside of me.

My cry this time was of pleasure.

My breath this time left my body in a torrent of ecstasy, any remote thought of holding back on what I wanted from him long gone from my mind. All I could see was *him.*

All I could feel was *him,* thick and pounding inside of me, and I could not fathom how I could ever live without it.

Each thrust gave me life.

Each dip of his hips reassured me that what I needed to survive was *him.*

We had only time.

We had only need, and frustration, and desire.

The pleasure was so great, the moment of our reunion so powerful, I found myself slipping into a fuzzy black, my eyes rolling to the back of my head, my neck falling limp in a picture of death by lust. Death by ravaging of the man who was as much a part of me as my own soul.

"No, you don't," he gritted, picking up his pace as my legs let loose at his sides, and I began to sink into the ornate flooring of the castle I was raised in.

"You're staying right here with me," he growled and slid one hand behind my head, pulling on a fistful of my hair, the dull pain bringing me back to the light to relish in the exquisite release that tore through my very bones in a shedding of all I had held inside for weeks.

"*Karus,*" he groaned, pushing himself inside over and over, again and again and again, seeking his own oblivion and finding it as his mouth met mine once more. His tongue pressed against mine, daring me to meet him one more time in what we were so masterful at making together.

He slowed finally as my senses returned in pieces. My lungs burned as if I had run miles without stopping. My legs shook as if I had climbed a mountain. He did not move from me as he gasped into my neck, and I squeezed his chest to mine.

I would not let go.

How could I ever let go.

He motioned to slide out of me and lift himself off my body, but I held on tighter. "No. Please." He moved his head to look at me, and I at least allowed that. His bottom lip was bleeding and his eyes were a wild blue that matched the magic that still surrounded us. "Just stay here a little longer."

He smoothed the hair matted to my face in sweat and caressed my cheek with his thumb.

I swallowed and blinked my tears away, letting them fall down the sides of my face without any effort from me to stop them. "I'm sorry," I choked. "I never should have gone. I'm so sorry. I love you."

Pain crossed his face and he leaned down to kiss me softly. I tasted the blood on his mouth and savored it, the sharp swell of iron helping me focus even more.

He pulled away from my lips and slid out of me, rolling to his back and tucking me onto his chest. He grabbed my trembling leg and draped it over his hips as I always loved to do.

I buried my face in his neck and whispered, "Please forgive me.

Please say something." I wiped at my eyes and continued hurriedly, "I know it is difficult to love me. I know I don't make it easy, but I—"

He lifted my chin, forcing me to look into his eyes and cutting me off. "It is not difficult to love you, Karus. It has *never* been difficult to love you. What is difficult is keeping you safe. Often from yourself. It is difficult not to lock you up and keep you from your own reckless decisions. It is difficult to not tether you to myself with a leash or a chain, so that I can watch over your every move. So you cannot get yourself into situations like this."

He sighed, gathering his thoughts, his jaw tightening again. "That is what is difficult. It is easy to love you. It is easy to give my heart to you, regardless of how much you or I break it."

I hated myself. I hated witnessing what I knew I had done to him. Seven years of torture from one reckless decision. Two more weeks of the same from my determined curiosity and fierce self-ishness.

"I don't deserve you."

"I don't believe that, but it doesn't matter anyway. You have me."

I kissed him again and believed it still.

He pressed his forehead to mine. "Are you hurt?" he whispered, the crackle of his powerful cage akin to a fire burning in a dry summer heat.

My lips trembled and I pushed his hair behind his ear. I couldn't speak of it yet. I couldn't admit the truth of what I had witnessed and what I had learned. The looming pressure of leaving this intimate place he had made for us pressed on my thoughts. I knew we had much to face outside of it.

But at least we'd face it together.

"Okay," he murmured understanding me entirely. "You can tell me when you're ready."

He sat up, bringing me with him, our clothes in shambles, our hair matted and streaked with sweat. He pulled the sleeves of the pink dress back up my shoulders, realizing what I wore for the first time.

Raising a brow, he chuckled and buttoned the remaining one, just enough to cover my bare chest. He smoothed the ruffles of the collar gently as if to preserve the delicate lace from the aftermath of our ravishing of each other's bodies.

"It's borrowed."

"I figured."

"It's very pink and unflattering on me."

"I didn't seem to notice. *Sarchio.*" His enchantment worked in a slow turn. The buttons that had flown across our space hovered in the air, encased in his blue light, mending themselves back onto the dress, the fabric smoothing out from its puckered state.

I grinned, laughing softly, watching his eyes alight with the mischief I loved. "*Sarchio,*" I mumbled back, smiling myself at the repair of his shirt while he stood and pulled on his pants, offering his hand for me to rise as well.

He pulled me close, his hands caressing my back as they should always do and I lifted my arms around his shoulders. My eyes fell to the cut of his lip and I lifted a hand over the wound. "*Sarch*—"

"No." He caught my hand and brought it to his broken lip. "This stays. We don't mend this. Let them see."

"She'll be more than willing to try to punish you now. Maybe even punish both of us."

"If you'd like to leave, I can send you back to Felgren." He moved back from my body and made a movement with his hands I had not seen before.

A glowing viridescent portal opened in our magical enclosure— just my size.

"I've never seen you do that," I gasped.

He shrugged. "I told you once that portal magic is rare. I had only begun my lessons on portals before Heimlen died. I had to learn the rest myself. If you'd like, you can return to Felgren and I'll deal with this mess here."

"You won't go with me? Why don't we just leave right now and handle this mess from our home?"

He shook his head. "That's not how my portal magic works. Only one living heart can enter each portal before it closes, and I cannot make another for a while. It takes a certain kind of power that I have not completely mastered."

I thought about the black portal the Blightress had lured me into. She must know portal magic Rev did not.

Tangling my fingers into his, he brought them to his lips, leaving delicate kisses on each of my knuckles. "If you go, I will be able to follow in a day or so. At least I'd know you'd be safe. I cannot leave without righting things here."

"You think I'd leave you now?" I scoffed, "You think I'd leave you to get through all this mess on your own?" I shook my head and shrugged. "Chain? Leash? You've got it."

He pulled me back to his chest, the portal closing in a loud *thwap*.

"Ready?" he murmured into my ear, kissing my temple.

I moved to his side to face the dais he had kept us hidden from and slid my hand into his, pulling my hair back from my face. "Next to you, Baron Revich, I'm ready for anything," I said with a tired soul, but renewed confidence.

He smirked and our crackling walls began to fall.

He let them down slowly, and we both watched as our enflamed enclosure melted away, revealing what we would have to face, but what we could face together.

PART TWO

CHAPTER 18
SAELYN

I was almost seventeen, and I lived for Viridis.

Actually, I lived inside of Viridis. I had been so clever to pull together four of the silky benches, each an entirely different color, all with the claws and talons of varying monsters. I liked to imagine that the bestial feet intricately carved into the four legs of each bench were creatures who watched over me as I slept.

Pah-Pah disapproved of my occasional choice of rest, but did not tell my mother. She had grown anxious, jittery, and difficult to speak to in the last year and did not need to be bothered with where her daughter chose to sleep.

She still held immense power and wielded it for our people, but it seemed rote now. It seemed as if we all were there, but she was not.

We no longer took long walks in the forest together. We no longer ate breakfast each morning side by side to plan out our days. I'd watch her do her duties and wring her hands together, squeezing them until they turned white.

To cope with this change in my mother, I spent more and more of my days in Viridis. I had learned even more control of my magic and practiced among the great courtyard each morning, afternoon, and evening. The only person who ever really noticed my absence was Pah-Pah, who made sure I was fed and still scrubbing my teeth each morning and night.

If anyone had been my caretaker, it was him.

"You're like a father to me, Pah-Pah." I told him one morning as we sat together in my favorite hall.

He grinned wide and chuckled. His wrinkled, dark face lighting up in my admittance. "You know, Sae, you've been as much a daughter to me than any I might have had a part in making. Life is funny that way. I did not know I would have you to care for one day, but here you are, beautiful as the first day I cradled you in my arms."

I slumped into my hand, my elbow resting on my knee. He had brought hard cheese and apples for our first meal of the day and I munched contentedly on a slice of the crimson fruit that I had layered with a chunk of crumbly cheese.

Mouth full and manners lacking, I asked, "What should we do for my birthday? It's coming up with the next silver moon and I think you and I should celebrate."

He stiffened oddly.

"What is it?" I stopped my chewing and straightened, intrigued by his sudden seriousness.

"I had forgotten it was so close. How many days is it now?"

"Thirty-seven if you count the rest of today, which I suppose we must."

He nodded. "Yes, we should have a special celebration. Do you have anything in mind?"

I grinned, but not too wide. I didn't want him to say no to all of the ideas I had planned.

"I'll think of something. We can plan a whole day and night of it."

He nodded again and raised a well-groomed brow my way. "Thevin will be back for the summer by then, will he not?"

I blushed. "Yes."

"And do you think you'll tell him how you feel this time?"

"No."

His face softened. "Saelyn, no happiness was ever had without a risk being taken."

"I don't know any happy people who became so from taking a risk."

"You know me."

"What risk did you take?"

He nodded toward the vast courtyard. "I chose to come here. Felgren is not the place I have always called home, and by taking that risk, I have found myself to be happy."

"And my mother? Was she ever happy?"

"Ah, Saelyn, you are too observant. You notice too much for your young years, and I fear one day you will find yourself in trouble because of it."

I picked at the skin of my apple, ripping pieces off each slice in one long strip of red. "I'm right, though, aren't I? No risks they ever took made them happy. My father is dead after all."

He reached across the space between us and pulled me into an embrace, smoothing my hair back and kissing the top of my head just as he did when I was little. "Your parents took risks and were very happy. We do not know what our future holds when we take the uneasy step of moving toward the unknown, but we do know what our future holds when all we do is stand still."

I glanced up from his chest to look into his golden-brown eyes. "And what's that, Pah-Pah?"

"The same, Sae. The same life we have always lived."

His words filtered through Viridis's breeze and I sighed. The barest brush of my name whispered through the birch trees, and I wondered if I'd ever be brave enough to step forward and take any risk at all.

CHAPTER 19
REV

I was ready.

I would guess the Queen was not.

In the last sixteen days since I had arrived in her court from Felgren, she was not convinced of my love for the woman she raised who left her castle seven years prior. She refused to see that what I had done was to keep Karus safe, not to deceive the Queen for nefarious purposes.

Queen Rina was possessive of her, wanted control over her life. I knew that now.

Even the way she refused to accept her name from "Ash'Arah" settled into the back of my mind. I knew we would be on dangerous ground as soon as Karus set foot in Hyrithia.

I had tried diplomacy at first, resonating confidence and ease in my words, taught by the man who had caused so much pain and death in this city years before. But Queen Rina was never going to trust me. She would never believe me again—at least not without the help of Karus.

As I gradually released the walls I had created around us, I watched Karus steady herself once more.

She was good at it. I'd seen it many times in her years in Felgren how she'd inhale fully while her neck and back would straighten and an undeniable strength would radiate from her skin as if obstacles to her desires did not exist.

Fuck, I loved her.

She'd told me she didn't deserve me which I'd decided to write off as exhaustion. I'd get her alone tonight and show her exactly who deserved who.

"That was quite a display of power, Baron Revich." The Queen's voice, authoritative yet worn, filled the throne room in the silence of our reveal.

She didn't know the half of it.

Or, possibly, she guessed the whole of it.

No fewer than twelve of her guards were surrounding us, longswords drawn as if we were a threat to their city and queen.

"I see you have deceived the crown yet again."

Captain Yarah picked up the broken amethyst band from the mosaic floor and brought it to the dais for the Queen's inspection.

"I did not deceive you, Your Highness. You made assumptions about amethyst dampening all power from Felgren, and, under-standably, I did not correct you."

Her dark eyes narrowed and she stepped off the dais toward us.

Karus moved in front of me swiftly, letting go of my hand before I could tighten my grip. "I have returned to Hyrithia, Queen Rina, to defend the Baron of Felgren and his actions regarding my health and whereabouts these last seven years. No trial or council of the leaders of Arcaynen will be needed once you have heard what I have come to say."

"Ash'Arah, my dear, I have no doubt this man has besotted you with his words of flattery and his well-crafted lies, and I—"

"Karus." She stepped forward, pushing her way through the drawn swords to reach the Queen as if their sharp edges were a mere nuisance. "My name is Karus and you will address me as such. I have much to tell you and you have much to learn, so I advise we speak privately, Your Majesty."

The slightest hint of amusement filtered through the guards and pride tore through my chest watching my love demand the respect she deserved.

The Queen lifted her chin, just a few feet away from the young woman she thought to be dead only weeks ago. I admired her strength as well.

"I cannot allow—"

"ASH!"

A door to the left of the throne room flew open and the Prince stumbled forward. His tunic hung off one shoulder in careless dishevelment, his call slurred, and one of his eyes sporting a blossoming bruise.

Geyrand entered the hall behind him, and I nodded to the man I had grown to like, even if every ounce of me was annoyed he'd ever known Karus at all.

Karus turned and her face lit in a direct beam of pure sunlight as she gasped, "Philius!"

"Leave! All of you! At once!" the Queen demanded and guards sheathed their swords, hustling out of the room one by one. Captain Yarah remained by the Queen.

Karus ran to the Prince and fell to her knees just as he collapsed to the floor in sobs so desolate it hurt to hear them.

"You were d-dead," he sobbed into her hair and she squeezed him, shushing his cries with whispers I could not hear.

Queen Rina's gaze met mine. She stepped forward, ignoring her drunken son and his reunion with the woman he loved as a sister. "The Council of Arcaynen will unite in two days' time, Baron Revich, regardless of what she has to say."

I nodded, shoving my empty hands into my pockets to tighten in a fist. "I'll be there to attend it." I smirked as irritation narrowed her eyes. "You have nothing to fear from me, Your Highness. I only seek peace and to strengthen the ties between Felgren and the great cities of Arcaynen. I have been open and honest with you, and Karus will corroborate the history of the last seven years. I will wait for you to speak to her alone, but then,"—I stepped closer, our eyes meeting with the same determined spirit borne to us through circumstance —"I will not let her out of my sight."

"If she is any of the same girl I raised, she would never allow it. You really think you can possess her, Revich?"

I snickered and grinned, knowing Karus had no problem feeling a possession of *me*. "Don't worry. The feeling's mutual."

CHAPTER 20
KARUS

"Sing to me of the sweet, blue sea.
Sing to me of Hyrithia.
Whisper to me of the grass that's green.
Whisper to me of Hyrithia.
In the fields of wheat and grain,
Through the halls of the castle,
I did find what I'd choose to claim,
As my love for Hyrithia."

The song of our childhood returned to my lips easily in the very room I had slept in countless times. The Prince's enormous bed, carved from the wood of an oak tree, still groaned at the foot, and the notches from our rough play as children, were still embedded in the four carved posters.

His room was unkempt, reeking of wine and stale clothes. I sighed heavily into his dark coils while he slept off his drunkenness. I continued to hum the song we would sing as children when we had little to no comprehension of the futures which awaited us.

Philius and I had been inseparable as children, and though we fought just as much as blood siblings did, we also grew together in our formative years as best friends, learning about our world side by side.

That all changed when Queen Rina had begun to raise us differently. By the time we had both turned seventeen, the Prince was off to parties and balls with the wealthy people of Hyrithia. There, he would make connections and learn what it was to be royal. His future daughter, after all, would someday become queen.

I had been put to use.

I was to help with the fires in the castle and tend to the fruit trees in the Queen's gardens. We drifted apart, and that's when Geyrand and I had grown in our own bond. Both of us were suddenly taken from our greatest friend, and we had found comfort in each other's company.

Now, as I gently slid out from under Philius's arm, I pulled his covers up over his chest. I paused at his hands, studying the black lengths of his fingers that melded into his mahogany wrists, the obsidian lines working their way up his arms.

If Heimlen was somehow still alive, I would kill him myself.

Seven years later, he remained the villain of my story as well as so many others. I only hoped the people of Hyrithia knew the truth of their "Savior".

I kissed the top of the Prince's head and left. I did not know how he lived his current life, but I could guess at it. That was a conversation he and I would have when he was rested. For now, I had a queen to subdue.

Queen Rina and her captain were waiting outside of his room as I closed the door quietly and breathed deeply. I turned to face her. Only the three of us stood in the hallway with the edge of night forcing its way through the great windows in their gilded frames.

"Where is Baron Revich?" I asked, feigning a vigor I did not feel.

"He is in his rooms," the Queen answered, watching me with careful observance.

"Not a cell, then?" I knew I should not start this conversation in such a way, but my patience with this entire situation had grown irreversibly thin.

"You will remember who you address, Karus of Felgren." Captain Yarah stepped closer, moving in front of the Queen with a sharp glare.

"Leave us, captain."

The woman showed the slightest bit of indignation before storming off down the hall, leaving the Queen of Hyrithia and I to whatever came next.

"Karus," she spoke softly, but firmly, as if trying out the sound on her tongue.

I nodded slowly and moved from the door, stepping closer to the woman who raised me, sheltered me, hid me from the world, and hid my potential from myself.

I wondered then if I still loved her.

I wondered if what had broken between us could ever be mended.

In all of our time apart, we had both faced the world and its adversities, confronting decisions and circumstances out of our control.

Behind the door lay her sleeping son, before her stood her adopted daughter. I was much changed from the one she gave to the man who had hurt her children and her people.

I had convinced myself she didn't know. I had been assured at the time of my own discovery of Heimlen's heinous deeds that the Queen did not know the origins of the Black Fever that had ravaged its way through her city.

But as we stood there together, silent in the royal chamber hall, I was not so sure. She held a painful, guilty expression and before anything else was spoken, I needed the truth.

"Did you know?"

She stiffened, opening her plum painted lips slightly and raising her chin. "Did I know what, Karus?"

"Did you know what Heimlen had done?"

"This is not the way to begin this conversation."

I shook my head in disbelief and spoke slowly, "You gave me to the man that killed thousands of your people. It is a simple question to answer. Did you know at the time of my departure from Hyrithia that he was the one who had created and spread the Black Fever?"

Her jaw clenched. "The Prince would have died."

"*I* would have died." I stepped forward, my hands shaking. "I was *seconds* away from dying that night in Felgren."

"I was deceived by the misinformation of your death. I have been living with this guilt of sending you to a monster for the last seven years, and this is how you greet me? This is how you speak to me, knowing I have suffered greatly at my decision to save my son and send you away, hoping with every piece of a mother's heart that you would survive under Heimlen's rule?"

My lips trembled and my eyes welled with burning tears. "*You* sent me to my death. My life as a sacrifice was Heimlen's only intention for my power in Felgren." I scoffed and pulled my sleeve under my nose. "And you would put to trial the man who saved me. You would condemn and judge the very person who stopped me just in time from destroying myself. The man I love and will bind my life to. You say you were deceived; I say we both were saved. Without Revich, I would not be here today before you with my memories returned and my head clear of its darkest spaces."

"He lied. He claimed you were dead. If he was so noble and good, he would not have deceived your mother, your brother. Look at what has become of Philius. Look at what Revich's treason has left in its wake. Open your eyes, Karus. Your love for him is irrelevant to the damage he has caused."

"You blame him for the state of your son?" My blood was heating, my anger showing itself, pricking my fingers in a green glow. "And what of the state of your daughter? Who do you blame for that? What punishment do you place upon yourself for giving me away to a man who was willing to murder?"

"I had no choice."

I laughed, wiping my cheeks. "I see that, My Queen. I see that it was my life or his, and that was no choice at all."

I took a deep breath, shaking my head. "*Revich* had no choice. He knew that if he told you the truth, you would have fought with all you had to bring me back to Hyrithia. And then where would I be? What state would I have continued to be away from him?"

"He—"

"He *saved* me. He saved me from Heimlen, he saved me from myself, and he saved me from you." I stepped closer and spat my next words. "You will *cease* this trial, you will make amends with the Baron of Felgren, and you will tell the world of what he has done."

"The trial will—"

"The trial will not commence!" My voice echoed through the hall in a visible glow of emerald light. "You will meet with the leaders of Arcaynen and tell them you were mistaken. You will relate our story, and they will welcome Revich as the Baron of Felgren who is good, and powerful, and leads with the intention of making this isle a better place for all who live in it."

She swallowed roughly and steadied her breath. "You have much changed. I see that you did not heed my lessons of self-sufficiency."

"No, I did not, and I stand before you now, stronger because of it."

She placed a hand on my cheek, a single tear sliding down her face. "I will think on your words. There is much you have yet to know." She stepped away and quickly wiped the tear from her chin. "Now get some rest. Baron Revich sleeps next to your old room."

Turning quickly, she grabbed her gold satin skirts and swept down the hall in dismissal.

I did not watch her go.

I had somewhere to be.

I slipped silently through the castle, turning corners and winding my way down stairs, not bothering to reminisce on my childhood home. My heart pounded through my chest at the thought of being alone with him, and I began to run, passing servants who lit the sconces and lit my way to the only future I would ever choose.

I rounded the corner of the guest room hall and saw his back. His head was bent, one hand in his pocket, the other at his neck as he paced before the bedchamber doors.

"Rev," I whispered, breathless and on the brink of being the happiest woman alive at the sight of my lover waiting for me in the dark.

Nothing could compare.

He turned as I ran toward him, lifting me as our bodies collided, no words said or needed as our lips touched for the thousandth time.

And for the thousandth time, the world stood still. He in my arms, me in his and it was just us two. Just our souls living as one, living in the peace of knowing that this was right, that this was good, and needed, and the most powerful thing we could ever wield.

I didn't want to dwell on what I'd just learned. I didn't want to ruin the moment of happiness on his face with talk of how the mother who raised me knew she sent me to a monster.

So, in the true nature of myself, I said nothing.

He pushed me against the stone wall, and I slid from his lips, moving my head back for air in an attempt at clarity for my thoughts.

He pushed his body against mine, harder, his tongue finding its way across my throat in the promise of the pleasure to come.

"Rev?" I questioned, working so hard to keep myself from falling into that place where time did not move as he moved inside me.

"Yes?" he replied, hearing my inquiry and choosing to listen and work at the same time, gently unbuttoning the top two brass buttons on my frilly gown.

He was a talented lover, I'd be the first to admit. He kept me poised against the wall with one arm slung underneath me, while working his way down my dress with the other, all the while brushing kisses across my collarbone and neck.

"I don't want to wait any longer," I breathed, pulling him closer while trying to explain my actual intentions for the night.

He chuckled, "Neither do I." And moved back to my mouth, his hand now sliding up my skirts instead.

"What I mean is," I mumbled on his lips, realizing I had not been very clear. "I don't want to wait to become companions.

Tonight," I finished before I was past the point of coherent thought. "I want our ceremony to be tonight."

He finally understood my words and pulled his face back to beam at me. His smile would slowly kill me—death by suffocation, for I could hardly breathe in the presence of it.

"I love you," he stated simply.

It was my turn to grin stupidly, laughing in the perfect state of bliss underneath him.

He let me slide down from the wall and pressed his forehead to mine. "Alright," he murmured, getting down to the basics of our task. "I cannot leave the castle. And we need conduit magic to complete the ceremony." He lifted his head and looked down the hall in deep thought, pushing both of his hands flat against the stone wall behind me. He leaned forward and spoke while I stared in awe of the beautiful creature I was gladly trapped under. "Of course, Clairannia will attempt to skin me alive if she misses it…" He looked back to me, smirking. "She probably knows how to do it, too."

I shook my head. "I don't care. She can skin us both, but later. After we are companions." I stroked his smooth face, my thumb brushing his lips as he kissed it. "We have my magic. We have all the magic of the Baron of Felgren. We don't need a conduit and we don't need to wait." I straightened my spine and kissed him gently. "No more, Rev. We've waited long enough."

He took my hand and held his lips to the bend of my fingers, kissing my conduit ring and nodding. "I'll take this." He slipped the teardrop emerald from my finger and turned me around, guiding me to the door of my old room.

"What's your plan, Baron Revich?" I giggled, as he opened the door and gently pushed me into the place I used to call my own.

"I'll meet you back here in one hour. Bathe, dress, I don't care— I'd bond my heart to yours either way."

I laughed and began unbuttoning my dress even more, teasing him as I backed away from the door and further into the room.

"You're exquisite, Karus, but your attempts to lure me further into this room are in vain. For I, the Baron of Felgren, have a task to complete of the utmost importance."

I nodded, leaving the front of my dress half opened, the soft curve of my breasts teasing what I knew he struggled to resist. Placing my hands behind my back and stepping forward to him in the doorway, I whispered, "I await your return then, my love." I kissed his lips gently and slow, suddenly cursing myself for stopping what a part of me cared solely about.

He held the sides of my face, his tongue easing its way into my mouth to caress mine, and then mumbled, "I lied. I shall never leave this room if I do not leave now."

I laughed on his lips and lightly pushed him back, beginning to close the door. "I'll see you in one hour. You'd better not be late."

He took the door handle and murmured as he closed it, "Don't worry, I won't be."

CHAPTER 21
REV

Before I left the hall, I entered my borrowed room to just breathe. I was never disciplined around Karus, and tonight was no different.

By the Blightress, the way she felt pressed up against that wall, her breath leaving her body so rapidly, her lips red and full as she tried to speak…

I had learned some restraint in her presence in the last seven years, and I used it now, pacing my room, rubbing my face and attempting to focus. Thoughts of her undressing in the room next door and slipping bare into a warm bath did not help my current state, so I entered the washing room to splash cold water on my face.

She wanted to become companions tonight, and I felt no different. I'd bind to her anywhere, anytime at this point in our lives. If she was willing to throw all the planning for the ceremony we had already done out the window, so be it.

It was true, Clairannia would be the most hurt, followed by Figuerah and Pompeii, all three of which had helped us plan decorations and vows of binding. Clairannia herself was going to lead the ceremony as the conduit we'd chosen to conduct it.

I'd never heard of a completed companion ceremony with just the two to be bound, but I was more than willing to try.

I did not know where she had been the last sixteen days. I did not know what she had been through, but I was ready to listen when she was ready to speak, and if that was not now but after we were bound as one, I could accept that.

More focused, or as much as I ever would be for the night, I left the room, headed to the kitchens.

I'd been able to find my way around the castle and learn its halls somewhat while I was imprisoned there, waiting for Karus to land. Not long after I had found the rhyzolm in the grass, her pulse had dispersed. The pull from the stone was of her landing in varying places on the isle. First Hyrithia, then to the Spire, it would bounce across the Attatok Mountains, the Hallow Marshes, never landing more than a few moments before being pulled elsewhere again.

I couldn't make sense of it, and what had initially led to panic, then led to a precision state of doing everything I could to find her. And that meant enrolling the resources of the powerful influence who was the Queen of Hyrithia.

I knew she would want to help, but I was also aware she would distrust me after learning of my lies.

Her attempted imprisonment, however, I did not expect. And though her band of amethyst did nothing to dull my power, I stayed to keep what little trust she held in me still.

I had to become resourceful in leading the expedition to find Karus. I had grown friendly with the guards and servants of the castle, channelers who I could sense with the rhyzolm.

Geyrand had been the most useful, quickly arriving after learning Karus lived, and I would forever be in his debt for finding her and bringing her back to me.

"Baron Revich!" Mierah almost dropped the kettle in surprise as she brought it to a teapot on the table in the castle kitchens. She set the kettle on a stone tile and put her hand to her chest with a demure grin.

"Good evening, Mierah. I require your assistance." I placed my hands in my pockets and gripped the rhyzolm. Good. Karus was still somewhere upstairs.

"Me?" She shook her long black waves and moved around the table. "Shouldn't you be with Ash—I mean, Karus right now?"

I inhaled in a hidden sigh. Mierah had done her best to flirt with me over the past weeks since my arrival, and her dislike of Karus was evident. I was cordial enough to her, sensing she held some channeler magic, but I was growing tired of her coquettish ways.

It's true, I had used her fascination and attraction to me to be able to explore more of the castle and make more allies. She had been very useful, and though I did not wish to deceive her, I'd made it very clear her attempts at flirtations were useless.

"I just left her actually."

Her face fell and she turned back to the table.

"Do you know of styris tea?" I asked hurriedly.

"Of course, but why would you need…" Realization lit her eyes and she frowned. "You plan to bond to her? Tonight?" She shook her head and crossed her arms, the unblemished olive skin of her face reddening.

"I do." I stated simply, growing tired of this conversation already. "Where can I find it?" She huffed and spun around, her dark plum skirts and apron spinning with her. She headed to the dried goods pantry, and I helped myself to finding two mugs and a tray.

I filled another kettle with water and set it on the stove to heat, looking around for something that could suffice as a small dinner.

I heard Mierah rummaging around as I ladled two bowls of whatever soup had been made for the servant's dinner that night. I couldn't even think of eating, elated as I was, but I knew Karus had to be starving.

I cut two slices of bread from the fresh loaf on the table and gathered everything, ready to bring them back to my room before heading out to gather everything else we'd need for the night.

"Here." Mierah slapped a cheesecloth satchel onto the table, tied with a piece of twine. "That should get you through the night at least," she huffed.

I raised a brow, amused at her anger. It looked like enough styris tea to get us through at least a week. "Thank you, Mierah. And thank you for your help since I arrived. I wish you well."

I turned to leave with the tea and tray when she called out to me. "I hope she deserves you, Baron Revich. From what I know of that woman, she doesn't."

I stopped and turned back around. "You'd speak so poorly of a woman you have not known for seven years?"

She scoffed. "I know people don't change as much as you'd think. I know that when she lived here, she did not value her position as she should. She was selfish and reckless. She led Geyrand on and on without a second thought, and I would not be at all surprised if she did the same to you."

I wanted to laugh. I wanted to chide at her words, seeing now where her anger truly lied.

"You cared for Geyrand, didn't you?"

She pursed her lips and raised her chin. "Not just me. We all did. We all care for each other. Each of us who serve or guard the castle. Ash was neither. She didn't belong with us, and she certainly didn't belong with him."

I smirked. "No,"—I turned around again, done with our conversation—"she certainly didn't."

CHAPTER 22
KARUS

I was not being reckless.

I told myself again and again as I raised my hood and slipped out of the side entrance to the servants' quarters. I remembered all of the secret doors of the castle, and I knew this one would be the least used tonight.

Thankfully, after a quick bath and changing of my clothes, I had only had to slip by five guards, choosing another route to this door each time I heard them walking or speaking to one another.

I didn't know what would happen if I was caught, so I'd rather I wasn't.

I took a glance into the armory to look at who was on duty tonight. Then I ran through the training courtyard and slipped out the side door of the stables, steadying my gait to match the people of Hyrithia out for the night markets.

I suppressed my prideful grin at yet another successful sneak out of the castle, even many years after the last.

I had thirty minutes left to reach the lumens and get back to my room before Rev knew I had left. I was sure I could do it.

I stepped up to the gates of Hyrithia and pulled off my hood, swiping at my white-streaked hair and pulling it to one side, hopeful I would be presentable enough to be remembered.

"*Lynden,*" I whispered harshly, knocking on the iron-fortified door that led to one of the two guard towers. I heard a rustling before the door opened slightly, revealing the face of the burly man, his beard bushy and twinged with grays.

"Ash?" He stepped back and opened the door wider, joy lighting his eyes and he grabbed my shoulders and pulled me into an engulfing embrace. He laughed and pushed me back to see my face.

I grinned sheepishly, remembering the guard as overtly friendly to everyone, including me while I had lived here. "Hello, Lynden. It is good to see you again."

He laughed again, his large belly jostling in the movement as he said, "Come in! It is good to see you as well! I never thought I would again!"

I nodded and stepped inside the small room. It was humbly furnished with a small fireplace and a few wooden chairs. It smelled divine as something bubbled over the fire.

"Karus now, isn't it?" he asked, gesturing to a chair for me to sit.

"Yes. I wish we had more time to catch up, but I'm here to ask for your help."

He chuckled and shook his head, no surprise on his face. "I will do whatever you ask, as long as I am within the oath of the Hyrithian Royal Guard."

"I have not been ordered to stay in the castle by the Queen, if that's what you're asking. I need to see the lumens. They need to begin their journey back to Felgren tonight. I would not ask for your help if I did not trust you, and I am in a bit of a hurry."

He paused and rubbed his chin. Seven years had wrinkled his pale face in laugh lines. I had always enjoyed Lynden's company. Everyone did. He was generous in his affection and joyful demeanor. I was lucky it was him on duty tonight.

"I don't see why that can't be done. Though, if I am asked, I will tell the Queen the truth."

"Of course, old friend. I would not have you lie to Her Majesty."

"Alright then. Follow me. I'll admit, I'd like to see these massive beasts up close myself."

He led us outside to the portcullis and took a key from his pocket. He glanced back to me and then to the door of the other guard tower, bringing a finger to his lips and I nodded.

The black door that was cut into the iron portcullis opened and I stepped through it, bringing my fingers to my lips and giving a loud whistle. I tried to imbue it with my magic, hoping that it would reach far enough to their ears.

I grinned wide as I heard the pounding of paws the size of dinner plates across the grass. I braced my legs as they reached me, ready to steady myself if they decided to topple me. Parvus jumped up on his hind legs but did not knock me over this time as Rauca nipped at his back.

"Hello, handsome," I greeted him and rubbed his snout as he sniffed me eagerly. "Hello, beautiful," I greeted Rauca and she sniffed my hands in earnest, whining again at the scent of Rev. "Don't worry, he is safe and misses you, too."

I reached into my cloak pocket, pulling out a leather bag. "I need you to return to Felgren. You must get this to Figuerah or anyone else there. We need their help."

Parvus sniffed the bag and looked up to me, gently clamping his teeth onto the leather, perking his head toward the south where Felgren lay.

"Yes," I whispered excitedly. "Good boy. Get there as quickly as you can, and I will see you when you return with the conduits." I scratched behind his ears again and bent my head to his. He attempted to lick my face, but I knew his moves well and backed up just in time to avoid his wet kiss.

Rauca tilted her head back and howled. I shushed her quickly, giving her more love and reassuring her that her rider was alright. Parvus trotted down the dirt path with the bag in his mouth, whining for Rauca to come along.

I watched as the giant wolves ran off into the night and sighed, thankful something had gone right.

When I turned back to the iron gate, Lynden stood in shock. "I didn't know they could be so…tame."

I chuckled and slapped a hand onto his shoulder. "Honestly, they're little more than cubs half the time. Every channeler or conduit bonds to their lumen and we…understand each other."

"But…how?"

I shrugged. "It's just a part of the magic of Felgren. Parvus and Rauca will return in less than two days, hopefully. Will you keep an eye out for them for me?"

He stared out into the night as if he could still see the lumens, though the clouds over the moon made it unlikely he could see anything at all. "Sure. I'm happy to help."

"Thank you, Lynden." I hugged his brawny form in a quick squeeze and patted his shoulder, my inner clock warning me that I needed to get back to my room. "It really is good to see you again."

He laughed and locked the iron door behind us. "You haven't changed at all, old friend. It's good to see you, too."

I smiled and left, knowing full well of what he did not realize. I had changed. And as I slipped back into the castle and up to my room, I assured myself, through all the faults I still held, I had and would continue to change for the better.

CHAPTER 23
REV

I grinned like a fool.

A fool in love, a fool ready to bask in the rays of someone else's light. Not just anyone's, but hers.

I chuckled to myself, standing in the washing room connected to my bedroom. I scrubbed at her emerald ring with a paste one of the channeler guards had given to me when I'd asked it of him.

The guards used it to shine their armor and the servants used it to shine the silverware. I used it to clean whatever was caught in Karus's conduit ring. I had noticed that a cake of black *something* was embedded in every crevice and I would not place it on her finger tonight unless it was free of whatever she had just gone through.

Where had she been? Why did she leave? What could have forced her to leave Felgren and yet let her set the rhyzolm in the grass so that I could find her?

I shook my head and kept scrubbing with the soft-bristled brush I had borrowed as well. She'd tell me when she was ready. I was impatient to know, but more so, I was thankful that she was here, in the room next to mine.

She was about to *be* mine.

And I hers.

Companion bonds were strong, and sure, they could be broken, but it did not happen often. I knew ours would not. After what we had already been through, I knew there was nothing, *nothing*, that could break what we shared.

When we were bonded as companions, our connection would be endless. The magic of the bond would pull on us at all times. Even without the rhyzolm, we would share some sense of the feelings and place of the other.

Our *liberum* marks on our wrists would dissolve, and we would be free to create children.

I wanted that. I wanted to share that with her, but not yet. Styris tea would prevent it if only for a short while at a time.

I thought of how we had ravaged each other in the throne room and snickered at myself. There I was, a thirty-year-old Baron of Felgren, and I wanted her more than I ever had in my early twenties. If anything, I had only grown in my desire to kiss her, taste her, feel her writhe underneath me.

I put my tools aside and dropped the ring into the water basin to soak. I looked into the mirror and let out a long breath. Thinking of her made my eyes swirl with blue. They swirled with the color of the ocean as she had told me time and again—a place I had never even seen. They only hinted at blue when I was near her. Or when I was thinking of her.

I shook my head. What a Baron I had turned out to be.

The power of the Baron of Felgren seeped through my eyes most of the time, causing my irises to turn fully black. But somehow, my original deep blue often resisted around her. I remembered Heimlen's gray doing the same thing on occasion, and I wondered if this warring had happened to every Baron before me.

Heimlen would have seen it as a weakness.

I saw it as a strength.

If my love for Karus was strong enough to challenge the most powerful magic on Arcaynen, I was heartily ready to accept that.

I wondered how her eyes would look black if she accepted the Baronship with me. It would be the biggest downfall, but maybe I'd get to see the green of them again when she was loving me.

I lifted the ring out of the water to inspect its shine. I used a soft cloth to dry it and slipped it into my pocket. I gathered the ribbons and flowers I had managed to use my connections here to find and stepped up to the door of my room, absolutely ready to begin this night. I'd come back for the food and tea later.

I opened the door just as Karus's fist raised to knock.

She lit in mirthful laughter, tilting her head back, exposing more of her beautiful neck and chest. She held a tray in one hand and wore something a bit more fitting than the rosy pink dress she'd found me in. This one laced up the front, pulling her breasts taught and lovely, the deep copper accenting her eyes and making her smooth skin glow in the dim light of the hall.

I stepped forward to slide my hand around the back of her neck. "You are…" I shook my head, unable to contrive a word that could even come close to describing her beauty.

"Yours?" she whispered, lifting her lips to mine, wrapping her hand around my arm that still held onto her.

I breathed in her scent, lavender and rosewater, as she pushed me back into the room.

"Are we doing this in here?" I asked, setting the flowers and gold ribbons on the small table. I took the tray from her hand and set it next to my own.

"If you don't mind." She shrugged timidly, and I realized she must have memories in her old room she'd rather not recall tonight.

I shrugged as well, inspecting what she had brought. "I don't mind at all. I'd bond to you in a lumen den if need be. Speaking of…are Rauca and Parvus safe?"

She nodded and paused. "They've been through a lot."

I watched her choke slightly on her last words, but I would not pry. I picked up the small bag of styris tea I had brought and compared it to hers, smirking and raising a brow her way.

She picked up the mums and lifted them to her nose, chuckling. "I see we've both been busy preparing."

"Indeed. How did you find the tea?"

"I used to live here. I know where it's kept. The question is, how did *you* find some?"

My lips twitched. "I've been busy and resourceful while you've been away. Thankfully, that hard work is paying off." I inspected the hard cheese and fruit she had brought as well. "Would you like to eat first?"

"Absolutely not."

She slipped her long fingers through the gold satin ribbons, four in total, and brought them to her chest, looking at me with precious vulnerability. We held each other's gaze in silence, and I remembered those times she would come to my study after she had found the rhyzolm in the forest. We would say so much in those moments without speaking a word.

Back then, she had looked at me with curiosity and confusion, though always with a hint of desire. Desire to know me or desire that seeped from somewhere deep within, I never knew. My gaze had always been one of longing, frustration, and hope.

"I love you," she said, keeping her eyes on mine and stepping forward, ribbons in hand.

I nodded. "I love you, too."

I knew what she meant. I knew the simple words were not enough to express what we felt, but our hearts spoke the truth louder in their steady silence deep within our chests.

She smoothed the ribbons out on the table and raised her right hand to me. I took the emerald ring from my pocket and slipped it onto her forefinger. She laughed lightly, grinning up at me without inhibition as I clasped my fingers around hers.

She inhaled long and loud as she picked up the first ribbon, exhaling softly through her full, ruby lips. "Ready?"

"Yes," I murmured. I wanted to shout through the streets that I was ready to bond to this woman. I wanted a public declaration to all of Arcaynen that I loved her and would want her all the days of my life. But I could see what this meant to her. Just her and I together, alone, where we loved each other best. The time would come soon enough for me to be able to shout to the rooftops of my soul singing her song, but here, in this borrowed room, she needed me...just me.

Finding the center of the ribbon and placing it over our joined hands, she carefully wrapped one end around her own wrist and then to mine, beginning the words to the bonding we had both been practicing.

"In this binding, I share with you my hopes and desires."

I took the other end of the ribbon and repeated her movements, first wrapping the long end around my wrist and then hers. "In this binding, I share with you my hopes and desires."

She bit her bottom lip in pure joy, and I shook my head. She knew I struggled to resist that.

I picked up the next ribbon, placing it over the other, managing to tuck one end under what was already wrapped around our hands. I understood why this was so much easier with a conduit to conduct the ceremony, but I managed to tie the ribbons together in a loose knot with my left hand.

I repeated the wrapping again, reciting, "In this binding, I reveal to you my strengths and weaknesses."

She took her end, wrapping it around us once more, and repeated, "In this binding, I reveal to you my strengths and…" she paused, swallowing hard. I lifted my free hand to her face as she looked to me and finished, "…weaknesses."

I wanted to kiss her, but couldn't yet, as my thumb caught the single tear that slipped down her cheek. If we were to get this ceremony right with just us two, we'd have to stick to tradition as much as possible for the binding to set.

She opened her red lips slightly and took a deep breath before picking up the third gold ribbon. She managed to tie it around the others and proceeded to wrapping while vowing, "In this binding, I offer you my past, my present, and my future."

I repeated her movements, vowing the same. "In this binding, I offer you my past, my present, and my future."

I trembled slightly, picking up the last ribbon. This was the final test. We'd know if the bonding worked with this last piece of gold. In traditional companion ceremonies, the last ribbon would be imbued with the conduit's magic, glowing as it was tied and wrapped over the other three.

I held the ribbon toward her and she took one end, closing her eyes and breathing deep. I watched as her brilliant green power raced down the length of the ribbon, meeting my own deep blue in the middle.

"Karus. Look," I whispered. She opened her eyes to watch as our power met and began to entwine, each tendril running down the length of the gold satin in a twirl of binding.

I slipped the ribbon under the other three and finished the ceremony. "In this binding, I promise my love to you, Karus, and all of the endurance I have to share it for all of the days of my life."

The ribbon flashed a brilliant blue, and Karus repeated my wrappings and words, "In this binding, I promise my love to you, Rev, and all of the endurance I have to share it for all the days of my life."

It flashed a brilliant green before each coil of power melded into one swirling piece of teal, the shade warm and soft, emitting a dim glow in the low light of the room.

Karus looked up at me with a beaming smile, upturning her left wrist before laughing and revealing it to me.

Her *liberum* mark was gone, and I lifted my own wrist to see that mine had left as well.

"We did it," she laughed with fervor. "We really did it."

I laughed with her, our hands still bound as I leaned down just an inch or two to kiss her lips.

It was a difficult task, our grins so wide our teeth clashed. Instead, I bent my forehead to hers, basking in the elation of the moment of our binding.

Companions. We were companions and bound to each other for the rest of our lives.

It would take time to sink in, I knew, but in those moments of joy, and laughter, and love, I fought with all I had to remember my heart standing before me. Her eyes were a gentle glow of green, her cheeks pink and burning from her smiles and laughter at our success.

I turned to the tray, placing the tea infuser over the brown mug as I poured the styris tea that had been brewing into hers. I repeated with my own and handed her the steaming brew.

She sniffed its contents. Neither one of us had ever tasted the tea since we had never needed it in the past.

She lifted her mug to mine, tapping its surface. "Here's to us, Rev."

I smirked. "To us."

We sipped the warm contents at the same time, both breaking out into laughter at the bitter taste.

"Couldn't they make it a little sweeter or something?" she asked, taking another sip and grimacing.

"I'd guess if they did, there'd be a lot fewer children on the isle. I think the bitterness is the point." I took another sip and then decided to down the whole thing in one go. She looked at me in surprise and I smirked again, shrugging. "Feel like joining me on the bed, Karus?" I winked at her and laughed as her face fell from amusement to lust. A small moan escaped with her breath and she mimicked my gulp, downing the rest of the tea.

Placing her mug next to mine, she followed as I lead us to the large four-poster bed, our hands still bound together. They would be until morning as was tradition. The consummation of the companion binding was meant to be tricky with hands entwined for the whole of the evening—the first difficult task the couple would have to navigate together.

I sat on the edge of the bed and pulled her to me. She lifted her skirts with one hand and settled herself over my lap.

"I need you to know something, Karus," I started, lifting my free hand to her neck, rubbing my thumb across the base of her jaw.

"I'm listening, Baron Revich." She leaned into my touch, the candlelight in the room reflecting off her eyes.

"From the moment I saw you, felt you, I've wanted you. It has never been a choice to love you. Never once did I have to stop and think about whether I did or did not. Your soul has spoken to mine through time and loss, and I have welcomed every second of it."

Her eyes brimmed with glistening tears, and she placed her free hand over mine still stroking her face.

"I am still healing from that loss, and I wake everyday thankful that you have come back to me. If I have realized anything these last sixteen days, it is that we deserve each other."

A soft cry left her, and she lowered her head in what I could only recognize as a sense of shame and guilt as tears spilled down her face. I kissed the top of her white streaks of hair, ones that I had helped in making. I gently lifted her chin and shook my head. "This is my soul speaking to yours, Karus of Felgren. My companion, my love, we deserve each other. You and I. I will show you every day of our lives that what we deserve is happiness, and love, and a future of good things. Together. Regardless of what we will face next, we face it together. Promise me that, Karus."

She swept forward, urgent, needy, pressing her lips against mine, pushing me to lay back on the bed, and I kissed her in return with just as much urgency.

"I promise, Rev," she breathed against my mouth. "Together. I promise."

I shifted my right hand to slip my fingers through hers under the ribbons. I never wanted to hear her speak of not deserving this. I never wanted her to think that she was worth less than what we shared together. I would make her see the truth. If not tonight, then every night for the rest of our lives.

I would worship her body, kiss and touch every inch of her skin until she understood what she deserved. And then, when she finally realized her worth, I'd do it all again, because *that* is what I deserved.

CHAPTER 24
KARUS

R ev managed to touch every inch of me that night.

Every brush of his lips, every caress of his fingers, felt like a rush of power and fire all at once. I glowed over him, under him, tucked into his body as if we were one shape, one being, joining rhythmically with every new position we managed even with our hands bound.

I no longer attempted to restrain my power. It seeped from my skin unbound and wild, flowing between us in green tendrils. I welcomed it, moving against him with it. I would not dampen myself when he did this to me. I would not confine what was mine to show and his to witness in the joining of our bodies.

I wasn't sure how long we'd been like this.

I wasn't sure if an hour had passed or four as we wove together in our first night as companions.

His thrusts were picking up on top of me again while he lifted my leg, pressing it to my torso with his left hand, holding my right hand above my head, bound with his. I thought I might perish.

I had found the bliss of release three times already and shuddered to think of what the budding fourth would do to me.

I writhed underneath his body, begging, screaming for him to finish me off right there; a life cut short by unfathomable pleasure.

He stifled my cries with his mouth, his tongue finding mine and settling in to kill me with a final wave of ecstasy I was barely conscious for.

He groaned on my lips and the sound hardly registered. I was already too far gone into some space where stars danced behind my eyes, and a resounding pulse beckoned me into a state of tears and trembling limbs.

He rolled over beside me and pulled me to him, our chests meeting bare and slick with sweat. He reached down and pulled the blankets over us. My blood ran hot, but I felt as if I'd be cold forever as I shivered, my teeth chattering uncontrollably.

I felt as if I'd never return to the normal I had known, forever marked by what he had done to show me just what kind of together he meant.

I laughed as I trembled and cried, understanding with great clarity that I was never to question those things again. Or, perhaps I would, if it meant I got this.

"It's alright," he murmured, recognizing in my face how lost in thought, and bliss, and rapture I had become. "I love you, Karus," he spoke into the night, now silent from my moans and pleas of more.

I slipped my leg, shaking still, over his hip as I always did, tucked in beneath the man who was my sky. The man who held me regardless of my brilliance, my dim, or the complete absence of my glow. I nodded, ready to slip into my dreams which could never compare to the one who held me.

CHAPTER 25
REV

I woke slowly, my need for rest warring with my need to comprehend where she was going with those soft kisses.

We had woken once together, both of us needing to relieve ourselves in the washing room after all that tea in the span of night. We both giggled in exhaustion as we were still bound and stumbled back to bed only to collapse onto each other and back into deep sleep.

The tea had worn off by now and from what my stirring mind could tell, where she was headed with that mouth, we wouldn't need more just yet.

Her fingers grazed over my stomach as her kiss lay soft and gentle on the underside of me, hard and ready for whatever kind of pleasure she was going to put me through again.

I kept my eyes closed and waited to see which Karus she'd bring.

Coy and slow?

Rough and fast?

Ah, it was languid and teasing this morning, I realized, as she flattened her tongue and licked all the way up only to lazily kiss the top of what I wished I could slip into her as uninhibited as I did the night before.

"Fuck," I breathed, which only led to some new torturous shape of her tongue before she slipped all of me into her mouth.

I gathered her hair in my left hand, our rights entwined over my stomach while I kept it out of her face as she worked, taking her sweet, sweet time as payback for what I'd put her though last night.

I'd never seen her so shaken, and I'd made it a new goal in life to see that a few dozen times more.

Somewhere in the depths of my mind, where logic was locked behind a fortified door, I wondered if we actually had time for this.

Knowing her, it was probable she knew we didn't, which made the precarious way she'd bring me to an edge before backing off and grinning up at me all the more exciting.

"If you keep this up, we'll be in even more trouble."

She wrapped her free hand around me and sweetly kissed what she slowly stroked, her eyes watching me in a challenge.

"Come here," I tugged on our bound hands with only the thought of pulling her on top of me to lose ourselves in rapture together.

"No, no, Baron Revich," she mumbled with the same lips that I would have moaning in a moment if it was up to me. "We've had no tea and are surely late to this morning's chastisements already."

I sighed as she squeezed our bound hands together and began her confident strokes again. "At least bring yourself up here to me. Remember what we did on the top floor of—" I sucked a breath through my teeth, feeling the warmth of her wet mouth take all of me in again. "Of Viridis?"

I heard her muffled laugh as I slipped out of her mouth while she lazily stroked me up and down. "I do remember that. And if my memory is correct, you were supposed to be helping me research the Baron who discovered the use of rhyzolm."

"I don't care what I was supposed to be doing or what we should be doing now, just come here." I yanked on our hands again, and she giggled as I successfully pulled her up to my chest. I rose slightly to catch her mouth and kiss her deeply. I rolled my tongue delicately across hers, giving her a glimpse of what exactly I'd like to do next.

She pulled away, laughing and resuming her strokes, this time faster and with a tighter grip. "I'm just giving you what you deserve, Revich."

I think I might have actually growled as I grabbed her neck, bringing her mouth back to mine. She pushed me back down onto the bed and left my lips quickly, her mouth otherwise occupied in my final release.

I relaxed, breathing heavy, still exhausted from the night before. She kissed her way up my stomach and chest, settling her head on my skin.

"In a moment, Karus, I plan to return the favor."

She exhaled heavily in a moan and stretched her body against mine. "I'm quite sore, actually. I think you've done enough for the next twelve hours."

I stroked her cheek and closed my eyes. "In twelve hours, then."

She laughed and made her way up to my chest, kissing my neck, then jaw and cheek, before settling her lips across mine.

The knock came first, followed by a sharp, "Baron Revich of Felgren." I sat up quickly, startled by the intrusion.

"What is it?" I called, Karus coming up with me.

"Your presence with Karus of Felgren is requested in thirty minute's time in the Queen's study."

I raised a brow at Karus and she grimaced. I had not been taken to the Queen's personal study yet and could not predict if it was a good sign or bad.

"We will be there in thirty minutes," I called, grazing a finger along Karus's jaw. Her skin was soft and pale, smooth except for the raised freckles that occasionally littered her face and neck.

We heard the man outside our door clear his throat and then continue, "I am to escort you both to her study."

"There's no need." Karus replied, pulling my fingers to her lips to kiss. "I know the way."

The man paused before we heard his decision at the sound of his footsteps leaving the corridor.

"What do you think this is about?" she asked. "Surely, the Lady of the Spire and the Madame of the Mountains have not arrived yet."

I shook my head and ran my fingers down her neck, then her chest, and took ahold of her left hand. "No, my guess is she's heard a rumor and wants to hear the truth herself." I kissed her wrist where her liberum mark had graced it for years before last night.

"How would she know so quickly?"

"I could not gather all we needed last night alone, my love. Servants talk. I think Mierah especially would have been willing to do so."

"You got all of this from *Mierah?*" she scorned.

"Yes, we've met."

"Oh, I'm sure she *loved* meeting you." She shook her head and clenched her jaw.

"Am I detecting you do not like Mierah?" I didn't know if that was jealousy that crossed her face just now, but I was enjoying it.

"It started with Mierah not liking *me*. I'm surprised she helped you at all." She paused and looked back to my face, her eyes flitting down to my bare chest and broad shoulders. "Actually, I know exactly why she helped you. And no, I don't doubt that she got word to the Queen immediately about the kind of tea you needed."

Her anger and irritation rolled off her, and I realized just how much I enjoyed it. For so many years, I watched Karus emit little to no emotion at all. She would recite the same answers to my questions in my study each day—her body like Karus, her mind not.

"Let's go prove the rumors true, then. The Queen probably thinks I've entrapped you somehow. Maybe we can convince her I have not."

"Oh, you most certainly have, Baron Revich. The difference is, I came willingly."

"And many times over."

She tilted her head back and laughed before falling into my chest.

I chuckled and smoothed the top of her hair.

She lifted her head to meet me and pulled our right hands up between us. "Are you ready?"

I nodded and began to help her untie our bonds. We pulled gently at the gold ribbons and slowly unwound them. They left red marks on our skin, and we both rolled our wrists, finally free of the physical bind, but never of the invisible one.

"Come on." She pulled me up to stand next to her.

I stretched my arms up high, popping them and then settling them back down and around her waist.

She reached over and grabbed an apple from one of the trays, holding it up to my mouth to take a bite before sinking her own teeth into its red flesh. "I'm taking you out to the market and my favorite stall after we speak to the Queen. I hope it's still there."

"And what if the Queen does not wish me to leave the castle?"

Karus huffed, taking another bite and chewing ravenously. "This nonsense ends today. She's had plenty of hours to think on what I said to her last night, and if she does not yet understand, I will make her."

Karus always had a fire that burned for what she loved and who she believed in, and, though it had been months since she had woken, I had not seen it flicker as fiercely across her face as I did now.

"I believe you, love." I leaned in to kiss her once more. "I believe you."

CHAPTER 26
KARUS

We half-ran down the halls and corridors, my satin slippers softly clicking on the long red carpets that lined our way. I pulled again on Revich's hand to keep up, not wanting to show any sign to the Queen that we were two adults who could not even make it to a meeting on time.

I fussed with the ties across my dress, pulling at the cream ribbon that slipped through each loop, sometimes twisted, and making for a haphazard appearance. Or at least one the Queen would notice.

I was finally able to twist the ribbon so that it lay flat across the front of my chest and looked over to see Rev watching me with confusion.

"What?" I exhaled, starting up the second to last staircase before our destination.

"I don't know…it's like…like I can feel how nervous you are. More so than what you're showing right now on your face." He pulled on my arm to stop only a quarter way up the stairs.

We'd passed several guards and servants on our way, and two more carried trays of pastries and small meat pies up the stairs, passing us by.

"And now you're starving. Karus, I think I can feel everything you feel." His smile widened. "Close your eyes."

I did, curious and taking a deep breath.

"Without looking, how am I feeling right now?" he asked softly.

I leaned in closer. I smelled the familiar draft of the castle, but also him. Earthy, pine. Even away from Felgren, he smelled like the fresh breeze of the forest and the upturned earth of a new sapling. "You're feeling…sorrow." I twisted my mouth into a frown and moved closer, reaching up to find his cheek. "Sorrow and a hole. Like there's a hole, right here." I opened my eyes and moved my hand to his chest over his heart.

His grin was brilliant, his black and blue eyes glassy. He bent down to kiss me. "It's true then. We can sense each other's emotions and desires. I didn't know it would be this strong."

"I don't think it typically is," I murmured. "What was that?" I patted at his chest where I had sensed that he was so wounded just now. I could not feel it again, but it was so real, as if someone had dug under his ribs and yanked out his heart, leaving behind an expanse of space that echoed through the world in a longing to be filled.

His smile fell and he rubbed the back of his neck. "I thought of what it was like when you were there, but not there. I wanted to see if you could feel that from me."

I pushed my forehead into his, holding back from crying right before meeting the Queen to discuss how well and healthy our relationship was. I sniffed. "How long did it feel like, Rev? Seven years outside of Felgren—how long was it for you?"

He brushed his lips across my forehead and pulled me to his chest. The castle staff whispered to each other about this scene of the Baron of Felgren and the woman who was supposed to be dead, holding each other on carpeted crimson stairs.

"An eternity, Karus. Just one eternity."

CHAPTER 27
REV

Somehow, I resisted from bursting into the study ahead, declaring my love, devotion, and life for this woman who writhed in nerves and poorly subdued anger next to me.

Her dark clouds raged around her thoughts, and yet, I could not be more elated. I could not be more proud, committed, or sure of what our future held together and the happiness we would share.

This whole trial and question of my intentions with Karus was nothing more than a trying charade of formality I would see through for her. I could have left these castle walls at any time in the last seventeen days, but stayed, waiting for her to land.

Even if the Queen and leaders of the isle decided I was guilty of…whatever they deemed unacceptable, we would not stay to hear my sentence.

The Baron of Felgren was indispensable to the isle. The Queen knew that. Barons had trained conduits for centuries, and conduits were necessary to keep our way of life going.

The Queen needed me.

I did not need her.

After Karus's knock, I already had my hand on the doorknob when we heard the Queen bid us to enter.

My companion glanced at me one last time, her face set, a flame licking her eyes, and I smiled smugly, ready to watch this unfold.

Her hand squeezed mine as I opened the door, and we stepped into the room.

The Queen stood at her desk, her dark face taut in a disapproving stare as she watched us.

It was an expensively furnished room with wide, cushioned chairs that encircled a short table. The trays of pastries that had passed us earlier were now set on its glass surface.

The Queen and Karus stared at each other, neither willing to give an inch, and I felt like an intruder, watching what was brewing between these two powerful women.

"Did you consider—" Karus spoke just as the Queen said, "I have more—"

They both stopped mid-sentence, the tension palpable between them.

"Do you mind if we sit, Your Majesty?" I gestured to the puffy violet-cuffed chairs near the table. "We're absolutely famished this morning."

I kept my face straight as Karus turned to me in irritation, and the Queen slid her lower jaw to the side, gathering patience to deal with anything I said to her.

She gave a short nod, and I led Karus to a chair, handing her a plate and picking up my own.

We'd only had time to share the apple this morning, and I was well aware part of Karus's anger was from hunger.

I bit my lips inward trying not to laugh as she hastily began piling her plate with small pies filled with sausage and gravy.

I plucked some sort of egg pastry from the tray and sat back into my chair.

The Queen joined us, taking nothing for herself. "I have more questions for you, Karus." She paused and glanced my way. "You as well, Baron Revich."

I nodded and began chewing. If anything, I was presenting myself in the worst possible way. But I was angry, too. And this show of indifference would get under her skin the quickest.

"Is it true, then?" Queen Rina glanced down to Karus's left wrist.

She held it up, so the Queen could see the unblemished underside, no longer holding the curved *l* from a *liberum* mark.

"How could you complete a companion ceremony without a conduit to conduct it?"

Karus ate furiously, swallowing and swiping her thumb across her lip. "We had my magic. We had Baron magic. We did not need a third."

The Queen narrowed her eyes on me as if I had forced her into it. I was cool and collected in my next words. "What is it you think I have done to your ward, Your Majesty? She sits before you now, whole and happy, and yet you still question my intentions?" I placed my plate on the table and leaned forward. "What did you expect when you let Heimlen take her? Did you think she would not change? Did you think she would not grow? Did you think the same woman who left would be the same one to return to you?"

She struggled to hide it—the effect my questions had on her—but I noticed the shiver that worked its way through her body as I voiced the very things she refused to consider.

"I could have helped her. Prince Philius, Geyrand—we loved her, and we could have helped her. You didn't even let us *try*, and now my son spends his days drinking and starting fights in taverns."

"So that's why you're angry." I nodded slowly, falling back into the puffed chair. "That's why you put on this sham of a trial? For what? For protecting the woman I love from never returning to me?"

"What have you told her, Rev?" Karus set her plate on the table and turned to me. "How much of this story does she know?"

"Enough."

"You didn't tell her then. You didn't tell her what I did to cause the loss of myself."

I gritted my teeth. I hoped I wouldn't have to.

Karus laughed in realization, pointing my way. "That man protects me even now, Queen Rina. Even at the sake of himself, he chooses to protect me from any potential harm." She reached across the chair, offering her hand.

I took it.

The Queen watched us, her wrinkles plainer on her face, the bags under her eyes, swollen with sleepless nights, more obvious. I wondered who the woman was that Karus once knew because I was convinced this woman was not her.

Karus cleared her throat and swallowed. "I hope you've set aside some time, Your Majesty, because I have some things to tell you."

I WATCHED KARUS AS SHE TOLD HER STORY, *OUR* STORY, LEAVING OUT some of the best details in my opinion.

But perhaps we shouldn't push any more buttons.

I glanced at the Queen occasionally, to see how she was taking in all of what had happened to Karus after she left. But really, I just wanted to watch Karus retell her life. I had recited this very story to her not too long ago, and it had been emotionally draining.

But the love of my life sat straight, her long torso held high, towering over the Queen's. What I could feel from her was… resilience.

When Karus spoke of what I had done to bring her back—all the searching for the rhyzolm, staying away from her to give her time to adjust to life with Moira, the questions in the study—I shifted in my seat, reliving that time with each word she spoke.

I hadn't told anyone but Karus that much of our story, not even my channelers. There were people who had lived it with me and knew, but I had only sat down and told her. And though I meant to speak of it someday, it cut through my chest sharper than I expected, hearing her retell some of the most painful years of my life.

She stopped mid-sentence, explaining how I had taken her to Viridis when she'd asked and how she'd fallen back into the dark after seeing it so corrupted.

Karus turned to me abruptly, her mouth parting slightly as her eyes furrowed. I met her stare, realizing I was a beacon of heartbreak right then, and she could feel every bit of it.

"Sorry," I spoke under my breath, producing a small smile. She rose from her chair and came to mine, bending over me, encasing me with her hands on both arm rests.

She brushed my lips with hers lightly, saying between just the two of us, "We can stop. We can stop here and go back to our room."

There she was. There was the woman I deserved. The one I called home.

I cupped her face with my hands, straightening to meet her with a kiss. Her hair fell into my face with the scent of lavender and rose mixed with what was just *her*.

I pushed her hair behind her ears and kissed the tip of her nose. "Never mind me, love. We stay until she has the story she needs to understand what happened."

She nodded and went back to her seat, taking my hand in hers again.

I turned to the Queen. Tears ran down her cheeks in a shimmering stream.

She took a handkerchief from her pocket to wipe them away and asked, "How—how did you find your memories again?"

Karus nodded toward me. "I found the rhyzolm that Rev was searching for. Holding it awoke the feelings of our past and memories began to return to me. He used that same rhyzolm recently when he came to you for help. And that day, after seeing Viridis... I..." She glanced back to me and continued, "I heard a voice speaking to me inside my head. It told me to wake. And then I did. And I remembered. I knew who I was. I knew something of what had happened. Rev, Moira, Clairannia, and Figuerah filled in the rest."

"Who was this voice? Who spoke to you in your mind?"

I watched Karus carefully. We had discussed this many times, never coming to an answer that made sense.

She squeezed my hand again and bit her lip, pausing before she said, "I know now who it was."

I cocked my head in surprise and she continued, staring right at me.

"It was the voice of the Blightress."

CHAPTER 28

KARUS

Watching Rev's reaction as I admitted who had woken me from seven years of knowing nothing of who I was, tore at me just as much as I guessed it would.

His lips pursed and he brought his hand to his mouth, covering any raw emotions he felt.

He could no longer hide from me, though. We were now bound, and though I couldn't explain why our companion bond was so strong, it was blatantly obvious to me that his reaction was confusion, fear, and anger.

Confusion for how it was possible, fear for what I had gotten myself into, and anger that I did not tell him earlier.

I squeezed his hand and turned back to the Queen, not ignoring him, but needing to see her reaction.

She was too still in hearing me speak about a woman who should have been long dead, and I frowned.

"You know, don't you?" I shook my head, recalling what the Blightress had casually mentioned about excursions funded to her land by the Queen. More and more I understood the countless number of details about my life and its origins that had been hidden from me.

Nodding slowly, she took a breath and answered, "The Blightress lives. Yes, I am aware of this."

Rev pulled his hand from mine and bent forward on his knees, rubbing his face.

"*You are* aware *of this*?" I laughed in disbelief. "Tell us, Your Majesty, what else do you know that could change the world we live in? What else have you hidden from me about my past and my parents?"

"I hid things from you to protect you."

"Oh, how ironic." I nodded toward Rev who continued to rub his face while listening to us bicker. "Is that not the same thing you're putting the Baron on trial for?"

The Queen sighed at my short temper and spoke softly, "I have decided to not proceed with a trial."

Rev barely looked at her before turning to me, his hand back over his mouth, his eyes black as obsidian.

I cringed. I knew there was much he wanted to say to me, but not in the Queen's presence.

She continued her inquiry. "How, Karus? How do you know it was the Blightress who woke you?"

I swallowed, my throat suddenly dry. If I was going to relive what I'd been through and heard, I might as well do it now. Rev would have to know eventually, and the Queen apparently knew plenty about the Blightress already. "Because that's where I've been for two weeks. I followed the Blightress to her lands where I… discovered some things. Things I did not know were there to find. She told me things about myself and my past."

Rev shook his head, his hands gripped so tightly in front of him, his knuckles turned white. "You found the Blightress in Felgren and decided to follow her around for *two weeks*?"

Oh, I was in trouble.

His voice came low and dangerous. I shivered, part of me infatuated with his anger, part of me dreading the talk we would have later.

I wasn't angry in retaliation. I deserved every emotion that was flitting off his body, and I had spent my last few days thinking about how I'd bear every bit of his rage if only I could be with him again.

I opened my mouth to answer, but the Queen spoke first. "I was unaware that she could travel outside of her domain. All of my reports say that she never leaves the confines of the Northern Steppes."

I replied quickly. "She wasn't so much in Felgren as she was… under it."

"*Karus.*" His eyes darkened further toward me, and I fidgeted my hands in my skirts.

"Let her speak, Baron Revich. You can scold her later," the Queen spat.

He bent his head in defeat, running his hands through his hair. When he looked up, he sat back in his chair, quiet, black eyes locked on me, gesturing for me to continue.

The Queen nodded in my direction. "Go on, Karus. I must know exactly what happened and everything she told you."

I slipped my fingers under my legs, sitting on my hands to ground them as best I could. Revich worked hard to keep his emotions in check while I told my second story of the morning.

I told them of the hole in the forest and how the lumens had fallen in and broken their legs. I spoke of the tunnel encased in blight and the portal she led me to. "It was a difficult choice, Rev," I confessed to him, his dark eyes continuing to pierce my skin. "I knew you'd be angry, and I knew you'd be scared, but I felt like I needed answers and there they were, right in front of me. She knew so much about me that I did not. She spoke to me in my mind, and I knew there was something there between us. I knew I'd only find out what it was if I followed her."

His expression didn't change. I was hoping he'd soften a little when he heard why I had chosen to leave.

"Did you find your answers then?" The Queen asked. "You were there for so long, I'd imagine you and the Blightress would be friends at this point."

My anger flared. I was glad I had chosen to sit on my hands. "No." I turned to face Rev. "No, I did not choose to be with the

Blightress for two weeks. The portal I stepped into…it slowed time and wouldn't let me leave. What felt like only a few hours in the portal was fourteen days outside of it."

There.

Finally, a slight movement in his jaw. I breathed a sigh of relief.

"How did you escape?" The Queen's questions were more hurried now.

"I remembered the portal to Viridis. It wants your true name, the one that truly belongs to you before it will let you through. I thought this portal might want something as well. So, I started speaking. Telling the black void that I needed to get back to you."

Rev squinted as if a dagger had sliced through his chest.

"I told the portal that I was leaving to find you and that nothing could stop me. I was angry. I screamed and yelled and when I showed that anger, it spit me out."

"And you saw the Blightress and her land?"

I paused. The truth was, I didn't know anything about how Queen Rina knew the Blightress existed. I didn't know what those excursions she was accused of funding were, and I didn't know how much she knew about my parents. "Yes. I fell out of the portal and found myself in her land." I did not describe the cave, the beating heart that hung there like a pustule, pulsing and red. Later, after Rev scolded me, I would tell him about the beating heart that fueled the Blight.

"What is her land like? What creatures did you see there?" she rushed on.

"It was a swamp land. A forest of infested puddles and over-grown fungus. There was one creature…" I trailed off remembering the trees that came to life and their earth-shattering roars as they chased me on the back of Parvus.

"Yes? What was it? How did you escape?"

She leaned in closer to me now, and I narrowed my eyes. "What do you know? Why do you assume I was in danger?"

She replied, "I know of the syphoners, Karus. Many channeler souls of Hyrithia have fallen to them. She keeps the channelers alive and takes their magic to fuel her own."

Syphoners. I shuddered to think of what that creature would have done to me had Parvus not shown up just in time.

"Have you heard enough for one morning, Your Majesty?" Rev spoke quietly, turning his gaze to the Queen.

She scoffed. "Not nearly enough, Baron, and I should think you'd feel the same." She turned back to me. "What did the Blightress tell you of your parents?"

"She—she said they had come to steal her power. She said you funded them to travel into her land." I took a deep breath and let it out slowly. "She said she tore out my father's heart in front of my mother."

Rev let his grief for me fly in the space between us, and I looked his way with a small smile.

"He is dead then." The Queen spoke slowly, looking just past me in a daze. "I did not know that at least, Karus. I did not know your father's fate, and your mother was too delirious to tell us anything. She didn't know about you before they left. Arah never would have gone."

A cold sadness welled in my heart hearing those words from the mother who raised me about the mother who bore me. I had gone all my life knowing very little of my parents, and I had accepted that a long time ago. "I would like to know more about my parents, but not now, Queen Rina."

She nodded solemnly.

"Why didn't the Blightress kill Arah as well?" Revich asked. "Why did she leave Karus's mother alive? What are these excursions you've been funding and why?"

"I will explain, Baron Revich. I will wait, however, until my fellow leaders arrive. There is much to discuss, and all of the rulers of the isle should be there."

She looked up at him as he rose from his chair to pace then turned back to me, pressing for more answers. "How did you escape her? How did you leave her lands?"

I stood as well, ready to leave. I needed to speak to Rev alone. "She let me go. That was our deal when I followed her underground. I would listen to what she had to say, and she would let me and the lumens leave safely. She promised not harm us and would let us go as soon as I asked her to, which I did when I realized how long I'd been gone." I grimaced and glanced at Revich. "I just didn't think to specify where."

He shook his head, his hands shoved in his pockets, radiating anger and more prominently, fear. We both stood with the table between us and did not speak.

Another one of our wordless conversations passed through our gaze until finally, the Queen cleared her throat. "I believe that is enough for this morning. Karus, Baron Revich, I request you do not leave the city until the Lady of the Spire and the Madame of the Mountains arrive. They are due here tomorrow evening, and we will continue this discussion then." She rose and stepped closer to me. "It is good to have you back here, Karus. We all have missed you. Philius has missed you." She took my hand in hers and patted it gently. "I have missed you, my daughter." She embraced me, and I patted her back, still unsure of how to feel in her presence.

Rev held a hand out to me across the table, and I moved to it eagerly. I wanted to get through the harsh words he undoubtedly had to say so that we could begin to move past what I had done.

The Queen gestured toward the door. "The Prince will be awake soon, and I have some things to discuss with him before you speak to him again. Why don't you show Baron Revich the market, Karus? He would enjoy seeing Hyrithia in all its beauty. You have not walked our streets before, I believe?"

Rev wound his fingers through mine and my heart jumped in elation. He couldn't be too upset with me if he was willing to still hold my hand. "Actually, I have, Queen Rina. But I was not able to truly admire your city at the time. There was something to distract me." His smile lifted to one side but did not last long.

We left the study, and he led the way back down the stairs. Instead of heading toward the room we shared, however, he walked us right out of the castle doors, nodding to the guards posted there as if he knew them.

I was surprised to see they nodded back and addressed him respectfully. "Baron."

"Just how many friends have you made here in two weeks?" I inquired, remembering Rev's charm never did fall solely on me.

He pulled me into the dusty cobbled streets, loud and busy with the mid-morning hustle of merchants and traders coming from all over the isle. The air was filled with shouts and laughter and an autumn chill that made me wish we had stopped for our cloaks. The copper dress I had chosen to wear for our companion binding was not meant for walks through the open marketplace, and the laced bodice was a bit too formal for such a casual stroll.

But casual was not at all Rev's pace. He seemed to have an idea of where he was going, his long legs and stride dashing under the two bridges that connected the most prominent inns in the city.

The inns of Hyrithia were always full, packed with traders and inventors, people who came to the hub to let their ideas be heard and their plans be seen to light.

"Are you going to speak to me at all, or are you going to lead me silently along until you think I've had enough?" I huffed, my breath billowing in a white cloud in front of me as I rubbed my arm for warmth with my free hand.

He turned his head back to me at that, his black waves threatening to unbind from the piece of gold ribbon tying back his hair. At least he wore the clothes of a Baron: long pants, boots, a cream shirt, and black vest. *He* was layered. Raising a single brow, I got the sense of annoyance from his face, so I shut my mouth and remained silent.

Fine. If this was what he wanted, I'd give it to him. I didn't like it, but I didn't get to choose how he felt about my leaving with a woman who wasn't supposed to exist, let alone still be living after centuries. Not to mention a woman who had murdered my father, captured my mother, and was legendary in her wrath.

Instead, I let him lead us around to different stalls on the busiest market street. He held my hand tightly at each one he stopped at, never acknowledging me there, but not letting go either.

At one point, I tried to yank my hand from his, but he seemed ready for the attempt and held it firmer still.

At least his hand was warm.

I sighed and studied what he purchased. So far, he seemed to be gathering supplies. He slung a satchel of fruit and bread over his shoulder. We stopped at a dairy shop built into the street where he bought three different kinds of cheese, talking friendly all the while to the full-bosomed woman at the counter who didn't seem to even notice me.

Irritated, I was pulled out from the shop's entrance and pulled into another, this time filled with dresses and women's undergarments. More curious than frustrated now, I watched as he caught the eye of the clerk and whispered something in her ear.

She grinned and looked at me, her brown eyes alight with what I could only call vulgarity. I pursed my lips and frowned at the back of his head, wanting to yank him around and demand he speak to me and explain what he was doing.

I huffed loudly, my attempt to gain his attention and favor unsuccessful as he ignored me. He brushed his free hand against several different warm, wool dresses as if he was considering their purchase, and I wished I was wearing one of them.

The woman returned from a back room, bringing a package wrapped in thick, brown paper and bundled in twine. He took coins from his pocket, depositing quite a few of them into her hands, and her eyes gleamed with excitement.

"What is that?" I couldn't help but ask as we left, curiosity buzzing far more than the vexation I was signaling to him loud and clear.

His answer was to swing it over his shoulder and continue briskly ahead. His fingers on his right hand looped under the string while the fingers on his left still wrapped through mine.

I thought of lighting the paper on fire, just so that he would have to turn and speak to me, even if only to yell at what I had done.

At least I might be warmer.

"Don't even think about it, Karus," he said back to me, his voice casual and loud as he led me back down the street toward the castle.

The last stall he stepped up to was one of traveling supplies. There were knives, rolled blankets, canteens—anything one would need to cross the isle by horse or foot. I glared at the back of his head now, wondering how much longer he was going to punish me this way.

I thought he would want to sit and discuss what I had done. I thought he'd yell a bit or flash his black eyes at me a time or two, and I would have to console him and convince him that I was never going to be so rash again. I would kiss him and lean into him, and he would fall to my wiles as he always did and we could move past my mistake. But whatever this form of discipline was, it irked me to no end.

He knew very well that I was a curious soul and that this leading me around, buying the most random of items, hardly saying a word to me, was a punishment in itself.

He picked up a thin bit of rope and paid for it, chatting with the trader about its typical use and strength.

Rope?

Was he serious about a leash?

My cheeks burned at the thought. Surely, I was mistaken there.

He adjusted his grip on the bundled package, sliding the length of rope in between the twine, and striding off again, pulling me along with him.

This was *not* supposed to be our morning. This was *not* supposed to be how we spent our first day as companions, and I was fuming. I should have been leading *him* around. I should have taken him to my favorite stalls, ones I had recognized through this torturous walk.

I hoped my glare seeped right into that mass of black hair and hit him square in the face.

He paused on the street and looked back at me, grinning wide.

I stood straight and resolute, putting my free hand on my hip.

He tilted his head back and laughed, pulling me closer. He pressed his cheek to mine whispering, "I know how this irritates you, Karus."

I shivered hearing his breathy words. He turned back around before I could reply. I bit my lower lip and thought of what he could be planning.

Was he going to take me on a trip somewhere? Did he gather

supplies to take back to Felgren after we spoke to the rulers of the isle? And what exactly was in that paper bundle? And rope?

I pulled my unbound hair to the side and tangled my free hand in my skits.

It was more than irritation. I hated this.

Of course, only Rev would know how to get so deep under my skin and rattle me relentlessly after what I had done.

As he led us to one of the inns, I started to defend myself. How was I supposed to know that I would be gone for two weeks? I planned to be gone for only a few hours. And I left the rhyzolm there for him. I made sure he knew I was alive, and he could follow me wherever the Blightress led me to.

Also, I thought, indignation settling in, I had both Parvus and Rauca with me, so surely, he would have known I had some protection that was more than just my magic.

He was speaking to the clerk at the front desk of the inn. The man nodded and provided him with a piece of parchment, quill, and ink while Rev began to write with his free hand, his other still squeezing mine.

I rolled my eyes and turned to look elsewhere. My power was beginning to bud again at my fingertips as I stared at the fire in the massive hearth of the tavern room. A performer strummed a lute and sang jauntily for a small crowd at the tables. The patrons ate their midday meal, half of them drunk already.

The inns in Hyrithia were well-known for their entertainment and care of their guests. Some of the wealthiest people of Arcaynen came through these doors and this inn, The Spinning Wheel, was no different. It was one of four that bridged to each other over the busy market street, hosting some of the most famous inventors, writers, and people of commerce on the isle.

During the Black Fever, I remembered how quiet the inns and streets had been, how echoing a single sound would ring through the streets as the people stayed in their own homes, fearing catching the disease.

Thoughts of Heimlen creeped in like an itch that could not be scratched, and I watched as the fireplace burned brighter.

Rev finished speaking to the clerk and turned to me, watching the flames flicker in gusto as well. "Is that for me? Or from something else?"

I was running out of patience with his brand of punishment and tried to free my hand once more to no avail. "So, now you'll speak to me, but won't let go?"

He smirked again. I convinced myself it had no effect on me. "Is that what you'd like, Karus? You want to be free of my touch?"

I raised my chin, suppressing a shiver. "Yes."

He released my hand. I wiped it on my copper skirts, the sweat from holding his so long stuck between my fingers.

He placed his hand on my back instead and gently, but determinedly, pushed me forward to an empty table where he pulled out a chair, gesturing for me to sit.

I realized he no longer had his parcels and glanced back to the clerk who was now gone from his desk.

I wouldn't say another word. I wouldn't ask what we were doing here, why he had purchased all of those things, or what he was writing.

I could be stubborn, too, but I was wary of how much longer he'd last than me.

Rev called over a young man, asking for the midday meal for us both as well as two tankards of apple ale.

I frowned and shook my head. He knew I had no real taste for alcohol and only sipped wine on occasion. He watched me with a lazy interest, then turned his chair to face the performer, tapping his hand on the table to the rhythm of the song. I ignored it and turned as well, crossing my arms and legs, my foot bouncing up and down, but not to any tune I heard.

"Listen did she to my songs of love,
Hear them did she and muffle my pleas.
'Twas in her room when she tore off my shirt,
and I slid…to…my…knees…"

The musician sang the last word long and low as he worked the crowd. Men and women cheered and held their cups in the air, splashing apple ale all around the tables and their clothes.

As he continued to strum, a woman sashayed from behind a curtain, plucking her own lute and joining him in song.

"'What would you like?' he whispered to me,

Knees on the floor, holding the key—

To what I would have in just one minute more—"

"—Or three!" The man chimed in and the crowd burst into laughter again.

I had not expected such a lewd song to be played so early in the day at The Spinning Wheel, but the crowd of guests seemed to have no complaints. The musicians faced each other and played their duet faster.

"I filled her request as best I could."

"He did not disappoint, and stood over me."

"I might have passed out."

"He slid to the floor, felled like a tree."

"And when I awoke, she was there still."

"Loving this good, I'd…never…foreseen."

She slowed the last line and sang the last note long and high as the crowd gathered around to sway. At the last strum, the two performers paused, stepping closer and letting their lutes fall to their sides, their voices harmonizing slowly together to end their song.

"What began as a dalliance,"

"I'd forever preserve."

"For she holds my heart,"

"And he's what I deserve."

I gasped and glanced at Rev who was already staring at me across the table.

Guilt swept through me for the hundredth time since I had left through that hole in the ground and my gaze softened.

He lowered his eyes to his upturned hand across the table, then back up to my face. I placed my own in his and he swept his thumb across my wrist, turning back to the performers.

I followed and grinned as they kissed on the stage, riling the crowd in cheers and whistles. Coins were thrown onto into an enormous hat below them.

"Here you are, friends." The young man returned, placing two wooden bowls of a shimmering cream soup and two mugs of apple ale on the table. His pale complexion did not match the black tips of his fingers, nor the dark veins that ran up his wrists. I looked back to his face. He could not have been more than twenty, which would have made him a child during the Black Fever.

I realized I was staring and swiveled my head back down to the food he brought. Fighting back the sadness and anger that threatened to spill out of me, I gave my thanks and took a long swig of ale. It bubbled and fizzed in my mouth like a crisp apple exploding on my tongue and, surprised to enjoy the taste, I kept going, filling my belly with bubbles. I drained the large mug and slammed it on the table, out of breath and holding back a belch as I hiccuped instead, sweeping my sleeve across my mouth.

Rev's lips were parted as he gave me a look of bemusement. I shrugged, picking up my spoon and dipping it into the stew filled with potatoes, soft, sweet onions, and enormous clams brought in from the nearby sea.

We ate together in our own silence, though the room was hardly that at all. The performers began a new duet, this time about companions trying not to kill each other, traveling from city to city.

It was witty and amusing, inciting even more of a stir of laughter and shouts from the crowd, but I kept my head down and ate. The alcohol seemed to swim through my veins and my almost empty stomach. It traveled down my legs, making them fuzzy before settling into my head. I was no longer able to concentrate on much as the sound of the songs seemed to play right next to me, yet far away. I looked up at Rev in an awed expression, my eyes wide and blinking in realization.

"Are you alright?"

I nodded, the movement sloshing my brain back and forth slowly as my vision tried to keep up.

"This ale is stronger than I expected. I'm not surprised at this crowd, nor at you right now after downing the whole thing."

I swear he was trying not to laugh at me, and I sat back and glared. "It wasss you...who bought it for me to drink so don't say you're surprised that I did."

He brought his hand to his mouth and rested his face on his elbow, covering what I knew was a smile because his eyes lit with humor, creasing at the sides.

I took my hand back from his and swept it through my hair, leaning back in my seat to stretch. My belly was full and my body was suddenly exhausted and heavy.

He pushed his chair back and came to me, offering his hand again to pull me up from my seat. I shook my head once in a defiance I was determined to continue for the rest of the day and stood on my own, wobbly but upright.

He instead laced his arm tightly around my waist, pulling me close to his side, so close I almost fell into him, defiance suddenly be damned.

He walked and I stumbled out of the tavern room and not to the doors of the inn, as I expected, but instead to the wooden staircase that climbed up and over a good hundred floors. It seemed like a hundred floors, at least.

"Oh, no," I muttered, my head falling back and squinting up at what I knew I could not currently climb.

"You'll make it, love. Here—" He pulled my arm around his shoulder, gripping my waist even harder with his strong hands that I knew very, very well.

We began our ascent to what I could only hope was a room to rest in. I seemed to no longer care about anything but finding a place to curl up and sleep.

I think we climbed for an hour, patrons chatting as they passed us down the stairs. We were overtaken by many of them on our endless journey, some of them looking back at us to give a knowing smile.

On what must have been the eightieth landing, I fell back against the wall, slapping a hand to my forehead in need of collapsing.

Rev was in front of me immediately to keep me upright, and I swore I heard him laughing into my neck as he kissed my cheek. He turned around, pulling my arms over his shoulders and bending slightly, grabbing the backs of my knees from behind.

"You ken-not be s…serious, Baron Revich."

"I am entirely serious, Karus, my love. Now hop on."

I less hopped and more sprang too high, almost knocking him over as he laughed and stumbled, but caught my legs nonetheless. I rested my head on his shoulder, my arms hanging loosely around his neck as he carried me on his back up an unfathomable number of steps.

We reached the top. Me, a parasite of sorts, who made no effort to make the journey easier as my eyes lulled, and I struggled to stay awake. He, a panting strongman, his workout admirable and impressive. He set me down gently on the final landing and turned quickly to catch me if I fell.

He breathed heavily and grinned, wiping sweat from his brow, and I smiled, laughing at what, I couldn't articulate.

"Do we live up here now?" I asked in confusion, my head lolling to one side as I fell into his arms, pressed against his chest. He smelled of warmth, and earth, and home, and I struggled not to cry then and there, though I wasn't sure why.

"We do for now. Come,"—he kissed my hair and pulled me upright again—"let me show you where you'll live for the next two days."

Curiosity forcing its way through my drunken stupor, I let him lead me hand-in-hand to the room at the end of the hall. He pulled a silver key from his pocket and turned the lock.

When he opened the door and pulled me through, I sobered slightly, trying my best to concentrate as I squinted around the room that was so lovely and welcoming. I burst into laughter for reasons I couldn't explain.

A table for two sat in one corner that led to a set of doors and a balcony that overlooked the city. His parcels lay on the table next to a vase of the same burgundy mums that he had found for our binding. The table also held two mugs and a kettle, along with a bag of what I assumed was styris tea.

A door at the back of the room led to a washing room and an ornately carved armoire stood tall against one wall next to an unlit fireplace. Even a bookshelf graced the room, filled to the brim with spines of varying colors and embossments.

I stepped toward the massive four-poster bed, lightweight cerulean curtains tied back on each side and draped in the top center, bowing slightly.

I laughed, the sound flooding the room as each note of it escaped my lungs rapidly in a hilarity only I would likely understand.

I turned to him in a sly smile. "But, my dear Baron…you've pro…you've procured a room with only one bed." I chortled at the slur of my own joke, falling into his chest again.

His chest rumbled, and he wrapped his hands across my back, my palms pressed close between our bodies. I wanted to curl up into him and sleep for days, never processing what I knew he was angry about, never dwelling on what else about the Blightress I needed to tell him, and never once losing myself to the guilt of the disease that had caused so much death in this city.

He pressed his lips to my forehead for a long moment, breathing deep before sliding his arm underneath my legs to take me to the bed.

He sat me there gently, kneeling before me, pulling off my slippers one by one. I wiggled my chilled toes, wishing the fireplace was burning bright.

"*Incendo*," he muttered, not even glancing at the fireplace laden with neatly stacked wood, its orange embers dying slowly from the last time it had burned. The logs burst into a flutter of fire, the first crackle of wood resounding in the room.

I grabbed his vest and pulled him to my lips, kissing wide and lazy, my head swimming through a vast ocean, but stopping to enjoy this.

He kissed me back, but not for long, pulling away with one of his incredibly heated side smiles that had my body aching and tingly.

I tried to bring him back, but he resisted, pulling away from my attempts to keep him close. He walked to the table, picking up the paper package there.

I squinted, doing what I could to focus, my mouth agape and curious as he unbundled the twine and so frustratingly slowly unbound the paper.

He lifted tiny silken straps of a green so deep, it mimicked the pines of Felgren on a moonless night. The nightgown slid swiftly off the table and he held it high for me to see.

My eyes brightened at the cupped neckline trimmed in soft, black lace. The silky high waist cascaded into a shimmer of green with a hem lined in the same black material.

"You didn't order that today." I closed my eyes and shook my head, trying to gather my thoughts. "She didn't just have that in the back room for anyone."

"She did not."

He brought it closer for me to touch, and I gasped when I slid my fingers over the silk, my conduit ring a brilliant emerald accessory to such a beautiful gown.

"Can I wear it?" I looked up at him standing over me next to the bed and a wave of desire hit my body, flooding me with heat and an ache to touch his bare skin. I didn't know if its origin was me or the man standing over me, holding the most beautiful nightgown I had ever seen.

"I hoped you would."

I shot him a delighted grin—a woman charmed by her lover. I picked at the ties to my bodice, wiggling out of my sleeves clumsily, standing to pull the rest of the dress and my undergarments off my waist.

I managed to out of the dress and kicked it aside, unclothed and excited to slip the soft silk over my skin.

His eyes roamed over my body, and he clenched his jaw, filling his lungs fully.

"Oh," I murmured, looking down at my bare breasts, my skin exposed and prickled. "I'm naked." I giggled, the truth of it hilarious, though I wasn't sure why.

He shook his head and huffed. "Yes, I see that, Karus."

Grabbing the hem of the gown, he pulled at the opening, helping me slip my head and arms through, letting the full length of it fall to the floor above my toes. I looked down, my face jubilant seeing my curves accentuated by the cut and the detailed lace that showed my creamy skin through its pattern.

"It's so beautiful. Thank you," I managed to whisper in the firelight.

He said nothing while I swished before him.

He stepped away, back to the table and poured from a pitcher into a cup, bringing it to me. "Here. Drink all of this."

"What is it?"

"Just water. You'll thank me when you wake."

"Are we going to sleep?" I mumbled, bringing the cup to my mouth. The water was cold and welcome, filling my belly with its weight and quenching the thirst from traveling at least one thousand stairs.

"Yes. You are going to sleep."

I finished my drink and swept a hand over my lips, handing the cup to him and turning excitedly. Climbing into the bed, I slipped under the mound of white blankets and sheets.

The cool cotton slipped over my legs, and I moaned in pleasure. My head was suddenly too heavy to keep upright as it landed on the pillow.

He pulled the covers up to my neck, tucking them around me.

"You will not sleep with me in this great big bed?" I questioned, my eyes too heavy to keep open any longer.

"Sleep I would not want in this great big bed," he whispered close to my ear, pulling my hair back from my face and kissing the base of my jaw softly.

I hummed and left him, falling into a place empty of thought or decision in a single bed at the very top of the tallest inn in Hyrithia.

CHAPTER 29

REV

Mumbling each title aloud, I continued my list in the soft quiet. *"Felgren's Power Unraveled: A Look into the Magic of Arcaynen. A History of Green. The Magic You Siphon: Understanding What You Wield."*

For the last seventy-five minutes, I had tracked time by glancing at the small clock on the fireplace mantle. The woman I was bound to continued to sleep off her drink, tangled in the sheets of the only bed in the room.

I grimaced, my thoughts roaming to her again. I fixed my gaze on the parchment and continued my list, adding, *Simple Secrets of Felgren Forest.*

That book had been partially destroyed by the Blight. Its thin black thorns had torn through the last third, but my channelers could still learn from its pages as soon as we returned to Felgren.

In my fuming, distracted thoughts, I had paced the room for too long before deciding to put myself to use. The list of books the four channelers would be given to study had become a distraction in itself, and as I finished it, I dropped the quill on the table and leaned back in the chair. My eyes darted immediately to the bed.

I rubbed my face and neck, gathering my hair and tying it back in a small knot with a piece of gold ribbon.

I still seethed.

When Karus had admitted she knew who had woken her months ago, I had not expected *that*.

How?

How could the Blightress be living? How could an ancient woman have power over Karus's mind and speak to her there?

The Queen knew.

Somehow, she was the least surprised to discover that the forewarned force of hate and anger on the isle was a living, breathing, centuries-old woman.

I stood quietly and walked to the doors leading to the balcony. I watched the streets bustling in the late afternoon through the paned glass. I saw the tops of apartment buildings and the turrets of the silvery-blue castle. The view expanded further still, the grassy green hills leading to rows of farmland, and beyond the fields of reaped wheat, lie the sea.

I tried to think of my channelers back home, wondering if Clairannia and Figuerah were tired of their task. Before I had left for Hyrithia, I had convinced them to not only stay in Felgren, but to continue my work for the time I'd be gone.

There were no doubts in my mind that they were capable of helping train the channelers. They had helped me before when I was so lost, but they had lives of their own they needed to return to.

The three of us had grown in friendship over the years. We all loved Karus and wanted to see her here with us again.

By the Blightress, she still didn't understand.

I frowned at the thought, coming to the conclusion that I would need a new phrase of cursing now that I was aware the Blightress lived and had trapped Karus in a portal for two weeks.

I had so many questions, so many thoughts to consider and speak to her about. I wanted to know every detail of her time after deciding to follow that woman into that hole.

Ah, Karus.

I would make it abundantly clear when she woke. I would

ensure she held the knowledge I had understood for years. She would keep it deep within her so that she would not make such a decision again.

She would not do this to me—to us, again.

She stirred in the bed, turning over, her arm stretching under the pillow.

My clumsy heart skipped a beat, and blood pulsed rapidly through my veins at the idea of her finally waking.

But her eyes stayed closed, her breathing slow and deep.

I turned back to look out the glass doors.

I'd keep waiting then.

It seemed I was always waiting for her.

And I'd still not grown tired of it.

I imagined I never could.

CHAPTER 30
KARUS

My head hurt, and my eyes were sore as if something pounded behind them.

I brought my hands to my face and applied pressure with my palms to the underside of my eyebrows, the pain subsiding a little.

My stomach churned, clams and ale mixing within, and I swore I'd never eat them again.

I sat up slowly and he was there with another glass of water in his hand as he sat on the bed next to me.

I took it without question, gulping the liquid eagerly, the stale taste in my mouth subsiding somewhat.

"Thank you."

"You're welcome."

"How long have I been asleep?"

"Almost two hours."

I nodded, then regretted it, my neck suddenly strained. "Why do people willingly do this to themselves?"

"They enjoy the loose feeling of being drunk. Everything is funny. You had plenty to joke about yourself."

I groaned. "I didn't know drinking all of that would hit me so hard."

"You drank an entire tankard of ale on an almost empty stomach. I didn't think I'd need to warn you."

"I'm not blaming you."

"I know you're not blaming me."

I scoffed and rubbed at my face, declaring, "It's not like it's your job to protect me, Rev."

"The fuck it isn't."

I looked up at him at that.

Yes, he was still angry.

Yes, I still deserved it.

He rose from the bed and brought a plate to my lap. He had sliced crusty bread and added cured meat in between. "Eat. I'm sure you don't feel like it, but it will help."

My mouth turned down in disgust at the idea, but seeing the admonishment clearly written across his face, I took the plate and bit into the food he made for me.

I forced myself to chew, watching him watch me as if I was a child on the brink of a particularly rough scolding.

He cleared his throat and spoke, "There's a hot bath waiting for you, if you'd like."

I swallowed the food and said dimly, "Are you sure I've earned it?"

"Probably not."

I wasn't getting off easy after all. I had hoped that his chastisement would be swift and him leading me all around the market had been enough to lessen the anger that sparked toward me and my recklessness.

That was apparently not so.

I took another bite and sighed. He rose from the bed and walked toward the washing room, undressing as he went. He unfastened his black vest and tossed it to a chair near the fire. He bent and pulled off his boots, then untucked his shirt. I admired how much better he fit into his clothing in the last few weeks.

I watched with an attentive thrill as he kept his back to me and pulled his shirt off his shoulders and arms. He didn't even turn to give me a smirk or some witty remark to get me to follow. He just left the room, his muscled back exposed, his hands beginning to work at the button of his pants.

I could have melted into a puddle in the bed watching him leave. Instead, I tossed the plate on the bedside table before scrambling out of the sheets to follow him.

I didn't get far, stopping and holding my head that ached and sloshed at the sudden movement. I gripped one of the bed posts and steadied myself.

I thought of every spell enhancement I knew. I wracked my brain for every lesson Clairannia had ever given me to stop this dizzying nausea.

A smile crept over my lips as I realized that it was Figuerah who likely had taught me the solution. "*Compaynen*," I whispered, the green essence of myself slinking up to my eyes, and swirling into my mouth. I swallowed it, my stomach settling immediately as my head of ocean waves calmed.

The spell sounded so much like "companion" meaning to settle and be contented. Figuerah had explained that she used it often to calm wild beasts or comfort mares and ewes on the verge of giving birth.

I stretched, feeling more like myself, but still aching in places lower than my stomach.

I followed Rev into the washing room. A circular window was cut into the back wall and looked out to the tops of golden shingles that blazed in the afternoon sun. A basin and silver mirror were against another wall and a long tub, big enough for two, filled the middle of the tiled-floored room.

Rev was already in it, his arms on the side, his head back and eyes closed.

I couldn't believe I was bound to this man, this powerful Baron who loved me so fiercely, regardless of everything we had been through.

"May I join you?" I asked, seductively pulling one of the thin straps of my nightgown down my shoulder.

He didn't even open his eyes to watch as he muttered, "Yes."

I bit my lower lip, confirming once again that, no, this was not going to end the way I desperately wanted it to.

I moved to the basin and splashed my face with water. Then, I swirled minty paste in my mouth, spitting it out into the bowl, which, to my surprise, held a drain. Hyrithia was known for its advancements, but I did not expect an inn to have one.

"I really need to pee," I stated, turning back to face the tub.

"Then pee," he directed, and I stepped over to the latrine, oddly embarrassed at once again doing something so private in his presence.

This man had licked every inch of my body, and I still reddened at the thought of relieving myself in front of him.

When I was finished, water washed it all away—more evidence of Hyrithia's advancements since I had been gone from the city. I padded back to the basin to wash my hands with the small bar of soap left there.

"Better?" He grinned, his eyes still closed leaning back in the tub.

"Yes." I dried my hands and turned around to face him. "Are you sure you're alright with me getting in?"

"Yes."

I rolled my eyes and huffed. Apparently, he wasn't done giving me only a few words at a time.

I slipped out of my gown, hanging it on a hook by the door, and stepped into the water. The steam rose to greet me, too hot, but I wouldn't complain.

In our rooms in Felgren, we had often warred at the temperature of the bath we'd share. He always wanted it scalding—I, more subtle warmth.

For once, I appreciated the heat as I sat, slipping my legs over his on the opposite side. The scent of eucalyptus oil swept through the air as I mirrored him, laying my head back against one end of the tub. I pulled my long length of hair over my shoulders, knowing it needed a soak as well.

Closing my eyes, I did my best to enjoy the warmth. I should have known it was a futile attempt, however, as I quickly peeked at him through one eye, trying to predict what was next for us.

He hadn't moved, hadn't even touched me as I settled my body in front of his. I closed my eye again and swallowed. I was ready to be done with this. I wanted him to speak to me again and forgive me.

"I'm sorry, Rev," I confessed. "I'm sorry I left. I'm sorry I was gone for so long." I shook my head, remembering the utter torment I felt tumbling out of that portal in a foreign land, feeling ashamed and foolish for ever entering it.

"If I could go back to that day, I would not have followed. I would have run to you for help. We would have figured out what to do about the lumens. We would have figured it all out together." I reached out my hand to place over his on the side of the tub. He didn't even open his eyes to acknowledge what I said, and I gulped at the lump in my throat.

He didn't know that it was torture for me, too. He didn't know of the terror and anguish I had felt while trapped in the Blightress's lands. He didn't know because I hadn't told him.

"It was awful," my voice trembled. "I didn't—I didn't know where I was or what to do. I haven't even told you half of what I saw there and she—" I bit my lower lip, muffling a cry of sobs, my eyes squeezed shut in remembrance of how much I hated her. "She told me so many things I had not even asked. By the time I sat to listen to her, I no longer cared. I only wanted to return to you. I only wanted to go home, Rev. And—and I understand that I was so foolish to ever leave."

He sat up quickly, the water sloshing over the sides of the tub as he pulled me to meet him in the middle, squeezing my hand in his. His grasp was tight and my eyes flashed open to see his eyes so beautiful and blue, the edges black as night.

"No, you do not understand. You *still* do not understand. Where you go, you do not go alone." He shook his head in disbelief. "A Chain? Leash? Karus, there's a fucking *lifeline* that connects us, and the decisions you make will affect me. *That* is why I am angry. That is why I will do what is necessary for you to understand that your survival is mine. Your well-being is mine. Your life in danger, your heart broken—all mine to share."

He grabbed the back of my neck, pulling me closer while my lips trembled, and tears streamed down my cheeks.

"What else would you have me do?" he continued in desperation. "Tell me what I must do to make you see that I do not *breathe* if you do not *breathe*. My heart does not *beat* if yours does not *beat*." He clenched his teeth and spoke through them, "*I do not live if you do not live*."

I cupped his cheek, my fingers pressing into his skin so he could feel me there. I needed him to know I heard him. I needed him to know his heart had spoken to mine, and I had finally listened. "You've done enough," I breathed, nodding and letting it sink in. Finally, I was beginning to understand that his suffering was real and tangible, and though I had not really lived those seven years, neither had he.

He led me through that market to show how his choices affected me. His constant love, and care, and pursuit to return my memories had affected me, too.

His life and mine had always been bound. From the first day Heimlen had given him his task to find me, our lifelines were linked, and I was the one who had not understood that enough in that moment. I had not stopped in that field of clover to admit that whatever path I chose, I chose it for both of us.

"I understand, Rev." I kissed him, bringing myself closer to his chest, my legs wrapping around his waist in the heat. "You've done enough…and I understand." I pressed my hand into his chest. "You breathe, I breathe. You live, I live."

His mouth slammed into mine at the same moment he slid his fingers into me, the water easing his way as he curled them forward. I gasped in rapture, clinging tightly to his arms. My cries were muffled by his mouth as he continued the motion quickly, rising within me unparalleled indulgence in his ability to please me.

I came quick and hard, rocking on his fingers as they curved forward easily, slick with my body's reaction to him.

"Let me show you living, Karus." He lifted a cup to my lips. I had no idea where it came from or what it was, but I gulped it anyway. The bitter taste of styris tea gone cold trickled down my throat.

He took the cup from me and downed the rest, tossing it over the side of the tub. The clank of copper hit the tiles—something neither of us cared for or heard as he pulled me on top of him. All of him.

I rode my high again in the water, now splashing out of the tub in waves over the side. I didn't hold back. I slammed onto the thick of him over and over, bringing a guttural moan from the back of his throat.

I had little room to move and, in my frustration, I slammed my hand on the side of the tub, wanting more, needing more than I was getting in our confined space.

Knowing what I meant, he lifted us out of the water, my legs wrapped around him. He stepped over the edge of the tub, bringing us to the puddled floor, wet and warm.

There we were again, two lovers consuming each other on an ornate pattern of floor tiles, this time in spirals of ocean waves. Each edge cut into the skin of my back, and once again, I didn't care as long as he filled me with everything I wanted.

All I'd ever want in this life—I was sure of it—was him. He only assured me more as he nipped at my neck and circled a thumb over my hardened, swollen center.

I cried out again, unsure if I could handle this, unsure if I was breaking, my soul leaving my body to be swept away into the steam, never to return to the flesh that writhed in utter ecstasy on the washing room floor.

"*Rev*," I pleaded, "*Please.*" I was beyond desperate for his pace to quicken and release me from the edge of bliss that I longed to tumble over.

He grabbed both of my hands in his, stretching my arms over my head, similar to how we had done when we were physically bound.

He didn't hold back, he didn't wait, he slammed into me,

rocking my entire body with his—kissing me with his fire that only flared for me.

Just me.

And as we slipped into the loose state of an earth-shattering end together, I relished in the glory of understanding everything he wanted me to—that even in these moments of undiluted pleasure, we were one.

I was his, he was mine, and we lived as the other lived, deserving this, deserving the pain of life, the joy of happiness and completion. I'd love him forever, tiled floor or not, and not once, not ever again, would I take that for granted.

His breath was mine, his heart, mine—his life was my mine and mine his to the end, to the very day we no longer drew air into our lungs, whenever that day would come.

CHAPTER 31

REV

After we cleaned up the water on the floor, and after we fed each other cheese, fruit, and bread, we were back at it again.
This time on the one bed in the room.
This time with rope.

CHAPTER 32
KARUS

"Black flowers bloomed along the roots of the Blight. Their centers were blue and they glowed. I'd never seen them before, and I think they bloomed from me." I opened my eyes to watch Rev's reaction. I wanted to see the wonder and worry on his face rather than just feel it.

Bundled close together, our bare bodies no more than warmly entangled limbs and torsos, we sunk into the bed while the fire crackled in a lazy heat we had not attended to for hours.

He traced his fingers up and down the length of my back as I spoke, spilling everything out of me. Finally, I more than wanted to tell him what I'd been through and done—I *needed* to tell him. I needed my other half, my piece of me that had endured so much, to know what I had just gone through. I needed him to hear me tell this story and know that I regretted every bit of it.

He watched my face carefully, his eyes soft and loving like he couldn't believe I was there, tangled up with him.

I swallowed. "I really didn't know, Rev. I didn't know following her would trap me there. The lumens had gone through, and she left after them, and I didn't know what to do. I thought of turning around and trying to find my way back. I thought of you and what you had already been though and what we had done to each other when we were so young and—"

"Karus." He brushed my cheek. "I breathe, you breathe. Ready?"

He inhaled through his nose and I copied. He filled his lungs and let the air out slowly through his mouth. I followed his lead and found a place of clarity again.

"Better?"

I nodded.

He pulled on the small of my back, bringing me closer and pressing my stomach to his. "We don't have to talk about the portal. What happened when you discovered how to leave it?"

"I fell out into a cave. It was dark and wet and enormous. Rev, there's something I didn't want to say…in front of the Queen. I—I didn't know if I should tell her."

He nodded, waiting for me to explain.

"In the cave…there was a heart. It hung from the top." I squeezed my eyes shut, remembering the pulse. "It was red and glowed and it beat every second I was there. It was massive…"

The smallest sigh came from his chest as he asked, "Do you think it's what you feel when you touch the Blight?"

"Yes. Yes, I know it is. And I know it's hers." I shook my head and brought our clasped hands to my face. "How did she get like this? How is she still alive?"

"I was hoping you'd know those things."

"Once Parvus saved me from those creatures, I didn't want to listen. I didn't care about her story anymore. I just wanted to get back to you." I slid my leg up over his hip, settling in where it fit so perfectly. "I'm sorry. I'll say that a thousand times again. If I could go back, I swear I would not have gone."

"You can't change time, Karus—"

"I know, I just need you to know that I would if I could."

He chuckled. "Ah, you didn't let me finish. When I lied to you about Heimlen, about what was under his gloves, I knew I had made a mistake. The minute you left the room, I began to unravel, trying to convince myself I really had done it to save you. I tried to convince myself that by lying, we would be able to destroy the Blight and it would never endanger you again. I left not long after you did to find you and undo what I had done. But I couldn't. And I certainly didn't expect you to be with Heimlen. After I finally searched his rooms and found the journal, I ran out of the Fortress doors to see the night sky lit in brilliant sunlight."

He reached out to wipe a tear that slipped down the bridge of my nose. He had never told me this story before.

"It was then that I wished I could go back in time. In that very moment, I understood what you had done because of the decision I had made. I made a selfish and foolish choice to lie, and the repercussion of that lie lasted seven years. I wished every day that I could go back to that night and tell you the truth and listen to what you wanted to say. But I can't. And I never will be able to. So all I can do is move forward. All I can do is keep loving you. All I can do is keep lifting you into the sky to shine. Because you shine so bright, Karus. You make mistakes, and you don't always think ahead. You're too curious by far and stubborn as well."

I grimaced hearing my faults laid bare. The truth of them I already knew.

"And I fucking *love* you for it. For all of it. You drive me crazy, you make me angry, you give me love, and joy, and hope. You make me feel like I can do anything and be the Baron who makes real change."

I brought my face to his, our lips brushing so softly, gently, as if we really could stop time and just be.

"Did I mention you're irresistible?"

"No, you did not."

"My mistake." He lingered on my lips before asking, "Did you know I chose that study for its desk?"

"Its desk?"

He nodded. "When I was training as Baron, I assumed I would take over Heimlen's study after he passed."

"But you didn't want to be reminded."

"No, I have been back there only once."

"Why did you choose your study for the desk then?"

"It was the biggest desk I could find in the Fortress. There are several more rooms that could have acted as my study. One of them is the library the channelers use now. But that study—the desk was so long and wide that when you came to me each day, it was the best barrier between us. The sun would stream through the window and light your face, and I cherished every second of it. If it weren't for that desk, I would have been too tempted to reach for you. Many of those days, I could barely look at you for fear of what I might say."

"You're still healing," I murmured as I traced a finger down his cheek.

He grabbed my hand and kissed the inside of my wrist. "I'm still healing."

I wanted to pull him closer, bring him to my chest and let him hear my heart. I tucked my arm under his neck, and he moved his lips to mine.

Fire rose from the embers always lit within me, and I wondered if I'd ever get enough of him. I wondered as his fingers trailed across my breasts, down my side, and over the curve of my hip, if I would ever not want this—if I would ever not need this.

I didn't think so, but I still had more to tell him.

"She was angry with me. She was angry with you."

Rev stopped his trek and pulled his head back to look at me.

"The Blightress somehow knew what you had done. She called it your betrayal. And she claimed…she claimed the power of the Baron of Felgren was once hers."

His eyes furrowed. "Hers? She said that a Baron's power comes from her?"

"Yes. And she said she wants it back."

He exhaled fully. "Fuck."

"Yes, fuck." I repeated. "Have you heard anything like this? Do you know the origins of the power of a Baron?"

"All I know is how it transfers. The moment Heimlen died, I felt it come to me. It came in a voice on the wind that had no gender or substance other than extreme power. It was incessant, constantly nagging in my head as I carried you back to the Fortress."

"What did it say?"

"It asked if I would accept the power of the Baron of Felgren."

"What happened when you said yes?"

He paused, uncertainty flickering across his mouth. "I felt as if I could make the world shake. The power…it was intense and terrifying. I spent years after discovering what I could do with it."

"You know, Baron Revich, I think you're much more powerful than you ever let on."

He chuckled. "I currently have no need for this much power. It couldn't give me in all those years the one thing I wanted, so it has its limits."

I frowned. That was true, but the Blightress had been able to wake me. She had been able to connect to my mind and help me remember, so if his power was hers, why couldn't he do the same?

"She also said that she gave some of herself to me. She could sense that I was growing in my mother's womb, and I reminded her of something she had lost." I bit my lip, realizing what I had not yet processed. "Do you think that means I only have this power because of her? I can only feel the pulse of the Blight because I am a part of her?"

"Regardless of where your power comes from, it is yours alone. You wield it, you harness the strength to use it. She owns no part of you, Karus, and you owe her nothing."

I wasn't sure he was right, but I knew one thing for certain. "I won't let her take it from you. I don't care if a Baron's power was somehow once hers, she can't have it back. I promise, Rev, she won't hurt us. I won't let her."

"No, she will not. I don't know what the Queen will have to say tomorrow, but let's keep this to ourselves until we know more. We need to get back to Felgren, but we can stay here for as long as you need."

"Thank you. After we hear what the Queen has to say, I will give my goodbyes." I followed our breathing again, inhaling through my nose, filling my lungs with the warmth between us. "I want to go home," I exhaled.

"You have been missed. Clairannia, Figuerah, and Moira especially are still worried. You'll probably hear more scolding before the week is done."

I twisted my face in another grimace.

"What aren't you telling me?"

I opened my mouth to start, then bared my teeth. "I—I think they're actually on their way here."

His eyes squinted. "And how is that so, Karus?"

"Last night, I was able to get a message to them. I sent Parvus and Rauca back to Felgren with a letter explaining what had happened and about the trial. I wanted them here to help me defend you."

"And when did you find the time to send a message with the lumens, Karus?"

I wasn't sure if he pulled my leg higher up his waist, pressing himself hard and warm into my belly, out of reprimand or approval of sneaking out of the castle.

"I…um…" I didn't know. I didn't care to remember or I just plainly couldn't. My mind focused instead on his fingers that traced over the curve of my backside, finding their way to what was slick between my legs with want for him.

"You left your room after I left you, didn't you, Karus?"

I swear he said my name each time like he was saying what it meant. Like he was saying *beloved*—*his* beloved.

"Yes," I moaned. It was all I could say, my body taking over all rational thinking as I basked in the light pressure and rhythm he circled over the sensitive skin between my legs.

How many times had we done this since reuniting in the throne room of the castle? I barely remembered even stopping—all I knew was pleasure. All I knew was the shape of his mouth as it opened over my breast, his tongue flicking each peak, causing my pulse to race and my breath to steal time in its rapidity.

We couldn't stop or keep our hands from each other. It was like those two weeks we spent holed up in our rooms in the Fortress after seven years apart.

"Come here."

Fuck, fuck, fuck.

I obeyed immediately, letting him guide my hips up and over his face as he wrapped his hands over my thighs and slammed my body onto his mouth. I gripped the headboard and wanted to scream. I wanted to alert the entire city of Hyrithia that this man could do whatever he wanted to me, and I'd be right there, a willing participant.

Yes, he held far more power than the Baron of Felgren.

He held me.

CHAPTER 33
REV

Moonlight streamed across the wooden floor of the room, spilling from the balcony window in a silvery haze.

I sat on the edge of the bed, running my fingers through my hair and gasping for breath. My dreams were not always as pleasant as my waking moments.

Karus said I was still healing, and she couldn't be more correct. When she had been gone for sixteen days, I could barely sleep. I had kept myself so busy in the search for her that I would pass out in a dreamless doze for only a few hours each day.

Now that I had her back, the nightmares would commence again. They had plagued me for seven years, each one filled with either the terror of losing what was right in front of me, or the torture of having back what I needed most in this world and could lose again.

I rose from the bed, carefully slipping into my pants, not bothering with a shirt. Karus slumbered deeply, her arms still spread in the shape of my body. She had clung tightly to me since passing out after my trek across every one of her curves.

I hadn't slept long according to the clock on the mantle, the fire below it mere cinders now.

"*Incendo*," I murmured, quietly slipping another log into the flames.

I walked to the balcony doors, careful not to wake her, though I knew she slept deeply after the two night we'd just had.

I stepped out into the cool night air. The sweat from my nightmare chilled my skin instantly, and I regretted not grabbing a shirt after all.

But the slight breeze was a welcome jolt back to a place where I could focus my thoughts.

I didn't know what the Queen would say.

I didn't know what decisions we'd be left with.

I didn't know the Blightress's intentions with Felgren or the world, let alone the woman I was bound to.

All I really knew was what I had and what I was going to keep.

I wanted to move on, move forward, and no longer dwell on what we'd been through. I wanted to train my channelers and seek solutions to the hard lives people lived in the Hallow Marshes. I wanted to conduct the conduit trials in one more year and have four new conduits. I wanted to do my duties as Baron of Felgren with Karus by my side as my equal. I wanted babies, and laughter, and joy. I wanted to train multiple groups of channelers at a time.

With Karus's help as a Baron, we could do it. She wanted to take the conduit trials even though they'd be trivial for her. She only needed to pass one to become a conduit, and I suspected she'd pass all four. But the most important trial would be the Baron Trial. If she could get through that, she'd have the choice to accept the Baronship with me.

I couldn't move back time. I couldn't move it forward either, but I once again found myself wishing I had that power.

I bent forward, gripping the metal rail of the balcony, watching the street below. The orange glow of the tented lights along the street looked warm and welcoming as my mind raced through what I would have done differently—what my life and Karus's would be like now if her mind had never fogged, and if her memories had stayed.

It would have been seven years of love, and fights, and bliss.

What kind of conduit would she have become? What kind of Baron would I have been?

Impossible to say, but I knew that what we'd been through had at least provided us with strength. And perhaps, in some small comfort, that would be enough for us to get through whatever our future together held.

"You're spiraling."

By the heart of Felgren, her voice was beautiful.

No, that wasn't the right curse to replace *by the Blightress*, but I'd keep trying.

I turned my head, still leaning against the rails, not ready to go back inside and try to sleep again. "Sorry I woke you."

She gave me the slightest shake of her head, her skin pale in the soft half-moon light. Her nightgown hugged her chest and hips in such a way that I didn't mind the nightmares if it meant she came to comfort me looking like this.

"I didn't hear you. I felt you." Her eyes flickered over my bare chest and she turned, running back inside. She returned moments later with a cornflower blue quilt bundled in her arms.

"Not a shirt?" I asked.

She silently shook it out, grabbing the corners of each end and letting the cotton fly in the breeze. She draped the quilt over my shoulders and pulled each end down, slipping her body inside our cozy bundle.

"I can't get this close to you with a shirt." She took a deep breath at my neck, her lips gently brushing against the stubble left at my chin before she settled herself there, humming our song, *The Sun and the Moon*.

I didn't want to say anything.

I didn't want to listen to anything but the gentle hum of her voice and feel the warmth of her breath at my neck.

We swayed as the moon lowered in the sky, my arms wrapped around her, pulled to my chest on a balcony in the place she was born, but not the place she belonged.

"There you go again," she scolded, lifting her head and wrapping her free hand at the base of my cheek. "Will you tell me what you're thinking?"

I sighed, kissing her forehead and mumbling into her hair, "It's everything. Everything we've gone through, everything I want for our future. It feels like we're at a pinnacle, Karus. It feels like…" I trailed off, not wanting to say it aloud. "It feels like the only thing left is to lose what I've gained."

I wrapped my arms tighter around her, pulling her body so that all of her bare skin, all of her silk nightgown, brushed against me. "If I can stand here with all I've ever wanted, all I've ever needed, doesn't that mean that the only thing I have left is to lose it?"

"And what would Baron Revich of seven years ago say to that?"

"Baron Revich of seven years ago had not yet lost."

"But look at what he gained." She pulled her head out from under my chin and traced a finger along my brow. "You said I couldn't go back. You said I need to move forward, and the same goes for you. We don't dwell. We don't do anything but learn from our mistakes and move forward. I am happy. I am loved, and I love you, Rev, with more power and strength than I was capable of before. No more spiraling. No more nightmares. You wake from them, you wake me. Your thoughts run down a path that leads to the darkest of nights, you take me *with* you. *That* is how you heal."

She jabbed a finger at my chest.

"Ouch," I chuckled.

"You breathe, I breathe. You live, I live, and you don't get to have it just one way, oh, beautiful Baron of Felgren." She shook her head in a defiance of any thoughts I may have had at keeping my pain to myself. "You heal, I heal. We do all of this together. Your decisions are my decisions, too. You cannot explain all of this to me and then go off on your own to dwell on what could have been or what pain you still could face."

Ah, she was turning my words back on me now. Clever, clever woman.

Correct woman, perfect woman, talented woman…my thoughts trailed as I wrapped my hands, now warm, across her neck, cupping her jaw and lifting her head to meet my lips with hers.

I kissed her in reverence and desire. Her lips parted and her tongue brushed mine as time slowed. My thoughts found a path and headed straight for it. This was perhaps the only time I could control time.

Right here, with her mouth pressed to mine, the world slowed to a standstill until we were done. Until we had exhausted our physical bodies, our souls never quite satisfied to an end.

"Karus?"

"Hmm?"

"Are you warm enough?"

"Not nearly enough. Got any ideas?"

"More than a few."

"Revich, I swear, if you go slow this time, I'll unravel into insanity."

I laughed and brought a cup between us from inside, wisps of my magic holding it in the air.

"We were so clever to make this tea in a batch ahead of time." She gulped half the cup, her eyes daring me to do everything she knew I wanted to.

I finished the rest and sent it back to the table through the open doors, lifting her nightgown and pulling on her legs to wrap around me.

"*Caloren*." Warmth bloomed around us on the balcony as I carried her to the wall of the inn. The quilt fell from my shoulders, and I adjusted it to cover her back.

I held her there against the stone, taking my time to rearrange the quilt so that she would not be scratched.

She quirked a brow.

"What kind of a companion would I be if I let your skin break against a stone wall while loving you?"

"I'd almost think you'd planned this."

"What can I say? I am a careful man, Karus." I pulled the quilt higher up her back and around her shoulders. What I had planned to do to her that autumn night in the top room balcony of the tallest inn, I planned to do without needing to stop for comfort adjustments.

The heat from my magic enhancement only added to the flush I felt as the azure trails of warmth spread between us in a luxurious haze.

I held her against the wall and began.

Her legs wrapped around me, and I pressed my hips into her, hard, helping keep her off the gray stone floor. I smoothed the hair off her shoulders with one hand, the other tucked underneath her. My fingers traced the skin of her neck, following her collarbone until I hooked a finger under one of the delicate straps of her nightgown.

She watched my face with building hunger as she followed to the other side and we both lowered one strap down, down, until the top of her gown gathered at her waist. She brought her arms up around my neck, and I took a moment to just look at her.

How many times had we done this since we'd bonded?

I'd heard of the companions' leave of course. It was well-known that after a bonding, the couple often went away for a few days to settle in. I had not quite realized that this was what the settling was really about.

"At least six." She rasped and then cleared her throat, reading my face. "This will be our seventh."

"And for you? How many times have you come over or under me?"

She bit her lower lip and tilted her head upward. I swallowed and waited.

Cocking her head to the side she said, "I'd guess maybe eleven? Twelve?"

"Aren't you exhausted?"

"No." She shook her head and slid her hands back down my chest, slipping a finger into the waist of my pants. "No, I'm not."

"Alright. Let's see if we can get to fourteen."

CHAPTER 34
KARUS

"I'm not sure I understand reality anymore," I spoke softly in the late afternoon light.

When did we arrive in this room and what was life even like outside of it? What kind of torture was his lips leaving mine, his body separated from my skin?

No wonder newly bound companions often made a child within the first few months of their ceremony. We couldn't keep up with the amount of styris tea we needed and were constantly making more. Both of us were living in a stubborn spree of begging the other to drink it whenever one of us got even a slight inkling of desire, which was constant.

It was ridiculous, really, how many times we'd pleasured each other in less than two days. And I didn't know where our stamina even came from. Just when I thought we were done, just when I could barely walk through the room, he'd say or do something and I'd be pulled instantly. That chain, that leash, that lifeline was always tethered, always pulled taught with just a look or grin from either of us, and we'd be back at it again.

"Mmm, I'd be happy to help you with understanding reality, Karus." He continued his journey down my right thigh, kissing me softly every inch of the way with that incredibly talented and wicked mouth of his.

I was slumped in one of the cushioned chairs next to the fire, still catching my breath from what he'd just hosted me through. His hands were still pinning my thighs to the arm rests as he kissed his way up my other leg, starting with the very base where I was most ticklish. I squirmed in delight and wanted more of his touch, his skin, his mouth—I wanted it all and I wanted it forever, not caring a bit about whatever was going on outside of this room.

"You see," he began, pulling my body to the edge of the chair and tucking his hands under my knees, pushing my legs back even further on the armrests.

I delighted in being so exposed before him. I relished in having no control of how I was positioned or what he was going to do next.

He bent forward, the hard length of him easily slipping inside of me, so slowly and fully that I whimpered. My body begged to move forward, begged for all of him completely, but I was still locked under his hands.

"The reality of our situation, Karus," he explained as I struggled to comprehend any of what he said, "is that for some reason, our bond has only heightened our desire for each other."

"Are you just explaining what I'm already fully aware of?" I gave a high-pitch whine as he pulled himself away and then slammed back in.

"I guess I am."

He tightened his grip on my legs, and, desperate to find my own movement, I pushed my body higher off the chair, my arms lifting me from the cushion. "Alright, keep talking."

"As I was saying,"—he exhaled swiftly, his mouth shaped like a whistle as he tried to control his thrusts—"I believe the reality is that...possibly for the first time in history, two of the most... powerful magic wielders have bonded."

I nodded enthusiastically, my lungs working hard to keep me going. "Uh-huh."

"And my theory is...fuck."

"What?"

"I don't remember."

"Okay," I laughed, my head falling back as he groaned, his pace quick, my body melting underneath him.

I reached for him, grabbing at his shoulders to lift me up into his arms. His hands left my legs, grabbing my backside and pulling me to him with his mouth on mine, hot and breathless.

I lifted myself off him, turning to push his body into the chair. He fell in a loud *whoosh*, grabbing the backs of my thighs to pull me back on.

I settled in and pressed my chest to his face where he gladly stayed, cupping my breasts with one hand and squeezing my hip with the other.

"I think you may be right, Baron Revich."

He flicked the peak of my breast, his teeth lightly grazing each one. "Uh-huh."

I pulled myself back, finding the angle I needed and gripped his legs, my nails digging into him. He held my sides so tightly as we both found our ends, our tether pulled so taut, I wouldn't be surprised if we heard an actual snap.

I crashed into him, my face pressed into his hair, both of us heaving at all the fine work we'd just done.

I kissed the top of his head, his eyes, his nose, leading myself down to his mouth as my body shook with the release of a woman somehow still upright.

Pushing his hair behind his ears, I smiled down at him. His eyes had never been so blue for so long, and I knew I did that.

I pulled myself off the chair and instantly collapsed to the floor, laughing.

"Okay, no more, Karus." He bent down, pulling me into his lap. My legs shook, and I wondered how I'd ever stand again.

"We need to get you something real to eat and keep our hands off each other for a little while."

I nodded, grinning stupidly up at the man I'd happily go back on that agreement with.

He managed to pick me up across his arms and brought me to the washing room, where he himself stumbled through the doorway. We both laughed as lovers who didn't know when to quit.

He filled the tub, sitting me down inside, and left the room to gather our clothes and bring us both water to drink.

I washed and we talked about what we were craving most, settling on a little tavern in the town square where they served savory meat pies topped with flaky crust.

"But no more ale." I shook my head and rinsed my neck. "I cannot take another experience like that right now."

I stood and he was there with a warm white towel to wrap around me as he stepped into the tub to wash.

He brushed my cheek and said, "I'm sorry my actions led you to drink like that."

"No…no it wasn't you." I sighed and dried off the rest of my body, reaching for the copper dress to wear again—the only one I currently had. "It was his hands."

Rev stopped his scrubbing and turned to me.

"The server's hands were black. He had the Black Fever, and he must have been very young at the time." I pulled the towel tighter around me. "When I saw the black tips of his fingers and the black lines that ran down his wrists…" I stepped into the dress and began to tie the ribbons across my chest. "I just felt this guilt. Like I had a part in all of that pain."

"You know you didn't."

I sighed. "I just wish I could have saved everyone. I wish I could tell every one of those victims and their families that I would have gone with Heimlen freely if I had just known what he would do— what he was capable of to get me there."

He nodded and splashed water over his face, taking the towel I handed back to him.

"What does the world think happened to Heimlen, Rev?"

He dried his hair with the towel, then pulled it across his waist, tucking one end. "I told all of them the truth. All three of the rulers know what he did. Unfortunately, it hasn't helped to build trust between Felgren and the rest of the leaders of the isle. It's going to take a lot of work to build that trust again."

"You'll do it. I know you will." I kissed him and continued to braid my hair, pulling the length of it behind me.

He pulled his fingers through his own hair, the black strands curling slightly, wet and shining in the soft afternoon light.

He was a beautiful man, the Baron of Felgren, and I loved to watch him do the most mundane things, like tie his hair back in a gold ribbon. The fact that his torso was bare and I got to watch little trickles of water slide down his chest, toned and sharply defined, was just icing on the cake.

"What?"

"Oh, just admiring the view."

"Dammit, Karus, you need to eat. So do I. Stop that."

"Alright, I'll stop." I finished my hair and untied the ribbon at my chest. I pulled tightly on each end, forcing my breasts to push further together in two curvy heaps of soft skin.

I glanced up to see if it was working and concluded it was as his jaw twitched and he rubbed the back of his neck, shaking his head.

"I'm sorry. I really will stop."

"More than half of me doesn't want you to."

"What's the phrase, though? Absence makes the heart grow fonder? Maybe you'll enjoy me more when we return to our room."

"I don't see how that could possibly be true."

"We need more tea. And cloaks. And we need to make the meeting in the castle tonight. We have some responsibilities to take care of, Baron Revich."

He pulled me close, brushing my lips with his thumb. "Alright. Let's see if what they say is true."

His lips pulled to the side, just a few inches from mine, and it took every ounce of strength I had left to not push him back against the wall and tear the towel off his waist to taste him again.

"You said you'd stop."

"I'm trying."

"Try harder."

"Harder?"

"Fuck, Karus."

"I know. I'm terrible at this."

"Let's focus. Where can we get more tea and cloaks?"

It worked. My mind started humming again, sorting through years of memories I had spent in Hyrithia.

"The dress shop where you bought the nightgown had cloaks, and the tea..." I walked the streets in my mind. I could see the city square behind the inns, which centered on a massive fountain that froze over in the winter. I knew a shop of drinks, warm and cold, and I was fairly sure they sold styris tea.

"I've got it. There's a place near the tavern. If they're still there, I'm sure they sell the tea."

He pulled his shirt over his chest, his pants already on and buttoned. I handed him his black vest and he smiled, slipping it over his shoulders and adjusting the fit to button across his stomach. My eyes flickered across his strong arms as he rolled each sleeve slowly, exposing his wrists and the slightly raised veins that traveled down each one.

"How many steps are there to the bottom, Karus?"

"Hmm?" I looked up to his face, knowing he had asked me a question.

"How many steps did we climb to get here?"

Confused, I tried to remember the climb the day before when I had drunkenly stumbled up them with lots of help.

"A few hundred? A thousand?"

He chuckled and grabbed my hand, leading us out of the washing room and to his boots and my slippers, handing them to me to put on. "Let's go and see, shall we?"

ONE HUNDRED AND FIVE.

There were one hundred and five stairs down to the main room of The Spinning Wheel. There were five levels, each with a landing and hallway with eight rooms total, four on each side.

That was it.

The day before I could have sworn we had climbed an entire mountain to get to the top floor, and today, I laughed when we reached the bottom, leaning into Rev as he snickered into my hair, pulling me closer.

We stopped at the front desk when a new clerk waved us down. She handed us an envelope with the royal seal, and I looked to Rev in question.

"I wrote to the Queen yesterday about where we'd be and where she could find us when she knew the time of the meeting."

I nodded, looking over his shoulder at the letter inside.

"Ten-o-clock? They must be arriving late, then."

He slipped the letter back into the envelope and pocketed it, clasping my hand again and squeezing. "I'd think the conduits and Moira would arrive by then, so it works in our favor."

I exhaled heavily as we walked into the street, heading first for the clothing shop. The air was slightly warmer with the sun doing its best to heat the market through the crisp of autumn. We stepped into the dress shop and picked out our cloaks. Rev chose a deep blue while I picked out a dark red in the color of the mums he'd chosen for our bonding. We paid the woman at the counter—the same one who had given Revich the package the day before. With a knowing smile, she winked at us, moving on to help another patron.

Now bundled in warmth, I led him through the alley near the inn, coming to the street on the other side.

"Don't look yet!" I shouted, coving his eyes so he couldn't see the great fountain in the square.

"Why not?" he chuckled.

"I want to dance with you at the fountain. The water sprays are timed to the music and there's a courtyard for it. So, let's eat and buy our tea first. I want you to dance with me with enough energy to twirl me around."

I turned him toward the tavern, letting my hand fall from his eyes, where he grabbed it and kissed the inside of my wrist. I squeezed his fingers and leaned in closer to his shoulder, clasping his arm to hold him as much as I could.

The music echoed through the square as we left it behind us. I pulled him into the tavern built into the street, one of the many shops that connected through shared stone and archways.

"The Salted Herring?" He read the wooden sign as we stood below it, the shape of a long, gray fish carved into its weathered surface.

"I hope they still make it," I said, giddy with excitement at revisiting one of my favorite haunts in Hyrithia.

I pulled him through the door and a wave of savory dishes and puffed pastry hit my nose. My body urged me to sit and consume everything I possibly could.

It was packed for a late afternoon, but we found a corner table and a middle-aged woman came to greet us.

"Hello, dears, what can I get for you?"

I swallowed, recognizing her immediately as Ninah, the woman who had apparently been serving patrons of The Salted Herring for decades now.

My cheeks burned, wondering if it was at all possible she'd recognize me, but her gaze landed firmly on Revich instead.

She put a hand on her hip and tilted her full head of gray hair that frizzed into a top bun. Her brown eyes and freckled face widened into recognition. "Aren't you the Baron of Felgren?" She nodded toward his vest. "You're wearing the Baron's clothes, and your eyes are all black."

I smirked at Rev, watching him politely smile and nod.

"I am the Baron of Felgren, yes." He held his hand out to her and she took it. "Revich. Nice to meet you...?"

"Ninah. My name's Ninah and you can have anything you'd like. On the house. The Queen may have her issues with Barons, but we Hyrithian's are in debt to the late Baron Heimlen."

My spine chilled and Rev's eyes darted to me as he finished shaking her hand and put his on top of mine.

"Thank you, Ninah. Can I ask, what dish are you most known for? What has been on your menu the longest?"

"That'll be the fisherman's pie."

He looked to me in silent question, and I nodded slightly, not really registering what she had said.

"We'll have two, please. And water. Perhaps a pitcher?"

"Sure thing, love, but I'll be bringing just one pie. It's big enough to share."

She curtsied slightly and left, moving quickly to the counter.

Rev brought both of his hands across the table to hold mine and I sighed. "I'm fine. Really. Are you alright?"

"I've had seven years to process Heimlen's betrayal and manipulation. You have not. It'll take you time to get used to hearing his name."

I nodded again and vowed to control my anger at the praise he received from the same people he sentenced to die.

"I breathe, you breathe, ready?"

I bit my lips, closing my eyes and taking a deep breath, letting it out slowly through my mouth.

Ninah returned with a pitcher and two cups, her eyes darting back and forth between the two of us before shrugging and turning away.

"Wood," he sighed, his black eyes glinting in the dim tavern lights as he tapped the table.

"Wood?"

He nodded. "There's always some kind of wood between us, not letting me get close enough to you."

I looked down at the worn surface, dented and marked from thousands of tankards and plates over many years. "Like your desk?"

"Like my desk."

I rose and walked around the table's edge, slipping onto the bench where he sat. I pulled his arm around my shoulder and nestled into him, getting that sultry scent of earth and pine needles freshly snapped. "What's a piece of wood between two lovers?"

He lifted my chin and kissed me soft and sweet.

"There's something I've been wondering. Remember how you said that you thought our bond was so strong because we are both powerful?"

"Mmm hmm."

"I had another thought. What if what the Blightress said was true and we both carry what was once her power with us? What if the reason our bond connects our emotions, our very thoughts at times, is because we wield the same power that came from her?"

He tilted his head back against the wall to our quiet corner. "I don't know. She could have been lying about her power. Maybe we don't yet understand her motives."

"But you know this isn't typical. You know bonded companions don't feel this deeply. What if two pieces of her power are now combined again and that's why we sense each other like we do?"

"If that were true, wouldn't you have felt more of a bond with Heimlen?"

I thought for a moment. "There was certainly...something. Not love, but a mentorship. His magic was leaving him anyway. The only reason he was still alive was from siphoning life from Sylva." I shuddered, remembering the moment he took the rest of her life with a kiss. "You were already growing in power by the time we met. What if our magic from the Blightress was calling out to the other, bringing us together like this."

"You might be right about the bond. It's possible her magic embedded into you and if a Baron's power originally came from her as she claims, the two sources combined would make something already strong, stronger."

He tightened his grip on my shoulder, bending his forehead to mine. "But I have no doubts that no matter who you were or what I became, I would have loved you regardless."

I nodded, kissing him long and slow.

"Here you are—fresh, hot fisherman's pie."

Ninah set an enormous pie and two forks on the table, and before she turned to leave, she warned, "Careful, loves. It's hot." She winked before leaving us to our meal.

"Are we that obvious?" I laughed, picking up my fork and handing his over.

"How could we not be?"

I turned to the pie in front of us, ready to dig in. This pie was different from what I'd usually choose when Geyrand, Philius, and I would sneak off to eat here in secret, away from our lives in the castle.

I had always been a pastry lover. Flaky crusts, creamy sauces in the middle, enhancing the richness of the vegetables and meats inside. Even Lia's cinnamon buns were my favorite sweets to devour, but this fisherman's pie, I realized, was a bit different.

Its round surface was topped—not with pastry—but a thick layer of potatoes, boiled, seasoned, and mashed before it had been baked in the brick oven at the front of the tavern.

Each tiny peak of potato was golden brown, covering the surface and crusting on the edge of the pie tin. Each valley of the creamy mass of root vegetable was a soft yellow. Steam rose from the dish, seeping into my nose as I leaned over, inhaling more of the savory aroma.

"Mmm," I lilted, biting my lip and poising my fork to dig in.

Rev shifted next to me, adjusting in his seat and craning his neck to look across the tavern.

I followed his gaze. "What is it?"

"Just looking for a clock."

"Why?"

"Honestly, I don't think I'm going to make it to ten."

Heat flushed my cheeks, and I shifted as well, suddenly uncomfortable in all my clothing. My dress was too tight, my breasts too confined, and I sighed, crossing one leg over the other in a tight squeeze.

I wasn't going to make it either.

I let out a long breath through my lips, my eyes wide, my mouth in a grimace. "Fork. Pie. We can do this."

Before he could answer, I looked away, focusing on eating—something we both badly needed to do. I scooped up a heaping bite, gathering soft potato, creamy sauce and white fish onto my fork, blowing gently before shoving it into my mouth.

Salty, savory, enriched with herbs—I closed my eyes and chewed slowly.

The flavors of my childhood slid over my tongue, summoning unbidden memories and reminding me that some small part of me would always live here in the place I was raised.

"*Rev.* You have to try—"

He was leaning away from me, his elbow holding the weight of his head as he covered his mouth with one hand, his eyes slowly fading from black to a deep blue.

Well, fuck.

"This is pathetic." I tossed my fork onto the table and crossed my arms, squeezing my legs again to relieve the ache between them. "We can't even eat pie together now?"

Silently, he removed his hand from his mouth, gripped his fork, and without taking his eyes off me, scooped some of the dish, blowing lightly before carefully opening his mouth to take a bite. I watched, transfixed, as he slowly pulled the fork from his lips.

He took his time chewing as I gaped at him, our bond forcing me to watch with rapt attention. I was no more than a puppet. I could do no simple thing unless he pulled my strings in those moments where my body knew only his touch—wanted only his mouth on mine and other parts of me.

He swept his tongue across his upper lip and I thought I'd melt to the floor.

Is this who we were now? Would it ever subside? We'd never get anything done. We'd never be able to function as a Baron and conduit once I passed the trials, let alone as two humans who had responsibilities.

Get a grip, Karus. I found some hope in the stubborn trait buried deep inside my soul, and I blew air out of my lips harshly, turning back to the pie steaming on the table.

I took my cup and drained it, the cold water cooling my desire the slightest fraction. I decided not to look at him again until my belly was full.

He chuckled beside me, shifting slightly away so that we did not touch.

Good.

No, *bad.*

My body screamed that a great insult had just been made against it and demanded I scoot closer to him.

Again, my iron will rose resolute in my chest, and I stabbed at the pie—this time with more force than I'd meant. I scooped more of the peas and potatoes, shoving another bite into my mouth. I'd forgotten to blow, and my tongue burned as I rolled the bite around, quickly opening my mouth and breathing in short puffs to cool it.

"Don't burn your tongue, you'll need it later."

"Dammit, Revich, I was doing really well just now. Why would you say that?" I still didn't look at him.

"I apologize. Please go back to diligently ignoring me."

I stared at the pie and watched as he reached for more.

Don't look, don't look, don't look.

I cleared my throat and took another bite, this one filled with pearl onion and more flaky fish.

It was delicious, better than any of the pies here that I could remember, but with this pull toward Rev, I could barely enjoy it.

"You seem tense."

"Well, that's because I am," I snapped back. I took another bite, the tines of the fork hitting my teeth.

"Can I help you with that?" His voice was low and seductive, beguiling me into finally turning to look at him.

I attempted to swallow the lump in my throat and rasped, "I really don't see how."

My cheeks flushed in embarrassment, and I looked around the room. Over half of the tables were filled with people talking and laughing while Ninah darted all around refilling tankards.

"Can I at least try?"

"We're in the middle of a crowded room," I whispered, my eyes flicking around again, weighing the risk of what I knew he suggested. I caught Ninah's eye and she headed for our table.

"Everything good, loves?"

Rev grinned, nodding and replying, "It's delicious, Ninah, thank you." He waved his fork in the air casually and continued, "In fact, I think we'll be a while in finishing it. I'd like to savor every bit of warmth if I can. I'm not sure when we'll be back here to experience this pleasure all over again."

His wordplay was not lost on me, and I gritted my teeth.

"I'm so glad you enjoyed it. I'll be sure to let Orvan know. He'll never stop talking about how much the Baron of Felgren enjoyed his fisherman's pie."

"Please do. Now, if you don't mind, we'd like to finish before it grows cold."

Recognizing it as a dismissal, she nodded, turning quickly, and rushing through the tables, no doubt to tell Orvan himself.

"You could have been a little nicer."

"I've no patience to be nice right now, Karus." He wrapped his arm around my waist and pulled me close. "I'm going to need you to sit over here."

He grabbed my hips and slid me over his lap, pausing just a moment, before ungraciously plopping me down on his other side.

"What are you doing?"

"Pull up your skirts, Karus."

I obeyed immediately.

He leaned into the table, his back facing the room as he casually forked another bite. His hand found my leg quickly, pushing aside my undergarment and sliding a finger softly between what ached for him.

This was one way to create new memories in this place, I admitted, opening my legs wide, gripping the table, and attempting to steady my breath.

He scooped at the pie again, this time bringing his fork to my mouth, at the same time he slipped two fingers into me.

I muffled the cry that tried to escape my lips and swirled the food over my tongue, almost choking in an absolute lack of aptitude for eating while being pleasured in a public tavern.

I don't know how he managed his position, his fingers curling so quickly and right where he knew I wanted them. I gripped his arm, digging my nails into his skin, my head bent forward before quickly falling back to hit the wall behind us.

"If I could get away with it," he whispered, his breath leaning in close to my ear, "I'd be under this table right now."

I whimpered, biting my lip. Two of his fingers slid around my swollen center and I burned, pulling a leg up closer to my chest to give him more room to touch me.

He took another bite and then fed me another, ensuring his movements were slow, taking his time, building within me an edge I was thrilled to meet. I shattered, only three bites later, my lungs at their capacity as I opened my eyes, expecting everyone in the tavern to be watching us.

I blinked, finding my focus, relief washing over me as no one so much as glanced our way.

He withdrew his fingers, sucking each one casually.

My chest heaved up and down and I laughed, looking up to the wood beams above us, satisfied, but likely not for long.

I pulled on the back of his neck, kissing him hard, my tongue lazily sweeping over his. I ran my hand down his leg, ready to return the favor when he caught it, squeezing my fingers and placing them on the table.

"Oh, so you can touch me in a tavern, but I can't return the favor?"

"What was it? Absence makes the heart grow fonder?" He shook his head and took another bite. "I'm trying it out, remember?"

I laughed, scooping more pie. "And what was that just now? You abstaining?"

"You can't expect me to abstain completely, Karus. Besides, I'm enjoying this place. Happy to make some first memories here." He winked at me and took another bite.

I laughed and shook my head, loving The Salted Herring now more than I ever had before.

CHAPTER 35

REV

Karus led me outside, her fingers woven through mine, laughing as she pulled me toward the music of the square. Her eyes reflected in the descending sun, and her breath came warm and sweet when she stopped in the middle of the street to kiss me.

She stretched her hands through my hair, the pads of her fingers pressed into the roots, like her heart pressed into my soul.

She laughed for no reason at all other than loving me, and I grinned, knowing why my own chest rumbled with hers.

"Do you hear it?" she whispered on my lips, looking into my eyes as if I was about to be introduced to something magnificent.

"Yes, I hear the music, Karus."

My beloved.

She brushed her lips along my cheek, whispering in my ear, "Will you feel it with me?"

The violinist streamed her music into the cool air, her arm moving the bow rapidly across the strings as her body swayed and hummed with the music.

The fountain behind her was massive, filling the square as water shot from raised spouts across each end, timed to the song. The square was full of people darting in and out, calling to each other or stopping to dance on the marble tiles laid in a pattern of a golden sun.

I stood in awe watching the fountain play with the notes flying high and low across it.

It really was magnificent.

She laughed again, her arms sliding around my waist. "Gears under the fountain. When a musician is chosen to play, they come each day for seven days, and their songs are timed to the sprays."

"And there's no magic involved?" I pulled her closer, watching how effortlessly plucked notes of the violin synchronized with the spray flying through the air to the spout on the other side.

"No magic. Just a beautiful invention. This only happens every other week. It takes another seven days to get the gears set up for the next musician's set. Do you love it?"

"Yes. It's…incredible."

She quirked a brow in my direction. "How's your dancing, Baron?"

"Not the best, I'm afraid. Didn't really have the time or means to learn in the Hallow Marshes. You?"

"Good sir, you are speaking to the ward of the Queen of Hyrithia. I was formally trained since the age of six."

"Are you any good?"

"Absolutely not."

We laughed in the shining sun as the music stopped, and the crowd clapped. The musician bowed low and nodded, thanking those around her before picking up her bow once more, stepping on a raised stone at the fountain's base, and beginning something new.

Karus pulled me forward, refusing to let me stall any longer.

The sound of the strings being pulled tightly started the next round of sprays across the water, and Karus began the movement to a dance I did not know the name of, let alone the steps.

She led the way as she showed me how to hold her hand and place my other around her waist, her own clasped in mine. She gripped my shoulder as she guided us around the marble tiles.

Other couples joined us, young and old. Even a father and his daughter stepped into the paved courtyard as he twirled her around to the time of the music that he seemed to know just as well as his child's laughter. The sound lilted through the square and everything was perfect.

Everything was beautiful and right, and all I knew was Karus in those moments of joy, both of us stumbling a bit over our dance not yet perfected, yet perfect in that moment.

I pulled her closer, not caring what was traditional, not caring what was proper or common. She laughed in my ear as I took the lead and led her further away from the crowd.

I lifted her hand and twirled her around and around, her burgundy cloak and coper skirts flying in time with the music as she tried to keep up with her own feet.

We flew to the edge of the other end of the fountain where fewer people gathered and no one danced. Her laughter hit me hard and where it did best, right in my chest like a sharp pang of longing, sadness, and fear of what I could lose once more.

But I remembered what she said, and she was right. I was not ever going to heal this way if I did not stop these spiraling thoughts —if I did not stop these moments of remembrance of what little joy life held without her.

Instead, I chose euphoria in that moment.

I chose to love her in that space of time, dancing around a fountain to violin music. Dancing around her laughter and perfect beauty spilling green from her fingers as she held onto mine. The sway of her skirts were like the sway of our love, flowing through the world as a beautiful and mesmerizing thing to behold.

Her grace in her feet was impressive, considering how often she stumbled into doorframes or tended to miss a bottom stair. I loved seeing her like this.

I twirled her once more, readying myself to catch her if she flew too far, but she let go of my hand to continue spinning, her arms out wide, welcoming in the joy and the bliss of the moments we shared together.

She continued her trek, spinning too far and too fast, and I swiftly moved in, following her glide across the square just out of reach of the fountain.

She tumbled into a human statue, clasping onto its outstretched hand before falling into laughter, her chest heaving on the bronze frame.

I caught up to her and leaned in, laughing myself and asking, "Are you alright, love?"

"Yes! I'm alright. I didn't mean to spin that far before this good man caught me." She backed up, holding her stomach in laughter, her hand closed around the statue's bronzed gloved fingers.

I glanced up at the shining metal, and dread pooled through my veins in recognition. "Karus," I warned, pulling her away.

"No…it can't be," she whispered, her breath leaving her lungs rapidly from the dance or what we had discovered. I wasn't sure which.

His likeness was well done. The curve of his high cheekbones, the tuft of his beard, right down to the detail of his gloved hand that seemed to be reaching out toward the city as if in a gesture of aid.

I read the inlaid stone aloud below us, Karus's gaze still set on his face. "For his cure that saved our city, we honor Baron Heimlen with this likeness, the Savior of Hyrithia."

CHAPTER 36
KARUS

I knew I wasn't a good person.

I knew in that moment of disbelief that I had been through some trials in my life that could not be undone.

Maybe that happened to everyone.

Perhaps we all were born in the light until the dim and dark of the world reared its head and cast a shadow upon us. By then, we were forever marred, not something pure light or endless dark, but gray. Something that could be either.

It was the dark that flickered through me in those few moments.

If Heimlen stood before me now, in the flesh, not in molded bronze, I would have killed him.

I had no doubts of this. Some things are certain.

I don't believe I would have been merciful, either.

And I don't believe I would have found myself lacking in the revelry of his demise.

Rev still held me. His hand, which had just held mine to spin me around to the song, lay flat and wide against my stomach as he pressed my back to his chest.

He said nothing, though I knew he felt every murderous

thought, every sliver of rage that slipped through my heart until it festered, infected and painful.

My breath matched the rapidity of my pulse while my eyes flicked over the likeness.

It was a good one. His outstretched, gloved hand was worn, so much so that it was no longer bronze, but golden. I didn't doubt its discoloration was from the people of this city reaching back to the man who hid his secret under the very gloves they brushed for comfort and thanks.

I thought of what I could do.

One, I could fall to my knees and weep. I could shed many more tears for the pain he caused, the lies he fed, and the brokenness he'd helped cause in Revich. I could fall apart in the busy square and Rev would hold me close, whispering words of love and a future we still held, even after all that manipulation and loss.

But this was not the time to weep.

This was the time to rage.

I stepped forward, out of Rev's grasp and clasped the hand of the man who had taken me from this very city seven years before.

Just as I knew I could hold breath in my lungs, I knew I could destroy this piece of tribute. I knew I could melt this bronze into a bubbling puddle of metal and revel in doing so. I would savor the moments of destruction, watching him fall before me—the same woman he expected to fall to the Blight of Felgren.

Revich stayed silent, and it was the silence that stopped me.

I heard no words from his lips, no emotions from our bond.

He stood behind me, letting me choose. Letting me decide what was next—what path I wanted to take in those moments.

But I was no longer just one. My choices would affect him as well, and I knew the one I could not bring myself to take.

If I showed my power, if I demolished this loved statue of the Baron these people saw as their savior, guards would be alerted immediately. The people would be frightened at such a feat, and I would be taken to the castle cells. But Revich would never allow that to happen, and a struggle would ensue.

Rev and I would win the battle, and then where would we be?

For perhaps the first time in my life, I stayed my hand.

I inhaled fully, holding my breath, making my choice. The wrath within me raged and fought, budding sparks of flame rattling against my chest, screaming to be free—to burn every ounce of Heimlen's memory left behind in his death.

I turned around to face Rev. His eyes showed the very darkness that threatened to consume me. My head jerked in a short flicker of *no*, enough to let him know I would not give into my rage. I would choose *us* over Heimlen. I would choose to follow the very words Rev burned into me the night before, and I would recognize our chain, our leash, our lifeline.

Our lips found each other's hard and heedless of where we were, who we were, or what our lives had come to be.

We stumbled to the fountain. We bumped into people who either shouted or snickered, neither one of us caring in the least.

I don't know how we made it to the inn.

I don't know how we made it up the one hundred and five steps, but I do know we almost didn't. My laced front hung loose with Revich's hand warm and rough inside, my breasts on fire contained in their cotton cage, begging to be free halfway up the staircase on the third landing.

I pulled at the waistline of his pants and found my way inside, gripping him tightly, forcing a deep rumble from his chest. He let me stroke him, his cloak pulled over our bodies as another couple passed us, quickly leaving the scene we displayed.

We hadn't uttered a word to each other, and words seemed insignificant and trite as he gripped my arm tightly, pushing me back to the stairs. Up we went, my feet finding purchase on each step that rose behind me. His body somehow guided us, though his mouth was still pressed to mine, our tongues flicking over teeth and lips and any surface that could bring us closer together.

We reached the fifth landing, my hand still stroking him tightly, and he tore at my skirts with a sharp rip.

I freed him quickly and gasped as he thrust inside me once again, my back pressed to the wall, a mere ten feet from our door. My head hit the wood behind me, and I saw stars, slumping forward as he lifted me from the wall. My thoughts swam in confusion for a moment before I heard a click and we tumbled into our room.

He slammed the door shut with his foot, and I kissed him again, the pleasure snapping me back to the moments I needed to bathe myself in.

We fell to the floor, the one bed forgotten and ignored, both of us preferring whatever surface was closest over cool sheets and soft bedding.

He gripped both of my hands in his, clasping my wrists together above my head, taking control of our bond, his hips digging into mine as we rocked on the floor to our borrowed room.

I turned away from his mouth, the moment too great. The burning in my soul of hatred and anger found another outlet that I let fill me completely. I watched as my magic escaped, lifting from my skin as he pulled at my dress, the copper fabric ripping at my sleeves, freeing my chest and giving me the room I needed to breathe.

We still said nothing as my magic found its way to his face in a caress, touching him as he wouldn't allow my hands to do. His eyes turned bright watching me on the cusp of something beautiful and great, a power in itself that we created together. Something I'd share with him again and again and again, never knowing when to stop, never caring either.

I found my climax almost screaming in a carnal bellow—my slip into a release just as great as all the others we'd shared here in this room. He followed it close behind, the waves of pleasure from my peak continuing to ride swiftly through me as he pounded hard to find his own.

We gasped together, the room suddenly cold and dark, our passion releasing us and giving way to moments in time moving forward again.

He let go of my wrists, and I found his neck as he fell on his back beside me. I wove my hands through his hair, kissing him again, words too much of an effort to say while our bodies heaved together.

We held each other in those few minutes that passed, our line pulled taught once again.

"You know," he breathed, "I'm becoming quite fond of floors."

I laughed into his chest as he continued.

"No, really. I don't think I've ever seen so many up close and appreciated their artistry and use. The tiles of the throne room are magnificent, the mosaic in our washroom is a beautiful display of art. Even here,"—he knocked his knuckles against the hardwood underneath us—"this wood is beautiful. See the grains of red that wind through these chestnut pieces?"

I rose slightly and turned my head to look, tracing my finger on the pattern of knotted wood. I nodded, "Yes, and the ceilings."

"Ceilings?"

"The ceilings of these places are impressive." I pointed upward. "This one is so intricately designed to support the weight of the roof above. Each of these wood beams has a purpose. And the throne room? Have you noticed the dome above that curves so gracefully to allow the light to stream through? Though I didn't see much of it while I was there."

His laugh rumbled into my hair, and I chuckled into his neck.

I inhaled heavily and murmured, "We forgot the tea."

"I know."

"It probably wore off."

"I know." He sighed and brushed my cheek. "We won't do it again until we're ready."

"Yes, no more." I paused, thinking of a solution. "You know what we need, my love? We need a flask. You keep one in your breast pocket full of styris tea—that way we can't ever find ourselves needing it again."

"Ah, brilliant, Karus." He kissed my forehead. "Beautiful, brilliant Karus."

I fell into his chest, slipping my bare leg over his hip possessively.

"What are we going to do, Rev? How do we let these people know what really happened with Heimlen?"

He sighed heavily. "The truth is, Karus, I don't know when the right time will be to inform them. The Queen knows and there must be a reason she has not put a stop to this. There must be a reason she lets her people admire the man who killed their loved ones." He stroked my hair, pausing. "I would have defended you, you know. I wouldn't have let anything happen to you…if you had destroyed it."

"I know." I rose my head to tuck his hair back from his face. "But I chose us. We'll find a way to reveal the truth together. You and me." I took his hand and kissed his fingers. "You breathe, I breathe, Rev. You live, I live."

CHAPTER 37
REV

Her dress had seen better days.

She bit her lower lip as I mended it, the second dress I had ripped open since our reunion.

Once again, we exited the inn and received more than a few stares, including a creeping blush up the cheeks of the inn's clerk as we passed.

I doubted I was acting like a Baron at all. But really, what example did I have?

The truth of it was, I didn't care.

We had three hours to waste however we wanted. Karus led us to the shop to find more styris tea, and just as importantly, a small flask that fit in my inside vest pocket.

The night market was beginning to open, and we walked the streets, hand-in-hand. As the daytime stalls came down, new ones erected full of lanterns and dark corners.

The city venders were efficient with the merchants calling to each other, laughing and joking as they set out their wares. The taverns were packed with hungry guests filling in to eat their dinner and warm themselves by the roaring fires.

Neither one of us were hungry after the unforgettable fisherman's pie, so Karus led us to a bakery that served a warm drink she called calpomum.

"Alright, now stir the bottom like this."

We sat at a small table on two backless chairs while people filtered in and out to purchase breads and sweets. I followed her instruction, picking up the delicate, thin spoon and swirling it in the bottom of my clear mug. The motion brought a swarm of spices to the top.

She nodded excitedly. "Now, this next part is important."

She glowed before me. Whether her magic appeared or not, this woman was no less than a beam of light straight to my heart. Her eyes lit with joy, her lips red and full. "I'm listening," I acknowledged with amusement.

"You take this,"—she held up her stick of cinnamon—"and you have to drink fast because sometimes you get a stick with a hole in it and your calpomum will just spill out the sides."

She took mine from the plate we were given and inspected it closely. "Perfect."

She handed it to me, and I took it, placing it in my drink and bending along with her to take a sip through the cinnamon straw.

Warm notes of clove, apple, orange, and cinnamon, rolled on my tongue and coated my throat as I swallowed.

"Good?" she asked in a brilliant grin.

I nodded and cleared my throat. "Very."

"I'm sure I could teach Lia the recipe when we get home."

Home.

I reached across the table, my hand open for her to take, and I brought her knuckles to my lips. "Yes. Home."

Voices grew louder near us and we both turned, hearing the word *lumen* and *conduits*.

"Two of them and one creature from the forest with skin green as the grass and wings! Actual wings!"

Karus looked to me and bit her lip.

I nodded. "Time to go."

If the bakery on the market street was already abuzz with the news of arrivals from Felgren, we needed to be at the castle before the meeting to fill them in.

Wrapped tightly in our cloaks, we hurried along the night market. The scent of jasmine and sandalwood floated through the air as the lanterns lit our way in the dark.

When we arrived at the castle, I recognized one of the guards, who nodded and opened the doors for us. Karus was right. I really had done my work the last seventeen days.

The foyer was full, servants and guards filtering in and out, groups of them speaking quietly and hurriedly to each other before a higher ranking officer told them off.

I spotted Mierah near the grand staircase and took Karus's hand, headed to her.

"Mierah, did a group arrive from Felgren?"

She turned from the guard she was speaking to and they both looked over us.

Mierah's eyes darted back and forth between Karus and I before she rose her chin and nodded. "Yes. The Queen is meeting with them now in the throne room. The Lady of the Spire and the Madame of the Mountains are due to arrive within the hour." Her eyes swept back to Karus with a look of smug distain.

"Hello, Mierah," Karus greeted warmly with a patience I did not share. "I hope you are well."

Mierah glared. "I would be if your little green creature hadn't decided to rip apart all the fresh flowers I just put out in the foyer."

We looked behind us to see that the enormous vase looked as if something ravaged through its petals. They were strewn about the floor, several blooms completely destroyed.

Karus brought her hand to her mouth to hide her amusement. We both knew exactly who had done that and for what purpose.

"It isn't funny," Mierah continued. "They will be here soon and I have to find replacements or I could be punished. So, thanks for that, Karus. You return here after seven years and still you are a thorn in my side."

My brows rose in surprise. I'd never heard anyone speak that way to Karus. I glanced her way to give her the chance to tell her off before I did.

She sighed heavily and stepped closer. "I don't mean to laugh. Moira is…well, she doesn't think like we do."

"I don't care. Now, if you don't mind, I actually have use in this castle and work to do."

I opened my mouth, about to be yet another thorn in her side, when Karus squeezed my arm, addressing her again.

"You may not like me, Mierah, but I will still help you. And only because I feel responsible for Moira while she is here. She does not know this culture or these customs. She is a fae of Felgren and only wanted those petals for a new skirt."

Karus motioned for her to follow as she stepped back to the vase. The guard I didn't recognize and Mierah followed. I watched in pride and love as Karus brought her hands around the flowers, her emerald magic lifting the petals fallen to the floor and around the table. She didn't even need to utter any words of magic to mend them. Her power brought each cream petal of each rose back to its place on the peduncle. A few of the petals were missing, but it was hard to notice.

The guard looked impressed while Mierah crossed her arms and glared.

"This is the part, Mierah, where you give your thanks to Karus for saving your ass," I chided.

"Thank you," she murmured, turning swiftly to leave.

Karus shrugged and took my hand again.

"May I escort you to the throne room?" The guard asked, gesturing the way.

"Yes, thank you," Karus answered and we followed. "Would you happen to know if the guard Geyrand is still here? He lives to the north on the boarder of Hyrithia."

"Of course. Geyrand is in the throne room as well. The Queen has called him to the meeting with all the leaders of Arcaynen." He glanced back to us. "And he is not a guard. He is the Commander of the North. He leads the entire guardship there."

I looked questioningly at Karus and she shook her head, confirming neither of us had known of Geyrand's title.

He moved past the guards at the crimson doors, which had been fixed since Karus had burst through them less than two days ago.

We stepped inside hand-in-hand, and Karus called to her friends.

"Clairannia! Figuerah!" She rushed to them as they turned, both grabbing ahold of her, all speaking at the same time in relief and general chastisement that seemed to follow Karus everywhere.

"Moira!" Karus held out her hands, and the faerie landed in them wearing a floral skirt of cream rose petals. They pressed their foreheads together grinning wide, Karus's smile enchanting, Moira's full of razor-sharp teeth.

They began to speak all at once, each of them somehow able to keep up with the others.

"We got your message—"

"And then Rev felt like you were headed north—"

"There's so much to tell—"

"Even believe that they weren't sure I should come—"

"Ran! We ran to the den—"

"It was so hard to just stay in Felgren—"

"I'm so sorry! I can really explain—"

"So I said, 'Of course I'm coming, I don't care what those humans think—"

They continued excitedly, exasperated, all four of them continuing each conversation with each other, commenting accurately on what another had just said. I shook my head laughing.

They all turned to me, and I cleared my throat. "Apologies. Please continue."

"Karus, where *were* you?" Figuerah, the most piqued of them all, put her hands on Karus's shoulders as they slumped.

She turned to the Queen. "May we have a moment, Your Majesty? We'll return in time for the meeting."

Queen Rina sat on her throne and nodded. "You may take my sitting room if you'd like." Without much of a breath, she added, "A word, Baron Revich."

Karus turned and smiled, her eyes bright as she put her arms over Clairannia and Figuerah's shoulders, leading them out of the room. Moira sat on her arm, her long, green fingers combing through the chestnut and white strands of her hair.

Beloved, indeed.

"Commander Geyrand has informed me of how he found Karus in the north. He is aware of…the circumstances by which she got there."

I glanced to Geyrand who stood beside Captain Yarah. His face gave away nothing as he met my stare.

"He will be with us at this meeting. It is essential the guards of the north are kept in communication of the threats that lay upon Hyrithia."

I nodded, slipping into the role of the Baron of Felgren with ease. "Agreed, Your Majesty. I look forward to this meeting and hearing how Felgren can help your great city. Karus and I have plans to leave tomorrow morning. My channelers will be waiting for their instruction to resume."

"Yes, I'm sure you have many duties to attend to, Baron. Though I was hoping Karus would stay a few weeks longer and spend some time with the Prince."

I smirked. "You are, of course, welcome to ask. I do not make decisions for her."

"I will." She paused a moment, glancing around the room and lowering her voice. "The Prince is unwell, Baron Revich. I do not doubt you have noticed in the short time you've seen him here. I will do *everything* I can to help him get out of this and that includes begging your companion to stay with him. Karus can help him heal. I know it."

Ah, so she chose to tug on my heartstrings to see if I'd persuade Karus to stay.

She might be right. The Prince might be able to find his way through his constant drinking and stumbling into tavern after tavern if he could understand where Karus had been for seven years and why I chose to tell them she was dead.

"As I said, you are welcome to ask. Now, if you'll excuse me,

Your Majesty, I'd like to speak with my conduits and ask after my channelers."

"You may go, Baron. I will call for you when it is time." She dismissed me with a wave of her hand.

"I'll show you to the Queen's sitting room." Geyrand stepped toward the doors, and I moved in beside him, my hands in my pockets, my back straight.

We walked through the door to enter another long hall.

I spoke in the quiet, "I want to thank you, Commander, for fulfilling your promise and bringing her back to me."

"Geyrand. And it was as much a promise to myself as to you, Baron."

"Revich," I replied, remembering his short way of speaking. "I know how much you once cared for her, and I know how much she still cares for you. You and your family are welcome to visit Felgren anytime you'd like."

He stopped a moment, his hand outstretched toward me. I took it, his grip as strong as mine.

"She loves you."

I nodded. "I know."

"It tore her apart, whatever happened in that land."

I swallowed tightly, our hands still in a firm grip.

"But nothing seemed to eat at her more than getting back to you. I've seen her angry before, Revich. I'm sure you have, too."

I chuckled in agreement.

"But I've never seen her look like that."

"Like what?"

"Like she did when she was ready to tear this castle down to get to you."

My heart beat furiously, uncomfortable that I was so far away from her. "She is a powerful woman."

"She is. And she needs you."

I nodded again and moved forward, clasping him across the back, thankful he was there to catch her when I could not. "She has me, Geyrand." He slapped my back just as heartily and I repeated, "She has me."

CHAPTER 38

KARUS

Each one of them had different reactions.

Each one of them was angry, relieved, or excited in their own way.

Moira's wings beat furiously as I spoke of the Blightress's land, of the Grower, of the monsters that had chased us in the woods.

Figuerah was furious I had followed her into that hole in the ground. Like Revich, she thought there were better options than blindly following an ancient woman into a blighted tunnel.

Then there was Clairannia. She was upset for me and had plenty of empathy toward what I had been through, but was angry for an entirely different reason.

"Karus, I really am sorry for what happened to you, but did you *have* to do it? You really could not wait until you were back in Felgren? All that planning, all that preparation and you go and do the ceremony without us?" She huffed and fell into one of the saffron chairs. "And in that! You wore *that* to your own ceremony? Your gown just arrived and you chose to show up in *this*."

She pointed to my laced-up copper dress which had been mended enough through magic that it looked a bit frumpy.

I looked down and pulled on the lace. "It's not so bad. It looked a lot nicer during the ceremony. Besides," I stated, putting my hands on my hips, "it's not like Revich cared what I was wearing anyway."

"I'm sure he didn't," remarked Figuerah.

"Yes, yes, he loves you regardless of what you wear and all that, but *Karus*. He would just die if he saw you in this gown—it's *gorgeous*."

"Let me guess. You brought it with you."

"Of course, I did! Your message said, and I quote, 'P.S. Rev and I are going through the companion ceremony tonight. I'm sorry, but we can't wait any longer.'" She huffed again. "I don't even know how you were able to do it yourselves, but I was not going to let you get away without seeing his reaction to you in this dress. I told you years ago that your love story would end up like this, and I refuse to let you get away without some kind of public party."

I laughed and bent down to hug her in the chair. "For you, dearest, for you." I kissed her cheek and she grinned. She'd always had a love of romance, and who was I to deny her the ending she wished for?

"I don't know how to say this delicately, so I'm not going to try." Figuerah interrupted. "Have you been using styris tea?"

"Of course! I mean, most of the time."

"What is styris tea?" Moira asked, sitting up from where she lay on the table, picking at the little cookies left there.

Figuerah sighed. "I know it's not my place to say, but a child right now would probably not be the best thing."

"I know. We do want children…eventually. It was only one time. We're fine. Right, Clairannia?"

She nodded emphatically. "It's possible, but extremely unlikely you'll be with child, Karus. Especially since your *liberum* mark just left your wrists. You will now begin to go through cycles of bleeding. It's complicated, but when people have their mark, their bodies do nothing to produce what's necessary to conceive a child. But…"—she rose and took my hand—"once your first bleeding begins, it's all very possible from there. Your body will begin to actively produce what it needs to make a child and not drinking styris tea…it could easily result in one."

I grimaced and bit my bottom lip. "What if just one of us drinks it? Is that enough?"

"You could do that. Though, I've been with plenty of mothers on their birthing days when only she or her companion drank the tea. Your best bet is to *both* drink it. Every time. And it only stays in your bodies for about two hours."

"Glad I don't have to take it," Figuerah mumbled.

"What is styris tea?" Moira piped up again.

Clairannia turned to her. "It's a drink that stops human bodies from conceiving a child when they come together."

Moira made a face of disgust and I laughed. "Is there anything else, then? Any other spells or things we can do to prevent a child for now?"

Clairannia shook her head. "Styris tea is your best bet. The *liberum* mark is impossible to re-implement on companions and nothing works better than the tea. If something else was easier, we wouldn't have new generations of children to take our places." She looked around at each of us, her medicus conduit side lecturing. "Our population has stayed at a steady number, if not slightly declining in the past fifty years. We actually need companions to *have* children." She turned back to me, nudging my hip with hers. "Just when they're ready."

I agreed, "When we're ready."

"Do you know what this big meeting is about, Karus? We thought we'd get here and have to defend you both. The Queen told us there would be no trial for Rev. She also said it was up to you what you'd tell us afterward."

"The Queen knows more about the Blightress than she's told us so far. I'm going to guess she wants all the leaders of the isle to hear the same information and discuss the next steps she has planned."

"I can't believe she has a Grower." Moira mumbled, hopping from one cushioned chair to the other.

"What exactly is a Grower? What can they do?" I asked, beginning to pace.

A soft knock came to the door followed by, "It's Rev."

Clairannia got there first, swinging it open and hugging him tightly, her arms stretched up high, her toes almost at a point to reach him.

He grinned wide and kissed her cheek before letting go. "It's good to see you."

She pushed his shoulder. "Yes, well, you've been awfully busy, I've heard. You know you're in just as much trouble as she is,"—she pointed back to me—"if not more so, because, honestly, I don't think Karus can help but do the first thing that comes to her head. But *you*—" she jabbed her finger in his chest and stormed, "you couldn't have waited another few days? I realize I'm being selfish, but *really*, Rev? After everything you've both been through, you had to do that without us?"

He glanced at me with an *I told you so* look.

"Clairannia…" Figuerah crossed the room to both of them, reaching up to give Rev a tight squeeze. "You're gonna have to get over this, girl."

"I know, I know. I just wanted to be there because I love you both, and I'm just…"—she wiped a tear from her face—"I'm just so happy for you."

I laughed and rushed to her side, the four of us embracing in one big hug, all of us having been through so much love and loss together. I caught Rev's eye, my own brimming with tears of happiness, and he leaned in to kiss me.

"So, Growers are the fae that grow things." Moira sat cross-legged on the table of sweets, a chocolate bun in front of her, licking her fingers. She continued, choosing not to join in on our embrace. "Their power comes from Felgren, of course, and their numbers wane and grow with the seasons. During Karus's winter, there were very few to be found. I don't know if that's part of why it lasted as long as it did, but lately, they've been popping up everywhere."

It was so rare to hear Moira speak of her own kind, we all turned to listen.

"That's why I'm surprised there was a Grower with the Blightress. We fae only stay in Felgren. Well," she added, shrugging, "most of us only stay in Felgren. Growers have the power to revive dead trees and rebuild devastation. They're the ones who've been helping Felgren return since Karus destroyed most of the Blight. They're the ones who kept track of its growth in the first place."

"Why haven't we ever seen one before?" I looked to Rev in question. He shook his head, confirming he had not either.

"They don't want you to see them, so you don't."

I puffed air out of my lips. "We really need to get back home."

Rev nodded, moving into the room and closing the door. "Thank you three for coming. I'm sorry you missed the companion binding, but we can celebrate when we get back to Felgren."

Clairannia and Figuerah looked at each other and then back at him.

Figuerah spoke first. "Rev, Karus, we can't go back with you. We need to return to our lives. Our people are depending on us as conduits, and they need us now more than you do."

I frowned. I wanted to keep them. I wanted them to stay with us in Felgren like we used to. I wanted to spend more sunny days in fields of wild buttercups with them, talking about anything and everything as we once did.

"She's right. We've stayed for a while now, and we need to return. They've been wonderful months, and I would not give up seeing you come back to us for anything, Karus."

I lowered my head and nodded. They were right, of course. They had lives that had gone on after they had become conduits, and we had no right to ask them to stay.

"I will miss you both so very, very much." My voice trembled as tears streamed down my face. I had lived in Felgren without them already. I had lived and loved Moira, but I had not lived as myself without them by my side.

"We'll write as often as we can, love." Figuerah grabbed my hands in hers. "Nyeimah needs me, too," she whispered, speaking of her companion—the same woman who had loved her before she'd trained as a conduit.

"I can't wait to meet her someday," I whispered, sniffing.

"We'll plan it. You can come visit me in the Attatok Mountains and then travel south to see Clairannia in the Spire. Nyeimah and I will come with you, and we'll be reunited again."

I squeezed her tighter.

Rev moved closer to me. "We'll plan for it then. As soon as we get settled back with the channelers. How are they?"

Figuerah answered, "Oh, they're fine. We haven't let them off the hook, and I think they're glad for a little break. Pompeii promised to watch over them for now. Though…" she trailed off, a slight smirk on her dark lips.

"Figuerah…" Rev lowered his voice in question.

"It's nothing. I just think you should get back quickly. They need your guidance, Baron." She turned to me. "And yours, Karus. We told them quite a few stories of our time together as channelers in training and they begged us for more."

"Your meeting will start soon, I think," Clairannia interrupted. "But before it does, you cannot meet the leaders of the isle in that dress, Karus." She looked to Rev. "And I've got something for you, too."

I laughed and pulled her close. "Anything for you, Clairannia. Let's see what you've brought."

I stood transfixed watching Clairannia adjust the delicate skirts and rearrange the fabric flowers of the most breathtaking gown I had ever seen. She draped it across one of the small couches, and her crimson magic flowed delicately between the petals of each one, ensuring they were unfolded and free of wrinkles since traveling from Felgren.

"Don't forget this," Figuerah murmured, pulling a headpiece out from the bag.

Clairannia laughed, taking it to adjust as well. "Like I could."

Moira fluttered to my shoulder, pulling the hair back from my ear so she could whisper, "I actually really like this one."

I nodded, my jaw still hanging open after the gown's reveal.

"Well, I think that's as good as I can get. C'mon, Karus, get undressed. We don't have all night like we *should* have had. Rev's clothing won't take nearly as long for him to get into."

"I don't…I mean…what do I say?" I stepped forward, my hand tracing the skirts. I shook my head. "How…just *how*?"

"Oh, I have my connections in the Spire. This was hand-crafted by one of the famous dressmakers there." Clairannia started untying the ribbons at my chest, and Figuerah pulled at my sleeves, urging me to keep moving.

"When I explained to her that it was for the first-ever companion of a Baron of Felgren, she dropped everything else and got to work."

Moira left my shoulder to straighten some of the blooms on the headpiece.

I shimmied out of my dress and stepped into the gown.

If Viridis was something to wear, it would have been this.

If spring in Felgren could be made into a dress, it would have been this.

The silk was a sage green, the same color as Moira's skin in the afternoon sun. The bodice hugged my breasts and waist tightly. Long trails of delicate leaves fashioned out of fabric had been sewn into the front, which spilled into long vines of blush roses. They fell down the front and sides of the skirts that bloomed off my hips.

A skirt of green moss spilled to the floor behind me, the hem littered with rose petals, leaves, and more vines that trickled behind when I walked. The length in the front hit the floor in a cascade of a sheer-white gauzy material and the sleeves began just below my shoulders, flowing out from my arms and ending in a bundle of sage lace that gathered over my wrists.

I turned to look in the gold mirror above the sideboard. I shook my head, again at a loss of words that I could ever wear something so beautiful. This was art. This was my home gathered into one stunning piece.

"What should we do with her hair?"

"What we can, I guess. When did she last brush it?"

"I've been busy," I laughed.

"I'm sure you have," Figuerah muttered, smirking in the mirror.

Clairannia took a comb and began to unwind my hair from the braid it had loosened from.

Moira flew to the sideboard, a small pot of red lip stain in her hands. "Can't forget this!"

I grinned as she flew to my lips and began to paint. When she finished, I said, "Moira, I'm surprised you're excited about this."

"No one more than me." She showed her teeth and continued, "This means you stay in Felgren. This means there will finally be a human with some sense who gets a say over what happens in the Fortress."

I bent my knees carefully as Clairannia reached up to place the headpiece on top of my now shining hair. It was akin to a crown of cream and blush floral blooms that brushed to one side, the circlet gold and glinting in the candlelight.

"The Queen of Felgren." Clairannia giggled, "It has a nice ring to it, don't you think?"

I laughed, "I'm not sure that's quite right. But we'll figure out something."

"Karus you are every bit a queen as any of the rulers on this isle. You've done more to save Felgren and magic than anyone." Figuerah lifted her fingers to my ear. "Now these are from the Attatok Mountains. Our goldsmith fashioned these just for you."

She clipped an earring onto my lobe, phases of the moon crawling up the sides. The other earring was crafted into the setting of a sun. Each one graced the full length of my ears, ending in a cuff at the very top.

Tears threatened their treks down my cheeks, and I widened my eyes and sighed, unable to keep the grin off my face.

I turned from the mirror and pulled my two friends close, my fellow channelers, lovers of Viridis and Felgren, lumens, and fields of yellow blossoms. "Thank you," I whispered, meaning more than for what I wore. "Thank you for loving me."

They both squeezed tighter and pulled back revealing, their own tracks of tears.

The soft knock came as we knew it soon would.

"I'll get it!" Moira shouted, flying to the long handle and looking to me in question.

I looked down at the masterpiece I wore one more time, swallowing the tears away, ignoring the butterflies in my stomach.

"Ready," I spoke with confidence, straightening my shoulders. "I'm ready."

CHAPTER 39
REV

Ah, Karus.

There she was as she always should be, draped in silk and roses, a picture of Felgren and Viridis as it once was wrapped up into one powerful woman.

She bit her lip. I don't think she was conscious she even did it, and I laughed, shaking my head.

I blew air out from my lungs, long and slow, my eyes taking in every detail of this woman. I flicked my gaze to Clairannia, one brow raised and she mouthed the words back to me, *I know.*

"But have not the strength," I spoke, reciting one of the lines from our song. I stepped into the room, hands shoved in my pockets, holding the rhyzolm tightly as it pulsed with a fierce pull, reminding me that I was near immense power.

I already knew.

She laughed moving toward me, her gown sliding across the floor. "Nor do I, my love."

We were inches apart, her chest meeting mine as I brought my hands to her face. "So I'll see you at dawn?" I whispered.

"Not just dawn," she answered, running her hands up my chest to my neck. "I'll see you at dusk, in the afternoon, all through the night. I'll see you every day, every evening, and all the time in between."

"Promise?" I brushed my thumb below her red lips.

"Promise," she returned, lifting her head to reach me, her lips soft on mine, as we took our stolen moments once again, the world coming to a standstill.

"Alright. How are we doing this?"

Karus and I walked through the castle halls, leaving the conduits and faerie behind.

"Are we going in quiet, just there to listen and gather information? Should we address our situation and let them know how we plan to move forward training conduits? Do they know you've gathered more than usual? Do they know you're training a male channeler?"

Her questions came quickly as she pulled me along with her, the skirts of her gown swishing over the carpeted halls, sliding around corners in a graceful ease.

I could do nothing but watch her.

She looked like a queen. A Baron in her own birthright, and I wished more than anything that she already was one. I wished that I could present her as a Baron of Felgren before the other leaders so that they understood her importance and power on the isle. I knew titles were important to all three of them.

She needed to pass the Baron trial first—after the conduit trials which she wanted to take.

I could not tell her the Baron trial was coming.

I could not warn her beforehand, or I would negate the outcome.

She stopped faced me when I had not answered any of her questions.

"I'm sorry. What?"

"Is this too much?" She gestured to her dress and her crown.

"No. This is a perfect representation of who you are in Felgren and what you mean to this isle."

"Then what is it? What's wrong?"

"Why do you think something is wrong?"

She huffed and tilted her head, patting my chest. "I can feel you, remember? Something is nagging at you."

I pulled her closer. She should always be this close. "It's nothing. Just anxious to get home. You are beautiful, you are strong. You don't need to be anything but you in this meeting. You tell as much or as little of your story as you wish. We will listen, we will answer their questions as we best see fit, and we will begin our journey home tomorrow." I kissed her forehead and mumbled, "I just feel sorry for the channelers."

She pulled back and grinned at me gloriously. "And why is that, Baron Revich?"

"Because once we arrive, they'll have to go one more day—maybe two—without me." I cupped her cheek, adjusting her golden floral crown slightly. "Because when we get home,"—I moved my mouth to her ear—"I plan to keep you."

"This way, Baron and Karus of Felgren."

The same guard who led us to the throne room had returned, finding us pulled close together in the brightly lit corridor.

Karus stiffened and I could feel from her that she did not want to move. Her hand gripped my arm and excitement breezed across her open neck in the form of goosebumps at my promise to love her when we returned home.

The guard cleared his throat when we had not moved to follow him, and I drew breath again, pulling away with difficulty.

Her cheeks flushed, and I kissed her temple before taking her hand in mine. I nodded to the guard in a silent acknowledgement that we would follow.

His eyes passed over our attire, Karus in her representation of the forest itself, and me in my Baron's clothing.

Clairannia had commissioned a new shirt, pants, and vest, the cut of each somehow perfect for my height and build. The black silk vest was patterned with tiny leaves and the gold buttons were each embossed with a sun and moon together in an embrace. The amount of detail she had commissioned for both of us was perfection, and I'd find some way to make up to her for the ceremony she had missed.

We passed through the throne room, its thistled mosaic floor gleaming in the soft light of lit sconces. Our steps echoed across the empty hall as we were led through the doors on the opposite side, up another staircase, and finally to a room near the Queen's study.

The guard opened the door and I thanked him. Karus stepped inside while I stayed in the hallway. The guard was as tall as me with brown and gray hair pulled back at the nape of his neck. His beard was trimmed short and the lines that creased at his brown eyes implied he laughed often. With my hand outstretched, I asked, "What is your name?"

"Mychael, Baron."

"Thank you for your help, Mychael. What guardship position do you hold here?"

"The Prince, Sir. I am one of Prince Philius's guards."

I nodded, the slightest pull of channeler power coming from my rhyzolm as I shook his hand. Its faintness was enough to tell me it was possible he did not know he had it.

"It's good to meet you, Mychael. I'll leave you to your duties."

He let go of my hand and straightened his shoulders. "They are here, Baron. The Prince will also attend this meeting." He nodded to the inside of the room where I saw Prince Philius embracing Karus so tightly, he was crushing the flowers on her gown.

I'd never seen him sober in my time here, and as I stepped into the room, Mychael behind me, I recognized the relief and pain on the Prince's face.

To give them space, I instead turned my attentions to the Lady of the Spire. "Lady Lamoral, it's a pleasure to see you again." I crossed the open room, my eyes quickly darting to the expansive table in the middle which held a topographical map of the isle.

"Baron Revich, you are looking well these days." Her sultry grin crossed her face as she rose from her seat to give me her hand. I kissed it lightly. "And I see why. It seems that you have been telling little lies and keeping this lovely creature,"—she nodded toward Karus—"all to yourself in that great big forest of yours."

I nodded, narrowing my gaze. I had met her twice before, traveling to the Spire to look for new channelers to train. Renn and Rell had come from her city, and she had been accommodating to my task.

She'd also offered herself up on a silver platter.

She leaned in close, looking up at me with sparkling blue eyes. Her golden hair had been slowly turning gray, and the lines of her face suggested she laughed often. She was beautiful, regal, and putting her efforts into a lost cause. She had been for years.

"The offer still stands, you know," she whispered at my neck. "You can always bring your lovely companion along if you'd like."

I stepped back. "You're better off, My Lady, seeking someone else to warm your bed. I am a one-woman Baron."

"Oh, that saddens me to hear. Your predecessor was not so. I do not see why you cannot follow in his footsteps."

"My predecessor was also a murderer," I retorted.

"It's not like they go hand-in-hand, Baron Revich." She smiled wide, her hand patting my chest. "This is a night of celebration! It's been decades since all of the leaders of Arcaynen were together in one room. And your companion ceremony!" She took a glass from the table and raised it high, before swallowing all of its fizzing contents in one gulp. "Come, I've brought my daughter with me. Do you remember little Lanna?"

I looked back to Karus who was now speaking urgently to the Prince, her brows furrowed as she gestured with her hands. The Queen also watched them from the back of the room where she stood with her captain and Geyrand.

"Lady Lanna, you remember Baron Revich, don't you?" Lady Lamoral leaned back to me and whispered, "Of course, she does. She talks about Felgren constantly."

I grinned and bent down to the girl's eye-line. When I had last seen her, she'd still been in her toddlerhood, running from her mother's throne room in ruffled skirts, battling with a wooden sword at one of her guards. Now, she stood taller, her chubby cheeks thinning out into that gangly look young children are known for.

"How are you, Lady Lanna? I see you did not bring your sword this time?"

She smiled and dimples formed on her cheeks. "My mother would not let me, Baron Revich. She said this is not a meeting of swords."

I laughed and nodded. "Well, your mother is quite right. I didn't bring a sword either and would hate to be underdressed."

"But you have magic!" She delighted, showing a mouth of two missing bottom teeth. "You don't need a sword! Can you show me some?"

"Lady Lanna, it is not polite to ask—" her mother began, but I was already on my knees and pointing to the floor before her.

"It is said that there are great fae warriors in Felgren Forest." My magic left my hands, forming wisps of wings and limbs, emulating a fae creature with a long pointed sword who thrust and cut through the air. "These creatures have great strength and cunning, once battling the monsters of Felgren and forcing them into hiding, dwindling their numbers greatly."

She laughed and clapped at my display of magic as I displayed a mock battle scene with the blue tendrils.

"Have you ever seen one in real life?" she asked, reaching out to touch the wisps of magic, her little fingers falling through the wings of the fae.

"I have not. In all my years as Baron, I have never seen such creatures."

Her face fell and a pout formed on her mouth.

"But," I continued, "that does not mean they are not real. There are many things in Felgren I have not seen, and many I likely never will." I chuckled when her blue eyes, the same hue of her mother's, looked to mine and sparkled. "When you are a great Lady of the Spire, you can visit us in Felgren, and we will look for these warriors together."

"Really? Are you really saying so? Or is this another one of those things that adults do where they make promises they do not intend to keep?"

I winked and raised my hand before her. "On my honor as a Baron, I promise you, Lady Lanna."

She giggled, bringing her hands to her mouth and watching me as I rose from the floor.

"You are quite charming, Baron Revich." Lady Lamoral put her hand on my arm and smirked. "I hope you intend to keep your promise, as I will hear of it for many years to come, I'm sure."

"I do, of course." I glanced back down to her daughter. "It's good to have something to hope for."

I turned to look at Karus again. The Queen was now in conversation with her and the Prince, and all three of them spoke in hushed tones.

The Lady of the Spire sighed. "Oh, where *is* that Madame Zoreyah? Just wait until you see what she brought with her."

Karus caught my eye, anger darkening the green hue of them. I tilted my head downward, a question if she needed me.

She shook hers slightly, her shoulders relaxing. She drew a deep breath through her nose, holding it a moment before exhaling through her lips. I kept her gaze and repeated another breath with her.

"Madame Zoreyah." The Queen moved to the door, welcoming the young Madame of the Mountains. She held her infant daughter in her arms, and, to my surprise, a black muri padded into the room beside her. Its large, yellow eyes scanned the room, stepping in front of Zoreyah in a protective stance, its feline face nudging her hip.

"My babe needed to eat and rest after such a journey, Your Majesty. Thank you for waiting for me to arrive."

"Of course, dear," Queen Rina replied, ignoring the enormous beast.

Karus gaped at the animal. The only time she'd ever seen one of the large cats, it was being consumed by the Blight.

The Madame bundled her child tighter into her saffron blanket and tucked her into the basket on the back of the muri, folding straps across to hold her tightly. The muri stalked carefully across the room, finding a quiet corner and lowering itself to the floor. It laid itself down, its cargo unmoving as it placed its head onto its paws and closed its eyes.

"Madame Zoreyah, you've met Baron Revich, I believe." the Queen gestured to me, and I bowed my head as she returned the nod. "And let me introduce you to the daughter I raised with the Prince. This is Karus."

Karus stepped forward, her hand outstretched. Zoreyah was young, no older than twenty, and she smiled quietly, her lightly bronzed skin tattooed in golden circles that draped over her arms and across her chest. Her dark, copper hair had been twisted into two large buns that reminded me of the pastry Karus and Moira loved to make with Lia.

"Hello, Madame Zoreyah. I am happy to meet you. One of my dearest friends is a conduit of yours in the Attatok Mountains."

She gave a small smile and took Karus's hand. "Yes, Figuerah is most loved. It is my people's hope that she returns to them soon."

Karus's shoulders dropped. "She returns very soon, Madame. She is here, in the castle, and ready to leave with your company when you wish."

Lady Lamoral rushed to the Madame's side, taking her hand. "Zoreyah, my lovely, please come closer to the fire and warm yourself. Motherhood becomes you, but it also drains the best of us."

"If everyone would take a seat, we can begin our discussion of the utmost importance to the isle." Queen Rina motioned for all of us to move closer to the fire and sit. Karus found my hand and led me to a pair of crimson chairs.

Geyrand and Captain Yarah moved to the Queen's side. Prince Philius watched Karus with his arms across his chest.

The Queen took a deep breath. She wore a gown of deep purple, her golden crown woven with her dark coils, similar to the Prince's. Their likeness was more obvious in the dim light—the long shape of their noses, the square of their chins. But the Queen's eyes were a dark chestnut, whereas the Prince's were a golden brown. They flicked between Karus and myself, then darted to our clasped hands.

"Though I am most grateful to see you all here, in Hyrithia, I do not welcome you with good news."

Lady Lamoral pulled little Lanna into her lap, wrapping her arms around her daughter.

"The Blightress has shown herself," The Queen began, "She has taken Karus to her land, claiming to seek more power."

I turned to watch the faces of the other leaders on the isle. Both women held the Queen's gaze with no sudden realization that the Blightress existed.

So, only the Baron of Felgren had been left out of this little detail.

"I would like to share with you what I know and we can discuss the correct call to action against her. I have been sending my own people on expeditions to the Northern Steppes for years now, with little success on information of the Blightress. The entrance to her land is filled with syphoners, and it is rare that my people return to me. They either die, or the syphoners keep them alive and she…feeds power from them. They do send letters to the guards of the north, and we have been able to piece together that her land is no longer a vast desert, but a marshland full of dangerous creatures."

She took another deep breath and nodded toward Karus. "It was Karus's mother who was last seen alive from this land. Almost thirty years ago, she returned, heavy with child, and covered in black ash. I was able to comprehend some of what Arah had been through. The Blightress could sense Karus growing inside her mother and chose to keep her alive, instead of murdering her as she had done to the rest of the expedition.

"There she kept Arah, feeding magic to her growing child while watching her mother slip into a mindless woman. At some point, Arah escaped with help. I do not know the details of this, but I do know that Arah was able to burn some of the syphoner fields and find her way to the guards of the north where they brought her to me. She died hours after Karus was born."

My fingers were being squeezed so tightly, I sent a sliver of my magic around our clasped hands, whispering, *"Compaynen",* in an effort to ease Karus's body. Her shoulders relaxed and she straightened, inhaling deeply.

"I raised Karus, then named Ash'Arah, alongside my son. It began as a way to watch this child who was born of her channeler mother and the meddling Blightress. I feared what magic she held, and I was correct in my assumption that Karus was powerful. At a very young age, her power began to manifest in ways I had not seen nor heard of from any channeler. Her anger turned to fire; her pain turned to withered fruit and wilted flowers in the castle garden. I chose to raise her to control those emotions and not rely on others for comfort, as I surmised that if she was ever broken, her power would manifest itself into something great and terrible."

All eyes in the room darted to Karus as if she might explode right then and there.

I wanted to take her into my lap. I wanted to hold her there, protect her from their stares and their questioning if she was inherently good or bad. Then I wanted to lash out at them all for daring to even consider it.

She stared straight ahead at the Queen, listening to the story of her origins that she'd never been told.

The Queen began again, "When Baron Heimlen came to me to discuss taking Karus to train in Felgren, I refused. Not only was the Treaty still in place, she was my daughter, and I would protect her from her own power at all costs."

"Except one." All of our heads turned to the Prince, his response low and dark.

The Queen ignored him and continued. "Baron Heimlen was willing to kill to bring Karus to Felgren. And yes, when my son was inflicted with the Black Fever, I finally agreed to his terms. He was to take Karus to train in Felgren until she passed the conduit trials, then she would return to Hyrithia and stay.

"I made this decision solely to save the life of my son and more lives of my people. Baron Revich has informed me that Heimlen was able to control the disease through channelers. He killed thousands of them this way, hiding from my people that he had the cure because he had created the disease in the first place."

She swallowed. "I, however, had guessed at the truth, but chose to save my son, knowing some of the risks Karus might face."

I turned to Karus in question. She nodded slightly, her eyes lowering to the floor.

I rose from my seat, taking a step toward the Queen. "You knew?" My nostrils flared, and I struggled to control my words. "You knew that Heimlen had murdered your people, and you let him take Karus anyway?"

It was shame that crossed the Queen's face, the first I'd ever seen from her.

"Yes, I knew. Or at least, I had guessed as much. He'd been sending letters for months, and the timing was too perfect for the truth to be otherwise."

Rage, disgust, disdain—I understood Queen Rina better now. I didn't hold back my scorn as I shook my head and said, "You call her your daughter, but you do not deserve the title of her mother."

Karus rose beside me and raised her chin, addressing the Queen, "There is a statue. In the market square. 'In honor of the Savior of Hyrithia'. Why do you let your people believe his lies seven years later? Why do you let his likeness stand before the very people he chose to die for his cause?"

"My people needed to heal," she answered. "They needed to believe that their loved ones had not died in a campaign to retrieve a channeler to Felgren. The people of this city needed to rally behind someone they believed to be a savior—"

"A savior because you lied to them!" Karus moved forward swiftly. "You let your people believe and continue to allow them to believe these lies. When will you tell them the truth? When will you decide they deserve to hear it?"

The Queen closed their gap. "Do you really believe for one moment, Karus, that they would not have stormed into Felgren had they known? If I had told them the truth, they would have demanded war. They would have wanted to fight for their people. We would have been right back where we were over a hundred years ago before the Treaty. When you stand by your companion's side in Felgren and help make the difficult decisions there, *then* you can talk to me of *choices*." She seethed her last words, cheeks flushing in anger.

Karus shook her head. "They deserve to know. Your people deserve the truth. They deserve it just as much as I did."

"What exactly happened in that forest?" Lady Lamoral broke the strained silence. "Baron Heimlen is dead; Karus still lives. What does all of this have to do with the Blightress?"

The Queen brought her attention to me. "Baron Revich, perhaps you would like to explain?"

I turned my body to Karus, who slumped ungraciously into her chair. I took both of her hands in mine and kissed them. She nodded, murmuring, "They need to know. All of it. Even the heart."

I cupped her cheek, leaned in and kissed her.

I didn't care where we were or who witnessed it. I'd choose Karus first every time I had a choice to make.

I stepped toward the Queen, any respect I had previously held for her gone, and I turned to the leaders in the room.

I gripped the rhyzolm in my hand, just to monitor the power before me. Madame Zoreyah had strong magic, Lady Lanna had potential, but Lady Lamoral did not contain any of Felgren's magic. "Baron Heimlen was a manipulator and a murderer. He groomed me to find the most powerful channeler on the isle, which led me to Karus. As his chosen heir, I did not know of his intentions and means to get her to Felgren. I was blind to all of it, though I should have questioned more of it.

"When Karus was brought to Felgren, she didn't want anything to do with it. At first, she fought hard to persuade us that she held little power and was useless to Heimlen's plans. But this rhyzolm,"— I pulled the stone from my pocket to display—"said otherwise. When a Baron searches for channelers to train, he uses one of these and it pulls him toward someone with great magic. You see, she would have been more convincing if not for the connection I felt through this stone every time she was near." I chuckled, dropping the stone back in my pocket, looking at her, "Actually, she didn't have to be near. I could feel her miles away while I was in Felgren and she was still here, in Hyrithia.

"She began to love Felgren and chose to stay once it was revealed to her that the forest needed saving. It was great news to me since I had already fallen so hard for her and couldn't imagine my life holding any joy if she'd left it."

Karus bit her lower lip and smiled at me.

I held her gaze for a moment and continued, "Felgren Forest has been under darkness for some time. A Blight. Black vines choke life and magic from its soil, and it has ravaged through thousands of acres for years. Heimlen needed the most powerful channeler I could find so that he could train her to fight the Blight with him. He intended to do this without either of them surviving the fight. His 'legacy' as he called it, would need to continue on, and he wanted to be known as the Baron who saved the forest.

"But Karus was more powerful than either of us knew. She could feel a pulse in the Blight—a heartbeat. We have since learned that heartbeat comes straight from the Blightress."

"How do you know this?" Queen Rina stepped forward slightly, hanging onto my every word.

"I did not tell you everything." Karus stood and moved beside me, taking my hand once again and for the millionth time, it fit perfectly in hers. "When I was in her lands, I had been spit out of a portal that ended in a cave. This cave held a massive heart. It hung from the walls and its pulse…" She shook her head. "It's her heart. She confirmed this to me."

Lady Lamoral pulled her daughter closer to her chest. "So, this heart of the Blightress beats through the Blight? But why? What does the Blightress have to gain from taking over Felgren with her vines?"

The Queen quickly replied, "Power. It is what she seeks after centuries."

"Not just any power," Karus corrected, "Power she believes was always hers. She seeks to regain the power of the Baron."

The Queen's eyes narrowed and her lips pursed.

Madame Zoreyah spoke, "What will she do with this power if she wields it?"

Karus shook her head. "We do not know."

Lady Lamoral stroked her daughter's hair. "What did you do about the Blight? Were you able to destroy it? And why did Baron Revich tell all of us you were dead?"

"I was able to use a spell that simulated the sun and caused the Blight to wither and recess. Heimlen died using what power he had left to keep the spell intact. Most of the Blight is gone, but hundreds of acres remain. And it has infested our library, Viridis." She looked to me, her eyes sorrowful, remembering what happened next. "When I used my magic to hold the spell, I began to fade. In order to hold it as long as I did to destroy as much of the Blight as I could, my memories left me one by one. And if Rev had not stopped me, I don't think I would have lived through that night."

"You couldn't remember who you were." Madame Zoreyah whispered.

"No. I held nothing of who I was. And anytime the ones who loved me tried to help me, I'd rage and fall to pieces. Eventually, I found friendship with a faerie. I lived in the Fortress with her each day, never remembering who I was or how I had come to the forest. For seven years, I did this. And every day, Revich held onto hope that I would return to him."

"Hope he didn't give us," the Prince spat, stepping our way, marred fists at his side. "He lied, Karus. He does not deserve you, he does not deserve our respect, he does not deserve his title."

His fist flew through the air and caught my jaw, twisting my head, causing me to stumble back.

Karus gasped and reached for me just as the Prince's fist reeled back for another hit. I was ready this time, catching it in my own hand, grabbing his other wrist before he could land another blow.

My magic flared over my fingers, pushing him back in his rage.

"You use your power to hold me? Why don't you try fighting fair?" he challenged, still pushing on my grip.

"You hold power too, Your Highness," I spoke calmly. "Why don't you use it?"

"Baron Revich, that's enou—"

"You know I can't. The only time it's come to me was when I learned about my sister, you fucking—"

"Bullshit," I countered, "You've barely tried, I bet. Use it now, Philius. Use it now to hit me again. C'mon, it won't be a cheap shot this time."

I was more curious than angry. I understood why he hated me, but I wanted to see if he could pull from the forest. I wanted to see if he could do what I suspected he could if given the proper training.

I dampened my power, only holding his fists by strength alone as he gritted his teeth. His eyes raged as a spark of orange light jolted through his hands to mine, sending me stumbling back to hit the table behind me.

I grinned in satisfaction.

There he was.

He lifted his hands again to send another blow but before he could even try, he flew back, crashing into the wall and slumping to the floor. Green tendrils of power encased his hands at his side and Karus stood over him.

"You will not touch him again." Her command came soft and powerful as her magic slipped over every inch of his body.

"He wanted me to—" he choked.

"I don't care, Philius," she interrupted. All I could see was her back to the rest of us in the room as she bent down closer to his body. "You will never seek violence against him again, do you understand?"

Chills flickered down my spine, and I tried to steady my heart beating furiously for her.

By the hands of the Spire.

Fuck, that was the worst one yet—probably because I was too focused on the woman defending me to be clever.

She turned quickly, her magic falling from his body as the Queen rushed to his side.

"Are you alright?" Karus brushed her fingers across my jaw, which I assumed would soon begin to bloom in purple.

"More than alright." I grabbed her waist and pulled her against me. "I'd say both of those displays were worth it."

She kept her back to the room and pressed her body to mine, her mouth on mine, her teeth scraping my bottom lip, pulling away from it slowly.

Ah, fuck.

"How did you remember who you were?" Lanna had slid off her mother's lap, holding her hands in front of her dress, looking up at us with curiosity.

I'd forgotten she was there and straightened immediately, pulling my vest down and running a hand through my hair.

The Queen rose with her son from the floor and Karus continued her story as if nothing had happened.

"The rhyzolm. I found it one day in the forest. I had lost it there years ago, and when I held it, memories started to return."

"So, you knew everything that had happened?" Lanna asked.

"Some of what had happened, yes. Some of it had to be explained to me. Like what happened after my memories had faded with the sun."

"But how did a stone return your memories?"

The little girl was asking the real questions.

"Love, Lady Lanna," Karus bent down to meet her eyes, holding out her hands for the little girl to take. "Love is the strongest power you can wield. Love can last through time, overcome pain and fear. Love was imbued into that stone and holding it, I remembered that I was loved."

CHAPTER 40
SAELYN

I would be seventeen in two weeks, and I was convinced I was the most hideous creature on the isle.

One particular raging red blemish had refused to leave my chin for days and *days*, and I would see Thevin again in just a few hours.

I knew I shouldn't care. I knew *he* wouldn't care…at least, I was trying to convince myself he wouldn't.

But as I searched the many, many volumes of the Magical Language Hall of Viridis, I became more and more irritated that my stupid face was not cooperating with me.

I found myself rubbing my chin again and rolled my eyes. No wonder it was pocked.

Usually, I didn't bat an eye at my appearance, choosing to let my long hair, long torso, and long legs fly free. The idea of prepping my appearance each day seemed like the biggest waste of time. But less than two-hundred minutes away from seeing Thevin again, I wondered if I should have taken the time to learn more about this.

My mother was of no use. She barely remembered to braid her hair each day, let alone line her eyes in kohl or add pink to her cheeks and lips. I had thought of asking Pah-Pah for help, since he always wore something lovely around his eyes, but I loathed the thought of more teasing.

Sighing, I let my focus settle back on my book.

Beauty in Magic: A Guide to an Effortless Appearance by Olyviah Destyn.

Whomever this author was, she had probably been gorgeous and wrote an entire book about it.

Inside were enchantments to make your fingernails grow long and strong, potions one could brew for shinier hair. I flipped through the pages eagerly, wondering if this beautiful woman had ever had to even deal with blazing red sores on her face.

"Demarcess: *to fade or wither. This enhancement can be used to subdue any type of imperfection on the skin. Use it wisely, however, as the spell can also wither your current state of being if you are not properly trained yet in your magical focus.*"

I scoffed, sure but also slightly unsure if that last part applied to me.

I set the book down on the bench and held the hand mirror up to my face. Of course, I had come prepared. It was one of my greater qualities.

I breathed heavily, focusing on the raging red of my chin and stated confidently, "*Demarcess.*"

The pockmark recessed immediately, fading to what looked more like a budding freckle on my chin.

Also, my heart slowed, and I felt my chest deflate.

Dammit.

The nerves and excitement I had felt moments before were nowhere to be found as I squinted at myself in a strange sense of confusion, my head swimming with murky waters.

Great. I guess I didn't have the proper training to avoid this part of the spell after all.

I grimaced, trying to focus as I moved time. "*Revertayden en tepiore.*" The seconds ticked backward, my chin once again marked and painful.

I didn't like moving time. When I had first discovered the spell by piecing together words of magic, I had used it often. I liked playing with the space between truth in its purest form and reversing it, winding the seconds back, changing a small piece of the world in my small, little way.

As I grew older, I understood what I played with. I understood that what I had done was discover a way to manipulate the truth into whatever I wanted it to become. I was very powerful, and that must remain a secret for as long as I could manage. My desire to see Thevin again without a marred face, however, was enough to convince me that moving time—just this once—wouldn't hurt anyone. I picked up the mirror again, but technically for the first time, and spoke the spell. This time, I understood that my focus needed to be more intentional on exactly what I wished to do.

The mark left my chin, and I took a few seconds more to just hold onto the spell, refusing to let it wither my mind as well.

Grinning with a clear face, I closed the book and patted its surface, hearing it *thwip* back to its proper place on the shelf behind me.

Realizing I was hungry, I casually walked down the steps into the courtyard. I admired a patch of lavender which was humming due to the visiting swarm of fluffy, striped bees and slowly made my way up the marble stairs to Viridis's portal.

The whisper of my name caught my attention from the tips of the birch trees that swayed, and I narrowed my eyes, wondering why it had followed me here. I usually didn't hear it for years at a time, but now it breathed twice so close to turning seventeen?

I shook my head and ignored it again, stepping into the portal and away from the mystery that had surrounded me since I was seven years old.

CHAPTER 41
KARUS

The minutes passed by as everyone gathered themselves.

Madame Zoreyah's newborn began to cry on the muri's back, and the black creature stalked over carefully.

The Prince slumped against the wall with his arms folded across his chest as the Queen spoke quietly to him.

I wondered briefly if I had been too hard on him. Not just on his body, but emotionally as well when I had slammed him against the wall.

In truth, I had hardly registered it was a choice I made. No one would be touching Rev if I was there to stop it, regardless of if Rev could handle it himself.

Lanna left my hands and shyly asked to pet the muri who purred loudly at Zoreyah's feet while she fed her infant.

"Such an interesting display of power, Karus of Felgren." Lady Lamoral walked gracefully to us, her long silk gown accentuating her eyes in a cornflower blue rimmed with white fur. "Tell me Karus, do you desire power? If the Blightress gave you hers, did she also give you her ambitions in this world?"

I watched as her gaze flickered to Rev's jaw, where a small cut, red and jagged, had not yet been healed. Her eyes then trailed up to his mouth where they stayed, transfixed.

What the fuck?

Nothing had happened between these two, I was sure of it, but she looked at him as if he was a meal to be consumed.

I twisted my jaw to the side and gritted my teeth. "I have many ambitions and desires in this world, Lady Lamoral. One of them is standing right in front of you."

She glanced to me and laughed. "Oh, Karus, don't take it personally. It must be the most obvious to you how handsome your companion is. Though I will say, you two make a *fine* pairing." She slid to my side, holding my arm and leaning in close to whisper, loud enough for Revich to hear. "It's a shame. He told me he's a one-woman man, though he could easily have two, and all in the same night."

About to tell her off for good, Rev beat me to it.

"Lady Lamoral, you've been turned down on several occasions at this point. I would think an intelligent woman such as yourself would have the sense to understand *no* when it had been implied, so let me be more direct."

He grabbed my waist, pulling me to his chest. "No."

She rolled her eyes. "Alright. I will not ask again. But know that my door is always open if *either* of you would like to come in."

I sneered as she walked away.

"Who does she think she is?" I stormed at Rev, watching her join Geyrand and Captain Yarah's conversation.

"I believe her and Heimlen had an…understanding when they met."

"And what? That means she gets to have every Baron of Felgren in her bed?" I shook my head, still irritated at her persistence.

"I'd guess she's not turned down by many men or women. I think it's gotten to her head a bit."

I rubbed my temple, reminding myself why we were here. "What are we going to do, Rev? We know the Blightress won't stop. We know where her heart beats in that cave. Do we wait for her to strike against us? What if there's something more dangerous than the Blight? What if she sends syphoners to the cities?" I touched his chin and whispered, "*sarchio*", watching as his cut begin to heal.

"I don't want to wait, but I don't think we should rush into this, either. If we're going to go after her heart, we'll need power. We'll need more conduits. And I have an idea."

He gripped my neck and kissed me, his thumb brushing over the golden cusp of moons on my ear.

"If we could all reconvene, I'd like to propose a plan." He checked in wordlessly to Zoreyah. She nodded back, her babe asleep again in her arms.

The room grew quiet, waiting for the Baron of Felgren to speak.

"We cannot sit around, waiting for the worst from the Blightress. We know she holds immense power. We know she seeks to return more of it. This threatens our way of life here on Arcaynen. We cannot risk Felgren's destruction and risk the magic we rely on. If anything, we need to be training more channelers—something I plan to do.

"But, for now, I ask this of you. Each of the three great cities will gather two of their most powerful channelers. We will come to give their Offerings a few months from now. They will be trained, knowing their task is to enter the Northern Steppes and stop the Blightress from stealing more power. I will also make inquiries to conduits throughout the isle if they wish to join us when the time comes."

"How are we to choose these channelers? Is that not the job of a Baron?" Lamoral crossed her arms at her chest, lifting her chin.

"Usually, yes, but if I was to take the time to go to each city and search for channelers, that time would be wasted when I could be training the ones I already have. I am asking for your help. I believe each of you great leaders possess the necessary skill to choose two channelers. Your conduits can help you as well. Karus and I will depart from Felgren when you have chosen. We will bring them to train and, hopefully, we will be ready to approach the Blightress. Keep in mind, these channelers need to know what they are getting into. They need to know that they come to train for a dangerous excursion into the Blightress's lands."

"It takes years to train a conduit. We don't have years," the Queen argued.

"It takes years to train a conduit in all of the ways and history of Felgren. Since we do not have that time, we will not spend it reading those books. We will spend it controlling their magic and harnessing the power of Felgren."

"I think it is a solid plan. I will begin the search the moment I return to the Attatok Mountains."

"I think it has holes," Lamoral sighed, putting her hands on her hips. "But…it's the best thing we've got so far. We can't sit around and wait to see her next move, and we obviously can't just shove our people into her lands and hope for the best, either." She eyed the Queen.

Rina clasped her hands in front of her plum dress. "I agree to your terms, Baron Revich. We can pause the Treaty and discuss its terms another time. I will begin the sear—"

"I've already chosen the channelers from Hyrithia, Your Majesty." Revich slid his hands in his pockets. "Mychael,"—he flicked his head toward the guard at the door— "and Philius."

The Queen gasped, "If you think I'd send my son—"

"It's not up to you, mother." The Prince stepped forward, facing Rev, loathing still withering on his face. "I accept."

"Good. Mychael?" Rev turned to the guard.

He flustered, clearing his throat. "Y-yes, Baron. I will accept as well."

"It's settled then." Lamoral clamped her hands together and sighed. "Now let's move on from this subject. Queen Rina, I am in need of a drink."

The Queen glared at Rev, then me, and back to her son who still met Revich's gaze.

Madame Zoreyah stood, her muri with her, and she excused herself from the room in an obvious state of exhaustion.

I moved to Geyrand as Captain Yarah took Lanna's hand, leading her out of the room.

"Do you think this will work?" he asked, taking my hands in his.

"I do. I believe in Rev. If he can just get more channelers to Felgren, he can train them quickly. I can help."

"I need to go."

"I know." I let go of his hands to embrace him one last time. "Please send word when Viv has the baby. I'd like to visit after a few weeks and do what I can to help."

"I will write to you." He brought my fingers to his lips, just like that fateful day before I left Hyrithia behind. "I'm glad I was the one who found you, Karus." He glanced toward Revich. "I'm glad I was able to bring you back to him."

"Me, too, Geyrand. Me, too."

~

REV AND I MADE IT BACK TO OUR ROOM IN THE SPINNING WHEEL, both of us exhausted, both of us sipping styris tea along the way. We fell into our one bed, sliding our hands over each other, undressing slowly, carefully, and slipping into the sheets.

We'd hardly spoken, our minds processing everything that had happened.

"How can I say goodbye?" I whispered as he held me to his chest, my tears free-falling off the bridge of my nose, only to land in a cold splash onto my other cheek.

"Clairannia and Figuerah know how much you love them. It is that love that has endured over years and that love that will continue to grow and nourish. Even when you are apart."

"I don't know Felgren without them," I sniffed, wiping my nose with my hand. "They have learned to live without me, but I still need them."

"You have them. You will write to them, and they to you. And if you ever wish,"—he pressed his forehead to mine—"if you ever cannot stand the thought of not being near them a moment longer, I can send you to them through a portal. You can visit for a few days."

I brushed his neck and kissed him.

"Of course, I'll be pining the entire time you're gone, but that's secondary."

I laughed, wrapping my arms around his neck, pulling my body over his.

He traced the lines of growth on my hips and murmured, "Do you believe in me, Karus?" His hands flitted up my waist before settling back down over my backside, his thumbs smoothing over my skin.

"If I believe in anything, it's you."

"And do you trust me, Karus?" He pulled my hips forward, sliding over the length of him, my body silken with the desire he continuously pulled from me.

"If I trust anyone, it's you."

He pushed me back, and I moaned at the friction between our bodies.

"Do you want to go home, Karus?" Pulling me along again, I instead shifted, slipping him inside my body, the movement forcing a breath through his clenched teeth.

"If home is anywhere, it's with you." I bent forward, sliding up and down, my mouth crashing into his as we loved each other one last time in the tallest inn, in the highest room, of the city of Hyrithia.

PART THREE

CHAPTER 42

REV

I had never been to the sea.

Yet, somehow, I knew it well.

The contrast of the white waves that folded into blue-green water I recognized without ever having seen it. The language of each crash was one I understood, speaking as if in constant greeting. The scent of salty brine was something that pulled deep from the place I had once called home.

Karus gripped my arm and beamed at me, her body buzzing with excitement as I gazed upon the vast ocean for the first time in my life.

I finally understood her reference to my eyes. I understood her love of the sea, how it called over and over to us, beckoning our souls to step into the life it gave.

The salted breeze brushed across my lips, and I pressed them to hers, the taste seeping into my tongue as if the ocean could not bear to let me ever forget its presence.

As if I could.

I wished we could stay longer. I wished we could set up a house on the cliff's edge—a quaint little cottage with a thatched roof where Karus and I would walk the beach everyday, collecting the shells long since broken. They glittered in the morning sun as the waves brought them to the shore, the ocean letting us gaze upon the beauty it brought and wonder at the power it possessed.

"You look good here, Rev." She pressed into my shoulder, sitting her chin upon it. "Well, everyone looks good at the ocean…but you especially belong in *this* light."

"I remember that," I chuckled. She had recited the first words I'd spoken to her as she'd stepped into Viridis for the first time.

"I think this might be your Viridis. I think you might have found the light you belong in."

"Ah, Karus," I took her hand and kissed the inside of her wrist. "I found that light many years ago."

I filled my lungs again with more breath than I ever had in my thirty years. "Thank you."

Her smile enchanted me, the perfect rival to the beauty of the sea.

"We didn't travel out of the way just to look at it, Rev." She was already pulling her boots off, tossing them on the sand and sinking her toes into the soft grains. She turned around and ran backward, her arms out and free, her hair whipping in the wind as a challenge for me to follow her movement.

She sprinted to the waves, and they lapped over her legs, soaking her skirts as her laughter flew through the air.

I loved her.

I loved this place.

I loved us.

~

We arrived back at the carriage, boots in hand, the bottom half of our legs soaked in seawater. Mychael spoke to the driver and two other guards while Philius watched Parvus and Rauca play in the tall grass on the cliff's edge.

"You'll be cold now, on the way to the village." Mychael's lips lifted in amusement seeing us attempt to wring out our clothes.

"We have magic for that." Karus shrugged, her cheeks flushed, her lips rosy. She called out to the lumens and the Prince, ready to continue our journey.

The four of us sat inside the ornate carriage, embellished with the long gold, crimson, and midnight blue tassels which represented Hyrithia. It had been a short journey to the sea; a detour Karus insisted we make, but one I'd never forget.

At our departure from Hyrithia, Moira insisted she fly ahead, claiming she had no patience to wait for a human contraption to slowly take her there. That was more than fine by me. I didn't want to listen to her complain on the road for two days about human ways of travel.

We planned to stop at a small village about a day's ride from Felgren and rest there at the inn. I squeezed Karus's hand as she looked out the window at the fields of wheat we passed, long since harvested for the year. The dry stumps rose from dark earth, an expanse of dreary rows of what would not bloom again until next spring.

She turned to me, and I glanced at the Prince and then back to her, a sly smile creeping across my face.

Her eyes darted to Philius and she rolled them, huffing loudly.

He rested his chin on one black hand and stared out the window while he tapped at his leg in clear frustration.

I'd been watching him carefully since his magic had sparked when he hit me, and I saw glimpses of it now in subtle orange flickers every few taps at his knee.

It was ironic to me that the Queen, who spoke of controlling tempers, raised two channelers whose magic came unbidden so often in a state of anger.

Mychael glanced back and forth between us and cleared his throat, breaking the awkward silence. "What is the Fortress like in Felgren? Is it akin to the Castle of Hyrithia?"

Karus shifted next to me. "No. It is much darker. Black. Black everywhere, but it's Felgren you'll truly love." She smiled at him, then turned her attention to Philius. "It's spring there, in the forest. You'll get to see Felgren for the first time at its loveliest."

The Prince clenched his jaw and nodded to her, then stared at me.

Obviously, we were not done here.

"And the training?" Mychael asked, doing his best to settle the tangible anger coming from the Prince. "What will that be like?"

I cleared my throat and shifted my attention away from Philius. "Were you aware you held channeler magic, Mychael?"

He shook his head. "My companion, she was always the one with the magic." He chuckled, "Solla always wanted to become a conduit. I used to wonder if Baron Heimlen would've given her an offering if she had not been born in Hyrithia at the time of the Treaty. She was so adept at helping in the fields and growing her garden." He glanced out the window. "There was this one tree. An apple tree. She would sing to it in the spring, and I swear the blooms would respond."

"What happened to her?" Karus asked quietly.

He exhaled heavily. "The Black Fever."

"I'm so sorry." Karus's voice broke and she reached across the cabin to take his hand. "If you'd like, we could set up a memorial in her honor in Felgren. Something you can visit to remember her. A place with her name so that she can be a part of the forest she wanted to see."

That was one way to pull on my heart, and I grabbed her waist, tugging her close, kissing the top of her head.

"If I could," she continued, "I would have every single channeler's name carved into a tall rock and placed in Felgren. To remember those who never got to see it, and those who died to save it."

"Thank you, Karus," Mychael rasped. "She would have loved that."

"So," Philius spoke, shifting in his seat, "what *is* training like, then? How do you plan to expose our magic when one of us didn't know we had it and the other can only summon it occasionally?"

I liked his directness. Philius got to the point—contrary to his mother. I studied him for a moment. He was the tallest of us all with bronze skin and black coils that he tied at the top of his head, letting them spill out in a thick mass. His physique was lithe like Karus, toned, but not particularly muscular, and I didn't doubt they'd both ran through the same fields and climbed the same cliff faces.

But where Karus held a humbleness, Philius did not. He was raised a prince, a future regent of the crown, a man whose purpose was to choose a queen and create an heiress for their family line. Life in Felgren was going to be immensely different for him.

"Felgren is the key to your power. I can teach you how to summon your magic from its roots. I can teach you how to listen to your truest self in its breeze. It may take time, but I have no doubts you both will find your channeler magic there."

"I want to be trained by Karus," he challenged.

I laughed. "I have no qualms with that. She is more than capable and can teach you things I cannot."

"Philius, don't be stupid. Rev can teach you better than I can. I myself need to train still. It's been years of my magic just sitting there unused."

"I trust you more than him."

"Well, I trust *him* more than anyone, so there."

"He's a liar."

"Oh, and you've never lied?"

"Not about something so important."

"What about your magic, Philius? Hmm? What about the fact that you had enough power to collapse an entire castle wall?"

"I couldn't control that."

"But don't tell me you didn't know it was in you. You kept that a secret, admit it."

"What if I did?"

"Well, that's a lie, then, isn't it? Omitting can still be lying. You never once told me you had magic, too. You know how lonely it was for me to grow up being the only one."

I listened to them bicker like siblings, realizing how very much they were. Karus crossed her arms at her chest, one knee hanging over the other while her foot bounced in irritation.

"I…I wasn't sure that it was anything. I was able to ignore it most of the time."

"Well, that didn't work in your favor because now you need to draw it out." She leaned in close, her body tense. "And Revich is going to be the one to help you do it. So I don't want to hear any more of this. He lied to save me, end of story."

"Maybe we could have saved you."

"You could not. We've been over this, Philius." She pounded her fist on the side of the cabin. "Driver, please stop. I need to get out."

The carriage rolled to a stop and she continued, "Stop telling yourself you could have saved me. Stop telling yourself you deserved a chance to try. Felgren is my home. Revich is my heart, and if you cannot see that by now, then you are blind to whatever doesn't suit you *as usual*."

She opened the door and flew out of it in one swift drop, storming through the broken fields.

The Prince glared at me before following her, slamming the carriage door, running to catch up to her.

Mychael grimaced, and I sighed heavily.

"In his defense," he murmured as we watched them argue in the field, their hands gesturing wildly, "the Prince really did suffer in the knowledge that she was dead. We all were grieving after the Black Fever—I did my fair share—but the Prince never even knew she'd been taken until he recovered. He didn't even get a chance to say goodbye and then she was gone. It broke him…something I suspect you know a little about."

I nodded slowly, listening, but keeping my eyes on Karus.

"I'm not saying I think you were wrong to lie. I'm saying the Prince will need more time to heal."

I bent forward on my knees, my body cold since she had left my side. "Me too, Mychael. Me too."

When they reached some sort of compromise and got back into the carriage, not another word was spoken, both of them resolved to look out the window for hours.

Mychael and I didn't feel the need to speak either as my own thoughts wandering to what Philius had said.

The truth was, I felt no guilt about lying.

I held no hesitancy in my decision, and I would not apologize for it.

Karus understood as well as I that love was the only way to bring her back, and the people she had left in Hyrithia would never have cut it.

I thought about who she'd been when she showed up for the first time in the Fortress. If I closed my eyes, I could remember that woman, resolute on proving herself useless and returning to Hyrithia.

I had waited and waited for weeks that turned to months for her to realize where she truly belonged. Even then, I was sure Felgren was her home.

But now that I was not wrapped up with her in The Spinning Wheel in Hyrithia, I worried.

I worried about the Blightress. I worried about her plans for Karus. She wasn't done with her, that much we both knew. What would she do with my power if she could somehow take it?

The answers must be in Viridis. There must be something we missed about her history. There must be some line, some small paragraph about the Blightress and the power she held. Something about her origins or how to really stop her as the first Baron had done hundreds of years ago.

Felgren was threatened. The power of a Baron was threatened; therefore, conduit training and Karus herself was threatened, and I would never let that happen.

If we needed to destroy her heart, fine. We'd do that. We'd do whatever we needed to save the forest and to save ourselves.

The carriage slowed through the village and the single inn was a welcomed sight.

The Fields and Forest was charming in a quaint way. Two storeys tall, its front was covered in creeping ivy. The shape of windows was cut out at the top rooms so that patrons could look out into the muddy street. It was still autumn outside of Felgren, and the ivy was in the midst of changing its hue from deep green to a brilliant crimson. Two chimneys at either end of the inn puffed tendrils of smoke into the early evening air.

As the carriage rolled to a stop, I opened the door, thankful to be able to stretch my legs. The two guards from the back of the carriage hopped off and did the same. They'd accompany us to the boundary of Felgren before returning with the carriage to Hyrithia.

Mychael stepped out next, followed by Philius who ignored me completely as I held the door open. He spoke to the guards and proceeded to the inn, his stance regal, his voice authoritative.

I was curious how much he'd drink tonight. Karus had warned him we kept no ale and very little wine in the Fortress. He hadn't been too happy about it. I eyed his trunk on top of the carriage, wondering if he'd stored any bottles inside.

I stepped in front of the carriage door and held out my hand. Karus took it while stepping down, exhaling heavily. I wrapped her arm around my waist, pulling her in, whispering in her ear, "He'll come around."

"You don't know the stubbornness of royalty."

"On the contrary. I think I've learned quite a bit about it the last few weeks."

"I'm worried he will always hate you. I don't want anyone to hate you."

"You can't force people to like me, Karus."

"The fuck I can't."

I laughed and watched her eyes spark in defiance.

"Let's get something to eat. Philius can mope and grumble to Mychael. I don't doubt we'll hear more of it soon enough." I kissed her lips and fit my fingers through hers, pulling her inside.

Warmth flooded our skin and the smell of fresh-baked bread filtered through the air, welcoming all guests to sit and dine at the worn tables of the common room.

Mychael approached, holding out a key. "I took the liberty to reserve our rooms ahead of our arrival. They only had three left, so I will stay with the other guards and driver while you and Karus take a room and the Prince takes the other."

I thanked him and led Karus to a table away from Philius. I'd seen enough of him for the day.

We sat and a young woman took our order of water and roasted mutton with vegetables.

Karus fell onto her hand, her elbow resting on the table. She rubbed her face and stared up at the wooden beams across the ceiling.

"What is it?" I asked.

"It's everything." She sighed again and yawned. "I just want to go home."

My heart leapt at the anticipation.

She opened her mouth to say more, but stopped, sitting upright, her jaw hanging open while looking behind me.

I turned. "What is it? What—"

A few tables away, in the back of the room, sat Talon and Ilyenna. Talon's eyes were wide and Ilyenna was chewing her lip nervously.

I rose from the table, clenching my jaw, sliding my hands in my pocket for patience. I had a feeling I knew why they were here.

I maneuvered between the tables and stood before them as they squeezed together. Karus slid up beside me, peering over my shoulder.

Talon cleared his throat. "Baron Revich, Karus…" He stood, bringing Ilyenna with him, their hands clasped. "It is good to see you are well. Karus, we were so worried."

My eyes flicked over my shoulder to Karus's face. She was biting her lips together, her eyes alight with excitement.

"You might be wondering why we're here," Talon admitted, taking a moment to swallow.

He waited for me to speak, and I waited for him to explain.

"You see, Ilyenna and I…" he started, lowering his chin and clearing his throat.

"We're companions," Ilyenna finished in her soft voice that rose lightly in the busy room.

Karus flinched with excitement, leaning on my shoulder.

I was not as amused.

I waited for more, my eyes narrowing.

"Yes. We…" Talon straightened, rolling his shoulders slightly. I noticed his two black braids were wound with white ribbons. I could guess what they were from. "We bonded last night. While…while everyone was away."

Well, fuck.

They'd only known each other for a few months and the minute they were out from under mine and the conduits' thumbs, they ran off to do this.

I took a breath, gathering patience.

"Please say something," Ilyenna pleaded, her soft blue eyes staring up at me. She was barely past twenty, Talon twenty-five. They seemed so young to do this.

Karus brushed in front of me and held her arms out to embrace Ilyenna, then doing the same to Talon. "Congratulations to you both. We will celebrate when we return to Felgren."

Talon grinned, relieved. "We hoped we could stay a few more nights—"

"You will do no such thing," I interrupted. "You will return home with us in the morning, and we will discuss your decision then."

Karus glanced back at me, a scolding look on her face. "Where did you find a conduit to conduct the ceremony? And how did you escape the clutches of Pompeii?"

"He was ill last night. He retired early, and we thought this was our chance because you wouldn't approve." Talon looked at me in appeal.

"I would not," I stated.

"Will you join us?" Ilyenna gestured to the table, and my heart pulled at the lightness of her voice.

These were two of my channelers, my responsibility, and I had failed them. I should have seen this coming, though I knew I would have done the same with Karus had it not been for the very different roles we had been in seven years ago.

"Of course, we would love to."

I glanced at Karus who was still grinning ear-to-ear. At least she could see some good in this.

We all sat, Talon and Ilyenna poking at their dinner.

"We were so relieved when the letter came that you were safe," Talon spoke first, looking to me and adding, "And we were anxious to hear about your trial, Baron. Clairannia and Figuerah made us stay behind, but we didn't want to. In fact, we thought we'd head to Hyrithia after another day here to see if there was anything we could do."

The same server, seeing we had moved tables, brought us two plates of mutton glazed in a rich sauce, roasted carrots and squash on the side.

I rubbed my mouth, defeated. "Alright. I'm angry. I suspected you two had some connection for a while, but I would not have guessed you'd go and do this. And in the middle of the night—sneaking out while Pompeii, your *caretaker*, was ill. I would have preferred we talk about this."

Ilyenna shook her head. "There would be nothing to say, Baron Revich. Please know we did not intend to hurt you or anyone. We only listened to our hearts, which led us here. There's a medicus conduit who travels from here to Hyrithia often. We found her last night and she conducted the ceremony for us. We didn't tell her we were channelers from Felgren, assuming she wouldn't approve."

"I'd imagine not," I started.

She continued, "But the truth is, Baron Revich, we knew you would not allow us to do this. Or it would at least take a lot of convincing, which neither of us wanted to do, so we took our chance when it arose."

Karus tugged on my arm and set her chin on my shoulder. "It's quite the surprise, but I'm sure you've made the best decision for yourselves. I hope Pompeii isn't upset. Did you leave a note or anything?"

Ilyenna chewed and nodded. "We told Rell and Renn. They promised to keep our secret until the morning when they would reveal it to Pompeii and the other servants. It's probably the first time they've ever kept a secret for so long."

I suppressed a grin. Ilyenna was probably right.

"Are you both doing well?" she continued as Karus dug into her food. "I mean, I'm sure there's so much to speak of, but both of you are out of danger?"

Karus nodded, gulping water. "Yes. We have much to explain when we return for everyone to hear, but for now, catch us up on everything that has happened in Felgren the past two weeks."

Talon cleared his throat, looking at me again. I softened my face and picked up my fork. He and I would have a serious talk later.

"It's only been a few days since you've been missing. There hasn't been a lot of time for anything exciting to happen."

"We did read about the history of Barons, though," Ilyenna spoke excitedly. "We went on a hunt through the Fortress, searching for each one's portrait." She paused and tilted her head at me. "Yours is the only one we couldn't find. Well, Heimlen's was missing, but we understand why that is."

Karus turned to me, wrapping her hand around my shoulder, no doubt trying to get me to relax a bit more. "You still don't have a portrait hanging in the Fortress somewhere?" she scoffed. "We'll have to remedy that the moment we return, Baron Revich."

She leaned into me again. Her charm was working. I felt my shoulders drop under her touch.

"It wasn't ever a priority," I murmured.

She bit her bottom lip, her eyes flicking over my chest and arms, then back up to my face. She tucked a stray strand of hair behind my ear. "Well, we'll have to make it one."

I shifted in my seat, unsure why her words sounded so sultry or how she managed to distract me so swiftly, leaning her head to the side, exposing more of her creamy neck.

I took my plate in my hands, and she immediately did the same. We stood, both of us knowing exactly where we needed to be and it was not here in this crowded room.

"Talon, I'd like to speak to you alone." I nodded toward the stairs, and he furrowed his brow.

"Ilyenna," Karus spoke, "A moment, please?"

Talon rose from his seat and followed me toward the staircase. I balanced my plate of food in one hand and embraced him with the other. He patted my back and repeated, "I'm glad to see you both unharmed."

I jostled his shoulder, speaking firmly, "I don't think you should have done this. But I am happy for you both. Do you have styris tea?"

He nodded, looking down at his boots. "We got some today. I hope you'll forgive us, Baron Revich."

"I already have, Talon." I patted his shoulder and glanced back to Karus, her own plate in her hand as she held Ilyenna close. "I'll meet you both here in the morning. I'd like to get home before sunset tomorrow."

He nodded, watching Karus approach. She slipped her free hand in mine, and we left upstairs without a word, both of us eager to fall into bed, both of us needing to be close, both of us almost home.

CHAPTER 43
KARUS

I was first out of the carriage, first to the border of Felgren with Parvus and Rauca at my sides.

I stood at the edge of endless green. An unfathomable line of power, that I now recognized as part of me, raced along the ground. One side of this strip of land was dull—a dirty array of muddy grass that was mostly beige. The other line was filled with tall trees that reached up to the sky. I'd never see the tips unless I was back in my channeler room looking out the slanted window. Even then, I could never see the edge of the vast wilderness that lay across Arcaynen's southeastern corner with acres upon acres of trees, and flowers, and fields.

The pull to enter the place that kept me alive was impossible to resist, so I stepped forward, my boots traveling from one edge of mucky brown patches to the blissful soft underbrush of Felgren Forest.

I'd never traveled through its barrier by foot. The sweet scent of newly budded golden daffodils and white apple blossoms filled my lungs as I took a heavy breath, renewing my soul with my home. Birdsong lifted through the air in a chorus of new life and the warm, sunny days to come.

Parvus and Rauca ran ahead, jumping up and into each other, just as relieved to be back in this place which fueled us all.

I bit back tears of relief, memories flooding within me of the rainy spring day I had followed the Blightress underground. But that field of clover was acres away, and I had changed since I had entered it.

Rev stood behind me, his small pack slung over one shoulder, the same sense of relief across his face that I knew was brandished on mine.

We grinned at each other in absolute joy, both of us laughing as we came together, wrapping our arms at each other's waists.

"Let's never leave again," I declared, watching his black irises turn blue.

"Let's never leave for at least a while."

"Let's never follow strange, ancient women underground."

"Agreed. Let's."

I paused in my response, gritting my teeth in remembrance of what I had done, trying to make light of the choice I had made and failing. "I'm sorry, Revich," I whispered, my breath heavy.

"I know." He pulled me closer to him. "We're moving on from it. Don't dwell. Just be here with me."

I took a deep breath with him, my hands on his chest, feeling it expand slowly over my fingers. I glanced over his shoulder, eyeing Talon and Ilyenna approaching hand-in-hand. "How much trouble are they in, Baron of Felgren?"

He looked behind him and murmured, "Plenty."

"And what will be their punishment?"

"Cleaning out the lumen den…and Pompeii."

"Pompeii?"

"Yes. They will take care of his every need for a week at least. They will wait on him hand-and-foot until he is well, and then they will continue to do so until I feel they've gained some contrition for their impulsivity."

I giggled into his shoulder. "And what about me? What is my punishment, now that we're home, for my impulsivity?"

His lips brushed mine, then moved across my cheek, the curve of my jaw, his warm breath on my ear as he whispered, "You've suffered enough, Karus. Though, I have some ideas on ways you could take care of *me* if you still wish to atone."

I closed my eyes and tilted my head, wanting and needing more of his heated words that left me in a puddle at his feet.

"How far do we have to travel to get to the Fortress?"

Philius's question jolted my current melting into my lover's arms, and I blinked at him for a moment as Revich sighed and drew back from my neck.

The Prince and Mychael each held a handle of his wooden trunk as they lugged it through the trees.

Mychael's rich brown eyes were darting along every surface of the forest, taking in its immense beauty. I wondered if he could hear the whisper of it calling to his magic and settling itself into his very bones as it did on my first visit to its thread of life.

Philius only looked at me, the small frown on his lips he had held since we'd left Hyrithia ever present still.

"Karus and I will walk with you, if you'd prefer. It will take most of the day to arrive at the Fortress without riding a lumen."

"Why can't we ride lumens, then?" Philius asked, setting his end of the trunk down on the path.

"A lumen cannot carry that trunk and you. You also have not bonded to any of the lumens yet, and I think a long walk through this forest will be good for you."

He crossed his arms and grumbled, "Don't you have magic or something that can carry this to the Fortress? I've seen Karus use hers to carry heavy items throughout the castle. Don't tell me your magic doesn't work that way."

Mychael tuned into the conversation and grimaced, the lines of his forehead creasing.

I bit my tongue and let Rev handle it. I'd said enough to Philius in the past two days to go another week without having to argue with him again.

Revich slipped his hands off my waist, but not before giving me a squeeze and slid them into his pockets. He stepped toward Philius. "There are four of us here with enough power to lift your trunk.

Though, I see this as an opportunity for your first lesson." He addressed the channelers, "Talon, Ilyenna, please take Parvus and Rauca back to the Fortress, and inform the staff of our arrival by sunset."

They nodded and called the lumens to them, Talon helping Ilyenna onto Parvus before he climbed onto Rauca's back.

"And please inform Pompeii that he is not to help in preparations for our arrival. He is to rest, and I will see to him first."

They nodded and Rev added, "If he is in need of anything, you two will see to his requests. For a week."

Talon looked relieved more than anything and Ilyenna responded, "We'd be happy to, Baron Revich. We will do what you ask and see you this evening."

They whistled to the lumens and they were off, the pounding of the massive beasts' paws thundering over the dirt path.

Rev returned his attention back to Philius. "If you'd like to reach the Fortress without needing to carry your trunk, you'll have to work with Mychael and summon your power to do so."

Philius huffed. "How?"

Rev shrugged. "It's simple, really. Stand on the ground that feeds your power and let it fill you with the knowledge you need. Felgren speaks to each channeler and conduit in different ways. You must discover how it speaks to you."

"I don't hear anything," he replied curtly.

I met Revich at his side, gathering patience. "For me, it was the breeze within the tips of the trees. It felt like my name was being called on the wind, something I did not yet know myself, but Felgren was aware of. I felt myself being reached through ageless power that sought to settle itself within my very soul."

Rev beamed at me and nodded. "Yes. Like that."

A tendril of white encircled the handle that Mychael held, thin and wispy, but proof nonetheless of his channeler magic.

He looked down at his hand and laughed, shaking his head in surprise.

"Congratulations, Mychael. You've proven your position as channeler to be here."

I thought of the first time I had been asked to prove myself here in Felgren. Heimlen had led us to a small patch of earth and requested we each grow a flower from the thawing soil.

All three of us had done it, not yet knowing that was our first trial in Felgren.

Philius furrowed his brow at his guard, looking down at his own marred hand gripping the handle tightly. "What if I can't do it?"

"Then you can turn around and catch your carriage back to Hyrithia," Revich answered, now crossing his arms at his chest—something I rarely saw him do.

"I don't want to go back."

"Then summon your magic to carry the trunk," Rev replied.

Philius fought back a retort. I could see it in the tension of his body and the way he slid his jaw to the side as he had always done when we were children.

We'd both been taught to hold back our anger. We'd both found ways to suppress it, and I wondered if he'd rebel upon that demand of the Queen's just as I did.

Mychael's magic was thin, and he still needed to hold the handle to keep the trunk upright, but I was proud of him for heeding our words. He glanced at me and I smiled, watching his face light up in a similar grin. He was a handsome man, at least ten years older than me, a few strands of gray littering his brown, shoulder-length hair that curled at the ends. His beard and mustache were flecked with grays too, leaving him looking more than a bit dashing, and there was a kindness to his features. He was probably the oldest channeler ever to be trained in Felgren.

We stood for a few minutes, waiting for Philius to prove he belonged in Felgren as he glared down at his hand wrapped around the trunk's side handle.

"It's not working," he said bluntly, not looking up.

"We noticed," Rev replied, quickly adding, "Would you like to hit me again and we'll see if you can summon the strength?"

I knew what he was doing.

And it worked.

Sparks of orange light shot from Philius's hands. His side of the trunk lifted suddenly, the weight off-balance as one end flew into the air and they both let go. The trunk crashed to the ground in a thud. I wondered how many bottles of wine he'd undoubtedly brought were now broken.

I'd never seen a channeler or conduit's magic express itself like his. Typically, it displayed in thin tendrils like smoke around the magic wielder's hands as they used it for tasks. But Philius's magic sparked like the initial flare of a fire about to burst into flame.

"Well done. You've both shown your suitability to be here. You may follow us to the Fortress."

Rev turned from them, slipping his hand into mine and continuing down the path.

We walked in silence for a time, and I took those moments to bask in the late morning sun and fill my soul with Felgren.

I stole a glance back at the two new channelers. Mychael's magic still swirled around the handle of the trunk while Philius seemed to have lost his.

He glared at the back of Revich's head, and I rolled my eyes, turning away.

"Was I this stubborn when I arrived here?" I mumbled.

"You had more reason to be. You had been forced to come here. He has not. Though, I understand his frustration. His power only shows through anger, and when you arrived, yours flowed from your skin easily and without your knowledge."

"Not when I first arrived." I frowned.

He squeezed my hand. "Yes, it did. The very night I met you, your magic slid from your hands to catch the vase you had knocked off the table before I caught it."

I met his eyes with disbelief. "I don't remember that."

"I'd guess at the time, you didn't believe you were so powerful and didn't notice those things as I did. Do you remember growing the crocus in the forest before I took you to Viridis for the first time?"

"Of course."

"You sat on that hard ground with your eyes squeezed shut and green magic rose from every surface of your body. You were trying so hard not to use your power, it instead left you in excess. That's what had confused me for weeks. You were obviously powerful, but denied it continuously, pretending you held very little."

I thought for a moment in silence. I remembered trying to hold back what was mine to wield here in Felgren in those first few weeks on its soil. I remembered pretending, feigning a difficulty in summoning the power that I had always possessed.

It wasn't until Heimlen had shown me the Blight that I'd decided to test my own limits, and prove that I was strong enough to save Felgren.

"And what about you?" I asked. "Has your magic ever left you without summoning it?"

He slid his eyes to mine as we walked. "No."

I raised a brow. "Just how powerful are you as Baron of Felgren? I don't believe I've seen the extent of it."

I felt his hesitancy at my mention of it. I felt the pull from our bond to suddenly protect me and keep me near, yet something was amiss.

"What are you not telling me, my love?" I asked, my eyes narrowing.

He cleared his throat quickly and replied without answering, "What would you like to me to show you? The power of a Baron is very strong indeed."

I stared ahead, thinking. "Could you move the trees if you liked? Diverge a stream?" I grabbed his arm, and pulled myself closer to his warmth. "Could the Baron of Felgren move the very earth we walk and transport us right up to the steps of the Fortress if he so wished?"

"Yes."

"Alright then, let's see it. Show me something new. Something I haven't seen you do before."

He responded to my challenge immediately, nodding ahead of us as roots of the opposite towering pines broke through the earth, rising upward to wind together across the path in an archway. Clomps of dirt fell as a woody vine slid along the intertwined roots before blooming into great heaps of purple wisteria that hung heavily down the archway.

My jaw dropped at the display, and I laughed, letting go of his hand and running to the proof of his power. I gripped the sides of my waist and asked, "Was that simple for you, Revich?"

"A Baron's power is most easily called upon in Felgren. I'm not sure I could do something like this outside of it, or to trees that did not grow here."

I lifted a purple hanging strand of petals to my nose and breathed in the sweet smell of fresh blossoms. I lifted my hand in the air, calling to the monarch nearby. She landed on the ring of my forefinger, stretching her wings in and out slowly before finding the wisteria and fluttering to its petals for a drink.

I looked to the sky in a wordless call to more of them. Moments later, a swarm of orange and black wings flew to the blossomed archway.

"We can do it, can't we?" I whispered, coming back to him, wrapping my arms around his shoulders while Philius and Mychael set the trunk down on the path to take a rest. "We can build our lives here, training channelers together. We can provide the isle with more magic and make people's lives better because of it."

He pressed his forehead to mine. "Together, I believe we could do anything."

I closed my eyes, inhaling his warmth of fresh pine and woods— the life of Felgren. "You breathe, I breathe," I spoke, our phrase of tethered lives now settled between us.

He hovered over my mouth, his breath familiar and sweet. "You live, I live, Karus."

Our lips met in slow admission of our strength together, our love of this forest, and our desire to see it thrive.

We could do that. Together, we could do anything.

We stopped every once in a while to allow Philius and Mychael to catch their breath.

Mychael's magic was still weak, but present all the same to help him on our long trek to the Fortress.

Philius, however, couldn't keep his magic flowing and his forehead was streaked with sweat.

We sat near a small stream, only another hour's walk to the Fortress, and I began to recognize more of the details of my home.

Offering Philius an apple, I sat next to him on a rock while Mychael and Rev spoke together of Felgren's history.

"You're lucky you get to bring this at all, you know," I mentioned, my boot lightly tapping the trunk. "When most channelers come here, they cannot bring anything from their homes, let alone an entire trunk which I'd guess is filled with wine." I raised a brow at him in a challenge to deny it.

He bit into his apple and eyed the trunk, before looking back at me, shrugging.

"Also," I continued, "the Baron of Felgren typically dresses you in formal clothing that suits your personality, and a conduit ring"—I lifted my right hand—"is formed on your finger."

"You think I don't know that?" he huffed, chewing with his mouth open just to annoy me.

"I wasn't sure you remembered. It's not like we saw Offerings growing up."

He cleared his throat and murmured, "I'm sorry I missed yours."

"It's not like it was a *real* Offering. I didn't have a choice, and you were still in bed from what almost killed you. Of course you weren't there."

"I'm still sorry for it."

I nodded, sighing. "Why did you agree to come?"

"Well, I wasn't exactly fulfilling my duties at home." He took a last bite of the apple and threw the core into the stream, watching it bob up and down as it was carried away. "Besides, I don't trust him. And I want to see you safe. Like I should have done."

I blew air out of my lips, exasperated by this continuing conversation we came back to time and again.

He laid back against the rock, his hands behind his head,

soaking in the sunlight. He reminded me of the orange and white cat we once kept hidden in his room so that the Queen could not take her away. She loved to bask in the sun, too.

"What would he have to do then?" I asked, looking for a way out of this endless argument. "What would Revich have to do to earn your trust?"

He shrugged one shoulder, eyes still closed. "Turn back time?"

"He can't do that."

"Then I will probably never trust him."

"You're impossibly stubborn, Prince Philius." I crossed my arms over my chest.

He peeked one eye open with a slight smile. "Oh, you're one to talk."

"I know I'm stubborn, but at least I'll admit it."

"I'll admit I'm stubborn, too, then."

I tilted my head back and groaned.

The sound caught Rev's attention and he turned to us, in question.

"Let's keep moving," I said, standing and thinking of all the ways I could return Philius's grating remarks using my own short temper.

Rev slipped his hand into mine, and we continued our journey forward, the Fortress soon in sight.

The black towers joined the tops of the trees, and though they once had felt looming and dark, I couldn't help but smile seeing them again. The Fortress was such a contrast to the forest, but I no longer minded as I once did. Now, it felt more like a place of rest and recovery. Now, I saw the Fortress as shelter from the elements, a place I could curl up into with a good book and a good lover.

The windowless structure met us in its usual defiance of the green that surrounded it, though creeping vines of ivy still fought their way up its black stone steps.

Rev put his arm around my waist and pulled me to him, kissing the top of my head without a word.

He turned to meet Philius and Mychael. "Welcome to your new home, channelers. We'll get you settled in the tallest tower,"—he jerked his head to the dark stone spire that rose high into the waning blue sky—"and then we'll meet in the dining hall for dinner."

Mychael's eyes widened with awe as he gaped at the structure. Philius took an air of indifference, but I saw right through it. He was curious, and I hoped for the hundredth time then that Rev was right—that this new life would help him let go of the one he left behind.

Rev stepped closer to them both, holding out his hand first to Mychael. "It's tradition for the Baron of Felgren to bestow new clothing and a conduit ring onto channelers before they enter the Fortress."

Mychael nodded and took a step forward to grasp his hand. Instantly, his attire changed from that of a Hyrithian guard to a new channeler of Felgren. Sleek black boots replaced his brown riding ones. Fitted pants, the color of deep green verging on the edge of midnight blue, wove over his legs. Lastly, a black shirt clung tightly to his chest and rose halfway up his neck along with a fitted vest in the same color.

I smiled, a small laugh escaping me as Rev glanced my way, one brow raised, and I bit my lips together.

Mychael, the former royal guard, was quite handsome. And it showed now even more so in the waining light of Felgren.

He took his hand from Rev as his conduit ring appeared on his right forefinger in a band of gold, offset with a middle ring of mother of pearl.

"That was...fascinating," he finally spoke, pulling on his vest and sleeves.

Revich shrugged. "It's a subconscious part of you who chooses the garments and the ring. I just have the power to give them to you."

He turned to Philius without a word, holding his hand out in question. Philius glanced to me first and took a deep breath, taking it in his. A suit of emerald soon hugged his tall form. Bands of gold-embroidered flourishes cuffed his wrists and climbed up his over-coat, spilling onto the collar at his neck, stiff and upright. He looked more like royalty than I'd ever seen, and I smirked slyly, crossing my arms as he gazed in awe at his new attire.

He pulled his hand away and held it up in front of his face. His conduit ring contrasted his blackened fingers in a brilliant flash of iridescent orange opals that spun through a band of silver in a pattern the shape of a flame. He twisted his hand around, his face falling slightly as he shoved his hands in his pockets and looked up at the Fortress once more.

"You both look so handsome." I slid my arm through Philius's, our arguments not over, but my heart at a truce.

He stumbled forward with me as I yanked him up the steps of the Fortress, my simple white dress snagging on the stone. I pushed the heavy iron-lead doors open and welcomed him to my home.

CHAPTER 44
SAELYN

I would be seventeen in seven days, and I glared at the checklist I'd written.

Cake. Check.

Clean dress. Check.

Colorful garlands. Check.

Invitations…empty box that seemed to mock me in its lack of pigment.

I tapped my fingers on my chin and then quickly stopped, remembering I would just summon more blemishes if I continued.

Since starting my preparations for my birthday celebration, I had decided I wanted to invite everyone. I wanted all the servants, all the people I knew, to be there and we would have one giant party with music, and lights, and delicious food from the kitchens. We'd been living such a rote, dull existence for so long now, I wanted to change that. I wanted to celebrate the new arrival of summer. I didn't even care that the party was on my birthday.

But as I continued to stare at the list, my thoughts crept once again to my mother. I hadn't told her my plans. I hadn't even confessed I wanted a party to begin with.

All my past birthdays had been small, quiet gatherings—if

gatherings really at all. Our home felt its darkest on those first days of summer, and everyone seemed to tip-toe around as if in mourning.

I knew some details of my birth. I knew it had been hard on my mother, coinciding with the day my father died, so I had stayed quiet too. I'd usually hold my mother's hand those nights as she, Pah-Pah, Thevin, and his parents gathered around to eat my favorite strawberry cake together in the quiet.

She never seemed to want to let go of me on those days, and I'd gladly held onto her.

I wasn't sure how she'd react to an invitation to a grand party, and I didn't want to hurt her, so I had done everything in preparation except send the invitations to everyone I knew, which was really not many people at all.

As if my thoughts summoned her, a soft knock came to my door, and I quickly shoved the checklist into a drawer in my desk.

I could feel her presence at the door and called, "Come in, Mama."

She entered quietly, smiling my way and closing the door behind her. She walked to my bed in the corner, picking up the wooden lumen I still kept on my nightstand.

She cleared her throat and spoke, finally looking at me. "I just spoke to Pah-Pah. He let slip that you're planning a grand celebration for your birthday this year."

I gulped and nodded. Her voice was low and quiet, and I couldn't read her tone.

"Saelyn, my Little Love, I think it's a wonderful idea."

"Really? You're not upset with me?" I rose and rushed to her, throwing my arms around her shoulders, breathing in her scent.

"No, I'm not upset. I know your birthday has always been…a more sorrowful day, and I am sorry for that. But seventeen is a big year, and we should celebrate together. All of us should celebrate *you*."

I looked up into my mother's eyes as they lightened and wanted to cry. I wanted to snuggle up with her in her giant bed in the room next to mine like I did as a small child. She'd wrap her arms around me and stroke my hair at her chest under the soft blankets, and I knew I was safe and loved.

"I didn't mean to hide it from you…I just—"

"You didn't know if I'd be upset by it." She pulled me back to her chest, wrapping her arms around me. "I'm so sorry, Saelyn. I did what I could to love you, but I'm afraid it wasn't good enough."

I suddenly had the thought we weren't just talking about my solemn birthdays. "What do you mean, Mama? I know how much you love me."

"Do you?" She sniffed and wiped a hand across her face. "Do you know just how much you are loved?"

"Yes," I replied simply.

She laughed, and I didn't know why, but I followed just the same.

"Well," she began, sniffing more and pulling me back to see my face, "everything will be better soon, you'll see. This will be the biggest celebration we've ever had. Show me what you've done so far in preparation, and I'll help you with the rest."

I couldn't smile wider, rushing to my desk to pull out the checklist, and then show her the paper garland I had painstakingly cut and glued together to hang through the trees with the other banners and lanterns.

As I looked up at my mirror, I saw my reflection, though my eyes looked sad and worn, full of a pain I did not currently feel. Frowning, my reflection followed the movement and a pale woman behind me mouthed my name as I heard it whispered in my room.

I turned quickly, my heart racing, expecting to see her standing there beside my mother where she just had been in the mirror.

"Saelyn? Are you alright?"

I licked my lips and grabbed the top of my dress, my heart still pounding. "Did you see her?"

My mother looked around the room, moving closer. "Who? See who?"

"That pale woman who stood beside you just now. I saw her in my mirror. She whispered my name."

My mother stilled, her face draining of its typical rosy hue as she looked around the room again, even checking under my bed, frightening me more than she likely intended to do.

After a few moments, she took a deep breath and closed her eyes. "Why don't you sleep in my room tonight. Like you used to. I'm sure it was nothing, Little Love. Just a trick of the light or maybe you're tired from running through the fields with Thevin all day."

I nodded, eager to leave.

I gathered my nightgown and wooden lumen, taking one last look at my room as I followed her out and shut the door, wondering who that woman was and if I'd ever see her again.

CHAPTER 45

REV

Karus burst through the Fortress doors shouting the name of everyone she'd ever met here in Felgren, and just as I would have done, just as I would always do, they came running.

Moira flew.

Only Pompeii was missing, and I was glad of it if it meant he was getting some rest.

In a burst of joy that was green, she hugged every one of them, introducing each to her brother and his former guard, quickly explaining our plan to train more channelers. She left out exactly why, but no one seemed to care as grins spread across their faces, and they all agreed how happy they were to see her safely back home.

"Oh!" she continued, "And one more thing. Baron Revich and I…we've gone through the bonding ceremony. We're companions."

An outcry of excitement, and some small disappointment that they'd missed it, filtered through the gasps and squeals. I kept my hands deep in my pockets, my fingers toying with the rhyzolm as I watched her glow.

I watched the people who loved and cared for her extend their congratulations and embrace her, Moira sitting at her shoulder. Karus was the only human I'd ever seen her touch.

I liked to think there were moments in time that I could hold onto forever.

Memories I could brand into my soul, so that I could keep them and pull them back to me when times were dark.

I'd had some of them in those seven years of waiting.

Her first look upon Viridis.

The night of our first kiss under the light of the full moon and the nitor moths.

The night not long after when I had declared my love for her, no longer willing to keep it to myself another minute.

There were several more I looked back upon often, but those three were my favorite. In those years of missing her, like old friends, they'd sheltered me when the storm of pain and loss threatened my horizon for the foreseeable future.

And this moment, this one I told myself to hold onto as well.

Lia caught sight of me leaning against the black stone wall, and she smiled with tears on her face. I pushed myself off and walked to Karus's side, receiving hugs from everyone, Philius excluded.

Even Moira's lips curled into a grin, though still with the hint of menace she couldn't quite ever rid herself of.

"Should we have a party?" Rell asked in buzzing excitement, her red curls bouncing just like her sister's as Renn said, "We have two companion bonds to celebrate!"

Talon caught my gaze sheepishly, and I nodded. "Yes, we should have a party. After Pompeii is well." I addressed Lia then, "How long would you need to prepare cakes and food for a celebration?"

"And cinnamon buns!" Moira shouted with her long sage fingers cupping her mouth.

Lia lowered her gaze, mumbling to herself for a moment. "Three days, love. I could have something together by then with some help." She eyed some of the other servants and they all nodded.

"It's settled then. In three days time, we'll have a party. Then it's back to training for all of you." I met each of my six channeler's gazes in turn.

"We have three more days off?" Rell questioned, nudging her sister.

"You have three days to do as you please in the Fortress or Felgren. Rell and Renn, kindly show Mychael and Philius to their rooms in the tallest tower. I expect you to help them settle in for a few days and show them the dining hall and library. You may take them to the lumen den if you wish."

I turned to Talon and Ilyenna. "You two, come with us to Pompeii where we will discuss your further duties."

We all dispersed, Rell and Renn talking excitedly with Mychael and Philius who held overwhelmed expressions hearing them speak. It would take time to get used to their quick words full of too much information at once, but we'd all gotten there eventually.

Karus slipped her hand into mine, and we headed to the kitchens where Lia had already bustled off to, listing duties to the servants along the way.

"I'm going to be gone for a few days, Karus," Moira casually mentioned on her shoulder.

"Where are you going?" Karus asked.

"Just fae things in Felgren. The Growers have asked for a meeting, and since I am the official expert on all things *human*," she spoke the word in slight disgust, "I suppose I should be there."

"Alright. We'll see you at the party?"

Moira nodded and was off, flitting through the open back door in the kitchens.

We turned down the corridor that led to the servants' quarters. I noticed Karus's eyes flicker briefly to the third door on the left—the room Sylva had occupied years ago. The largest door at the end of the hall was Pompeii's and one I had rarely entered.

I knocked gently, calling, "Pompeii? Are you accepting visitors?"

We heard a weak, "Yes, please come in."

I opened the door, peering in at my Overseer and friend. His room was simply furnished, though as colorful as its occupant always displayed himself to be. A red and gold woven rug lay under a modest sized bed of opulently carved wood with spindles on each corner. A dark purple chair sat next to the fire and a small wooden table with a single wooden seat sat nearby, a white vase of yellow daffodils casting a cheery mood throughout the room.

I neared his bed, my brows furrowing at how frail he looked there in a silky woven robe of copper trimmings. Kohl no longer swiped along his eyes as it had been every day I'd known him.

His hair was pulled back messily, another detail he'd always kept pristine, and I frowned further seeing his usual olive skin wan, his cheeks sunken.

I reached for his hand to feel his pulse, pressing two of my fingers into his veins just as I'd seen Clairannia do to her own patients. She'd taught me a thing or two from her apprenticeship after passing the trials and joining other medicus conduits in the Spire.

I was feeling for a steady, strong pulse and was met with a racing, erratic one. I placed the back of my hand on his forehead, searching for signs of a fever.

"How long have you been like this, Pompeii?" I questioned, nodding toward his neck, my hands hovering at each side. "May I?" I asked next, and he nodded weakly.

He cleared his throat and rasped, "Just a day, Baron."

I used my fingers to feel my way around the sides of his neck, something Clairannia had also taught me, looking for swelling or a gasp of pain, finding neither.

"Karus?" he whispered. "Is Karus well?"

Leaving Talon and Ilyenna in the doorway, she moved to sit on the other side of his bed and took his hand in hers. "Yes, Pompeii. I am here and well." She looked to me with the same worry I knew my own face reflected. "Can you do anything to help him?"

I nodded, brushing his forehead once more as a dazed look crossed his face. He was warm, but not feverish, though I could tell his mind was clouded. "Pompeii," I murmured, leaning in close to catch his gaze, "I'm going to use an enhancement spell to help you sleep. Then, I'll be bringing you something to eat. You need rest and food to give you strength."

He nodded slightly, his eyes already drifting.

"Talon and Ilyenna will continue to check in on you, but so will I."

I looked back to Karus and saw her magic pooling around her hands, clutching one of his.

"*Soporen,*" I spoke softly, helping him slip into a place of rest.

Before his eyes shut completely, he mumbled something I could not quite catch, but Karus instantly straightened, cocking her head at me.

"What did he mean?" she asked, squinting at his chest, pulling back part of his robe.

"I couldn't make out what he said." I pulled at the other side, seeing dark, swollen skin over his chest like a deep purple bruise.

She leaned closer, in confusion, lightly touching his skin with her magic, and mumbling, "I think he said something like 'laboratorium'?"

My eyes shot to her, wide in revelation. "*Fuck.*"

CHAPTER 46

KARUS

We raced down the corridor, leaving a bemused Talon and Ilyenna in the doorway. Revich pulled me through the foyer and down the hall that would eventually, after many turns, lead to the doors of Viridis. But we stopped short at a door halfway there, both of us out of breath, myself confused with a creeping sense of dread.

I bent forward, hands on my knees, looking up at him as he braced his palms on the black door. "What is this place?" I asked, heaving and pulling my hair back from my face. "What haven't you told me?"

"I was going to show you," he puffed, "the day you left Felgren. I was going to show you that night."

I glanced at the door, swallowing. "Show me what?"

He placed a hand on the latch, but paused. "Karus, I don't now what we'll find in here, but if it's what I suspect, I need you ready. *Simulair Solum.* Can you start it for me?"

My jaw dropped. "The *Blight* is in there?"

He nodded. "Parts of it. This is my laboratorium. I've been studying the Blight here for years, bringing different specimens together to record reactions. I'm no agricola conduit, but I knew I needed to do something in the time your memories were gone."

"And you just kept this from me?" I scolded.

"You've only just returned to us for a few months. I've been… slowly telling you things. Like I said, I intended to bring you here the same night you left."

"And what about in Hyrithia? You could have said something then!"

"We were busy."

I scoffed, reluctant to admit how simple that truth was. I folded my arms. "Alright. What do you think is in there, then? Why did you react that way when Pompeii mentioned this place?"

"The last specimen I brought was bark from the trees you grew in Viridis."

"What!"

"And a pit from the fruit."

I could hardly wrap my head around it. He'd been studying the Blight for years?

I bit my bottom lip, and he let me think. "You should have told me sooner."

"I should have."

"*Simulair Solum.*" I spoke the words to the spell over my cupped hands, a brilliant light illuminating the corridor in mimicry of the sun. I held the swirling mass of sunlight above me, keeping it small in the moment, no bigger than a bowl, but ready to expand its surface if need be.

Pride hit me in full force, coming from the tether between us. I looked up to see his eyes prickling with blue once again. I filled my lungs and nodded at the door.

He took my elbow in one of his hands, Cosensian Magic tumbling over the ball of light in brilliant blue for just a moment as he used his power to enhance mine. With his other hand, he slowly turned the knob of the door, pushing on it slightly, and to my reasonable dread, it caught on something behind the wood surface.

I'd seen this happen before on the day Heimlen took me through the small door that led from Viridis to Felgren. I had witnessed the Blight for the first time that day, and now, I had more reason to be afraid.

Rev pushed harder, my sun growing larger as both green and blue power wrapped over its surface, its glow streaming through what little space we could see.

I don't think I could ever forget that sound.

The raging hiss of pain.

The sibilant stream of recession coming from the Blight as it withered from the door and from the sun I held in my hands.

He pushed harder still, forcing his shoulder into the dark wooden door, gripping my arm, never letting go.

I felt alive.

I felt incredible power sifting through my blood. The scent of death poured from the room, and I pushed myself through the space Revich had made.

The room was brilliantly lit now that the sun itself radiated through the stone space, and I watched as thick, black vines recoiled from the floor, a long table, and chairs. It had been growing along the fucking *wall* even, and nothing pleased me more in that moment than to see it wither and shrink back to a shelf near the door.

This Blight was different from the one grown in Felgren. The wood was slick and pustules of black liquid popped sporadically as it diminished, flecks of the substance spotting my dress, flying to my face and hair, some landing on the sun and sizzling into a smoky black steam.

It took only a few minutes for the Blight to recess completely. A husk of the source lay dry and dead on a bed of broken glass.

I turned to Rev and he nodded solemnly.

He let go of my arm, moving closer to inspect what had caused all this in the first place. I tried to bring the sun back to a smaller size—bring it down to a pebble and release the spell.

My hands shook as I felt my power only grow once more, and the bowl-sized sun expanded instead to the size of a carriage wheel.

"Rev," I pleaded, my thoughts a swirling mist of panic. I'd lost control of my power once before and flashes of that fateful night began to flicker through my mind like pages of a book. It felt as if I was witnessing each second of holding that massive sun over Felgren in tandem with each second that passed in the room we stood.

His soothing voice echoed in the room as he faced me, gripping both of my arms. "Karus, bring it back in. You need to end the spell."

"I don't know how!" I shouted, a cold sweat brimming at my brow. My breath came in short bursts as the sun continued to grow, and Rev had to let go or be burned.

"Karus!"

I heard his fear and could do nothing for it.

The simulated sun was heavy, and I remembered that, too.

I fell to my knees as it grew to the size of the door and began to pulse.

"Rev," I whispered, terror gripping me to a standstill on my knees, memories of that night still flashing before my eyes.

And then…darkness.

I blinked on my back, wondering if I had fainted.

The sun was gone, but the heaviness remained, pumping through my blood rapidly and pressing on my chest in the dim room with only a sliver of light seeping in from the hallway.

No, that wasn't the sun's residual weight.

That was Rev.

"Are you alright?" he breathed above my face, smoothing hair back from my head and murmuring, "*Incendo.*"

I squinted in the sudden flare of light as the sconces along the walls flickered to life. I nodded, my eyes darting all over the room, my pulse still reflecting my panic.

"Karus." He cupped my cheek, easing off my chest. "I breathe, you breathe. Ready?"

I kept my eyes on his and inhaled long and deep through my nose, exhaling out of my mouth in the same beats as he did. I followed his lead four times before I felt my heart settle, and I sat up, taking his hand to rise off the floor.

A muscle ticked in his jaw as he looked over my appearance.

"That bad?" I asked, holding my arms out in front of me to see specks of black remnants of the Blight.

"Your hair. It has more streaks of white."

I touched my head, pulling strands in front of my face. There were certainly more of them, but I sighed in relief to find that the color still mostly held a chestnut hue.

"Is it hideous?"

"No."

"Are you…are you upset with me?"

He laughed sardonically and pulled me close to his chest. "Absolutely not. You were glorious."

"Why can't I break that spell?" I questioned, my cheek pressed to his neck, flecked with the same black spots of liquid that splattered mine. I traced a small burn there, whispering a spell to mend his skin.

"I wish I knew."

"You can't just knock me over every time I use it…though that seems to be the only thing that works."

"What makes you think you'll ever be using it again?"

I pulled back from his neck. "How else are we going to rid Felgren of the rest of the Blight? And Viridis? How will we return Viridis to what it once was?"

"Certainly not by that spell, or at least certainly not from you using it."

I scoffed. "I'm *fine*. It's the only thing we've found to work, and I can hold the spell longest. Unless you want to train for it."

"I think I will."

I huffed, folding my arms at my chest. "You know I have the power to do it. You know that with Cosensian Magic and some more training, we can clear the Blight completely."

He turned to the door and shut it, leaning back against its frame, his own arms crossed at his chest. "What I know is that both times you've used that spell, your hair has lost its color. What I *know* is that both times you've used that spell, you couldn't let go of it even as it grew beyond a weight you could carry."

"I can *do* this, Rev. I was brought to Felgren to do this."

"You were brought here to *die*."

The last word seemed to resonate through the room like a

promise never fulfilled by the man who still continued to haunt our lives.

"I'm sorry, Karus, I—"

I held up a hand. "No, you're right. What you said is true. But I refuse to believe that's the only way. It can't be the only outcome to destroying all of the Blight. I won't let it be."

He rubbed his face with his hands, pulling them through his black waves. "Let's go. We both are badly in need of a bath. I'll explain this"—he gestured to the laboratorium, destroyed as it was —"after we've cleaned ourselves up."

I nodded, my arms still crossed as he opened the door. I stepped out into the hall, breathing cool air, and he followed, locking it behind him.

"You didn't lock it before you left the last time?" I asked, headed down the hall.

"No one comes down here except Pompeii to—" He frowned and looked back at the door.

"What is it?"

He opened the lock and barreled inside. I followed, peeking around the door to see him pulling open a basket on a small table near the shelves.

Sighing he replaced the lid, finding the contents empty. "The towels. Pompeii must have come here to clean the towels I used with the last pieces of Blight. The one that evolved into that…thing." He pinched the bridge of his nose.

"Then you think…" I started.

"Yes," he continued for me, "Pompeii's sickness comes from the Blight."

~

MY BARE FEET PADDED ACROSS THE COLD STONE FLOOR. I PACED back and forth before the fire in our rooms, hardly able to even appreciate being back in them.

Our bath was hot and waiting, just how Rev liked it.

I had stripped down to my undergarments, having thrown my

dress into the massive fireplace, watching the ruined fabric flare and burn down to nothing.

If what we guessed was true, we couldn't risk others becoming infected. We'd chosen to isolate ourselves here after Rev retrieved the towels from Pompeii's room.

I rubbed my temples, thinking of all that could go wrong. Rev had been exposed for weeks now, so it was unlikely he would be affected. But Talon and Ilyenna had been in Pompeii's rooms.

What if they caught this blight infection as well?

What if it killed its host?

Maybe we were wrong. Maybe he fell ill from something else, but just as Rev had confirmed himself, I'd never seen Pompeii sick in the time I knew him. And the bruising at his chest looked eerily similar to the black hands of those inflicted with the Black Fever.

Rev stepped through the doorway, and I stopped my pacing. He held a bag in his arms, shirtless and with ill-fitting trousers that were far too small and emerald green, like Pompeii's livery. I concluded he had shed his clothing, stuffing it into a bag to reduce exposure as he walked through the Fortress.

Closing the door, he strode quickly to the fireplace, tossing the bag into the fire where it burst into flames, and smoke began to enter the room. He erected a wall of blue power around the fireplace to keep us from the fumes and turned to me. "Pompeii is still sleeping. He should be out for another few hours. I've informed the staff and the channelers. Talon and Ilyenna are isolating in Ilyenna's room as well." He exhaled heavily. "I just hope we're overreacting. Maybe it's nothing."

I shook my head. "You heard his rasp. You saw the dark bruise on his chest—Rev, what if this is something new? What if what I grew in Viridis can infect us all?"

"Then we'll find a way to stop it. We won't let it take him or anyone."

Tears welled in my eyes.

This was supposed to be a happy time.

We were finally supposed to have a moment to breathe back home and instead, our friend was growing weaker by the minute.

"How did Heimlen cure the Black Fever? His journals said you helped."

"I tried it just now. He pretended, Karus. He pretended to find a spell enhancement that would work and then left for Hyrithia immediately after." He shook his head. "It didn't work on Pompeii. I don't even know if it's a real spell."

"We have to search Heimlen's study then. There must be clues about how he really did it. Since he used the Blight to create the Black Fever, there must be a clue on how to cure this, too."

"I think that's a brilliant step forward." He began to unlace my shift, letting the thin strings fall at my chest before slipping them down my arms. It fell in a soft sigh at my feet, leaving me bare, my skin still flecked in places with spots of black. I stepped out of the shift completely and brought it to the fireplace.

He unbuttoned his too-tight, too-short pants and threw them in as well, letting the wall of magic disperse for just a moment to do so. I tossed in my undergarments, and we watched the flames flicker over what we couldn't risk getting onto anyone else's skin.

"Won't Pompeii be angry with you for burning his trousers?"

"After this, I'll commission a new wardrobe of whatever he wants."

I took his hand and we entered the washing room, the steam a welcome sense of normalcy. We stepped into the enormous tub, and I picked up a rag and bar of rose hip soap. I began scrubbing his neck, healing small burns on his chin as I went, kissing them away after using magic to return the skin to its usual sandy hue.

A bit of black stubble was beginning to show, and I brushed my fingers along the sharp line of his jaw, each prickle of rough hair catching on my skin.

He watched me touch him in a mixture of love, worry, and admiration he always seemed to project to me. I knew his concern was about more than this new illness. This was also about how the *Simulair Solum* spell affected me, and how he knew I was not going to back down from insisting I could use it again.

We would meet this impasse continuously, I was sure of it, and the best thing I could do right then was to show him that I was alright. I could show him that the spell had its setbacks for me, but that I'd made it through this time relatively unharmed, and I could do it again.

I took those moments in the steaming water to show him exactly how fine I was. I slowly, softly brushed the pads of my fingers down the hollow of his neck. They slid down his chest, following the lines of his ribs and over the plains of muscle that had shown more definition again over the past few weeks.

My palm slid over the hard length of him, and he inhaled slowly, his lips parting as I leaned forward to kiss him gently. My lips met his with each slow stroke of my palm.

He lifted his hands from the soapy water and slid them around my neck, taking the kiss deeper, pulling me to him. "I know what you're trying to do, Karus," he whispered low on my lips.

I slid my legs over his, pushing myself against him, my breasts pressed to his chest, his arousal pressed to my stomach. "I would hope so, Baron Revich." I wrapped my arms around his shoulders, kissing him deeply again.

He pulled away and lifted my chin, catching me off guard. "I know you want to convince me you're unharmed."

"I am unharmed."

"Then prove it. Show me, Karus. Show me you can take care of yourself." He took my hand and guided it between my legs, pressing my fingers to the center he wanted me to touch, holding my fingers and moving them in circles to show me what kind of taking care of myself he meant.

I did so.

Gladly.

He leaned forward, grabbing the rag and soap from the water to wash the Blight from my skin. I closed my eyes and released myself to his touch and mine, pausing a moment to dip my hair back into the tub.

"Don't stop," he ordered, bringing my hand back down to what was now slick between my legs. "You don't stop. You keep going. Keep touching yourself, and don't stop until you're ready to beg for me to slip inside you."

I gulped, a flood of excitement racing through me as my body ached to feel full and completed by him alone.

He slid the soap down my breasts, moving to my neck to kiss the dip into my shoulders. "I want to hear you beg for me, Karus," he whispered. "I want you push yourself to the edge until you can't live another moment without me…fucking you."

I wanted him *now*.

I was demanding in bed, and I knew that. I always wanted all of him all at once, quickly, greedily filling me, making me whole again while he pounded inside of me.

His thumb brushed my nipple before his mouth, hot and soft, covered it whole, and I groaned, my fingers moving faster in the water.

He scraped his teeth gently over the peak, and I grabbed the back of his neck to bring him in closer, to love me harder.

Gently, he took my hand from his neck, backing away from my breasts and kissed my palm, then the inside of my wrist, sending the trail of his lips down my arm.

My breath was short, my need for him screaming, urging to beg him to take me. He caught my eye with a small upturn of his lips as he watched the turmoil on my face.

To my horror, he rose from the water, stepping out of the tub and wrapping himself in a towel, leaving me there to please myself alone without the presence of him right beside me. Without his hard body over mine to complete the space I held in this world as my other half, the piece of me contained within him.

I gripped the sides of the tub to stand and he was there, guiding my hand back down between my legs and wrapping a towel around my shoulders. "Don't stop," he instructed again, but gently, as if he expected me to forget his command.

Just as I was about to break, just as I opened my mouth to beg for him to take me, he pressed his lips to mine, stopping the sound before it could register, urging me to keep going.

I gave a small cry on his lips in frustration, and he returned with the slide of his tongue over mine, rendering me incapable of speech, rendering me breathless as he bent to pull me up onto his hips. My legs wrapped around his waist, and my hand continued my pleasure, brushing over him in turn.

Dripping wet, he carried us to our bed, his mouth still over mine, one hand holding the back of my head as he laid me down, so heartbreakingly gently I wanted to cry, to explode, to plead for him to release me from this build that still rose within me.

He left my lips, pressing himself to my thigh to give me room to continue his bidding. He turned my cheek so it lay flush with the quilt below us. His breath traveled hot on the underside of my jaw as his lips skimmed over my skin, sending flares of pleasure throughout my body, enhancing each swirl of my fingers, now picking up a steady, continuous pace.

"Rev—" I began to plead.

"Don't," he growled, pressing his thumb to my lips. "Stop."

Fuck.

I was going to shatter and he wasn't even inside me. He wasn't even kissing me where I wanted him to, where my fingers now circled furiously.

I couldn't open my legs any wider, and unable to stop my impending release, the stretch of slight pain from trying to was hardly registered as my body rocked and I exploded with pleasure. My hips rose in an urge to find more, more, *more.*

I cried out, my blood rushing through my veins, the pain in my open thighs tight as I slowly released myself from the stretch of them.

"Beg," he ordered, fitting himself between my shaking legs, pulling my hands up above my head, and hovering over my body in a promise of the more I wanted.

"*Please,*" I rasped, my plea halfway out of my mouth before he thrust inside of me.

A deep moan escaped me, my body open and welcome to what it wanted, what I was absolutely willing to beg for on that bed, in that room, in that space of the joining of our bodies—the ultimate completion of who we were and what we deserved from each other.

He gave me what I wanted finally as he drove in and out with a wild inhibition, himself consumed by what would always be the truth between us.

My nails dug into the skin of his hand, which pressed mine to the bed leaving marks I knew would stay for hours.

"*Rev*," I pleaded again, breathless, the second release stronger than the first as he slammed into me impossibly fast, and I lost myself to the time it took for him to give me what was promised.

He collapsed onto my chest, both of our lungs heaving. I gulped, my breath leaving in small moans, his face buried in my wet hair.

"We're terrible at this," I puffed.

"I'd argue otherwise."

"I mean the tea."

"Fuck."

I rubbed my face in frustration.

He slid out from me and pulled my leg over his hip as I crashed into his chest. "It'll be alright. We won't do it again."

"That's what we said last time," I mumbled.

"We can't seem to keep our word."

"Because we've gone so long without needing it." I huffed, pressing my cheek against his chest to listen to his pounding heart. "We just need to get into a pattern, that's all."

"What if I drink it all throughout the day, so we don't have to stop and worry about it ever again."

I shook my head. "Clairannia said that isn't good enough. It's not potent enough to ensure there's no child if only one of us takes it, and it's pretty reliable if both of us do."

He lifted my chin to look him in the eye. "From now on, we don't risk it. We keep each other accountable. We won't forget again, Karus, I promise you."

I believed him.

CHAPTER 47

REV

Dawn came and though I could not see it from our rooms, I could feel it in my chest, urging me to leave the warm bed, leave her soft body curled into mine and get up to help Pompeii.

Karus slumbered in the nightgown I'd commissioned for her, and I admired the rise and fall of her chest under green silk and black lace.

I gently smoothed away her hair which had caught on her lips and studied the streaks of white. There were several more pieces that littered the top and sides of her head, and my stomach fell, remembering both times she'd used that spell.

We both knew I didn't want her to attempt it again. I didn't want to see her lose that control.

I'd do it.

I'd practice the spell. I'd use it on the Blight. Maybe even on Viridis. She could use Cosensian Magic to imbue her power to me and we could try again.

But first, we needed to cure Pompeii.

And train the channelers.

And conduct the conduit trials.

And she needed to take the Baron trial.

There was so much to do. I wondered how much time we really had before the Blightress reared her head again.

I tried not to spiral, I really did, but then I realized how much I was as Karus shifted beside me.

Let her sleep, Rev, I reminded myself as I shifted away from her warmth and rose from the bed.

Spring was cold in the Fortress, so I stoked the fire before heading to the washing room to splash water on my face.

I didn't want to do what needed to be done today. We needed to search Heimlen's study for answers. We needed to check on the laboratorium to ensure she really did kill off that Blight. We needed to hear from Talon and Ilyenna that they were alright, that they hadn't caught this Blight illness from Pompeii.

I splashed my face again and drew a bath for Karus, filling the tub with water just warm enough to steam.

I felt a pull from her in the bed, a flurry of pain and panic. I rushed to her side as she sat up, her hand covered in blood.

"It's started," she trembled. "My bleeding has started again."

She pulled back the sheets to reveal a red stain on the silk of her nightgown. Tears streamed down her cheeks. "I've ruined it."

"No, love, Lia can get that out."

She sobbed and I pulled her to my chest. "It's alright. It's okay. You can do this. Are you in pain?"

She nodded, rising with me as I took her hand and led her to the washing room. I slipped the thin straps off her shoulders and she stepped into the water, a sigh of relief on her lips.

I kneeled down on the side of the tub and kissed her temple, holding my hand out for her to take. "Show me where it hurts, Karus."

She grimaced in pain and brought my hand to her lower stomach. "Here. Clairannia warned me about this. The first bleeding since getting my *liberum* mark would be the wor—" she bent over in pain, unable to finish the word.

"*Remolyn.*" I spoke the enhancement spell of loosening and relaxation. Tendrils of blue wove through the water, encircling her waist.

Her face eased instantly, her head falling back to the edge of the wooden tub.

"Thank you. I'll have to remember that one."

"You rest here. I'll check on Pompeii and speak to Lia. I'll bring you some breakfast. Do you need anything before I leave?"

"Please be careful around anyone. What if you carry the illness and it just hasn't shown up yet? It seems like it would have by now, but what if—"

"I don't think we can carry it. I keep thinking about what the Blightress told you. At least some of your power comes from her and unless she's lying, a Baron's power does as well. She made the Blight, so what if we're too connected to it to be affected by this?" I shook my head, sighing. There were too many questions with too few answers we'd be able to find without speaking to the Blightress herself. "I'll be careful, but I just have this gut feeling we're immune."

She bit her lower lip in thought. "I suppose neither of us feel ill. And we burned everything we wore in that room..." She nodded. "Please just be quick."

"I will." I rose and kissed the top of her head as she leaned back, closing her eyes. I picked up her nightgown, and headed to the bed to change the sheets.

"Wait, Rev, can you bring me something before you go?"

I turned back to her, stunned by her beauty. She gripped the sides of the wood, the water rippling around her shoulders, her hair floating out around her. Her cheeks were flushed red with the heat, a contrast to the bright green of her eyes in the flicker of the sconces on the wall.

I shook my head slightly. There were moments like these I still couldn't believe she was mine, that she was back, and that I could hold her at any time.

I didn't want to possess her.

That was a lie.

I wanted to own her as much as she owned me, and there lay the line I had crossed once before. I crossed it when I lied to her about

Heimlen and what evidence of his betrayal to us both had been hidden under his gloves.

I promised myself I wouldn't cross that line again. Not to save her, not to keep her. But in moments like these, when she took my breath away, I wondered if I was lying to myself because I would do *anything* to protect her. I would cross any line I'd ever established just to save her.

I cleared my throat. "Whatever you need, it's yours."

Her lips rose to the side, her eyes sparkling. "How about a good book?"

POMPEII'S BRUISED CHEST WAS A DEEP PURPLE, VERGING ON BLACK. His lungs strained with each breath he took. This illness had developed quicker than I imagined it could.

I tried everything I knew. I tried every medicus magic enhancement spell I'd learned in the eleven years I'd trained my magic.

Nothing worked.

His breath strained with a rattle at his throat in each inhale. He coughed again, and I caught the phlegm from his lips with a rag already stained in pools of black.

"Revich," he rasped, the effort to speak twisting his face. "You cannot risk—"

His cough began again, and I pulled him up to lessen the gasping of his chest.

"That's enough. I'm not leaving you here like this." I ended any more question if I should be with him. "Karus and I are going to look in Heimlen's study today. There must be something there about how he cured the Black Fever. I'd guess this illness is similar."

He let his head fall against the headboard and squinted my way. "You haven't been…in years."

I clenched my jaw hearing him struggle.

This was my fault.

I should have been more careful. I should have told him before I left to avoid the laboratorium while I was away.

"It doesn't matter. We'll find something. I'm sending a letter to Clairannia today. She might know a spell that can help you."

He took another full, rasping breath. "Don't want to… spread…"

More coughing, wheezing, struggling to breathe.

"I see you trying to warn me, old friend, and I will not listen."

He gave what I assumed to be a chuckle.

I brought another spoonful of Lia's broth to his lips, and he sipped it slowly.

I spoke to him of all that had happened in the two weeks outside of Felgren that was only a few days within. His smile was brightest hearing about how we had completed our companion ceremony without outside help.

"It brings…me joy, Baron."

"When you are well, we will celebrate." I wiped his mouth again. "So, you'd better recover soon because the servants and channelers are itching for a party."

His grin was pained but there nonetheless.

"Rest. I'll be back in a few hours to check on you again and let you know what we find."

He nodded weakly, and I helped him settle back against his pillow. "*Soporen,*" I murmured softly, his eyes closing and the tension in his body releasing.

I rose from his bedside, collecting the ruined pillowcase I'd found him under and the rag I'd used to collect the sludge coming from his mouth. I threw them into the fireplace, forcing the smoke up the flue.

This was bad.

No, this was terrifying.

Not only was I concerned for my friend's life, I worried for the rest of the staff. For my channelers. For Karus.

I had to trust my instincts. Karus and I shared a connection to the Blight through the Blightress. I didn't have time to panic that she would succumb to this next.

But Ilyenna? Talon? I'd sent both of them to take care of

Pompeii in their punishment, and I might have doomed them as well.

It was time to order a lockdown of the Fortress.

I stood outside of Pompeii's room, my mind struggling to remember the spell I needed. It wasn't as if I amplified my voice often. I closed my eyes, leaning back against his door, cycling through the enhancements I knew.

I'd been blessed in my thirty years with the gift of memory, able to recall pieces of my life in flashes of pictures, and my thoughts sorted through a book I had once read about conduits who had taken more leadership roles on the isle.

I could see the pages I had flipped through in Viridis, when it had been so much more than the husk it currently was.

There was the spell. *Amploren*: to project your voice.

Behind my eyes, I saw the word written in the book just as if I held it again in my hands under the Viridis light.

I cleared my throat and spoke, "This is Baron Revich," I began, blue wisps of my power flowing from my words, winding their way down the long hall and through the door to the kitchens.

"Please do not be alarmed. I am speaking to you after leaving Pompeii's bedside. He is very ill, and because I cannot be sure this illness will not spread, I am ordering a lockdown of the Fortress. Each of you are to stay in your rooms with the exception of Lia, who will continue to bring food to your doors."

She'd do it, too. I knew if I asked her to stop feeding the people in the Fortress, she'd ignore me anyway.

I gathered my thoughts and continued, my magic still flowing from my voice and booming through the hall. "I've spoken to each of you personally about the Blight that lives in the depths of Felgren. It is my fear that a form of this Blight has infected Pompeii. His lungs are bruised at his chest, and a black liquid seeps from his mouth when he coughs. Lia or myself will be at each of your doors at least twice a day, where you will confirm to us that you do not show signs of this illness.

"You are to stay in your rooms. I cannot stress this enough. Karus and I are seeking answers. We will keep you informed. I wish each of you well. Now, please, head to your rooms, and await answers from me."

I left the corridor for the kitchens, passing several servants heeding my orders. I nodded to each one as they scrambled through their doors.

Lia stood in the kitchen, barking orders to the few people there as they washed up and left. She nodded to me and turned, getting straight back to the dough she kneaded on her work table.

"For you and Karus," she informed, pointing to a tray of cinnamon buns and pastry-wrapped eggs and bacon—both of our favorites.

"Thank you."

She added, "Ilyenna and Talon are well so far. I checked on both of them already this morning."

"Lia," I chuckled, "I don't know what we'd do without you."

She kept at her work and responded under her breath, "No one ever does, love."

I took the tray and left as a few more of the staff passed through the dining hall, confident in the knowledge that I was doing whatever I could to keep my people safe, and knowing it was time to enter Heimlen's study.

CHAPTER 48
KARUS

"The four women who first trained with Baron Adaynth became the first mentors of the conduits he would produce, and it is said that most of them would continue on to become the first in lineage as the rulers of the isle.

The medicus conduit becoming the first Lady of the Spire, mentoring future healers. The first iumenta conduit becoming the Madame of the Mountains, raising livestock and connecting with animals of the region. And finally, the first Queen of Hyrithia is said to have been an agricola conduit and no doubt the reason Hyrithia is known for its finely grown grains and fruit trees.

It is unknown what happened to the first lapis conduit. Some sources say she ended up in the Hallow Marshes, her ability to find precious stone leading to the first discovery of rhyzolm."

I flipped back to the cover of the book. *To Train a Conduit: A History of the Conduit Trials* by Thalia Lighton. The book had been one of the three Revich had brought to me in the bath. One was about fishing, one a romance that tied music and magic, and this book, which was currently the most intriguing.

I flipped through the rest of the pages quickly, scanning for any sign of the Blightress. Already there had been more in this book about the first Baron, Baron Adaynth, than I had ever been able to find in Viridis.

If nothing else, I figured this book would be useful in my own preparation for the trials. I continued from my place.

"This tale would fit neatly into the story of the first four trained conduits by Baron Adaynth, but this author wonders, how often is history molded to fit neatly into a box that we all can wrap our heads around? Which of these stories are true, and which were created out of convenience, allowing the following generations the ability to hold onto something that cannot hurt them? Something that is easy to believe and accept with no doubts crossing their minds as they go on with their lives, raising their children, working in their towns, unaware that what they have been told may not be the truth—or at least not the whole of it."

I shivered despite the warmth of the bath. Everything I'd learned about the Blightress had been exactly this. Her truth, regardless of how much I hated it, was not what we were told as children.

Her wrath was not born from wrath itself as we all were led to believe. She'd told me as much, and I closed my eyes, thinking of some of the last words she'd said to me: *You are ever much a part of me as you are to the woman who bore you or the woman who raised you, Karus, and one day, you will be ready to truly listen.*

I wondered if what really mattered was where I had come from or who I would become. The woman I'd meet by the end of my life, a woman so changed by then, would I recognize myself now? Or would I look back at this woman and all she was, wondering which turns I had taken to become so changed.

The truth of my future would remain undiscovered until I lived it. I knew that. But what I didn't know, what I couldn't deem to understand, was how much the woman I was now held the direction of my fate. If I hadn't gone down that tunnel, if I had said no, refusing to follow the Blightress, would my future already be set on a different path?

And could the paths of our lives detour before finding themselves right back to where they had originally led?

Some things in life were certain.

My hatred for Heimlen and the path he had chosen was heavy in my chest each day I woke, and yet, I knew full well that some part of me was thankful.

If he had not taken me, if he had not found Rev and given him the task to find the most powerful channeler on the isle, would our paths have ever crossed?

I liked to believe they would. I liked to believe our lifelines had been linked the moment I had come into this world and that we would have found each other, regardless of the circumstances of our lives.

I chose to believe it.

I chose to believe some things were certain.

"This is Baron Revich."

His voice echoed through the washing room and tendrils of his magic floated toward me like smoke of an extinguished flame.

Startled, I looked for him, realizing quickly he was somehow amplifying his voice. I closed the book, setting it aside and rose from the bath, grabbing my towel and hurrying to the wardrobe to dress.

I donned my channeler skirts, white linen shirt and green vest, taking care to prepare my undergarments for my bleeding.

I braided my hair quickly down my back as the last of Revich's announcement faded from the room.

We had so much to do.

But first, I needed to head to the tallest tower because if I knew Philius at all, I knew he was headed down that endless staircase that very moment in search of me.

"TURN *AROUND*," I ORDERED, POINTING BACK UP THE BLACK STONE steps where Philius was indeed hurrying down, now dressed in traditional channeler clothing.

"What the fuck is going on? Where exactly have you brought us to, Karus?" He stopped on the landing, folding his arms across his chest.

Ignoring his questions, I retorted, "Stop with the dramatics. Turn around and get back to your room. You are not a prince of Hyrithia here, Philius. You are a channeler and you must listen to your Baron."

He leaned against the stairwell, his golden brown eyes challenging me just as they had as children. "And if I don't? Do we need to leave? Isn't the Blight the thing that almost killed you? What if you contract this illness and die, Karus? *You* should be in *your* rooms."

"I swear, Philius, if you do not get back to your room, I will force you there and seal your door."

He scoffed, "Like you could."

"She can."

I jumped, surprised by Revich's presence behind me in my attempt to get my brother to follow orders—something he'd never excelled in.

Philius's arms fell to his sides and he glared behind me.

"Your sister is right. You need to be in your room. We won't hide anything from you. As soon as we know more about this illness, we will inform you and everyone else here. I do not keep such secrets from the people under my care."

"But you'll risk *her*." Philius pointed to me and took a step down, closer to where I stood.

"If I thought Karus was in danger of contracting this illness, she would not be here on these stairs speaking to you."

It was my turn to glare. Like he had a choice.

"Revich thinks we cannot succumb to what Pompeii has due to where our magic comes from. Something"—I held up my hand to stop Philius from his next question—"you don't need to know about right now, but something I will tell you later. Now please, go back to your room and let us handle this. We're wasting time."

Revich didn't respond to my order, but waited with me to see what the Prince of Hyrithia would do.

He scraped his teeth together and gave short nod, turning and heading back up the stairs. He called over his shoulder, "I want

Karus to bring me my food. If I don't hear from her specifically, I'll find a way to get to her and *leave*."

I muttered an assembly of curses under my breath.

"That princely charm is endearing," Revich remarked, watching him leave.

"It always worked well on the Queen."

He slid his fingers through mine, turning us around and back down the enormous staircase. "How are you feeling?"

"Better. But worried. Let's get to Heimlen's study."

"We're eating first in our rooms."

"Forget food, we need to start our search."

"Oh, and you function so well on an empty stomach, don't you?" His dark eyes glinted with a playful smile.

"Fine," I relented, my stomach giving a well-timed grumble.

AFTER WE'D GONE THROUGH ALL THE CINNAMON BUNS AND EGG pastries filled with salty bacon and cheese, we stood before the solid black door with the emerald glass knob.

The alcove on the black stone staircase was easily missed, dark and eerie, even more so now that I knew exactly the kind of man who had occupied it.

I felt Rev's apprehension along with mine before he turned to me. "Are you ready?"

"Yes," I nodded, squeezing his hand.

He turned the key in the door and murmured, "For Felgren."

The lock clicked and he pushed the door open, more darkness greeting us like a past we could never escape.

We stepped inside, and I lit the lantern without a word, my green wisps of power flying to the wick, illuminating the room in a dim glow.

Rev's emotions were in complete turmoil, spilling from him endlessly in a cascade of anger, guilt, and betrayal.

"I never wanted to come back here," he whispered, his eyes

scanning every inch of the room he had trained in with Heimlen to become Baron of Felgren.

"I hate that you have to," I replied, my heart only filled with wrath for the man who had sat at the desk in front of us.

I took the key and stepped around the desk, lowering to the floor and inserting it into the hidden lock below the worktable. It clicked loudly and I rose to push the table forward, opening the secret door to this room I had discovered seven years ago.

I stepped inside, my magic again leaving my fingers to light the fireplace. It took longer than I expected, but eventually lit, filling the room with a low light.

It reeked of mold and dust, but I ignored the smell and ignored the looming memory of the night I had discovered the truth of Heimlen's manipulation. The walls were littered with portraits of barely clothed women, the canvases dark with a think layer of dust. I avoided the gaze of each of them, especially the one above the fireplace.

I moved quickly to the desk, snatching a journal off its surface. I remembered placing it there so long ago. I began sifting through the shelves of the bookcases, looking for any journals I had missed when I had originally ransacked this room for answers.

I knew Sylva, Heimlen's lover and life source, had burned most of them, but I held hope that she'd missed some.

Something here must allude to how he cured the Black Fever. I flipped open a journal and scanned the page. Seeing Heimlen's long scrawl, I wanted nothing more than to slam it shut and burn it, as the others had burned in that very fireplace where Revich now stood.

I turned my attention to him as he studied the portrait of a young Sylva.

"There's so much I should have questioned."

"Rev," I started, "we can take some of these and leave. We don't have to search for the answers here. We can take them to our rooms and—"

"No." He turned to me, his irises black as night, continuing, "No part of him leaves this room. I won't have him anywhere else in the Fortress."

"Yes, sir," I agreed.

A small smirk lit his mouth, and he came to the bookcase, reading their spines, thick with dust. Pulling a few, he headed back to the fire, sitting stiffly in one of the chairs. Dust puffed around him and he coughed into the stale air.

"Here, let me," I said, murmuring, "*Nitidus*" and watching as the chair's thick layer of grime disappeared immediately, the black fabric looking newly upholstered.

"Neat trick," he chuckled, leaning back to its surface and opening the book in his lap.

We stayed like that for hours, neither of us finding anything useful, checking in with each other every so often.

I had to stop myself from being consumed by a journal full of Heimlen's remarks on Revich's first days in Felgren as he trained in the Baronship.

"The boy shows much promise. His spirit is light and humorous, and his power is harnessed in his full heart. Already he makes friends with the Overseer and some of the channelers. They will go through the conduit trials soon, and I will bring the next few, hopefully including the one who can help me fight the Blight.

He is learning to use his rhyzolm properly. It led him to several channelers back in his home, but he needs more practice, more focus to really hone in on the one we need.

He has sworn to me he will be able to do this. Alas, I feel I myself am softening toward him. He will one day make a great Baron if I can just mold him into the man I know he can become."

I gulped at the lump forming in my throat, raw and painful. Furious, I wiped at the tears that fell onto the page, refusing to sniff at what ran from my nose and alert Rev that I was crying.

His head shot to me across the room and he rose from the tidy black chair. "What is it?"

Fuck, I'd forgotten about the bond for a moment—there was no hiding from him.

I wiped my sleeve under my nose and shut the journal. It had no use to us right then anyway. "It's nothing." I rose and added the journal to the pile of books I'd already skimmed through, adding, "He was just a bastard."

Rev turned my chin to meet his gaze as a flicker of blue traversed its surface. He cupped my cheek, leaning down to my lips, placing a soft kiss before a simple whisper of, "I love you, Karus."

My sobs came without invitation or welcome as I reached for him, falling into his chest, unable to do anything but cry there.

He wrapped his arms around me, and as my body shook against him, my mind whirled with all the pain Heimlen had put him through. I could face my own hurt. I could manage my own wrath and hatred for that man, but I could not take Rev from his. I could never protect him from those feelings of betrayal, and so, I felt I could never be the rock he needed.

"What's all this?" He tucked some of my loosened hair behind my ear. "Your emotions are something to be studied. They're changing so rapidly."

I laughed into his chest, breathing in his warmth. "I can't seem to help it. I just..." I squeezed my eyes shut and drowned out Heimlen from my thoughts. "I'm just...Rev, I'm so thankful for you. Please tell me you know that. I don't say it enough—not nearly enough." I pressed my lips back to his and pulled away to whisper, "I'm so thankful you found me."

His smile was brilliant, an utter perfectionist ode to all that was beautiful in a man, his now dark blue eyes looking at me like I was the absolute answer to everything.

"We deserve each other, remember? You live, I live."

I wrapped my arms around his neck and shuddered as I inhaled, forcing my body to calm. I nodded, running my fingers through his black waves. "You breathe, I breathe, Rev." I smiled above his lips chuckling as I whispered, "A fucking *lifeline*."

CHAPTER 49
REV

We spent a week searching the books in Heimlen's study before we moved on to the books in the library. We'd found nothing. Not a single hint at how we could possibly cure a disease created from the Blight.

Pompeii grew worse daily, though I could see him fighting. He could still use his magic, and I wondered what kind of conduit he would have become if he had ever trained.

So far, Lia had not taken ill, though she was the one to initially bring food to Pompeii before his illness had gotten worse. Just as I predicted, neither Karus or I had been affected. Talon and Ilyenna showed no sign of illness either, though they insisted they hadn't done more than leave soup on Pompeii's table when they saw he'd been sleeping.

Philius continued to sulk in his room, and Karus was sure to be the one to bring him food and tell him that she was still well.

I had tried several different spells of healing for Pompeii with no change in his condition. I wrote to Clairannia, hoping there was something she knew, something she could tell me to try.

Karus pushed for Viridis.

She did so subtly, mentioning the idea of bringing it back every so often in our search. She'd insist that it might still hold the key to curing this illness, just as Heimlen had once discovered something there.

"The books in Viridis are mostly ruined," I reminded her for what I was sure was the tenth time that day.

"*Mostly* ruined is not *all* ruined. We could go together. We could head straight to the medicus section and grab what we can and run." She held a stack of books in our current library to her chest, chewing her bottom lip.

I pulled on the back of my neck, tossing a book to the chair I'd been sitting in for hours. "Think about what you're saying for a moment. You want to return to the place where a version of the Blight grows that we know very little about. A version of the Blight that has infected Pompeii, who's been fighting it for more than a week now. The last time you were there, it came for you. I had to stop our excursions to retrieve books from Viridis because the Blight almost took Clairannia. It's too *dangerous*, Karus. We need to keep searching and wait for Clairannia to write back."

"But the spell, Rev. We can at least try *Simulair Solum* and—"

"And what? Put some pillows down to break your fall when I have to knock you to the ground again?"

She glared my way, setting her stack of books down and storming to me. "You could do it then. You could use the spell. I'll use Cosensian Magic to help. But this,"—she gestured to the walls lined with bookcases—"this is not working. There's nothing here. Heimlen found his cure in Viridis, and it might still be there, waiting for us to find it, too." She crossed her arms at her chest. "It's the best bet we've got."

I exhaled long and hard through my teeth. "Alright. We'll practice today. Maybe we'll hear from Clairannia and get some options to try from her. But let's get on the same page here." I pulled her body to mine, leaning back against the desk behind me. "You should not attempt that spell again. It's not just about the fact that you can't seem to break it. It's also about how you lost your memories because of it. That's not worth the risk and Pompeii would agree."

She placed her hand on my chest and held the other in the air.

"I promise not to use the spell without speaking to you first, Baron Revich. As your channeler in training, you can trust my word."

Her eyes glinted in amusement, and I bent forward to kiss her forehead. "Alright. Let's do this."

~

I HELD AN ORB OF BLUE LIGHT ABOVE MY HANDS, GLANCING AT SEVEN of the people who relied on me.

Karus and I agreed that because it had been over a week since the infection had started and no one else had contracted the illness, we could release the Fortress lockdown.

Each of the channelers sat on the fallen trunk of a dead tree covered in moss and lichen. They looked relieved to be out of their rooms.

"When you channel your magic for a specific spell enhancement," I began, my gaze flicking to each one of them, "it's essential you know exactly what you're trying to produce. Any wavering of any kind in your motivation can cause unforeseen results from your power."

"Like that time Talon tried to call an owl to perch on his arm and the owl dropped a dead quiphit on his head instead?" Rell giggled, elbowing her sister who laughed, both of them watching Talon for a rise.

He had his arms folded, Ilyenna's head resting on his shoulder. The slightest smirk twitched on his lips, but he kept his gaze on me.

"Yes, Rell, something like that. You must focus your mind on what exactly you wish to do. What is your purpose with your power in that moment? Siphon your magic and have a reason. If you do not, Felgren will guess for you."

I took a breath, my eyes catching on Karus for just a moment, sitting at the end of the tree, her hands wringing in her lap. Her anxious energy did not help, but I exhaled slowly, focusing on what I wanted to produce.

"*Simulair Solum*," I spoke, focusing back on my ball of light as it warmed in my hands, a defined brilliance of sunshine lighting its surface. I held it as long as I could, the heat and heaviness difficult to steady for more than a few minutes before I ended the spell, folding my hands closed to snuff out the light.

Karus and I had agreed the first thing I should focus on was the length of time I could hold the spell, not the size of the orb.

"Why don't you just use this spell in front of Pompeii and see if he's better?" Philius asked, sitting next to Karus, his own arms folded across his chest.

"I have. Briefly, but it was worth a try. This Black Lung illness is contained within his chest and sunlight does nothing for it."

Karus rose and began to pace. "What was the spell like for you, Mychael? The one that cured the Black Fever. You were there. Did it look like anything? Could you see it?"

He stood as well, his hand moving to his side where, as a guard, his sword had been sheathed. Remembering he no longer wore one, he rubbed his chin instead. "I was stationed at the castle at the time, but I didn't see anything. I remember the cries of relief throughout the city and the cheers, but…I certainly don't remember a glowing sun."

Karus nodded. "I didn't see anything either. It was as if one minute Philius was on the brink of death and the next, he was just sleeping peacefully."

The Prince slid his jaw to the side and looked my way. "How is it Heimlen was able to cure thousands of people at once and you can barely hold a spell for a few minutes? Are you less of a Baron than he was?"

It was the wrong thing to say.

Not just as a spoiled princeling to someone with greater power, but as a channeler to his Baron.

The shock had barely enough time to register to the other six of them before I called the wind to push them away from the fallen tree. The entire moss-laden piece of the forest rose, and Philius scrambled to find purchase.

He grunted in an effort to stay wrapped around the trunk as it lifted higher into the air. I tilted my head slowly, the trunk following the movement, rotating and threatening a vertical, upright position.

"Rev." Karus came to my side and touched my arm as the other five channelers either laughed or grimaced while Philius yelled for help, now slipping down the mossy surface of the trunk a good fifteen feet off the ground. His legs wrapped around the thick of it while his blackened fingers struggled to grip the bark.

I stepped forward out of Karus's reach, my hands shoved in my pockets, a grin on my face. I'd hoped I'd be the one to put Philius in his place.

"How is it," I drawled, "that a Prince of Hyrithia, born into a role of privilege and diplomacy, can speak with such disrespect and think there will be no consequence?"

"Help!" he shouted, sliding another foot down the tree as it came to a forty-five degree angle above the ground.

I heard a gasp from Ilyenna behind me, but I did not look back. I'd never had to do anything close to this with any of my other channelers. Each one of them understood their role in Felgren as well as mine.

Philius would come to that understanding today.

"Put me down!" His demand was confident, full of conviction that his order would be met as it always had been in his castle.

"You've not yet answered my question, but I will answer yours." I kept my eyes on him, high above me. "Heimlen took weeks, possibly months to find the cure to the illness he created from the Blight. He had access to Viridis and all of its books on medicus conduit magic. This cure will take time to find, but we *will* find it. And as for the *Simulair Solum* spell,"—I glanced back at Karus who watched Philius with unease—"even the most powerful magic wielder here cannot hold it for long, and when she does, she cannot seem to break it. It is the same spell that took her memories and would have killed her if I had not knocked her over and broken it for her."

Sixty degrees. He slipped further.

"So, yes, I cannot hold the spell for long, but you will not doubt my power again, nor my ability to put you in your proper place in this forest, which can be up there, dangling on that tree, or down here with your fellow channelers who understand what it means to respect their Baron."

Eighty degrees. He squeezed his eyes shut and orange sparks flared at his fingertips, singeing the dead wood as he began a slow slide downward.

I turned around to address my channelers and the most powerful one among us. "Our next task is to attempt to get into Viridis's medicus hall. I want each of you to head to the library, and research anything you can find on it. Many of the conduit memoirs mention it in their books. Start there."

I stepped in front of Karus specifically, ignoring the shouts from Philius that he could not hold on any longer. Her face was tight with worry, and I knew she struggled to hold her tongue. I kissed her cheek and whispered in her ear, "I'll handle this. Go check on Pompeii, will you?"

She nodded slowly with so much she wanted to say forcing its way across our tether, but she bit her lips inwardly and turned, following the channelers back to the Fortress.

I watched them go, a thin branch from a nearby willow tree snapping taught around Philius's ankle as his grip faltered and he began to fall. I let go of the tree trunk and heard it crash to the ground, turning back around to see him dangling a good six feet from the earth, his arms hanging, his black coils bouncing along with the rest of him.

"I hate you," he managed to spit, his breathing heavy.

"You don't need to state the obvious. But, since you're feeling especially angry, this is the time to practice your magic."

I pointed up to the willow branch wrapped around his foot. "You can come down when you break this."

He bent his neck toward his foot to see where he was held. "How do I do it? And won't I break something when I fall?"

I laughed. "Would you like me to get your pillow from your bed, Your Highness?"

He gritted his teeth and ignored my jab, reaching toward his foot, sparks of power flickering before sputtering out at his fingertips.

To his credit, he tried several times, ultimately failing and falling back down, his arms hanging while he closed his eyes to regain his breath.

I watched him carefully, fumbling with the rhyzolm in my pocket. It still buzzed behind me toward where Karus had left. I focused my senses and turned my power toward Philius to get another read on just how much magic he held.

The rhyzolm continued its slight pulse toward him. It hadn't changed since we'd entered Felgren, unlike Mychael where it pulsed steady, and stronger than when he had been outside of it. Every channeler I had brought here had grown in their strength the moment they set foot on Felgren's soil. Every one of them but the Prince.

"I didn't know," he mumbled, swinging slightly upside down in the breeze. "I didn't know you had to knock her down to break the spell. And I didn't,"—his eyes flashed open to look at me—"I didn't know she was the most powerful one here." He scoffed, reaching up to try to break the vine again. "Maybe *she* should be Baron."

I grinned, letting go of the Rhyzolm and folding my arms at my chest.

He didn't know how right he was.

He obviously loved his sister, just as he obviously did not really know her.

He fell back down to hang there, a grunt of exasperation sounding from his chest.

"Again," I ordered, my stare unwavering. "Try it again."

CHAPTER 50
KARUS

Blotting Pompeii's forehead with a cool rag, I hummed something soothing while he tried to keep his eyes open.

I'd woken him from his sleep, knowing he needed to eat, and helped him to his washing room to relieve himself. He needed full support, leaning on me the entire way there and back, his steps shuffling along the soft rugs on the cold stone floor.

When back in bed, he'd had another fit of coughing, black sludge dripping from his mouth. My stomach churned and my heart raced, innately aware that time was limited.

"Pompeii," I whispered lightly, "I promise you can sleep soon, but you must eat something." I held a spoonful of light broth to his lips. He opened them slightly to take it in, most of it dribbling down his chin.

I sighed, frustrated at how helpless I felt. I hadn't done it directly, but this illness came from me. Rev would argue it came from him and we'd both demand to take blame from each other, but I grew those trees in Viridis. I'd grown the new form of Blight and this was my power infecting my friend.

A knock came at the door, and I set the bowl of broth aside calling, "Who is it?"

"It's Mychael. I—I have something that might tempt your Overseer to eat."

Curious, I opened the door slightly, scolding, "You shouldn't be here. You can't come in. I won't risk it."

He chuckled sheepishly in an apologetic grin and held out a bowl for me to take. "I made this. It's the only thing my companion could keep down when the Black Fever infected her." He shrugged. "I wasn't much help in the library and Lia let me into her kitchens to make it."

"Well, that's a miracle," I admitted, taking the bowl and sniffing its contents. The savory scent of chicken in broth met my nose along with something sharp and sour.

"Ginger?" I asked.

"And lemon. Hopefully it can ease his nausea as it did hers. It usually takes hours to make, but did you know that Lia—"

"Can quicken cooking times," I finished, nodding and wanting him to leave to not risk infection. "Yes. Thank you, Mychael. This is incredibly thoughtful." I smiled up at him as he towered over me with a good five inches.

He inclined his head, backing away. "You're welcome. Glad to be of some use."

"I'll see you in the library when I'm done here." I began to close the door before adding, "Has the Baron returned with Philius?"

He shook his head. "Not yet. Should I check on them next?"

"No. Baron Revich has the situation under control, I assure you. Philius needs a good lesson on his role in Felgren and Revich is the one to teach it."

"So we saw. Remind me to never question the Baron's power."

"That's the thing, Mychael," I responded, closing the door, "You'll never need one."

～

AN HOUR LATER, REVICH CAME THROUGH THE LIBRARY DOOR, Philius behind him looking completely worn.

We all looked up from our books. I sat at the desk while Talon,

Ilyenna, Rell, and Renn lay in varying degrees of comfort over the chairs and couches in the room. Mychael was up on the ladder, reaching for books on the very top of the shelves.

I raised a brow, waiting for Revich to speak.

"Have you found anything?" he asked, ignoring the pressing question of what happened in the forest.

Ilyenna rose and handed him a book marked with a page about Viridis and how the conduit author suspected it lived.

He opened the book and skimmed the page. "We knew this already, but thank you, Ilyenna. Good work."

They turned back to their books while Philius joined them, taking one bound in red cloth from Mychael who offered it.

Revich came to the desk and bent forward, his hands palming the surface. "Nothing?"

I shook my head. "Nothing."

"And Pompeii?"

I closed my book, placing a strip of cloth on the page I had gotten to and sighed. "Mostly the same. Though, more full now, since Mychael made him some soup."

He turned to glance back at the former guard. "He made soup?"

I nodded with a grin. "Yes. And Lia even helped him."

He laughed shaking his head. "Well, that's a miracle."

"That's what I said," I whispered, leaning on my elbow, chin resting in my hand.

His eyes flickered across my face, landing on my lips. I flushed, sitting back, taken by the sudden heat from him.

"Wood." He rapped his knuckles on the desk between us, and I swallowed—previously tired and hungry, now wanting something completely different to distract me from what plagued my heart.

He reached into his vest pocket, bringing his flask of styris tea to his lips, taking a long pull before handing it to me, my arm already reaching across the desk for it.

He turned around and addressed his channelers. "Thank you for your steadfast research. You all deserve a rest. We'll meet on the

Fortress steps in one hour. Get something to eat from the kitchens and relax."

They left, Philius saying something to Mychael to make him laugh, patting at his back heartily as they walked out of the room together.

Revich watched each of them leave, Renn shutting the door behind her before he turned his gaze back to me.

I took an air of indifference, though my body was aching, begging for him to take me, right there on that desk and distract both of us from our frustrations and worries.

I stacked my pile of books and stood, holding back a smirk at his piercing gaze as I didn't meet it. I sighed heavily, unbuttoning the top two buttons of my vest and moving to leave.

"Where do you think you're going?" he asked, hands in his pockets, watching me.

"Who, me?" I replied, backing up to the door. "I'm doing as you requested, Baron Revich." I bit my bottom lip, just for him. "I'm going to our rooms to relax." I let my voice fall, soft and sultry.

He followed, taking my hand and throwing the door open, pulling me toward our place of rest.

MY LIPS GRAZED REV'S JAW, FRESHLY SHAVEN SINCE THIS MORNING, and I slipped my leg over his stomach, claiming what was mine. His breath still quick, his heart still pounding, I absolutely adored knowing I did this to him.

I pressed my cheek to his chest, listening to his racing heart steady as he brushed his hands over my hair.

I followed the definition of his muscles, my fingers rising and dipping over each one lightly.

"That tickles," he rumbled, jerking slightly as my fingers brushed his side.

I gasped, raising my head. "The great Baron of Felgren is *ticklish*?"

"Yes."

I shifted and pressed my mouth to his, coaxing his tongue to come back out and play with other parts of me.

He reached up to take my face in his hands, accepting my challenge to continue. "You're not done, are you?"

I shook my head silently, pulling myself up over his stomach, sliding my body along his skin.

A knock came at our door, and I cursed.

Rev kept his eyes on me, holding my hips and sliding my body back down his stomach. "What is it?" he grumbled, watching my face light up in pleasure as I slipped forward again.

"I'm sorry to disturb you." I recognized Jesslyn's muffled voice, one of Lia's kitchen aides. "But Moira has returned and is refusing to leave the kitchens until she speaks to Karus." She paused and I glanced down to Revich in frustration. "She says it's about the Growers? She won't elaborate—you know how she gets."

I slipped back down his body one more time, wishing I could stay there and take my pleasure one slide at a time, knowing I couldn't.

"Thank you, Jesslyn. We'll be right there," I called, hopping off of Rev and off the bed, my mood souring as I pulled on my undergarments and skirt, huffing to the wardrobe to pull a new shirt from a hook.

Rev sidled up behind me before I could put one on and wrapped his arms around my breasts, pulling my back to his chest.

He was still naked, a fact I knew from how hard he was against my backside.

"I'm sorry," he whispered at my neck, finding the curve of my jaw with his lips.

"You're not helping," I chided, grabbing my shirt and turning to hand him his.

The moment I did, he kissed me fully. "Absence makes the heart grow fonder," he replied, pulling slowly from my lips and leaving me dazed.

He took his clean shirt from my hands, slipping it over his shoulders and helped my arms into mine.

What a woman I had turned out to be.

Completely taken, no real sense of direction when he did this to me. A creature of his bidding, I'd do whatever he wanted in those moments where I saw only him.

I blinked rapidly, finding some strand of strength to recover. I cleared my throat as he buttoned my shirt so painstakingly slowly, grazing longer than he needed over the curve of my breasts. "Are you planning on being absent from this conversation with Moira?"

"Yes," he admitted, finishing the last button, one further down from where I usually buttoned my shirt.

"Don't you want to know what she has to say?"

"Of course. And you'll tell me." He walked back to the side of the bed where his pants had been tossed aside with little regard for potential wrinkles, and I watched blatantly. "I need to check on Pompeii. And then meet the channelers on the steps, just as I asked."

Tucking his shirt into his black pants, he donned his black vest, finishing the last few buttons and kissing me one more time. "Join us when you're done?"

I blinked again, clearing my senses and nodding. He took my hand, bringing the inside of my wrist to his lips, kissing it softly and pulling me along to our boots which had been flung across the room minutes earlier. We pulled them on and left our rooms, me regaining my dignity and Rev, watching me try, his upturned lips not at all helping.

I rolled my shoulders and entered the kitchens with Rev behind me.

"—without asking first, Moira. You know the rules of my kitchen and you will follow them."

Lia glared down at Moira with her fists tucked into her hips in a clear attempt to scold the unscoldable.

Baring her sharp teeth, Moira retorted, "I was hungry! You try sitting still and listening to your elders blabber on for days before getting to the important stuff!"

She pulled the buttered roll closer to her chest, hoarding the doughy treat with a tight grip.

"Moira!" I called, stepping down into the kitchen, feeling Rev's hand brush my back as he turned to the right, headed to the servant's corridor.

"Karus!" She didn't drop her roll, but instead flew to my face, knocking her forehead to mine.

I laughed, giving an apologetic look at Lia who huffed and resumed her work, once again wrist deep in dough.

I pulled a plate from the shelves and placed it on the small table near one of the few windows in the Fortress and gestured for Moira to sit while I grabbed some food from the communal tray.

Lia had strict rules in her kitchen about any passerby looking for something to eat. She kept us well-fed and always had fresh fruit and cheese on a tray that we could take from at any time.

What she didn't allow was the grazing of food she was currently preparing for a main meal, which was exactly what Moira had taken from—the basket of rolls and butter nowhere near the communal tray.

I bit into a yellow pear, catching the juice as it ran down my chin. "Tell me everything, my friend. Where have you been for an entire *week*?"

She stuffed her face with no concern for manners or pleasantry, bits of bread covering her cheeks, her long sage fingers greased with butter as she chewed loudly.

I ate almost as ferociously, rising to make a plate for Revich when he returned from Pompeii.

"Well," she started, licking her fingers and eyeing the bread basket Lia had moved closer to where she worked. "The Growers want to help you take back Viridis."

I choked on a piece of cheese. "What!" I gasped. "The Growers in Felgren can help with that? How? And why would they want to?"

She eyed my strawberries and I held one out to her. She folded her legs underneath her and began to pick off each tiny seed. I laughed having forgotten that little quirk of hers.

"We had a meeting with the elders. This season, they asked me to attend and I figured it had something to do with all of this,"—she gestured around to the inside of the Fortress—"but I had forgotten how long and boring those meetings are. The Growers speak so slowly, I slept most of the time, but then,"—she bit into the now seedless strawberry and chewed—"they spoke of the Blight. They've been trying to force it back, you know. Especially now that the sun stays in the sky longer each day. They said they haven't been able to do much and want to try something new."

"What do they want to try?" I waited for her to take another bite and chew.

"They want to experiment with pushing the Blight back and growing more forest at the same time. But they need your help. And they don't want to try it on Felgren first. They'd rather risk your library than the forest."

I thought for a moment, plucking at a piece of hard white cheese. "What exactly do they think could go wrong?"

She shrugged. "Something about growing too quickly permanently causing the soil to sterilize."

"Sterilize? Moira, do you know what that means?"

"Never heard of it."

"It means the soil would become barren. Unable to grow anything *ever*."

She wrinkled her nose. "Well, that's why they want to try it in Viridis first, I suppose."

"How do Growers…grow?"

"That's what they do. They grow things. I've told you before, Karus, if you'd been listening—Growers keep the forest healthy and new. They vary in shape, size, and numbers depending on the season." She eyed me with her large violet eyes. "And there are *a lot* of Growers this spring. More than we've ever recorded."

I tucked that detail away to think about later. "So, let me get this straight. The Growers want to come to Viridis and attempt to regrow it while we use *Simulair Solum* to push the Blight back? They really think that could work?"

She shrugged, wiping strawberry juice across her yellow tulip skirt. "I guess so. I've told them about Viridis before. At least as much as you've told me. I'm still not convinced it's really all you say it was."

"Moira, there's even more reason to do this. Pompeii is sick. And it's from the Blight that grows in Viridis. We need to access those books to look for a way to make a cure. That's how Heimlen made his cure for the Black Fever. The answer's in there."

"Pompeii is sick?" She scratched at the vines growing from her head like long strands of hair. "I kind of don't mind him sometimes."

I held back a laugh. "When can we meet with the Growers?"

"They've asked to meet tonight. Under the full moon. I'll be there to interpret, but it will take some time. They're slow talkers."

Nodding quickly, I was already thinking about what Rev would say. "Thank you, Moira, my dear friend."

She beamed, lifting her pointed chin, her sharp teeth startling to everyone but me. "Lia! Tell me that dough is for cinnamon buns!" She flew off the table, hovering over the cook's shoulder and sniffing the air as Lia tried to swat her away.

Grabbing the plate of food for Revich, I headed to Pompeii's room to deliver the news. He met me in the hall, taking an apple and my hand.

"How is he?" I asked, rushing to match his swift stride.

"The same. Still sleeping."

We passed through the kitchens, and I eyed Moira now sitting at the bread basket, chewing on another roll. Seemed Lia had given in.

We entered the dining hall and Revich asked, "What was Moira's news?"

"The Growers want to help us attempt to take back Viridis."

"The Growers?" He stopped, pulling my hand to stop, too.

"Yes. They want to attempt to push the Blight back further in Felgren and grow new life where it stands, but they want to try it on Viridis first. They're worried it could permanently sterilize the soil if they grow back what was recently diseased so quickly."

"So Viridis is the experiment? What if its soil becomes sterile?"

I shook my head. "That's all I know. They want to meet with us tonight. Moira will interpret."

"Great," he mumbled, heading to meet the channelers.

"We'll at least listen. Their magic is powerful in Felgren. And

Moira said there's more of them this spring than there ever have been on record."

A tug on our line. Revich watched me as I slowly realized why.

The winter I had been lost to myself, no memory of who I was or had been, was the worst winter in the history of Felgren. The longest, too. It had killed many of the trees, destroying whole rows of them. No wonder the Growers were en masse. They had work to do.

He resumed his fast pace through the foyer. "We'll go tonight, but I don't want to risk Viridis."

"We *need* Viridis, Rev. Regardless if we accept their plan, we have to try to destroy the Blight there. And soon."

He sighed and kissed my fingers clasped in his. "I know we do. Pompeii needs us. We're running out of time."

I LOVED THE MOON.

Silvery paths before us, she lit our way through the forest, a guiding light as we traversed the world she shone upon.

I followed Revich with Moira in front, her eyes reflecting in shades of blue, purple, and pink in the night. Revich gripped my hand tightly as if he'd lose me to the night if he ever let go.

We'd dressed in warm cloaks, but my cheeks still burned with the sharp chill of spring.

"We're almost there," Moira assured, flying backward in her tulip skirt and woven grass top, the cold having no effect on her skin. Her wings in the moonlight were glorious, sparkling things that caught my eye continuously as all the colors reflected in the soft glow.

Revich glanced back at me again, grinning. "Are you remembering, too?"

"What? The first time you led me out here and kissed me under the full moon?"

"Till dawn."

My cheeks flushed and my body responded to his voice, low and deep. "I remember."

We entered a clearing. A circlet of tall, skinny trees surrounded us. The soft glow of mushrooms sprouting from each of them gave the space an unearthly feel, their stems like fingers reaching out from the wood.

Moira flew to the center of the circle and landed on a boulder, cupping her mouth and emitting a high-pitched wail that had me gritting my teeth.

Revich looked to me with a single brow raised. I shrugged.

The movement began as soon as the ear-piercing call was over. Dark forms of creatures moved between the trees, coming to the center.

There were seven of them, each as unique as any human, some sporting the same mushroom-capped heads as the Grower I had met in the Blightress's lands, some with tall, leafy stems sprouting from their tops.

Each of them was built like a cross between a human and a tree, legs and arms as branches, their long torsos like a trunk.

I glanced at Revich to see his reaction, finding he had none. He stood there, still, his frame hard as he watched with little expression. But I could feel it. Through our bond, I knew of his apprehension for this meeting.

A Grower with a smooth mushroom dome of soft white began to speak. The speech was little more than murmurs of the wind, the light sway of branches as they crossed each other in forced movement.

Moira listened with rapt attention, nodding occasionally, once bunching her shoulders up by her neck before letting them fall into a deep sigh.

Revich and I stood there for what felt like ten, twenty minutes before Moira turned to us, hands on her hips. "They want to see the spell. The one that produces the sun."

Rev stepped forward, producing a ball of blue light over his palms.

"Not from you. They want to see the sun from the one who held it against the Blight." She stared at me, hesitancey on her face.

"No," Rev announced, focusing on the Growers. "It's too dangerous. She can't control its size, nor break it."

I bit my lip, crossing my arms. I hated that he was right.

Of course, I'd be willing to do it anyway. Viridis and Pompeii's life was worth the struggle and the danger the spell, but I waited to hear a response.

Moira turned back to the Growers, her screeching grating in the night.

A few more minutes passed before she turned to us again. "They say it must be you. First of all, they don't trust Barons,"—Moira eyed Revich with a sneer—"and second of all, we'll have only one chance to try this because the effort will drain them for the rest of the season. It must be done right the first time, before summer begins."

"I'll do it," I declared, stepping up beside Revich.

"She won't," he responded, still holding his light above his hands.

"Yes, I will," I returned. "You can help me break it. As long as you're there, I'll be alright. You won't let it grow too big. You won't let me go too far."

"No, Karus." His light disappeared and he turned my shoulders to face him. "Here we are again, talking about what's worth the risk. Viridis is not. They can use my magic or nothing."

"And Pompeii's life? Is that not worth the risk?"

"He—"

"Don't I get to decide what risk I'm willing to take? Finding a way to save Pompeii outweighs the danger, Revich. This is my choice."

"And your choices affect the both of us, remember? What if I can't get to you? What if I can't knock you down to break the spell? What then, Karus? What purpose is my life without the whole of you in it?"

"I'll be fine." My voice wavered. "You've saved me from this twice. You can do it a third time." I addressed Moira once more. "Tell them I'll do it. But not here. It's draining and we need to get this done as soon as we possibly can. Can they come to the Fortress tomorrow at dawn?"

Moria glanced from me to Revich. He shook his head, and she scrunched her face in a grimace. "Karus, maybe—"

"No. Not you, too. This choice is mine and I make it for Pompeii and Viridis. We have to try something and his time runs thin."

Rev stepped in front of me, his back turned to the fae. "Do you know what you're asking of me?"

My heart raced at the low timbre of his voice, spoken slowly, quietly, almost as if he hadn't spoken at all and the words came through our bond only.

I swallowed my nerves and straightened my spine. "I do. And I'm sorry, but I still make this choice knowing. I make it for Pompeii. I make it for Viridis and the future we share training conduits together." I reached out to touch his chest. "I make it for us."

I gave him a weak smile, his anger and worry unchanging on his face as I stepped around him. "Moira, please tell the Growers we will meet them outside of the Fortress doors at first light. We'll lead them to Viridis and get this over with."

She nodded, placing her trust in me and turned back to the assembly. I waited for her to finish her speech, glancing back to Revich once to see he stood behind me, hands shoved in his pockets, his jaw flexing as he stared at me. His eyes were dark. Black. All of the iris void of color and for a moment, just one moment, I hesitated again.

I trusted him. I trusted him with my life, because what he said, I knew to be true. If he lost me again, he wouldn't survive it, and yet I asked him to risk it with me.

I choked down the guilt heavy and solid in my stomach. There *must* be answers in Viridis. There must be a book we could use to find the cure, and though I knew many of them were ruined, I held the hand of hope that what we needed, Viridis would provide as it had before it was taken.

Moira finished and I watched the Growers, my eyes flicking to each one to show them I was not afraid. I wanted them to see that I believed this could work. That I held faith in them as well.

The leader gave what I assumed to be a nod, the movement jerky, head lowering and rising oddly.

"They'll be there." Moira's eyes flicked behind me and her face fell.

I spoke before she could voice her own concern. "Not you, too, Moira. I need your support here."

"Clairannia and Figuerah would not give it."

I almost laughed, surprised at her insight. "But you?"

"I don't like putting all my trust in him." Her eyes flicked back to Revich.

"Then put your trust in me."

She nodded, fluttered to me, and knocked her forehead on mine.

The Growers backed away slowly, disappearing into the circle of trees just as quietly as they came.

Moira bared her teeth in a smile. "I'll see you at dawn." She turned and followed them into the forest.

I rolled my shoulders, ready for the fight ahead of me and turned.

His dark eyes bored into mine, and I could no longer ignore the pain he held. The disappointment, the fear, the anger that hung heavy in the air around us.

We stood there, facing each other, yet another moment in time that seemed to still in our wordless conversations.

I finally spoke, "I can't do this with you feeling like that. I can't put everything into this task with what you're feeling right now."

"You'd have me lie, then?" he challenged.

"I'd have you trust me. I'd have you trust yourself." I stepped closer, my chest at his. I longed for him to touch me as he always did when we shared so much of the same space in this world. "Please, Rev." I blinked back tears. "I can't do this without you."

His body tensed. "Is there nothing I can say? Nothing I can do? Give me any other option and I'll take it. Ask anything of me but this and I'll do it. You want a library filled with life and books? I'll make one. You want a copse of birch trees and silk benches to read on? I'll grow them. I'll build them for you."

I slid my hands over his chest, his body responding immediately as he pulled on my waist. "You know that's not what this is about. You know our best bet at saving Pompeii is there." I lowered my head, taking a breath. "This is a choice. This is a risk, Rev, and I am asking you to take it with me and save our friend's life."

"We don't even know what book we need." He gripped my waist tighter. "There must be other things we can try. There must be medicus conduits we can bring."

"We don't have time."

"We haven't heard from Clairannia."

"All of the medicus conduits of Hyrithia could not cure the Black Fever, so what makes you think one medicus conduit has the answer?"

"She's not just any medicus conduit, Karus. She heads them all in the Spire. Something else you've missed since you fell to this same spell seven years ago."

His words stung, and I flinched at the harsh truth of them. "Then promise me you'll break it. Promise me you'll not let me get that far, and I'll believe you. Tell the world you won't let me lose myself again and I know you won't because you keep your promises, Revich." I gripped his vest, pulling him to me. "You won't let me get lost again. Promise me."

He closed his eyes and lowered his head. He drew a breath and whispered what I wanted to hear. "I promise."

He kissed all of me that night.

Every curve, every space of sensitive skin came under his touch as if he was saying goodbye. As if he'd never touch me again.

As if I'd ever let that happen.

Clairannia's letters were waiting for us when we returned that evening. The one addressed to Revich explained she did not have a solution to the illness, and continued to explain that the medicus conduits of Hyrithia still did not have an answer to how it was cured. They regularly studied those who had been inflicted and survived.

It was the letter addressed to me that tore my heart into more pieces.

"Karus, I can return to Felgren in two more months, but no sooner. I know you'll figure this out. I know you'll find a way to save Pompeii or at least keep him alive until I can come help you. My people need me here. There are rumors of strange occurrences in Hyrithia and I leave for the city in a few weeks, then I'll come to you. I'm sure I can convince Figuerah to come, too. But promise me, Karus, that you will wait for us and stay safe. I'll be on pins and needles awaiting your reply.

All my love,

Clairannia Lynns

P.S. When we arrive, we're having that celebration, and don't even think of planning it without me."

I folded the letter again, setting it back on my bedside table. Revich slept in our bed, tossing in a fitful sleep.

"Compaynen," I whispered, kissing his brow as the tension there settled and his breathing resumed at a steady pace.

I rose from our bed, pulling on a dark green robe over my nightgown. I paused at our door, looking back at him now sleeping peacefully. I took a deep breath, knowing what I had to do and do alone.

He needed rest.

I knew I did too, dawn just a few hours away, but I also knew rest would not come unless I had tried every option. Unless I had traversed every avenue I could think of to prevent what Revich so ardently feared.

I left quietly, my bare feet frozen across the black stone of the Fortress.

The kitchens were no longer warm and felt oddly foreign because of it. Holding my ball of green light above my hand, I rapped lightly on Pompeii's door.

With no answer, I stepped inside, immediately calling to the fire to relight, adding a few more pieces of ash wood to the flames.

I sat at his side, feeling his forehead, now flushed, too warm to deny he was getting worse. I knew he'd been fighting. I knew his channeler magic was strong, and he had fought this illness for a week before faltering.

I also knew that time was slipping from our grasp faster than we were admitting to.

I knew I had one last choice to make before I felt there was no choice at all.

Whispering words and spells of restful sleep, I left, my legs leading me up the endless staircase, passing Heimlen's study, passing the blank frame which had led to his rooms, passing the small alcove Rev and I had once used in our passion, just hours after we'd learned more about my connection to the Blight.

I reached the top of the staircase, hardly out of breath at all, and stepped into my old room.

I hadn't returned since the day I had woken. I hadn't returned since the day she spoke to me in my mind.

Little had changed, if anything at all.

My books were gone, now lining the shelves in the rooms Rev and I shared, my music box no longer on the vanity for me to ponder at its origins—I knew them.

My bed was neatly made, and my eyes flicked to the black stones that pressed together to make my ceiling. I remembered staring at them, confused at the emotions gifted to me by the rhyzolm, frustrated that I could not remember myself.

I moved the vanity chair to the slanted window, stepping on its seat and pulling the pin from the shutters. They swung open, and I caught them before they could rap against the stone and wake Philius, whose room shared a wall with mine.

I opened the glass pane and took a breath of the cool air, full of life and new beginnings of spring. My window faced north, the expanse of trees seemingly endless in the night sky, the full moon taking her slow decent to the horizon.

The Blightress was there. She was out there now, in her lands, plotting our downfall.

"*I need to ask you something.*" I stared out at the tops of the trees, finding the place within me which came from her, addressing it through our minds just as she predicted I would.

"*Little Sprout, I am so* pleased *to hear your voice.*"

I clenched my jaw and inhaled slowly, focusing on the jagged horizon. "*Can you cure what ails the Overseer of Felgren?*"

"*Is that who he is? My, my, I had no idea of his importance.*"

Venom seeped through my response. "*You did this, didn't you.*"

"*Didn't we both, my child? After all, I did not grow those trees in your precious sanctuary.*"

"*No, but you forced the Blight there in the first place.*" I paused, my eyes narrowing. "*How did you know those trees were what gave him this illness?*"

"*I know what the Blight knows. I see what it sees, feel what it feels.*"

I scoffed, "*Glad to know you suffered then, seven years ago.*"

Fuck. I was risking the small chance she'd help me with retorts like that.

I heard her laugh, just as beautiful, just as confident as what I'd heard before. "*Your short temper amuses me, so I will listen to your request.*"

I exhaled in relief. "*I'm asking you for the cure. I'm asking you to help me save his life.*"

There was a pause in our line, something I could feel, and I wondered if I'd lost her.

"*And in return?*"

"*What would you ask in return?*"

"*I would like to know you better, Little Sprout. I would like you to know me. One night each week. Hide it from your lover, I care not. One night where we speak, like this, and you hear me. I will listen to you, but you will also listen to me.*"

"*Done.*" That was no ask at all. I'd choose what to tell her and I'd listen to her story, which I decidedly did not care about, to save Pompeii.

"*I'll hold you to it, then. If you refuse, if you change your mind, I'll just come for you.*" Her tone grew with anger, "*I can easily take you, Karus. I can take all of Felgren, if I wish it.*"

"*Then why don't you?*"

"*I do not believe we've come to the point where all other options of returning my power have faltered. I told you once, you do not know me. Let me show you who I am.*"

"*Fine. How do I cure Pompeii?*"

"*I do not know.*"

"*This conversation is over.*" Furious, I began to step off the chair, my heart racing in rage.

"*Karus, I can tell you where to find the cure Heimlen used.*"

I gave a grunt of exasperation. She still spoke in riddles.

"*I know he used the Blight, my Blight, to make the disease; therefore, I saw him create the cure.*"

"*How? How did he do it?*"

"*The answer lies in a book. I saw a glimpse of him reading from the text and practicing his magic to counter what he had created. I assume it's what he used to produce the cure as I never saw him with any other text after that.*"

"*What book? Which one?*" I asked quickly, forgetting to dampen my tether.

"*Finding the Source: A Medicus Guide to the Art of Understanding Disease.*"

I huffed a sigh of relief. At least we'd know exactly what to look for if we could just get Viridis back.

"*It's a rather lengthy title, and I doubt the writing is very enjoyable.*"

"*You…you read books?*"

"*Should we continue this chat, and I'll list my favorites for you?*"

I huffed. I didn't like her sounding human. I liked her right where she was, a monster. "*If this really is what we seek, I'll keep to our deal. If not, I will close you out forever and destroy you.*"

"*What a delightful empty threat. I look forward to our talks, Little Sprout.*"

"Karus!" The door burst open and Revich stood there, breathless. He raced across the room, taking my hand into one of his, the other grabbing my waist.

He looked up at me, a wild fear in his eyes as he took in the chair I was standing on and where I was looking out into.

I searched briefly for any sign that the Blightress was still there in my mind and found that she had gone.

Good. I shut her out again completely and smiled down at my love.

"I know what we're looking for. I know the book we need."

CHAPTER 51
SAELYN

I would be seventeen in two days and fretted over the silliest things.

"No, no, like *this*," I corrected, exasperated with Thevin and his inability to correctly arrange a single paper banner across the trees.

"That's what I did," he grumbled, stepping down from the enormous tree stump, watching me correct the angle of the string.

"No, yours were all wonky and sad," I retorted, ensuring my correction would not fall by securing it around a low branch of the tree.

"You're all wonky and sad," he mumbled under his breath, catching me at the waist as I jumped down from the stump. I faltered slightly, but his strong hands held me steady, keeping me from falling as I landed into his hard chest.

By the love of my mother, I wanted to stay there.

My breath quickened and a red flush covered my neck and face. I could feel it there, creeping through my skin without permission as he grinned down at me, my hands pressed to his chest. The small cleft in his chin had become more charming now that his age had overtaken mine by over a year since he spent so much of his time outside of Felgren.

I swallowed, his hands still at my waist. "Am not," I murmured, not wanting to move away from his body, but doing so anyway. "Can you help me with these laynterns?"

"*Lay*nterns?" he laughed.

I giggled, shaking my head. "*Lan*-terns."

He nodded, picking one up and hanging it on a tree. "You always did struggle with names."

I pretended offense, "I was very small, and to be fair, Pah-Pah's name is not the easiest to pronounce."

He laughed and crossed his arms, looking up at the colorful banners and lanterns that now wove through the trees where the party would begin in less than forty-eight hours.

"I like it," he commented, glancing around at all the little details I'd added.

I grinned and found a low branch to hang another lantern as he finished, "It's very…you."

I blushed at that too, but turned alway quickly to calm my stupid heart down. "Busy and excessive?"

He laughed, walking to me and casually putting an arm over my shoulder. "I was thinking colorful and bright. Like the sun when it shines on a meadow."

If my heart beat any faster, it would burst from my chest. He couldn't just say things like that, but did more and more the longer he was here.

"Thank you," I murmured, taking a quick glance to look up at his face, seeing his clear, blue eyes already on mine.

"I mean it, Sae. It's beautiful." His eyes narrowed slightly and he brushed my long waves back from my face, his hand lingering by my neck.

"You've outdone yourself, Saelyn!" Pah-Pah's clap of approval startled us both. We turned to see him coming into the small clearing.

Thevin's hands found themselves in his pockets and mine wrung on my skirts.

"Thank you. There's very little left to do, but I keep thinking I'm missing something."

He shook his head and walked to me, his arms outstretched for an embrace, and hugging me, he whispered, "Looks like you have everything you need."

I think I'd die right there if Thevin heard that.

He pulled himself back as I pinched his arm.

"Shall we get some lunch? Your mother has set up something for us to share."

I raised a brow and looked at Thevin who shrugged, saying, "Sure. I could use some nourishment if I'm to keep working with this tyrant over here."

I smiled wide just as he did, loving his teasing, loving the way his cropped curls brushed across his forehead because I knew I was a goner.

Not only had I fallen madly in love with the one person I so rarely got to see, I had started to wonder if he was slowly falling for me.

"*Saelyn.*" My name brushed lightly on the wind and chills racked through my body, stealing my ability to move.

Pah-Pah turned to lead us back to my mother and Thevin frowned my way.

"What is it?" he asked.

My eyes darted through the trees, the flowers, the underbrush, looking for any sign of where my name had come from.

"Sometimes I—" I closed my eyes and shook my head. "Never mind. It's nothing."

I walked forward and he slid up beside me. "It's not nothing if it makes you look like that."

I shrugged, choosing to ignore whatever it was that was obviously haunting me. Whatever it was that had been haunting me for years.

CHAPTER 52
REV

The towering iron-leaded doors of the Fortress were waiting to be opened, but I didn't want to move.

My fingers wrapped through Karus's cold hand, and yet she was not close enough.

I did not want to do this.

Every part of my body begged to scoop her up and take her back to bed.

Every sliver of my soul warned me, screamed at me to force her behind locked doors and close her up to keep her safe from the task that faced us.

I could do it.

Just as I had argued with her since I found her on that chair in her old room, I could use the spell. I could light Viridis in sunshine and push the Blight back far enough at least to get the book we needed.

I could convince the Growers that—

"No." Her voice came swift and hard as she looked at me with eyes of viridian steel, feeling everything I felt, knowing exactly what I was so very tempted to do.

I warred with respecting her choice and demanding she make a different one, and there lay the parts of me that lied, pretending to promise to trust her every decision.

"You don't have to do this." I grabbed her waist and cupped her cheek, pulling us close and soothing my pulse having her so near.

"You promised," she began, tucking my waves behind my ears. "You promised you'd break this spell for me, and I believe you, Rev. You will not fail in this. I will return to you just as I am. And that is my promise to you."

Her conviction only made me further fear her loss from my life.

"Fuck that, we're going back to bed," I rumbled, reaching down to pull her legs up to me.

"We are not." She pushed my hands aside and broke from my heavy kiss, taking my face in her palms. "I've learned my lesson about choices. I know how asking you to help me with this is affecting you. But it doesn't mean we're going to agree on every choice either of us makes. I'm doing this for us, for Pompeii, for our future. I am thinking clearly. It's you who is deterred by our past and I understand why." She pressed her forehead to mine. "We will not fail. *You* will not fail."

She kissed me once more and reached for the handle of the doors. She pulled, revealing the coppery hue of the sun rising through the trees. She took a deep breath, looking back at me. "Viridis returns today."

I followed her out slowly. Moira waited on the stone newel at the bottom of the staircase, her wings fluttering madly as she spotted us.

One glance at me and she grimaced. "Karus, maybe we could—"

"Where are the Growers?" Karus interrupted, obviously done listening. "We need to move. We'll lead them to Viridis and get this done."

Moira scrunched her lips, but turned, calling in a screech toward the tree line.

Movement from the forest developed into the foreign shapes of the Growers' bodies, at least twenty of them in their varied forms moving slowly from the trees.

Karus nodded, addressing them all, "This way."

My head fell back, and I looked to the sky in a weighted exhale as Karus walked through the Fortress doors.

"Is she going to be alright?" Moira asked as the long line of growers clambered into the Fortress.

I clenched my teeth and looked to Moira who fluttered at my side. "I don't know."

It was the only real truth I could give her as we followed the last of the Growers through the foyer.

CHAPTER 53
KARUS

This would work.

It had to.

There were no other options with a chance at real success.

I'd be alright.

He'd be alright.

Pompeii would be alright.

Each echo of my steps across the stone halls sounded with the odd shuffling of the twenty Growers following behind me.

I didn't look back.

I only moved forward.

Rev's fear permeated the air, and I knew I was not the only one to feel it.

Our long, strange line of humans and fae finally turned and entered the massive corridor with a few short steps down to the doors of Viridis.

My green light expanded across the stone as I approached the black doors wound in trails of copper. They rose too far into the corridor for me to see their end.

I turned to explain how to enter Viridis, finding two Growers approaching the doors as if they already knew.

I addressed them, not sure if they could really understand me, or if Moira would need to interpret. "To enter, you must…" I trailed off as they ignored me completely, and each lifted their tangle of woven arms to the doors, one on each side.

I stepped back, witness to another of Viridis's secrets gone untold for centuries.

Their branches and vines grew, trailing up the stone, following the copper pattern. A variation of green leaves unfurled from each vine as they rose beyond what my eyes could see.

I glanced back to Revich who was just as surprised as I was while Moira watched as well, nibbling on her fingers.

We waited in bated breath as the doors came alive with each Grower, becoming one creature, one fae. I heard the click, the resounding evidence that the doors to Viridis were in fact ancient and sentient. A breeze, familiar in warmth and scent, lifted my hair and the doors pushed inward.

Viridis was still alive.

And it greeted me in the embrace of an old friend, never forgotten, ever a part of me and who I had become.

I'd bring it back today.

I was even more sure of it.

A dark expanse of tunnel formed beyond the doors and the Growers began to step inside, taking the lead.

"Did you know?" I started, Rev's hand closing over mine.

He shook his head in a rare silence, a small tick in his jaw.

We walked forward, following the Growers who seemed at this point to know more about Viridis and where it lie in Felgren than we did.

I expanded my light to shine above us, lighting the entwined tunnel which was narrow, barely wide enough for Revich and I to walk side-by-side. We stumbled over the branches wound below us, never stepping on a forest path. Peering through the woven thicket of twigs and vines, I saw glimpses of the Blight outside.

"I think…I think we're in Felgren." I glanced at Rev, his face the same hardened features as he eyed our path ahead. "You told me once that Viridis is in Felgren somewhere. And the Blight broke in through the door that leads to the forest."

He nodded, eyes straight ahead as we moved.

My boot caught under a vine and he was there, strong arms wrapping around my chest, grabbing me before I could fall.

I laughed lightly, pulling hair from my face and grinning at him, catching the sadness in his eyes which sobered me immediately.

If there was any time I faltered, it was then.

If there was a single moment I truly considered turning, running, with his hand in mine from this choice, it was in that moment of sorrow and fear across his face. It burrowed itself into the dull of his eyes, the straight line of his lips, the furrow of his brow.

I turned immediately, facing our path forward again, knowing myself. Knowing that if I saw that look once more, I would not have the strength to continue. Damned be Viridis, damned be Pompeii's life, and damned be the considerable guilt we'd both have to face.

We continued for five minutes which led to ten, leading to ten more. With every step forward, the rustle of new growth met our ears as the Growers in the front of the line grew their tunnel of life through the forest and through the Blight itself, proving their vast power.

The scent of the Blight could not be drowned out, meeting our noses as the unmistakable fetor of death.

At last, we came to the door I had met once before. The same old wooden door Heimlen had used to show me the Blight for the first time. The door that led from Felgren to Viridis. It lay at an angle, only one of its hinges remaining. The Growers expanded their tunnel to form a wide opening of branches, revealing the thick, thorny vines of the Blight that trespassed into the dark hall, which led to the second twin door in Viridis.

Moira's screech began as she spoke to the Growers.

"They want to start here. Obviously. They said this leads to

Viridis and that your sun can destroy the Blight starting here. They will follow you and regrow your library as you go. If this works, they can return to this door and cover it with their growth, which will hold the Blight off from coming back in. At least for a short time. Until you can help them destroy it all."

I pursed my lips and nodded, stepping up to the doorway, blocked completely by the obsidian mass of thick, spongy wood.

I held my hands out in front of me, an orb of cascading green held above my open palms.

I glanced over my shoulder, gathering strength to look at Revich one more time.

His gaze bore into my soul, begging me to stop, pulling on our bond so tightly, it strained on his end with thoughts of hesitation streaming down our tether, hitting my heart with full force.

I took a deep breath and turned to Moira, all twenty Growers watching me with spaces for eyes on their heads, eerie and fantastical all the same. "I can do this. We can do this together. It's our one chance." I swallowed firmly, lowering my voice slightly. "I just need enough time."

"I understand. They understand, too." She nodded toward the Growers, waiting for me to begin.

Without looking back and risking loosing what little confidence I held, I spoke clearly into the woven space protecting us from the Blight. "*Simulair Solum.*"

The sun burst into life, the orb of magic now warm and glowing, the Blight around us reacting immediately with that blood-curdling hiss.

I positioned the simulated sun close to the thickest vine, massive and strong, letting the sun loom next to its surface to watch as the light swept its way through. Crackles and pops resounded as it broke the vine down the center, cutting it off from where it led into Viridis.

Having a clear path forward, I closed my eyes and inhaled, taking Revich's words with me.

I breathe, you breathe.

I breathe, you breathe.

The sun grew, swelling to the size of the doorframe, destroying the Blight ahead as it went.

I could hold this.

It was heavy. It was weighing on my strength, but the weight was manageable. I stepped forward, the Growers shuffling behind as I entered the Blighted corridor. The ever present sizzle of the Blight in its own demise echoed off the stone as it recoiled and fell to dark ash around me. I picked up my speed, following the beat of my heart. Once again, I was destroying the very life of what the Blightress had sent to destroy Felgren.

I broke through the second door, meeting Viridis in full. Its life was hanging by a thread. Its breath snuffed out from the horrifying pulse of the Blight that wound through its once-gilded halls, entombing what was life, and beauty, and knowledge.

I ran, not daring to look back, unable to turn my head for fear of the faltering step I could not risk to take.

The Blight was powerless against my onslaught of sunlight as it fell into a recess of decay and ash that it deserved. Grotesque vines fell from the grove of trees in the central courtyard and tumbled down the hallways that rose above me. The sound of their destruction echoed in the glass dome high above, but I could not afford to look.

Anger, wrath, rage—each state of being bloomed in the sun I held as it grew and I could no longer focus on controlling its size and weight. I could only focus on the heat I produced myself, my own rampage through these halls, furious at what had been taken from me.

This was for more than Pompeii or Viridis.

I hoped the Blightress lay writhing somewhere as I hurt her.

I hoped she was in utter agony, feeling all the Blight feels, seeing all the Blight sees as the one she claimed as hers destroyed the very essence of who she was.

"Karus!" I heard Revich's call somewhere behind me.

I needed more time.

I widened my arms, filling the space with the sun I grew in the power I sourced from Felgren.

As the Blight hissed around me, it was replaced with life.

The Growers were proving their worth, continually replacing the abhorrent vines with blooms of red and yellow. With leaves unfurling in a brilliant green from the branches of the birch trees.

I laughed, a sound unheard in all the death and regrowth as I watched Viridis return to itself, imbued with life, and joy, and endless knowledge.

I took my final steps forward to face the thirteen monstrous trees I had grown. I filled my lungs again, the air a brew of decay and summer—Viridis newly returned warring with what now passed into nothing around us.

"It's almost over!" I shouted, hoping Rev heard me as I lifted the sun high into the dome above, its heat radiating upon my face. I moved it out of my way, so that it would not burn my hands and cheeks as it did the last time I'd held it this long.

I needed to see its brilliance lay waste to the final threshold of what grew in Viridis.

I needed, more than anything in that moment, to witness the destruction of what I myself had produced—the pulsating mound of fruit trees I had summoned months ago in my grief for Viridis.

I hadn't wanted to think about it.

I hadn't wanted my thoughts to linger on why or how I had been able to grow my own version of the Blight.

I faced those thoughts then though, coming to terms with the Blightress's truth that her power resided in me.

But as the trees began to fall, each one splitting down the middle, spurting black liquid down the white marble steps and igniting in a fire I did not mean to produce, I accepted the truth of myself.

I was a part of her.

I held immense power that came from her.

I was, in some way, *bonded* to *her*.

And I would wield that power she'd given me to her end.

I would devastate all she was and had now proven herself to be, sending her depraved growth to burn and crumble into nothing more than ash and soot at my feet.

I could destroy what I had produced.

I could prove that I was *not her*.

I could show myself that I would never succumb to the wrath I held inside.

CHAPTER 54

REV

My voice shattered through Viridis as I called her name once again in fear.

I sprinted after her, weaving through the Growers as they bent to the ground, their limbs sinking into Viridis's earth and replenishing it with life anew.

They'd stalled my ability to enter Viridis and Karus had gotten too far ahead.

Branches wrapped around my waist, pulling me to the ground as a Grower towered over me, hindering my effort to get to her, stopping me from saving the one soul that kept me alive.

Fuck.

That.

My power burst from my palms in a blaze of blue, blasting the Grower back from my sight, snapping its branched torso in two. A piercing cry of agony filtered through the courtyard as another branch caught my leg.

I raged, summoning a blue wall of power behind me. I snapped the branch on my thigh with my bare hands, throwing it to the new grass at my feet and sprinted forward, following the light of the sun before me.

Ten more Growers lay ahead between me and Karus.

"Move!" I roared, a line of azure flame, cold and static, piercing through their wall of thorns in their attempt to stop me from getting to her.

They wanted more time to bring Viridis back, but they did not understand the risk. They did not know that they would doom themselves—doom Felgren—if they let her fall.

Her sun rose higher into the dome of Viridis and I saw her arms open wide at the bottom of the marble steps, facing the trees she'd grown herself.

I tore through their brambles with my power and hands, now scratched and bleeding as more and more walls grew.

I could take them down.

I could destroy every one, but that would not get me to Karus in time.

She fell to her knees, the monstrous trees alight in her flame, and I screamed her name again.

She could not hear me, of that I was certain, as more walls formed ahead.

"Moira!" I thundered, seeing the flutter of her wings as I tore my way through another thicket of thorns.

Her violet eyes turned to me in understanding as she flew to one of the Growers blocking my way and whispered something in its ear.

It fell into the green grass in what looked to be uncontrollable, painful laughter, its wall of thorns falling with it.

She moved to the next and I didn't stay to watch as she used her magic to knock them down. I bent to the ground and summoned all of the power of the Baron of Felgren.

I had seconds to get to her—to break the spell before it broke her.

The earth erupted in a straight path of upturned soil, rumbling and sending the few remaining Growers flying back, leaving an open space for me to reach her and tearing through several newly healed trees in its wake.

I sprinted to her huddled form, my knees hitting the soft earth, just inches away from her. I smacked headfirst into a wall of iridescent magic I had not seen.

No.

I was so close.

I pounded on the shimmering force, calling for Karus to hear me.

The wall was not coming from her.

It was coming from *her*.

This was the Blightress's attempt to stop me from breaking the spell, and in my rage, I didn't stop to wonder why.

I slammed my palms flat on the shimmering surface, taking one last look at my love and closing my eyes, breathing in deep.

I summed all of the power of Baron. Each thread of magic I held inside and never needed to use.

"I need everything," I called, pushing harder into the Blightress's power.

"*It will not be enough.*" The same voiceless wind addressed my plea, finding its way into the cavern of my mind where it had dwelled for years.

"Give me *something*. I just need to touch her. I just need her to feel me to break the spell."

"*This is the one you'll split your power for?*"

"When she passes the Baron trial, yes. This is her." I felt a burning under my palms, but I still pushed all my strength. Karus's head fell back with her eyes closed, facing the sun as it began its descent toward her, the grove of trees dead and withered on the stairs.

"*She is…tainted.*" The wind whispered in my ear as the wall of shimmering colors began to crack, one minuscule hole beginning to form.

I took another breath and sought that power from the cavern in my mind. If the power of the Baron of Felgren wasn't willing to help me, I'd force my way in, pulling from every tendril of ancient magic passed down through the ages.

The strength of it swelled in my chest as a flash of the entirety of Felgren Forest unfolded behind my eyes as if I flew above it. I saw the top of every tree, the Blight that still took hold of the north-eastern quadrant, the river that flowed through the dense thicket to the west, and the black pinnacles of the Fortress itself.

I sucked in one more breath and sent it from my chest, down my arms, to the palms of my hands as the wall shattered into thousands of iridescent specks.

My arms wrapped around my beloved, and I pulled her lips to mine, gently lowering her to the ground. The sun flickered before it snuffed out in a cold reminder of its absence.

Her arms wrapped around my neck, her mouth opened on mine as my tongue slid over hers in relief and declaration—in promise—that I would *always* come to save her.

And as I felt her tire and begin to fall into unconsciousness, I left that cavern in my mind, which held precious secrets, ensuring I was heard before slamming the door on the essence that gave me the power of Baron. "She is *everything*."

CHAPTER 55
KARUS

J asmine and lavender.

A tickling breeze across my cheek.

I turned my head, eyes still closed, my skin meeting soft grass. The call of birds singing and the rustle of their wings flapping through the warm air broke a smile on my lips.

My eyes fluttered open, met with the brilliance that was the light of Viridis, streaming through the glass dome gilded in gold.

I stared up through the long branches of birch trees, their dance of limbs reminding me of a wave of hello, greetings from an old friend. The thin bark on their trunks peeled like strips of paper, and I reached out to touch the base of the tree I lay next to. Warm and solid, I could sense the power of this enchanted place returned. As it should be.

I sensed him there beside me and turned my head the other way. The warm light lit his face, his eyes closed, a soft smile on his lips. His arms were pulled back behind his head, his hands threaded through his dark hair.

"It's beautiful, isn't it?" he murmured, his voice gentle and light in the air.

I reached for him, tumbling over his chest to straddle his hips and bury my face into his neck. His arms smoothed over my back as I broke into sobs.

He brushed his hand down my hair, pulling me taut to his chest, continuing his observations. "I'd forgotten. I'd forgotten how Viridis makes me feel. I took it for granted. I never doubted it would always be here. I should have appreciated it more back then."

I laughed at his neck, nodding and sniffing. I wiped at my face before running small, short kisses up to his jaw, his chin, finding his lips and relishing in the feel of them pressed to mine in the sanctuary our mouths had met in many times before.

I kissed him deeply, breathing him in, taking my time to appreciate *him*. His touch, his skin, the way he pulled on the back of my thighs without realizing he did it, guiding me closer, always bringing me closer.

I pulled away from his lips to see his face. A few scratches at his brow and one longer gash at his right cheek had once bled and closed, leaving a slash of red across the surface.

I traced the line of crimson at his cheek while whispering the spell of mending, watching it close completely, leaving just a line of blood, the only evidence it had marred his face at all.

His hands slid over my hips as his gaze flickered over my hair. I didn't want to know the amount of white streaks it contained now.

I continued my pass of mending over his brow, speaking my piece as I went. "I love you, Baron of Felgren, Keeper of Promises, Savior of Powerful Women On the Brink of Self-Retribution."

He laughed at that, rising to sit, holding me to his lap by wrapping one arm around my back, hand sliding up my neck with the other.

"You did it," he said simply. "The Blight in Viridis is gone."

I grinned, glancing around us, but not for long before my gazed settled back on his face, rival as it was in this place of beauty.

"I had some help. How long was I asleep?"

"Just an hour or so."

I brushed my fingers through his hair, pressing my chest to his, my body reacting to the heat that pulsed through me. "And the Growers? Moira?"

"They've gone. The Growers sealed the door to Felgren as they left. Moira was difficult to convince to leave, but I assured her you were not lost and that you'd wake soon enough."

His hand slid from my neck down to my chest, unbuttoning the top of my vest.

"How did you know?" I closed my eyes and inhaled sharply at the soft press of his lips at the curve of my breasts. "How did you know I wasn't lost this time?"

"Our bond. You were there. Just tired." His breath was warm and heavy over my skin as his lips found my peak, pulling it into his mouth, his tongue a gentle caress.

I moaned, slipping my hand into his vest to pull out his flask, finding it empty.

"Fuck," I groaned, tossing it into the grass.

He pulled away from my breast and my body shuddered in his absence. "I should have made more tea this morning. Our routine was thrown off a bit."

"We shouldn't," I exhaled, biting my lip before I realized I was doing it.

His gaze flickered there, repeating, "We shouldn't."

"Clairannia warned not to risk it," I added, my breath refusing to slow.

He nodded. "We've risked it several times already."

"Though..." I trailed, using everything I had not to grind on top of what was hard beneath me. "We've made it through just fine in the past."

His fingers dug into my thighs, and his head fell forward. "Karus, I need you to get off my lap before I beg you to stay."

"Right," I said, lifting myself and buttoning my shirt and vest quickly, my skin burning, my body aching, screaming at our choice to separate.

He rubbed his face, pulling his fingers back through his hair and rose, slipping his hand into mine. "Right. Let's go find that book."

CHAPTER 56
REV

Viridis was in bloom.

And I could hardly fucking notice.

Seven years. I had seven years of experience not touching her, not staring at her like this. In all honesty, I had probably been terrible at that anyway.

After all, I only saw her once or twice a day, each time doing my very best to avoid her gaze, not willing to risk the effect I had on her then.

I hated how she'd fumble through her responses if I tried to speak to her. How Moira would scold me the next day, telling me she'd slept for hours into the afternoon, exhausted hearing my voice stray from what we'd agreed I could say.

Again, in all honesty, I recently faced a new plight.

I wanted to touch her always. Every second, every moment I breathed, I wanted her next to me.

She'd been out of my grasp for seven years, and now, I never wanted her hand to leave it.

Her eyes met mine as we ascended another staircase, both of us knowing exactly the level and section we needed to find.

By the breath of my beloved, she was beautiful.

The new white of her hair only beckoned her eyes to stand out further against her porcelain skin. The bow of her top lip and the gentle curve of her bottom, I longed to touch.

I didn't fucking care about the tea.

And if that made me weak, so be it.

I'd be weak for her.

But I'd stay strong as well, continuing up the stairs, just holding her hand. I'd find a way to be content with just that for the moment, if it was what she needed from me.

She watched me fight what we both wanted and her lips parted, her chest rising, flushing, a subtle crimson racing across her skin, her freckles at her chest.

I should turn away.

I shouldn't even look.

Maybe I'd be satisfied just to please her.

Maybe if I set her down on one of these steps and worshiped her with my tongue, it would be enough to satiate my burning desire that smoldered and seeped through any logical thought.

No, this *was* logic.

I wanted her. Here. In Viridis. Just like before.

I wanted to taste her, move inside her and hear her cries, her pleas for more.

Her breath caught as we reached the Medicus Conduit Hall. I hadn't even attempted to dampen my lust, and I knew it flowed down our line to her, just as hers found its way to me.

She closed her eyes and let go of my hand, her breath heavy as she stepped forward to the shelves where brilliant green vines trailed to the floor. I took a moment to observe the state of the books. They were mostly disheveled, black inking their pages and spines. I knew if we looked inside each of them, we'd find evidence of the Blight.

These manuscripts could not return to what they once were.

But we could work on that, replacing the ones lost to the Blight, filling the shelves with new works.

Her hand traced down the row of books, the pads of her fingers shuffling over each one as she tilted her head to read the spines.

I ran my hands through my hair, taking fresh Viridis air into my lungs.

"Here! It's here!" She pulled a thick tome from its place on the shelf above her head, its cover sticking to the book next to it. She peeled it away gently, sitting on the marble floor, the silk benches around us ruined and in need of replacing.

I sidled up beside her as she held the book open in her lap, scanning the pages for the answer we needed.

The book described common diseases, ones developed from others, changing and spreading over time—easily cured by any medicus conduit.

The second half of the book related the author's experience with magically produced diseases—whether created by accident or intent.

We skimmed those pages, both of us murmuring short passages to each other, continuing our search for how to cure our friend.

My eye caught on a passage and I pointed to it, reading aloud,

"Diseases created via magic are especially dangerous and can be cured with varying levels of success. The only way to completely cure a magical disease is to stop the heart of its creator. The power that was imbued into the disease will die with them.

However, through meticulous study, I have discovered another way to cure a disease, though only partially. Through this process, something of the disease is left behind in the physical or mental traits of each person infected."

"Philius's hands," Karus whispered. "The Black Fever was only partially cured because Heimlen was still alive."

I nodded and flipped the page.

"All magical diseases are created through parts of Felgren. I've seen cases where ferns or lichen were magically imbued to create an illness. This practice began as a way to find cures for certain ailments, but quickly developed into dangerous magic and was outlawed centuries ago.

A magical disease can be partially cured, if the piece of Felgren is destroyed. Then, the magic can no longer siphon through the object."

I leaned my head back against the shelves and closed my eyes. "If Heimlen used a piece of the Blight to create the Black Fever, how did he destroy it?"

"Fire. He used fire." Her line of sight was set across the courtyard to the enormous marble staircase. "I lit those trees on fire and they began to die. But we can't risk lighting all of the Blight on fire and possibly destroy all of Felgren. Heimlen must have known that, too." She rubbed her temples, sighing. "Heimlen was alive at the time of the cure, so there might be more to the survivor's traits than we realize. Their hands, yes, but here it says *mental* traits as well."

I knew we were both thinking of Philius.

"Since Heimlen is dead, wouldn't the disease be cured completely?"

I frowned, turning the page, looking for more answers and finding black, ruined pages. I shook my head, sighing. "I'd bet this author didn't know everything and anything else they did is destroyed. If the Blight played a bigger role in the disease, then it would be the Blightress whose heart also needed to be stopped to cure the Black Fever completely."

"But this means Pompeii should be mostly cured, right? The trees are destroyed and that's where his illness came from." She stood and gestured to the top of the white staircase where a portal would form for us to leave when we were ready. "Can you tell? If you try to connect to him wordlessly, can you ask him how he is?"

"Our connection has been weakened, but I'll try again." I stood and held my hand out to pull her up. I closed my eyes to concentrate, nudging Pompeii with my mind.

I felt a stir, as if he had been sleeping right where I'd left him this morning. The connection we shared as Baron and Overseer was still weak, but not as fuzzy as it had been.

"I think I just woke him. Let's go."

We rushed down the staircases and through the courtyard of new grass and blooms of lilac and lavender.

Viridis was beautiful. And it was ours to cherish and love once again.

And as Karus stepped through the portal at the top of the

marble stairs, I paused to look once more at our sanctuary, still heal-ing, but renewed all the same.

I liked this new beginning.

~

WE ENTERED THE KITCHENS AND STOPPED SHORT.

Lia was fussing over Pompeii, a bowl of soup in front of him at the small table, a sizable mound of crusty bread on the side.

"In all my years, I've never seen such a fuss over soup," she huffed, her black hair pulled back with wisps flying around her face.

"Pompeii?" Karus rushed to his side, sitting in the chair next to him, feeling his forehead, asking, "How are you feeling? We destroyed the Blight in Viridis." An enormous grin lit her face. "It's back."

He turned to look at me over his shoulder. Color had returned to his face, though his cheeks were still gaunt—nothing Lia's cooking couldn't settle.

"I am feeling on the mend, Karus. I'm sure I have you to thank for that." He patted her hand and took another spoonful of soup.

I sat on the chair to the other side of him. "It is good to see you up, old friend." I pointed to the book Karus had taken out of Viridis. "We were looking for this to help you, but when Karus destroyed the trees your illness came from, it seems the cure was already made. Though…" I trailed off, catching Karus's eye. "There's more time for that theory later. It is good to see you up again."

He thanked us both, taking a piece of bread and dipping it into the golden broth. "This is delicious. I'm told one of your new chan-nelers made it specially for me?"

"Yes. Mychael. You'll meet him in time and you can thank him yourself. For now, I think it's best you take the time to rest."

"I will do just that. I feel as if I could sleep for days. My chest is…" He opened the front of his robe to reveal the black bruising that was still marring his skin.

I leaned closer, analyzing the discoloration.

Just as the Black Fever still marked its victims, it seemed the Black Lung had done the same.

Lia rushed back to the table, spoon in hand and silently pulled three sand-colored stones from the bottom of the bowl, sitting them on the bread plate.

Each of us watched her in confusion.

She shrugged. "Sorry, love, I forgot to take these out."

"What are they for?" Karus asked.

"I use them to keep the soup warm after it's made." She left the table, returning to her chopping.

Pompeii cleared his throat and continued eating. "I'm glad to hear this did not infect anyone else in the Fortress. When I took the towels from your laboratorium, I thought nothing of the black liquid covering them. I became ill the following evening. I am sorry to say, I was not a good keeper of your channelers."

I laid a hand on his shoulder. "That is no fault of yours. I'll fill you in this evening after you've had more rest. There are many things to tell you."

"There always seems to be when you two are together." He winked at me, and I laughed.

Karus sat back, crossing her arms, exhaustion coming from her with or without our tether.

I rose from my chair. "I need to inform the staff and the channelers. You," I said, nodding toward Karus, "need to rest. And you," I patted Pompeii's back, "need to finish eating first, then go rest."

"And when do I get a rest, Baron?" Lia questioned boldly from the long counter where she chopped peeled potatoes into perfect cubes over a stone slab.

"As soon as you're done with those, Lia." I shrugged. "Take the rest of the day off. We can fend for ourselves for one evening."

She frowned, likely about to tell me off, but before she could, I kissed the top of Karus's head and headed to the servant's corridor to begin to right everything.

CHAPTER 57

KARUS

"I'm not cut out for this," Philius grumbled.

"You are. You just need more time," I reminded him once again.

"Time won't replace what isn't there to begin with."

I pursed my lips, a heavy sigh escaping me. It had been two more weeks of this resistance to everything Revich or I tried to teach my brother, and my patience with him was wearing thin.

After Viridis's return, Revich had found him drunk in his room with one of his last bottles of wine he'd brought in that trunk.

And now, without the drink to nurse his trauma and insecurities, he was irritable, temperamental, and generally a pain to be around.

In fact, I seemed to be the only one who would tolerate his presence longer than ten minutes. Even his old guard found excuse after excuse to leave his side, often headed to the kitchens or to help Pompeii as he returned to his duties.

"You have channeler magic, Philius. Revich can feel it."

He raised a brow and lowered his head, towering over me. I had always hated that no matter how much I grew, he always grew taller, even after I surpassed the height of most women I knew.

"Alright, listen. If you can do this one thing, I'll…" I huffed a sigh. "I'll take you to see the Blight."

He grinned, turning around to his task again.

He'd been asking to see the Blight in Felgren since the lockdown on the Fortress had been lifted. I understood his curiosity, but kept putting it off, having seen enough for one lifetime.

"But we're taking the Baron with us."

He tilted his head back and groaned. "Why? You're obviously more powerful than he is. I'm sure you can protect me, little sister."

"I've had enough run-ins with the Blight to know not to under-estimate it, nor its creator. And that's another thing,"—I jabbed my finger in his shoulder—"when we go, you are not allowed to speak about anything. The Blightress can hear and see everything the Blight can. We go, we look, we leave. That's it, *big brother*."

He shrugged and nodded.

The Blightress had not called upon me to have our first fireside chat. I hoped it was because she was still suffering from the abomination we'd cleared in Viridis.

"I can't get them to open," he complained, gesturing to the gardenia bush he'd attempted to grow in the past week. Five other woody-stemmed bushes grew in a stately row, each one grown by the other channelers and each one in a state of white blooms, their scent heavy in the late-spring air.

Philius's efforts, so far, had been in vain. His plant was yellowing at the leaves, and the buds were hardly more than the size of a pebble.

"We're going to try something else, then." I stepped up beside him as he looked longingly at the success of the others.

"Thank you," he said, relieved.

"We're going to try to summon your power straight from Felgren's soil." I knelt in my channeler clothing, light green skirts just warm enough for the season.

He gave a frustrated groan. "No, thank you."

"Get down here!" I yanked on his black-veined hand, and he tumbled to his knees with a glare on his face.

Ignoring it, I continued, "I want you to put one hand on the bud, like this." I gently lifted my hand to one of them, holding it up by the tips of my fingers. "And put the other in the earth, like this." I showed him how to stretch his fingers into the soil. I expanding my own until they were flat, my knuckles and conduit ring covered in dirt.

He played along, following my orders.

"*Floreyas*," I called to the bud. It grew in size before cracking and opening into an abundance of soft, silken white petals with a stark scent that hit my nose.

"Show off," he mumbled, holding a bud of his own and repeating the magic enhancement.

Surprise crossed his face when the bud grew in size, but filled with disappointment when it stubbornly refused to open, its sepals still tightly wound in a brilliant, waxy green.

"This is pointless." He lowered his hand from the bud and removed his other from the soil, flicking the dirt from his fingers and pulling off his channeler ring to wipe on his green vest. "I couldn't grow this flower if I had all the magic of Felgren. I'm not a channeler cut out for this. Something is wrong in the line of magic from Felgren to me." He replaced his ring on his finger, mumbling, "I should just go home."

I gaped up at him. He was certainly not the brother I remembered. He'd always had confidence, a laugh that filled the room and a lighthearted way about him that could lighten your own spirits.

Along with that came arrogance, and an assured sense of self of the man he was meant to become. After all the years we'd been apart, I wondered which of us had changed the most.

"Sit. *Down*." I yanked on his arm, jostling him back to the earth. "You think your line of channel from Felgren to you is broken?" I used my frustration to shape my words into something he'd actually listen to. "*Bullshit*. There's nothing wrong with your magic. It's your unwillingness to really try. To really put all of your efforts into these tasks we give you. You're stuck in the past, Philius, instead of growing in the present."

"And what? I'm supposed to just wear these channeler clothes, this ridiculous ring, and follow along like nothing happened? Like my sister wasn't given away by my mother and just left here to fend for herself? Like I didn't almost die by the Baron who took her? Now *that's* bullshit, Karus."

I scoffed. "Neither of us can change what happened. It happened. It hurt us both. Changed the lives of thousands of people, but here we are—together again in this forest that feeds us magic. We have a purpose here. We can train our magic and do everything we can to stop the Blightress from ever taking anything from us again. But, no. You choose to mope. You choose to whine and complain. Look around, Philius. No one wants to be near you but me, so push your damn hand back into the ground and produce a fucking bloom."

"I. Can't. Do. It."

Without a word I shoved his right hand flat on the earth and gripped his left in mine, placing his blackened fingers over the closed bud.

I filled my lungs quickly, letting my anger expand through me and sent my power to him.

He glared at me as if to say, *told you so*, before his orange light sparked under the bud and the bloom unfurled in a symphony of white.

He frowned, watching his magic continue to spark above his fingers.

"Keep going. Keep growing it." I ordered, continuing my flow of power to him.

He dug his hand further into the earth, mesmerized by the dozens of buds that formed, growing larger before bursting into a sea of white, the leaves of the gardenia bush no longer wilted and yellowing. The plant grew, wide and sturdy, overtaking all the others in size and blossoms, and we both stood as it reached our own height.

I let go of his hand, crossing my arms, staring at him with hope that this would help him understand his capabilities.

"You did that," he stammered, stepping back to look over the now massive shrub.

"No, you did. I used Cosensian Magic to give you some of my

power, but it doesn't work if there's not a direct line to Felgren through the recipient. You could have done this if you would just practice pulling power from this forest. I'm just showing you that you are not irreparably broken. You are bruised, Philius, and bruises fade."

He sighed, his brows still furrowed at the gardenia, glorious and pungent in his wake of power. "I'll try harder," he stated bluntly, crossing his arms at his chest.

"Good." I patted his shoulder and turned to leave. "I'll meet you at the lumen den after lunch. Revich will be free to go with us to the Blight then."

"You're still going to take me there?"

"Yes. Maybe seeing what we're fighting against will heal your bruises faster."

CHAPTER 58

REV

Toying with the rhyzolm in my pocket, I puffed air from my lips, leaning against the stone wall of Ilyenna's room.

No fever, no bruise across her chest, no sign of the Black Lung that had buried into Pompeii, but still, she was not well.

Talon pulled hair back from her face, his own full of fear.

"It's nothing. Really, you two don't need to hover over me like this." Her voice was firm, at least, and not raspy as Pompeii's had been.

Talon squeezed her hand tightly. "We're just concerned after what infected Pompeii."

I'd never seen him like this. I supposed even the strongest of men were soft to the ones they loved most.

I tried to voice his reasoning. "Ilyenna, I don't wish to worry you, but you've fallen ill not long after the Black Lung. We believe we've cured the disease, but we could very well be wrong."

A light knock came to the door, and Karus poked her head inside. "I heard Ilyenna's ill?" She looked at me with the same concern.

"I'm *fine*," Ilyenna grumbled, taking her hand from her

companion and crossing her arms at her chest in her bed. "Just tired."

"And nauseous. You couldn't keep your dinner down last night," Talon added, looking back at us.

Karus cocked her head, eyes narrowing. She opened her mouth to say something and hesitated. "Talon, Revich, I need a minute alone with Ilyenna please."

Talon sighed, bending his head forward, his two long black braids following the movement. He rose and left the room, an exasperated look on his face just for me.

I turned and left as well, waiting with Talon right outside the door. He paced back and forth across the hall.

"She's probably right. I'm sure it's nothing, Talon. Something she ate didn't sit well." I did my best to convince him, attempting to convince myself just the same.

"What if it's not? What if it *is* the Black Lung? You said you destroyed the Blight that caused it in the first place and—"

"We did. Pompeii is cured. This must be something—" I stopped my reassurance, confused. Karus was relieved, excited, and stern all at once in that room.

I pulled myself from the wall and waited for her to exit.

A brilliant smile lit her face as she opened the door. "Talon, Ilyenna has something to tell you." She was practically beaming with joy as she moved aside and let him enter.

She took my hand, pulling me down the hall to the staircase.

"What is it? What's wrong with Ilyenna?" I asked.

We got to the bannister that looked down many levels below to the foyer and she kissed me. "Nothing is wrong. Ilyenna is growing a child."

"*What?*"

She laughed, falling into my chest. "In eight months or so, the Fortress will host its first baby."

Relief and shock sifted through me as I wrapped my arms around Karus, shaking my head.

"How…how did this happen?" I murmured in disbelief.

She pulled back to look at me. "You know very well how this happened."

"Talon assured me they had styris tea."

"Ilyenna assured me that their first night as companions, they did not."

I huffed, trying to process what I'd never had to think about before. When a child came in several months, Ilyenna would still not be ready for her conduit trials. She'd need time to rest and they'd need help taking care of the baby. Maybe some of the staff would be willing to help take care of the child. We'd also need to move her and Talon to a room on the first level—

"Revich," Karus interrupted my thinking. "Say your thoughts aloud. I'd love to know what you're thinking."

"What does she need? What can we do to help her right now?" I pulled my hands through my hair, leading Karus down the stairs. "We need them to choose a room on the ground floor. She can't be walking up all these stairs several times a day. And what about her nausea? I'm sure Lia knows something that can help. She won't be ready for the conduit trials by the time the baby comes, so we need to enlist help from the staff so she can take breaks to train. Unless of course, she wants to spend more time with the baby, and—"

Karus was glowing.

I realized this when I finally glanced at her as we hurried down the stairs to get to the kitchens. Her joy had always shown itself as green. There was a warmth in the color that radiated from her fingers, often forming over her shoulders as well.

I stopped, pulling her to me. "You're glowing."

She laughed. The sound was the purest flutter of beauty I'd ever hear. "I don't know if you know this, my love, but you make me glow. It's almost always you. I know joy from you."

She kissed me, wrapping her arms around my neck, and I didn't hesitate to pull her chest against mine.

"You are the best Baron Felgren has ever seen." She kissed my cheek and pulled herself into my neck.

"I'm sure better ones will come along," I whispered into strands of white and chestnut hair.

"I mean it, Rev. You love and protect your channelers, your Overseer, and the people under your care better than any other Baron in the history of Barons. I know. I've read all about them. You're doing it. You're changing the Baronship for the better."

"We." I pulled her in front of me to smile at the glow still hovering over her. "*We* are doing this. Together."

She pressed her forehead to mine. "You breathe, I breathe."

"You live, I live," I promised.

~

RAUCA GREETED ME WITH HER USUAL NIPS ON MY ARM. I INSPECTED her for more evidence of what Karus had pointed out to me.

A new growth of vines wound under her belly, deep within the white fur. I glanced to Karus who inspected Parvus as well.

"Here," she sighed, pointing to a spot behind his ears which was sprouting small brown thorns.

"On Rauca's belly, too," I remarked, patting her head in reassurance when she whined at me.

"When Figuerah arrives with Clairannia, we need to discuss this with her." She laughed as Parvus jumped up, licking her face and almost knocking her to the ground. "At least their behavior hasn't changed."

Philius stood nearby, already saddling his own lumen, waiting in uncharacteristic patience.

I hopped on Rauca's back, past the need for a saddle to keep myself on. "Let's review this one more time. We ride to the edge of the Blight. We say nothing. We do nothing but observe. Save your questions for when we return, Philius. You do not touch the Blight, and neither does Karus. Agreed?"

"Yes, sir," Karus called, while Philius nodded.

I loved when she did that.

I turned Rauca, whispering directions to her, and she took off, her massive paws bounding over brush and branches, leading the other two on the quickest path.

She howled into the afternoon air, the other two lumens

returning her call in a cacophony of wolfish reports I couldn't comprehend.

When we reached the edge of the Blight, my heart thudded in a heavy apprehension. The line of dull black had been forced back by Karus seven years ago and here we met the extent of what her power had destroyed. Very little of the Blight had grown since then, including this particular acreage.

I had not returned to this edge of dark mist with her at my side, but she squeezed my hand in assurance that she would heed my words.

Philius dismounted, his face an open book of disbelief.

The Blight was monstrous yet remarkable in its expanse of black vines that wove over the trunks of trees, curling around each one in the maze of dark, smothering the life and beauty of Felgren.

Philius glanced at us and took a breath to speak, but Karus shook her head, reminding him of his agreement.

Karus and I watched him walk to the line where abundant green clover met the sharp thorns of black, spongy wood. He gazed out into the dark as if taking in what had inevitably been the beginning of all his life turned upside down.

He stood like that for some time, and I held Karus's hand so tightly, she flexed her fingers in a silent plea to ease off.

Our lumens hovered behind us. Philius's paced in obvious agitation while Rauca and Parvus rested nearby, drifting into a midday nap.

After giving him a few more minutes, I whistled and Philius looked back at us with an unreadable expression across his face. But rather than speaking his thoughts, he walked to his lumen to leave.

Karus and I headed to ours just as Parvus suddenly stood, alert, his snout sniffing toward the Blight, his ears swiveling in that direction.

Karus patted his head and moved to hop on his back when he bolted, bounding into the thick of the black trees and over thorns catching on his fur.

"Parvus!" Karus called, quickly slapping a hand over her mouth, running to the edge of the Blight.

I was not far behind, immediately wrapping my hand around her waist, not willing to risk her running after him.

She turned to me and shook her head, a silent promise she was not intending to follow.

We squinted into the mist, Rauca at my side, her tongue lolling out of her mouth in indifference. Confused, I pointed to Rauca and Karus shook her head, biting her lip and staring back out into the black abyss.

We waited for what felt like forever, but I knew was only a few minutes as Parvus's brown and black form bounded back over the thick branches, something hanging from his mouth.

He spat it out after clearing the last bit of thorns and returned to Karus's side, panting and looking to her for praise.

We stepped back, both of us staring at what he had brought.

A red rose, so dark the tips of its petals were black, lay on the earth, its thorny stem a deep green.

Philius shook his head. "Looks like the Blightress sends her regards."

CHAPTER 59
KARUS

We rode back to the lumen den in silence.

I'd failed Parvus and Rauca. That was obvious to me. When I had allowed her to help me heal them, the Blightress had used her power to influence their bodies and minds.

I knew she called him, and I knew she chose my lumen specifically. The moment we landed at the entrance to the lumen den, I gave Parvus a squeeze and left. Anything Philius wanted to ask would have to wait.

"Karus!" Philius yelled, dismounting from his lumen.

"Later," Revich responded. "She's got somewhere to be."

I'm sure he knew where I was headed—straight up the winding staircase to my old room in the tallest tower. I didn't know if I needed to be there to speak to her, looking out across the tops of the trees toward the north, but I wasn't going to do this twice.

I stood atop my old chair and pulled the pin to my window, slamming it open along with the place in my mind where our connection held by a thread.

"What the fuck *was that?"* I called wordlessly, the strong wind pulling my hair to play across my face.

"Just a peace offering of no hard feelings after that show in Viridis."

"How long have you been able to command the lumens?"

"Why do you ask questions you already know the answer to?"

I scoffed aloud. *"Parvus is mine. Rauca's is Revich's. You cannot have them."*

"Though, it seems as if I do, Little Sprout."

No one, not one single soul on the isle was able to enrage me like her. *"I'll find a way to break your connection. Just like we saved the Overseer, we will find a way."* I exhaled into the warm wind, then took a deep breath, searching for patience. *"I'm here,"* I continued. *"Speak. This is your weekly chat."*

"We'll have our chat tonight, Karus. I'm busy at the moment."

"Stealing babies, I presume."

"Not at all."

The connection broke. She was gone, and I stormed off the chair, shoving it back to the vanity desk.

I pulled my hair over my shoulder, catching a glimpse of my reflection in the dusty mirror. Dammit. I was looking more and more like her with each exhausting moment of my life. White streaks bloomed abundant not just at the top of my head as they had for years, but now more on the sides and the nape of my neck. My original chestnut color was still there, but I missed all of it, refusing to get used to this new reminder of what I continued to lose.

I yanked the door open, and Rev stood there, leaning against the wall opposite, hands in his pockets of course, emitting an air of protection and general reverence in my presence.

He quirked a brow at me, and I sighed. "She wouldn't tell me. I don't know how to break their connection, but I told her I'd find it."

"Do you think that counted? As one of your weekly chats?"

I shook my head, fumbling into his chest, meeting warmth and fresh-snapped pine...freshly tilled earth. I mumbled there, "She wants to continue that conversation tonight."

He rubbed my back. "I'll be here, if you'd like."

"No." I shook my head. "I'm not coming back up here every time. I only did so because I was desperate to find more answers.

She can use her power to speak to me in our rooms where it's cozy and warm."

He grunted in approval and we stood there for a few minutes, both thinking hard, but both relaxed in each other's arms.

"She can't have them, Rev."

"She won't. We'll figure something out. We're getting good at that. I'll have the channelers search in the Iumenta Conduit Hall."

"I'll write to Figuerah. Maybe she can get a letter to us before she arrives in two months."

"Let's focus on what we can do. We can search for answers. We can watch them closely. We certainly won't bring them back to the Blight again."

I nodded, my cheek still pressed to his chest. I would stay there for days if he'd let me.

"We can keep training. I tried to answer Philius's questions as best I could, but he said he had some just for you."

"Of course he did," I mumbled into his shirt.

"Karus,"—he lifted my chin with his fingers, sliding a thumb across my lip—"it's time for you to take the trials. If anything, your training is just a formality. We both know you'll get through these trials with ease. Once they're through,"—he cleared his throat—"you can move on to other…conduit things."

I nodded, not really wanting to think about the conduit trials, my body warming under his touch.

"I mean it, Karus. I'm setting them up this week. They'll be ready in two. I need you to take over some of the channeler training in that time."

I moved my hands from around his waist to press them to his hard chest. "I can do that for you, Baron Revich." The promise slid from my lips, low and suggestive, all of my anger and worry suddenly gone under what I chose to call mine.

His chest moved beneath my fingers in a rumble. "What else can you do for me?"

I reached for his flask, shaking its contents and finding it full. I backed away to the staircase that led down to the first floor.

He followed as he watched, black eyes filling with blue.

"Follow me and find out."

~

"Keep looking—that's too broad."

"It's all I can find."

I slipped off the golden bannister on the first floor of Viridis. I'd tasked Philius with helping me find a book in the Iumenta Conduit Hall specifically about lumens. I shoved the last bite of the beef pastry I'd snagged from the kitchens into my mouth and dusted my hands together.

I took *Creatures of Legend* from his hand and flipped to the chapter on lumens, showing him without a word that it was shortened to half a page. I'd read the book before and knew it wasn't what we needed.

"When you search Viridis for something in particular," I said, laying the book on the floor and patting it gently. It disappeared and slid back into place a few rows down, "you want to hold onto that thought tightly. Close your eyes and think. What do you really need to know? There are thousands of books here. Almost all the knowledge of the isle is at your fingertips. You just need to ask."

He paused. "We need to know about the magic in lumens."

"Right…keep going."

"We need to know how they make connections to their riders, how they can communicate."

"You're on the right track. Go ahead—ask." I smiled, waiting.

"Out loud?"

"No, no. Here." I took his hand and placed it on the shelf. "Let Viridis know what you need and let it guide you."

He looked doubtful, but did as he was told, closing his eyes and slowly slipping over books and verdant hanging vines. He found the end of the shelf and started on the next one down. He stopped when his fingertips hit a book pushed slightly forward.

"*Magical Creatures and Their Power: How Felgren Feeds its Fauna.*"

"Perfect," I praised. "Start there. I'll keep looking for something else."

Philius sat against the bannister, opening the book to begin skimming its pages. He still hadn't asked me anything about what he felt at the Blight, so I waited for him to begin that conversation when he was ready.

I tilted my head, my eyes darting over the spines in this section. It was fairly well-off compared to some of the other floors. Some halls of books had become shadowed remnants of where the Blight had grown over their surface.

I paused at the bloom of jasmine, white and pink blossoms falling over the top shelf to greet me. I leaned in to smell them, appreciating Viridis correctly. They began to grow, trailing down to fall upon a book second from the bottom floor shelf. I reached down and pulled the thin book out, reading aloud, "*The Moon-Callers of Felgren Forest* by Conduit Dynah Elspon".

"Moon-Callers?" Philius asked, still skimming his book.

"Wolves," I answered under my breath.

I opened the book, seeing the table of contents containing subjects such as *Lumen Magic* and *Great Communicators*. Once again, Viridis had provided me with exactly what I'd needed.

"Thank you," I whispered, grinning when a warm breeze swept past me.

I sat down next to him, folding my legs underneath me and opened the book to the introduction.

"I do not write to write well. I write this book to inform future conduits. That is all."

I laughed. I'd never read a conduit manuscript that had started like that. I flipped to *Lumen Magic*.

"I have studied lumens since the day I got here. These beautiful wolves should be studied by more channelers for their magic. When a lumen is born, the mother brings her pup (only one is born at a time unlike wolves outside of Felgren) to the Great Stream. I don't know why it is called the Great Stream. That name is simple compared to the fantastical names of things throughout Felgren. I am now realizing I am off topic."

I laughed again.

"Is it a humorous book?" Philius mumbled.

"It is actually, but I don't think she meant it to be."

I continued on.

"When her mother brings her pup to the stream, she holds their head in her jaws and bathes it in the water. I have seen this happen myself once while I was here (lumen pups are rare) and have read reference to this in some other books in Viridis.

After my research, I've concluded this is done to help the pup grow in magic. The water of the Great Stream is full of magic and power. I have bathed in it myself and drank its water, feeling stronger with both. I do not recommend bathing in the water unless it is summer or you will freeze your—"

"Philius!"

I glanced up from my book to see Rell and Renn tumbling up the stairs. They rushed to us, giggling as they continuously were, and stopped to catch their breath.

"Yes?" he asked with a smirk.

"All the channelers are getting together to visit Ilyenna and Talon. Mychael is bringing some of his soup and we're bringing these." Rell held out a bouquet of purple and white iris.

"And why are we visiting Ilyenna and Talon?" he asked, closing his book.

"Ilyenna's with child!" Renn burst.

He looked to me and I nodded.

Rising from the floor, he stretched his arms over his head, handing me his book. "Okay, what can I bring?"

"I don't know," Rell stated, shrugging.

"How about some wine for Talon? You know, to celebrate?" Renn smiled wide, sprouting dimples on her freckled cheeks.

"Did you come to find me just to see if I had some wine to share?" He crossed his arms, no doubt remembering what it was like to be twenty.

Rell gasped in mock surprise. "Why, we would never. How could you even ask us that?"

"So, do you?" Renn asked again, practically bouncing on the balls of her feet.

Philius laughed and began to walk with them. "Let's go see, shall we?"

"Not too much, Philius!" I called after them, wondering if I should intervene.

I decided not to. I wasn't Baron of Felgren after all. They were allowed to have some fun.

I skimmed over the rest of the lumen magic chapter. The author admitted there wasn't much research on how they got to be the size they became or how they had become so intelligent.

But the Great Stream was something to try. If it imbued magic into the lumens as pups, perhaps it could break a magical connection to the Blightress. It was worth looking into.

I stood and stretched myself, patting both books to return to their places on the shelves and finding my feet taking me to the Origins of Felgren section, fifth level to the west.

I pulled on the book I wanted, *Legends of the Blightress: A Collection of Tales Passed Down Through Centuries* by Layngden Roper, and found the page I needed to read again.

"If not ye wish to be dead out of the gates of Hyrythiah, wander not to the north of the cytydel where She blackens all life and styls all brything from thy chest. Her wryath consumes all after the fall of Felgryn from her arms and thy Bayron sayved us from Her eyvil."

I remembered reading this passage years ago in my channeler studies. I couldn't seem to move past the idea that a Baron, the first Baron in fact, "saved us from her evil".

Having met her myself, I could believe it, but something still tugged on me not to. I flipped the pages, again finding more of what I wanted.

"Without anger, She laughed in mirth.
*   Without love, She left them bleeding.*
*   Without hope, She walks the earth.*

Without fear, Her heart is fleeting."

I could pour myself into every line of that piece of lore, spoken down through the centuries in the Attatok Mountains, and still I would feel I could never really solve it. Was it so simple that to rid the land of her heart that fuels the Blight, we must give her nothing to fear? What exactly *did* she fear?

I rubbed my face, pinching the bridge of my nose, frustrated that everything was so complicated. Everything had an answer that I had to dig for. Nothing was open, and honest, and obvious, and real.

That wasn't entirely true.

Revich was all of those things and would continue to hold me like the sky he was and had promised to be all those years ago.

I closed the book and replaced it on the shelf.

I'd ask her tonight. When she called out to me, I'd listen as I said, but I was still too curious by far not to wonder at her origins as the Blightress. I just hoped I had the patience to shut my mouth and listen.

~

"Dammit." Blood swelled on the pad of my finger and I put it to my lips.

"Careful now," Rev eyed me over his book with amusement.

"I just haven't done this in a while," I murmured, checking on my wound from the small needle I had threaded.

The fire crackled and popped, warming our room as we sat in our chairs—mine the pillowy blue, his, the stiff black. My bare feet were tucked under his open legs, right where they belonged, and I wiggled my toes to get his attention again.

He glanced up over his book, *To Train a Conduit: A History of the Conduit Trials* by Thalia Lighton, and quirked a brow.

"How many times have you read that?" I tilted my head, avoiding my current task.

"Four."

I nodded, pushing the needle through the silky, light blue swath of fabric. I had promised Ilyenna that I would gather supplies and start her growth band for her, also promising to teach her how to embroider each moon.

We guessed she was a little over her first month of growing her child. Lia had been more than helpful, letting me use her box of thread and needles, also helping me cut and prepare fabric for the band that would tie around Ilyenna's waist until her child was born.

"Would you read it to me?" I asked sweetly, my mind trying to wander elsewhere. I wanted more distraction while waiting for the Blightress to call.

Rev smiled, pulling my chair closer and tucking my feet further underneath him. "I'd love to," he began with a wink.

My grin bloomed across my face, my heart skipping at least one beat whenever he did that.

He cleared his throat, reading, "The lapis trial is known as the most difficult. I would assume this is because it is rarely passed, as most channelers hone the power of health, animals, or plants instead of stone. I myself am a lapis conduit, and therefore, I do not quite understand this struggle, but this is how it has been proposed to me: the lapis trial is impossible to complete without adept lapis magic.

"The other trials can be passed, even if that channeler is not particularly interested in following that magic. For example, a medicus adept channeler can still pass the iumenta trial, but may perhaps still choose to apprentice as a healer. No such luck is had with the lapis trial, which is always the second trial each channeler goes through."

I interrupted his reading, pulling silvery thread up through the fabric. "Did Clairannia and Figuerah pass the lapis trial?"

"No."

I frowned. "It really must be difficult then. I would have thought they had passed them all."

"Mostly," he replied. "Clairannia passed the medicus and iumenta. She struggled with the agricola and gave up on the lapis."

"And Figuerah?"

He shrugged. "She passed all of the other three."

I set my embroidery in my lap and stretched my arms over my head. "Have you trained any channelers who have passed the lapis trial?"

"No, but I was hoping Ilyenna would."

"To help in the Hallow Marshes?"

He nodded, holding his place in the book with his thumb and flipping through some of the pages.

I watched the flames flicker and dance, wondering how many of the trials I'd be able to pass. I didn't feel particularly influenced by any stone but the rhyzolm. But I remembered the Blightress's implication that I held strong magic of all four types of conduits.

Rev cleared his throat and continued reading. "If the lapis trial is ever passed, the conducting Baron usually insists on that new conduit following that line of magic, due to the scarcity of it.

"I myself have apprenticed a few lapis conduits in my life and have helped in the opening of several gold and silver mines near the Attatok Mountains, also finding quarries of gems throughout Arcaynen before deciding to pursue other passions."

"I thought this was a conduit memoir," I mentioned, almost finished with the first half of the moon on the band.

"It is, I believe."

"But she speaks as if she wrote this years after she left Felgren. I thought conduits wrote their memoirs just before they left."

He flipped back to the beginning of the book. "It's dated as being written two-hundred years ago. She must have wanted to write something to add to Viridis later in her life."

I gave a sound of acknowledgment. "Did Clairannia and Figuerah write one?"

"No. Not yet at least. They spent a lot of their time researching ways to return your memories, and all of us got a bit side-tracked for quite a while in their training." He gave me a weak smile. "They've both assured me they intend to finish the memoirs they've started, though."

I sighed, looking up to our stone ceiling, wishing once again that I could change the past.

Rev rubbed the back of my calf and continued reading. "The

amount of time a Baron must place into preparing the lapis trial is greater than the other three. This is because a Baron himself often does not possess much of the skill needed to prepare the task that the channeler must face in this trial."

I interrupted again, "You obviously contain lapis magic. Have you struggled setting up this trial?"

"No, but I see why it would be difficult to."

"Is there any trial you had difficulty preparing?" I bit my lip, my curiosity distracting all other thoughts as I listened to him talk about his life as Baron. Something I wished I hadn't missed.

He rubbed his neck in thought. "The first four I did for Clairannia and Figuerah were all…strenuous to complete. Usually, the Baron in training prepares them with the help of their mentor, but that obviously did not happen. I enlisted the help of anyone I could. Both Pompeii and Lia worked with me to prepare them. And I didn't want to ask Clairannia and Figuerah to help in making their own trials, but they both insisted, and I lost that argument. It was… a difficult time."

I swallowed, understanding exactly why. He'd given the trials to Clairannia and Figuerah when I had been lost to time for over a year. No mentor, no lover who could remember him. I shuddered, thinking again of what his life must have been like.

I watched his face fall as he laid his head back against the chair, eyes closed, squeezing my ankle as if grounding himself to me, unwilling to let me go.

I set my work to the floor and climbed into his lap, placing the little green ribbon of fabric that marked his place into the book and set it down on the floor.

I straddled him, tucking my knees on either side of his hips and pressed my chest to his, holding the sides of his face.

I kissed him once with a gentle press of my lips. "Rev," I spoke softly, letting all of his pain into me through our bond, "take me with you. Don't leave me out here to live through this on your own. I come down that dark path with you, remember?"

His eyes flashed open in black pools of torment as they flickered over my face rapidly, as if he was assuring himself I was truly there.

"Where are you?" I smoothed his dark waves from his forehead. "Tell me what you're remembering."

He tightened his grip at my waist and spoke softly, "I tried so many times to speak to you." He bit down on his lips, squinting at me as tears brimmed in his eyes. "That day, the day they both would take the trials, I panicked. If they passed them as I knew they would, they would leave and another avenue of you returning to yourself would be gone. I didn't care who woke you, I just wanted you back." His voice cracked and he swallowed. "When channelers take their trials, the Baron cannot be there with them. He cannot assist them in any way. They take at least half a day to complete, so I wandered the forest that day, hoping to calm myself down." He looked past me, his eyes staring at the wall.

I brushed my thumb across his cheek, waiting for him to continue. When he didn't, I kissed him again, bringing him back to me. "Where did you go?" I whispered.

He closed his eyes again, furrowing his brows in remembrance. "To the muddy lake. The one where I used to find mudcopper fish for Heimlen."

He shook his head. The eyes that flashed back to me were dark, slipping a dagger into my heart as he spoke, a tear sliding down his cheek. "You were there. You were standing on the edge of the water with Moira, a long stick in your hand, swirling it in the mud like you knew. As if somehow, somewhere inside of your mind, you knew there were fish in that lake. And when I called your name, you smiled. It was the first one I'd seen in over a year."

He pressed a hand to my cheek. "But your face fell the moment your eyes locked on mine. The moment you saw me there at the edge of the lake, you were gone again, and I had to leave you. I knew what came next. The panic, the unstable breathing, sometimes screaming. I didn't want to leave you, but I'd only hurt you further if I stayed."

I sought the strength to reply, finding what I needed in my rage of what was done, not to me, but to him. I sniffed and wiped at his cheek, declaring, "I would give up every *single* thread of my power to save you from this." I tapped his chest over his heart, my lips trembling to release my words. "I know I can't and I know you wouldn't agree, but if I could give up my magic to go back, I would. Immediately, I would." I pressed my forehead to his. "I cannot do this for you. No one can. So I will stay with you instead. For as long as you need, I will stay right here with you. I will hold you, I will kiss you, I will remind you that I am not lost. That I am *not* leaving. That I love you, that I am yours." I kissed him gently, whispering above his lips, "I promise, Rev, you will never go through that again."

Wordlessly, he met my mouth, saying more with his kiss than he could by speaking. Sending love, and relief, and need straight to me. I welcomed all of it in to settle, blooming over my soul in that ever-present reminder of the lifeline held taut between us that had been growing for years and strengthened with each day.

Her voice came in the middle of the night.

"Are you there, Little Sprout?"

My eyes shot open, and I raised my head from where it had been nestled over Revich's arm and tucked into his shoulder.

His breathing was deep, undisturbed by my movement. I considered leaving the bed and speaking with the Blightress away from him. But I had asked him to take me with him. I had asked that we go down our dark roads together, and so I stayed, wrapping my leg and arm over him, pressing my cheek to his chest.

He adjusted his arm in his sleep to wrap around me, and I answered silently, *"Yes, I am here."* I watched the rise and fall of Revich's breathing, my eyes adjusting to the dim glow of the fire we left burning each night.

There was a pause, and I searched for our connection, thinking she or I had let it go before I heard in my mind, *"Something has happened. Will you tell me what it is?"*

I wasn't sure if she meant Ilyenna, and I certainly wasn't going to tell her about that, so I answered, *"What makes you think something has happened?"*

"Your power has grown. Something has fueled it since this afternoon."

I actually grinned, lifting my head to look at Rev, his face turned to the side, deep in slumber. I remembered the way he had loved me on the rug in front of our fireplace just hours before. I remembered how he kissed me, held me, worshiped every curve of my body before I'd done the same to him.

No, I was not at all surprised my power had grown since this afternoon.

I settled myself back onto his chest and returned, *"It's nothing you need to know about."*

I could hear her chuckle. *"A secret you'd like to keep?"*

"I keep all my secrets from you. You do not get any of them."

"I'm sure there are a few I could dig around to find."

"Don't. Don't even try. You want me to actually listen to you during these talks? Then you should actually speak about what you feel is necessary to tell me."

"I see you are still unwilling to speak to me calmly."

"You see correctly."

"You try my patience, child."

"And you mine, so continue. I'd like to get back to sleep."

"Alright, Karus, I'll start with this. I once loved a man who betrayed me and was the cause of our child's death."

My blood chilled, and a shiver crept up my spine to the back of my neck, an unwelcome heightened sense of dread sitting low in my stomach.

I cleared my throat, even though I was not speaking aloud. *"I'm listening."*

"Before I tell you this story, tell me what you know of my beginnings."

"Only what you yourself have told me. And there's a book with one small passage about you residing in the north, stealing people's breath after the fall of Felgren from your arms…"

"Is there more?"

"It mentions that Baron Adaynth saved Hyrithia and the forest from your wrath."

Maniacal laughter filled my head before, *"Is that really the story he gave them? I should not be surprised. He was always one for making himself into the hero. I myself am evidence of falling to the trap of believing him to be."*

I hesitated, wanting to ask more questions, unsure if it was a good idea. *"You loved him? You loved the first Baron?"*

"I loved him before he called himself Baron, yes. As I told you, we grew up together in Felgren. I loved him before he had any power, as I held all of it."

"Held all of what?"

"Power. Magic. I was the first wielder on the isle."

My breath caught and I licked my lips. *"You're saying you were the first channeler?"*

"As Visalia, I channeled nothing, for I was the first on the isle to have magic."

Revich stirred, turning toward me, and I accommodated his body with mine, attempting to dampen my racing heart to avoid waking him.

"That's your true name. Visalia."

"It is. Or at least it was the one I was given at birth. I do not mind being called the Blightress. It suits me well enough."

"You say you were the first one with magic. Did you take your power from Felgren like the rest of us?"

"No, Little Sprout. I gave my power to Felgren."

Revich's eyes flashed open. He blinked, watching me stare at his chin, my forehead creased in comprehension of what she was telling me.

"Is she speaking to you?" he whispered.

I nodded and sat up, continuing in my mind, *"You're saying the power in Felgren came from you?"* I shook my head and scoffed as Revich pulled himself up with me, taking my trembling hand. *"I don't believe you."*

"And why is that, Karus? Do you think I lie to you now in the dead of night during the little time you give me to tell you my story? That I seek to manipulate you into believing Felgren was born from me? For what purpose? Why would I choose that lie?"

"Are you alright?" Revich murmured, slipping the thin strap of my nightgown back up onto my shoulder.

"Yes," I whispered to him, my voice dry. I coughed and he moved to pour a glass of water from his bedside table.

"I don't know why you'd lie about this, but I do believe you're capable of it."

"I'd rather you believe me, but whether you do or not, it remains true. I was born with great power that Arcaynen had never seen before, and I chose to share it because I was a fool. I shared it with the forest I loved, the sister I loved, and the man I loved."

I gulped water from Revich's cup. *"Prove it. Find a way to prove that what you say is true, and then I'll believe you."*

"You will not like how I prove this to you."

"Try me."

"My sister can confirm the truth. Someone you already trust."

"Your sister still lives? Just as ancient as you?" I wrapped my arms around Revich's neck as his swept over my back. I would cling to him as my lifeline as I tried to understand exactly what the Blightress was saying.

"She was given some of my power, so yes, she lives, just as ancient as me."

I settled myself into Revich's lap, my face pressed to his neck, holding him tightly. *"Give me her name then."*

"Thalia was the name given to her at birth. Now, she now goes by another, and I believe you know her for her cinnamon buns."

CHAPTER 60

REV

Karus chewed on her bottom lip, her arms folded across her chest, one leg over the other at the knee with her foot jostling up and down. She stared across the kitchen at the dough tucked into a cold tray for Lia's morning cinnamon buns.

I had never paid much attention to Lia's magic. I'd assumed she was simply a channeler, brought to the Fortress to train, but not passing the conduit trials, had stayed to use her magic as the Fortress cook.

I had not guessed she was the sister of an ancient, evil woman who not only plagued my forest, but plagued my love, and threatened our home.

I paced, eyeing all of her tools, all of her stone slabs and gold utensils, coming to the conclusion that by not paying more attention, I had not figured out that she used lapis magic in her cooking.

"It's a bit early for you two to be up and about." Lia's voice came through the door to the servant's quarters.

I turned from studying the stone oven to address her, tossing the book in my hands across the counter. "Lia, we need to talk."

She read the title, *To Train a Conduit: A History of the Conduit Trials,* and sighed heavily. She bundled her thick, black hair back into a knot at the top of her head, a dark contrast to her pale skin, and picked up the book. "How do you know about this?"

"The book you wrote as Thalia Lighton or the fact that you're Visalia's sister?" Karus asked indignantly.

"She told you?" Lia shook her head, closed her grey eyes, and raised her brows. "That was not her secret to tell. Though, I'm not surprised. Why did she tell you this?"

"Lia, are you working with the Blightress? Are you helping her in any way?" I doubted it, but I needed to ask.

She huffed and moved to her tray of cold dough, lightly touching the round pastry and then whispering a spell to the metal tray to begin to warm it. "Of course not. I have not spoken to my sister in five hundred years. I am simply the cook in the Fortress."

"You are much more than that." Karus rose from the small table and came to Lia's side. "You have lived for how long, Lia? You're a lapis conduit? A powerful one?" She shook her head. "I don't think you're malicious at all. I think you're hiding."

"I am not hiding, I am merely living. I have done great things, seen terrible things. I just want to feed people and be left to live."

I cleared my throat, shoving my hands in my pockets to feel the rhyzolm. I'd never once used it to gain knowledge of Lia's power, but it hummed now in my palm as I faced her and said, "We don't wish to change that, but we ask for your help. The Blightress insists on telling Karus her story through their connection. Is it true she gave her magic to Felgren? To you?"

Her shoulders dropped and she bent her head. "Go sit down, both of you. I'll make us a nice cup of tea and something quick to eat, and we'll get this out of the way. I won't talk about my past on an empty stomach."

Karus frowned at me, and I shrugged one shoulder.

She slumped over the table, her chin in her hand, her fingers drumming on the surface while she gazed out the window at the smallest sliver of sun peeking over the earth.

I clasped my hands in front of me, watching Lia put things together. She set down a kettle, three cups, and a plate of dried meat along with Karus's favorite cheese.

Lia handed each of us a plate, pouring tea into our cups and taking her own bits of food, chewing on a strip of bacon and sitting back in her chair, staring out the window.

Once she had finished, she look a long sip of tea and a deep breath. Neither Karus nor I touched any of the food or tea, both waiting to hear her story.

"Visalia was born five years before me. By then, our parents were touting her around our village in the forest as a show, having her perform bits of magic here and there, using her to make money curing ailments and growing crops. Before I came along, she had no one to love, and I think that's why she took such a protective role in my life. She hoped I'd grow to love her, and I did."

She took another sip of tea, and I glanced to Karus, watching her struggle not to speak—to ask the many questions I myself wanted to say.

"We were inseparable, Visalia, Adaynth, and I. We did everything together in the spare time our mother and father gave her. She'd show off for us, too, of course, and we loved it. We'd spend time in the forest running among the trees, swimming in the stream. She told us one day she would give some of her power to the forest so that it could live with us, it could play as we did. And one day, she did it.

"She came home that morning exhausted, covered in dirt, waking me in my bed to tell me what she'd done. And so, Felgren lived. The first true channeler was born not long after that."

"So people were able to pull from the magic of the forest?" Karus asked, adding sugar to her cup.

"From what I know of it, I believe Visalia woke the forest. It became its own living thing, had its own soul. At that point, she did not control any of it and my guess is that the forest chooses those it gives power to." She shrugged again, as if this was all something simple to discuss over early morning tea.

Karus continued, sipping her own, "What about you? What about Adaynth?"

"Adaynth I know less about. I was not there when he convinced her to share some of her power with him. And I did not ask her to share it with me, if that's your next question." Lia took a bite of cheese and chewed. "Visalia was afraid of being alone. She told me she was going to live forever and that I had to, too. She couldn't imagine living without me. So, one night when I was twelve and she was seventeen, she gave me some of her power. It formed as lapis magic, and I've wielded it ever since."

"But how, Lia?" Karus asked, pleading in her voice. "*How* did she give it to you? She says mine also comes from her, but how?"

Karus's knee jostled under the table, rocking it slightly. I reached out and opened my hand for her to take. She did, stopping her rocking and inhaling through her nose with me, exhaling out of her mouth.

Lia's eyes darted back and forth between us, and she hid a smile under her cup. "To be honest, I don't know how she did it. I don't know how she does anything with her magic, really. It's not like mine. It wasn't like Adaynth's. Though…" she trailed off, watching me for realization.

I gritted my teeth and squeezed Karus's hand. "She gave Adaynth the power of Baron."

"She did. And it has passed down from one Baron to the next over centuries, settling from one man to the other."

I watched Karus. She didn't know I was working on the Baron trial, and I wondered if I should just tell her. Perhaps it was just a stupid tradition that the next Baron could not know they were being considered for the Baronship.

I kept quiet instead. I wasn't willing to risk it. I wanted her to be given the choice—one of the only things I felt I really could give her, was this. I could give her love and a happy life, but I also wanted to give her the choice of wielding the Baronship with me.

"She said Baron Adaynth betrayed her and killed their child. Is that story true?" Karus interrupted my thoughts, and I looked back to Lia.

"That story is…complicated. I do not wish to tell it."

"Did you and Adaynth…" Karus trailed off, her implication clear.

"No, nothing like that. I just don't care to relive the memory this morning, and I don't think it's relevant to what you need to know."

Karus continued her barrage, "What about the heart? Do you know about the enormous heart she keeps in a cave in the north? Do you know how she has been capturing the Queen's channelers and taking their magic, returning it to her?"

Lia shook her head. "I don't know about any of those things."

"Oh! Good morning Baron Revich, Karus," Jesslyn said as she entered the kitchens. "You're up early."

"Start on the cinnamon buns, please," Lia replied, rising from her seat. "I can answer more of your questions later. For now, I have people to feed."

Jesslyn got to work as I rubbed my face with my free hand, then snagged a piece of bacon.

Pompeii entered the kitchens, and to my surprise, Mychael followed. Not even attempting to suppress a grin, I sat back in my chair and chewed, watching Mychael kiss his cheek and leave, avoiding both of our gazes.

Karus caught my eye, biting her lips as Pompeii joined us at the table. His black hair, littered with gray, was pulled neatly into a bun at the back of his head. His golden eyes were lined in kohl as usual, which complimented his olive skin. "What is on the agenda today, Baron Revich? More trial preparation?"

I leaned in, just enough so Karus could still hear. "Are we not talking about *that*, Pompeii?" I nodded toward the door Mychael had just left.

His lips twitched and tilted upward. "I like him. He makes me smile. And he makes good soup."

Karus burst out laughing, unable to hide her excitement. "He won your heart with soup!" She covered her mouth with her hands as more servants entered the kitchens to begin their day.

"He has not won my heart, Karus, I just like him."

"It's alright, Pompeii. I think Karus has a crush on him, too," I teased.

She gasped and threw her napkin at me. "I do not! I can just see how handsome he is, that's all."

"Something anyone with working eyes can see," Pompeii murmured under his breath.

She looked across the table at me, shaking her head and heaving a heavy sigh. "Well, I'll leave you two to your trial preparation today. I have some channelers to train." She rose from the table and walked around it to kiss me goodbye, holding onto me longer than usual.

I didn't let go first.

"Meet me in Viridis for lunch?" she asked.

I nodded, and she left, giving Lia one last furrowed glance.

I leaned forward on the table, rubbing my face.

"She'll be ready." My Overseer saw right through my facade, and I wondered if he guessed about the Baron trial.

I set my eyes on him, my hand over my mouth in a frown. "I know she will be. She probably could've passed these trials the first day she entered Felgren."

He took another bite and poured himself some tea, nodding. "She'll make a great conduit." He rose a brow at me.

I sighed and drained my cup.

"The first two trials are prepared?" he continued.

"Three. Only the agricola trial is left."

"Ah. It almost seems pointless, doesn't it? All that work and she'll breeze through each, especially that one."

"She wants to prove she can. She wants to be treated like any other channeler and given the chance to prove she can become a conduit."

"She is much more than that."

"I know," I agreed, now convinced he knew I was working on more than just those four trials. I was glad he didn't ask me. I'd have to lie. "I just want to give her the choice."

CHAPTER 61

KARUS

Rain splattered my cheeks in the late spring downpour. Parvus was not particularly great-smelling when he ran in the rain, but he was getting wet where we were headed anyway.

Moira flew in front of us, skillfully dodging some of the fatter droplets. Six channelers rode behind me.

Ilyenna and Talon followed at a slower pace in the rear. Ilyenna insisted she was well enough and early enough on to be able to ride a walking lumen to the Great Stream. I agreed with her, though Talon moped, insisting she ride one of the oldest and slowest lumens.

Rauca ran beside Parvus, no rider on her back, and she sprang over log after log with ease. I'd found only a few curled vines around her tail this morning.

Parvus, however, was now sporting what looked like black seed pods from his inner hind legs.

"I hear it!" Moira yelled in front of us, over the sound of pounding feet. "We're almost to the stream!"

I looked behind me to check on the four channelers keeping pace. Rell and Renn were hunched down low, giddy grins on their faces as their lumens bounded forward. Mychael held a similar stance with a smirk on his lips.

Philius, however, looked practically green, the night's celebrations for the coming baby hitting him hardest, and I rolled my eyes.

He claimed to be too hungover to come with us, and I claimed if he didn't, he'd be sent to be Pompeii's personal assistant the rest of the day.

We arrived at the bank of the stream, and the rush of water hit my ears as Parvus slowed. It was less a stream and more of a raging river—Great indeed.

I pulled my hair from my face, tying it back and hopping down from Parvus. As the four channelers stopped as well, I addressed them. "Baron Revich would like you to feed your lumens today."

They looked at me in question.

"Feed them what?" asked Rell, petting her lumen's head.

I shrugged, remembering this task years ago. "Whatever they'll eat. The point is, you don't leave until they are full."

Baron Revich had led Clairannia, Figuerah, and myself to the middle of the forest during our training, giving the same few instructions.

This was an iumenta magic challenge, and it had not taken Figuerah long to catch and kill a quiphit for her lumen while Clairannia and I scrambled to find something our lumens would actually eat.

Revich and I had decided we could combine this lesson with what I wanted to try for Parvus and Rauca, taking the channelers to the Great Stream while he worked on the conduit trials.

"How do we catch something for them to eat? We didn't bring weapons." Mychael looked out at the raging stream and then down to his lumen.

"Your magic is your weapon. Find a way to catch some meat and your lumen will eat."

Philius slid down from his lumen, running to a bush to be sick.

"As soon as your lumen has filled their belly, you may go, and the rest of your time before lunch is yours."

That set Rell and Renn into action, and they set out between the trees with masses of red curls bouncing along.

Mychael walked up to the stream and bent down to peer into the water.

Philius continued to be sick.

When Talon and Ilyenna finally arrived, I filled them in, adding, "Talon, you cannot find something for Ilyenna's lumen."

"I can do it myself," she said.

"I know you can, but I also know he'll try to help you."

He frowned and helped her down.

"You go that way, I'll go this," she ordered.

"Don't go far," he muttered, reluctantly turning away from her.

She put her hands on her hips and watched him leave. Her blonde curls fell into her bright blue eyes, and she brushed them away, huffing. "He's become overprotective. I hate it."

"Don't be *too* hard on him. You've only just bonded as companions and now he has two lives to worry about. I'm sure he'll settle down soon when it becomes more routine."

She sighed and stretched her back. "Can you meet with me tonight after dinner? For an embroidery lesson?"

"Of course. I'd love to. I've started your first moon, so you can finish it. You're going to love the color of the band. It matches your eyes."

She blushed, red rising to her pale, slightly freckled cheeks. "I'd better get on with it. Do lumens eat fowl?"

"Yes. But I'll give you a hint. I said you needed to feed your lumen. I didn't say you had to kill anything yourself, but if you lead your lumen to a quiphit burrow or she happens to catch a flock of geese,"—I shrugged—"she'll be full, won't she? The trick is helping her catch them. That's where the iumenta magic comes in."

"I'll do my best. Thank you, Karus." She turned to leave, giving a wide birth to Philius who sunk against a tree, pressing on his temples.

I looked around for Moira, finding her flying above the raging waters, sticking her hand in the stream and laughing at the spray.

"Don't let it sweep you in, Moira! I'm not coming in there to fetch you out!" I called across the rush.

She laughed in her tinkling, light way and dove.

"Moira!" I ran to the water's edge, both Parvus and Rauca beside me watching where she went under. Cursing under my breath, I pulled off my boots, tossing them to the side of the bank and took two steps into the water before she shot above the surface, now naked and laughing at me.

"That was not funny. I was ready to dive in after you and probably drown."

"I thought it was very funny, Karusss." She spoke my name in that mocking way, a reminder that she and I were very different creatures.

"How did you manage to not get swept away?" I folded my arms and stepped back up onto the shore.

"I asked the stream not to."

"Oh, it's that simple, is it?" I chortled.

"It is if you're fae," she replied, diving back in again.

I huffed, looking down to Parvus. "What about you, handsome? Do you think you can swim in this?"

He looked up at me in his usual wolfish grin, giant tongue hanging out of his mouth before he sniffed the water's edge and whined.

"I know. It sure is fast. I don't know how Rauca bathed you in this as a pup." I patted her head.

Moira surfaced again and flew in circles above the water.

At least it had stopped raining.

"They won't go in," I stated bluntly, unsure if I could convince them with magic.

"Why don't you just calm the stream, Karus?" Philius asked behind me, wiping his mouth of spit.

"I don't know how to do that."

"I bet you can though," he replied, raising a brow at Moira who was now digging her feet just above the surface of the water, causing it to splash up over her sage body.

"Sure, I'll just wade in there and tell it to calm down so my lumens can take a bath."

He shrugged. "Okay."

I pursed my lips and stepped back into the water, unsure if I could really calm a river. That sounded like something a Baron could do, not me. I didn't even know what kind of magic that would fall under.

I held my hands above the surface, closed my eyes, and steadied my breathing. I thought of calm waters, of still streams, gently gliding over smooth stones. I peeked one eye open. Nothing changed.

"It's not working. Maybe I need to go farther out." I took another few steps, soaking my skirts up to my waist, my feet finding a hold on the slippery rocks below.

It was freezing. I knew exactly what Dynah had meant in that book about lumens. I tried again, thinking of calm, peaceful water.

Nothing but raging waves came over me, jostling me in place.

"It was worth a try, but I just don't have that kind of magic, Philius."

I began to wade back to the shore and slipped.

It happened so fast, I didn't comprehend it had happened at all. One moment my head was above the surface, the next it was under, water filling my mouth and nose as the rest of me tumbled through the rush, and I lost my way to the surface.

I only heard the gush of water as I tried to reach for something —anything to grab ahold of so I could find my bearings and take another breath.

The water swept me away quickly, carrying me downstream. My head finally breached the surface for a precious moment before I fell under again. The rage of water in my ears muted for a moment as it pushed me over a ledge, and I fell fast and deep to the bottom of the riverbed. My head cracked against something hard, and I fell limp, my lungs screaming for air, my head struggling to form thoughts.

It needed it to stop.

I knew that much.

The stream, the water, the rush and power, the heaviness that pushed me down needed to stop. I wanted it all to *stop*.

I opened my eyes, coughing, the sweet intake of cold, wet air filling my lungs before I heaved and more water left them. Large round stones, covered in algae sat nestled into their riverbed, suddenly exposed to the open air, just as I was.

I coughed again and continuously, watching water and blood drip down onto my hands as I felt for the gash at my temple.

"Karus!" Mychael was at my side, sloshing through what was left of the stream to get to me, grabbing my shoulders to look at my face. "Can you hear me?"

I nodded slightly, the movement painful.

"We need to move. Can you walk? It doesn't matter." He pulled me up, bending and lifting my soaking wet body over his shoulder, running to the shore.

He helped me down gently, the other channelers and Moira at my side. Philius brushed over my wound with the sleeve of his shirt, then ripped a piece with his teeth and pressed it to my head.

I turned and coughed again, somehow more water spilling from my lungs.

"Karus, where are you right now?" Mychael asked somewhere in front of me.

"At—at the Great Stream." I managed, blinking slowly, shivering before Philius's shirt covered me.

"What time of day is it?" he asked next, taking Talon's shirt and wrapping it around my legs, rubbing them up and down to warm my body.

I coughed, the jerking of my torso sending sharp pains to my head. "Morning."

I saw him nod, the twinkling of Moira's wings next to his shoulder.

"And what just happened to you?" he continued.

"I…I slipped and got carried away by the stream. I don't know how I'm not dead."

I heard Moira's giggle as she landed on my chest. "I know. Look!"

She pointed behind her back to the water. I lifted myself onto my elbows, squinting at the stream's edge.

A massive wall of water was forming, higher and higher into the sky. The rush of the river stopped right where I had been, exposing the riverbed completely. I gazed up at the wall of continual water as it grew taller than the trees, waiting for something.

"Tell it to let go, Karus. But slowly or we're all soaked." She crawled up to my shoulder and started pulling back my dripping hair.

"I did that?" I asked to no one in particular.

"Yep," Moira answered. "I always knew there was something strange about you, Karus. From that first day I met you."

I did what she suggested and watched as the wall of water slowly flowed downstream at the bottom of the wall, more and more of it rushing over the stones I had just landed on. Then the rest of it fell in a loud slap on the surface and the stream continued as if nothing had happened at all.

"I don't understand. I didn't use any magic to do that."

She laughed, the chiming of it hurting my ears. "You didn't need magic, Karus. You just did what any other powerful fae can do. You asked it to stop."

CHAPTER 62

REV

She was just wading there, waist-deep in the stream.

Her back was turned to me, her long chestnut and white hair curled, clumped and frizzy down her back as she laughed watching Parvus and Rauca swim after the stick she threw into the calm water.

She turned to me when I reached the riverbank, and her face lit into a glorious smile. Her green eyes sparkled in the late-morning sun in rendition of the glittering surface of the green-blue water.

"It's been quite a morning, R—"

I silenced her with a kiss, rushing through the water to her the moment she had smiled. The moment I assured my racing heart she was alive, she was well, she was still here.

I wrapped one arm around her waist, one hand at the back of her neck, and I did not let go.

If I let go, she could not be as safe as she was in my arms.

If I let go, harm could befall her, and then where would I be?

The raging, panicked man I had been thirty minutes ago when I was in the Baron trial, preparing the last few pieces?

Karus had almost died.

Within the span of a minute, I could feel her in Felgren and a moment later, she was struggling to breathe—her life fading in seconds.

Seconds.

Within seconds she would have been gone.

No waiting for her to return.

No easy seven years to get her back.

Gone.

"I'm okay. I'm alright. Rev, look at me."

She tried to pull herself back from my arms, which just fueled my grip. I pressed her head into the curve of my shoulder and would not let go.

If I let go, she'd look at me and say something about the fact that she was still here.

She'd assure me she was fine, as if my life hadn't just almost ended with hers.

For once, I did not want to hear her voice.

I did not want to hear her reassurance that she didn't leave me.

I just wanted to hold her body to mine and tell myself that she never would.

That whatever power brought us together would not be so cruel as to tear us apart again.

I chose to believe that.

I chose to cling to that hand of hope and hold her just a little longer.

CHAPTER 63

KARUS

I didn't say anything more.

He didn't want me to.

I'm sure Rev was tired of hearing me tell him I was fine.

I was becoming a bit irritated myself at always having to say it, apparently unable to keep out of harm's way.

So, we held each other in the now calm stream, the water moving over our legs, cold, but I kept our upper bodies warm. My green tendrils of power wove lazily around us, emitting warmth from the spell I had whispered.

His body was hard, a rigid tower of strength barely holding itself together.

I wouldn't be surprised if he produced a portal right in that moment and shoved me into some locked room where I couldn't leave, and therefore, couldn't get myself into danger—something I really seemed to have knack for.

Parvus and Rauca splashed around us, enjoying the Great Stream, though, to my disappointment, showed no improvements in their new physical features.

It had been difficult to convince the channelers to go back to the Fortress after my near-death experience, but after showing them how I could ask the stream to calm itself, they'd relented. It had helped that they assumed Revich would be here soon anyway.

Moira had told me she wouldn't be far, needing to tell the fae some things, which I assumed was faerie gossip for spreading word that a human with fae power was traversing around the Fortress, bound to the Baron.

I didn't count the minutes we stood there because they didn't seem to exist at all. Only the flow of water rippling around our bodies locked tight was evidence that the day moved forward.

I didn't mind.

Revich was my home, my place, the one I had fit into perfectly, completing my life with the love I was sure I was always meant to have.

He slowly pulled away from my chest, one arm still locked around my waist, the other still cradling my head.

"I—" he began, his eyes blue as the sea we had run through together.

I grinned, not able to show him anything but love on my face, and he pulled me back to his neck.

"No. I'm not done," he mumbled into my tangled hair.

I laughed and held him tighter. "You know," I murmured on the sandy skin of his neck, pressing my face there, kissing my way up to the line of his jaw, "I think I was made for this."

I kissed his throat as it bobbed, and he asked in a low grumble, "Made for what?"

"I think,"—my lips found his chin as he slowly loosened his grip on the back of my neck—"I think I was made to be loved…like this."

He stiffened, pulling me back to his neck again, and I sighed, not in exasperation, but in contentment.

This man loved me so fiercely, he couldn't let go, and that was not something I'd ever be tired of.

"You would have been dead." The statement came in a whisper at my ear, and I scrunched my face hearing it from him, knowing the amount of effort it took for him to admit it.

"Yes," I breathed, swallowing back the lump forming in my throat.

"You cannot die. You cannot just leave me like you almost did."

I nodded, a shiver running through me at hearing the demand in his words as if saying them aloud would force them to be true.

"If you'd just had…"

He didn't finish his thought, so I pulled myself back, confused by the fear and assurance he emitted in our bond.

"If I'd just had what?"

The stream parted around us, flowing upward into an alcove around our heads with a path leading to the shore.

I gasped in awe and delight, our water tunnel glowing with the blue light he held over his palm.

"If you'd just had me, Karus. This is the power of Baron. All of the elements of Felgren are mine to move, to shape, to call to my aid should I need it."

He pulled me through the tunnel to the shore. He let the open pathway fall and the stream returned to its great rush of water.

I no longer asked it for calm.

Parvus and Rauca shook water from their fur and nipped at their paws.

"I'm part fae," I blurted, biting my lip.

"What?" He turned me to face him.

"I don't know. I haven't let myself process what this means without you to talk it through. But Moira thinks so. When the stream swept me away, I couldn't do anything. I couldn't get to the surface, and it was moving so fast."

His face was a solid block of stone, the black of his eyes filling over the blue.

"All I could think was I wanted the stream to stop. I asked it to stop…and it did. A wall of water formed over where I was sucked under and…" I rubbed my face and mumbled into my hands, "Moira said only fae can make requests of the stream. And that by doing so and the stream listening, I am at least part fae."

I turned back to the water, hands on my wet hips. "But that

doesn't make any sense. You could manipulate the water and you're not fae." I looked over my shoulder with a sly smile. "Are you?"

"I didn't ask the stream anything. I willed it to move. There is no asking with the power of Baron. There is just doing."

"Well, fuck, I don't know then."

"You're taking the trials tomorrow."

It was my turn for surprise. "What! You said next week!"

He shook his head. "No. I'll finish tonight and you take them in the morning."

I narrowed my eyes and cocked my head. "What are you not telling me? Why are you rushing them?"

He slid his hands in his wet pockets, and I saw right through him.

"They're almost done. You should take them when they are. The magic doesn't wait around forever and pulls from me to work. It's why I couldn't produce a portal and just come to you immediately."

"And what happens after the trials?" I kept my hands on my hips, my chest meeting with his.

"We can move on from them."

"Hmm. And then what?"

He couldn't help it. He wound his arms around my back. "And then we keep living. Keep loving. We celebrate. We owe Clairannia something big."

I gave in too, wrapping my arms around his neck. "I can't wait to see her. To see Figuerah and tell them I've passed. We should have done them together, but…at least I've gotten there eventually."

He tucked my wayward hair behind my ear murmuring, "Eventually, I have learned, is far more acceptable than never."

PART FOUR

CHAPTER 64

SAELYN

I would be seventeen in one day, and I discovered I loved to dance.

Or at least, I loved to dance with Thevin.

Pah-Pah had revealed something he called a cylindrical turner, a device that played the sound of music through an enormous piece of gold shaped like a morning glory blossom.

He'd brought me an entire box of cylinders with tiny raised markings that flicked over wide, thin tines, playing notes that echoed through the golden flowerhead. He showed me how to turn the handle and music would play.

I'd never seen anything like it. Neither had Thevin when I took him to my room to show him the stunning invention.

"You pick one of these," I said, holding a gold cylinder with hundreds of raised markings, "and then you fit it in here like this." I snapped it into place, lowering the tines and turning the handle. "When it reaches a stop, you let go and listen!"

The music began to chime, fast and joyous, something my feet itched to move to. The handle began to spin backward, unwinding to play the song, and I took Thevin's hands as we spun around laughing. He twirled me around and around until I thought I'd fall, before catching me, which he seemed particularly good at, and I laughed into his warm chest.

He was at least a whole head taller than me, and I had to pull mine all the way back to really see him. A grin crossed his lips, revealing his one dimple, and his blue eyes shone bright with mischief.

I teasingly shoved him away, laughing with him and taking the cylinder from its home, pulling another one and snapping it into place before winding the handle.

The music began, soft and low.

"Oh, this one's slow," I murmured, reaching down to replace it.

He caught my arm and said, "Leave it. I like slow."

He pulled my hand to his shoulder, bent slightly to grab the other, and then placed it on the other side. He wrapped his own hands around my waist, and I gulped, my body sending a shiver through me.

I wanted him to touch me. I wanted him to bend forward and kiss me.

No.

No, I did not.

If he did, everything would change.

Like Pah-Pah had said, if we did not take risks, we would live the same. The same life we had always lived.

I wasn't sure this was a risk I was willing to take while not knowing the outcome of something blossoming between us. I was still content to stay here, never changing a thing, seeing him each day of summer and soaking in his laugh, his eyes that would twinkle in mirth, seeping into my heart to tug—jolting me from a steady heartbeat to a racing one.

"Tell me what you're thinking," he murmured, swaying us slowly around to the light tines of the song that filled my room.

"I'm thinking about the party."

He smirked. "Liar."

I shrugged, looking down as we moved slowly to the rhythm.

"Ask me." He nudged my foot with his.

"Ask you what?"

"Ask me what I'm thinking."

I huffed and rolled my eyes, doing my best to keep a ridiculously wide grin from forming on my face. "My dear friend, Thevin, what are you thinking about this very moment?"

"How beautiful you are," he returned.

No, no, no, no.

My heart pounded, furiously urging me to accept the risk it wanted to take.

I gave a small chuckle and said, "You should see my gown for the party. My mother wrote to a friend and had it specially made for—"

"I'm not talking about your gown, Sae. I'm talking about you. Right now. Right here." He lifted a hand to my face. "Like this."

I shook my head and swallowed. "Don't. Don't say that."

"I will say that. I will say it because it is true. And you should know it."

"Don't say anything else then."

"What if I want to? What if I have a lot more to say?" He grinned wickedly. "I thought you liked hearing my voice."

"Please," I begged, "stop. Stop talking like this. Nothing is going to change. I don't want *us* to change. I want to stay like this. I want to be happy here, with you, like this."

"What if there's more than this, Sae? What if I want *more* than this?"

I backed away, my arms leaving the place I wanted to stay forever, the music long since silenced. "You can't have it." I shook my head. "I won't risk losing you, Thevin. You're too important to me."

"You wouldn't be losing anything. We would gain something. Something already started that neither of us are going to stop."

"Please," I whispered, "don't."

"So, what?" He threw his arms into the air and then crossed them at his chest. "You want me to visit you every summer, and we'll dance to music and ride lumens through the trees? You'll boss me around, and I'll pretend to hate it? You'll smile at me, and I'll pretend it doesn't hurt, it doesn't pierce me and heal over, forever marking me with you no matter what I see out there? No matter how difficult the world is outside of this place?"

He chuckled and looked down at his feet, shaking his head. When he looked back up, his eyes were the brightest blue, like a lightning strike over a gray sky. "I can't do it, Sae. Don't ask me to do that because I can't. "

"You'll leave me," I whispered, my heart screaming in agony, watching him crumble and confess everything I myself wanted to say. "If it doesn't work. If you decide you can live without my smile, you'll leave, and I'll have nothing. *Nothing.* You're the best thing that feels real in my life, and I refuse to risk that. I cannot risk what you ask."

He backed up to the door, his face a picture of disappointment, hurt, and longing all wrapped up in his beautiful features. He opened the door, one hand on the knob, one arm leaning on the frame. "I don't know, Sae. The risk feels worth it to me."

He left.

He left me there with those words to pierce my skin and forever scar me.

I should have raced after him. I should have caught him in the hall and kissed him, admitting that I had loved him far longer than he knew—that I would risk everything just to see him happy. I should have reversed time, just by one minute and listened to more, accepted more, confessed more.

But I didn't.

And as the minutes ticked by and my spell could no longer reverse time that far, I just stood there, breaking my own damn heart, and listening to my name echo through the room in a numbing whisper as the tines clicked in a rhythm to the song's end.

CHAPTER 65
KARUS

Viv had the baby. A healthy girl we named Allyanna. Ashton is a good big brother when he wants to be. We would love for you to visit when you can. There is more news at the border, but I cannot write it here. Stay happy, stay safe.

Love,

Geyrand

T read his letter with joy, so pleased they were all well.

I picked up Figuerah's and read it too, my feet tucked up under me by the fire, no Revich there to warm them.

I cannot believe Viridis has returned. Karus, you did it. I'm so proud of you, I could shout it to each person I meet. Unfortunately, there are quite a few these days as Clairannia plans all these gatherings in Hyrithia. Nyeimah and I are exhausted, but we love her and come to them anyway.

We have a few more meetings to attend with the Queen and her royal procession before we can travel to Felgren. There's some news here that you and Revich need to know if the Queen has not written already.

Karus, I cannot wait to walk into Viridis with you. I cannot wait to show Nyeimah. Clairannia already has plans and two trunks of books on medicus conduit magic she'd like to add to that section. Her memoire is done. I should be able to finish mine while we're there and add it to the shelves as well.

I just want to see you. I miss Felgren, Karus. I miss it every day I am away, and I miss you. By the time you get this, I'll be there in just a few days, weeks for me out here. Regardless, know that no matter the outcome of the trials, you are a full conduit to me.

I love you, my dearest friend,

Figuerah

I let myself sob, tears splashing the letter and running down the ink in her messy scrawl. I missed her. I missed both of them, and again, I wished they were here for my conduit trials, as they had planned to be.

I wiped my tears on my sleeve and sniffed, folding both letters and sitting them on the table beside me.

Emotions tore through me as I sat alone in our room, watching the flames burn through a log of ash wood. Revich would be gone most of the night. He had insisted the trials take place in the morning and needed a few hours still to finish.

I had no real foretelling of what I'd face. Lia's book was a careful history, not a guide, and Clairannia and Figuerah had never told me what to expect, as was tradition.

We were supposed to go in blind, without knowledge of what we'd see or how we'd prove our magic for each type of conduit.

I pulled a midnight blue throw from the foot of the bed and tucked it in around me. I didn't want to get in without Rev, a ridiculous sentiment of romance, but I didn't care. Our bed felt strange without him in it.

I leaned against the armrest, tucked in like a ball to the seat of the chair and let my eyes fall, the day's events exhausting me past any more of my wandering thoughts.

I woke in bed. My back was pressed to Rev's chest as his arm draped over me, keeping my body pulled to him. I turned in his grasp, snuggling up under his chin, breathing him in, and kissing his chest to wake him.

He gave the slightest stir, and that was all the opening I needed, sliding my leg over his hip and pushing my self closer, my desire taking the reins of all thought.

"Karus," he rumbled, "you need to save your strength."

"Somehow," I lilted between kisses up his neck, "I think I can manage this and what the day has to offer."

"I mean it." He pulled on my chin, his eyes black as night. "There will be time to celebrate later. If you want." He sighed, kissing my pout lightly. "One of these trials is more difficult than you know. You need to dress and eat a full breakfast. Then we'll go."

"Fine," I sighed, untangling my leg from him, but not before catching a quick look at what I loved to see. "How late were you up last night? I don't remember getting into bed."

He sat up and rubbed his face. "Late. I brought you to bed only a few hours ago."

"Baron Revich, you need a nap today." I threw a clean shirt to the bed for him and dressed in my own clothes, nerves and excitement buzzing through my body.

By the end of the day, I'd be a conduit. I didn't know which kind I'd choose. I planned to go through each trial and decide after—if I passed them all—which type of magic I felt I belonged to.

Dressed, we entered the dining hall, our breakfast laid out on the table, courtesy of Lia. All my favorites were there—cinnamon buns, meat pies filled with gravy, pears, and crumbly cheese.

Rev poured us tea and filled his plate with bacon, eggs, and strawberries.

"Why don't you like cinnamon buns?" I asked, stuffing my mouth with dough still warm and soft, the icing from the treat coating my tongue.

"Too sweet."

Pouting, I offered a bite on my fork. "Just try it. How long since you've had one?"

"I've tried them before. Don't like 'em. Besides," he grinned, pointing his own fork at me, golden egg speared, "I get plenty of sweet from you."

"Gross," Philius muttered as he entered the dining hall, followed by Mychael, Rell, Renn, Talon, and Ilyenna.

I laughed and took the bite I had offered Rev.

Rell and Renn hurried to either side of me, sliding chairs out at the same time.

"Today's the day!" Rell began.

Her sister followed with, "How nervous are you?"

"I'm surprisingly calm, actually. I'm more excited to be through them. I've been here a long time without taking the trials, and I feel ready."

"How long will they take, Baron Revich?" Mychael asked, spooning eggs and toasted bread on his plate.

"It depends on the channeler, but I've found that most of them last all day, at times going into the evening." He eyed me. "That was Clairannia because she was so stubborn. She refused to give up on the agricola trial."

"How do you give up?" Philius asked, sitting across from Mychael and handing a plate of food to Ilyenna.

"You tap your conduit ring three times, return to the Baron, and you've failed that one."

He glanced at me quickly before returning his eyes to his plate.

I quirked my head and chewed on a slice of pear.

He really was hiding something from me. It kept trying to spill out of him, locked back into place, but slipping at times when he looked at me.

It must have been something with the trials. Something he couldn't tell me, likely because he was my Baron during them, not my companion.

"Well, I wish you the best of luck today, Karus," Mychael grinned my way and a murmur of agreements were sent out across the table.

I nodded and said my thanks, suddenly ready to be done. The whole one, maybe two cinnamon buns I'd eaten sat doughy in my stomach with half a pear.

Rev cleared his plate and I rose saying, "Shall we?"

He stood as well, grabbing one more piece of thick bacon. He held it out to me. "Yes, but eat this last thing for me, will you?"

~

REV HELD MY HAND AS WE WALKED THROUGH FELGREN. WE DIDN'T say much—me thinking about what I'd face, him probably thinking about the same.

We walked for some time, and I wasn't sure where we were going. I didn't ask. We finally broke through the pathway, and I recognized the massive burned maple tree atop the rocky outcropping with the gentle trickle of a stream running down the black stones.

Since my display of power over seven years ago in this place, the seeds I had produced had sprouted. Long, gangly saplings lined the shore, a bright green trunk growing from the burnt remnants of the great maple tree.

I surveyed the area while the memory of that fateful day slipped into my thoughts. It had been a cold awakening that my power was not all lovely and warm.

A brilliant flickering green portal hummed on the edge of the tiny stream.

He squeezed my hand in his. "This is the first place you really showed me what you can do. I set up the trials here to remind you that you are great, you are powerful, and you are beautiful, Karus." He nodded to the broken tree, the one I'd killed in fire. "But you also hold a darkness inside. Use everything you have to get through these trials."

I swallowed hard, nodding.

"Remember, nothing in there is real. Each one was set up by me for you." He cupped my face. "I followed every rule I had to. Every single one. If I strayed even the slightest, the trials would fail, regardless of how far you were in them."

"I feel like I should be more worried than I am," I laughed nervously.

"You'll be fine. Just remember for me, nothing that happens in there is real out here. You can do this."

I nodded again and he pressed his lips to mine, taking his time with each kiss, heating my blood as he was meant to do.

"I love you, Karus," he whispered on my mouth.

I kissed him one last time. "I love you, too."

I smiled, feeling the need to reassure him and not myself, looking into his eyes so black, I could see my reflection on the surface.

I let go of him and stepped toward the portal, flicking my fingers at my side, my feet bouncing, ready to face my first trial.

I rolled my shoulders and turned my head before I stepped into his portal, grinning and promising, "I'll see you on the other side."

I saw the mournful eyes of the man I loved staring back at me and ignored any inkling that what I was about to face would be my undoing.

CHAPTER 66
KARUS
THE IUMENTA TRIAL

I tumbled out of the portal.

They always seemed to spit me out, regardless of how I entered.

I fell to my knees, jabbing into sharp wood. A piece of it broke off, piercing my skirts and my skin. "Dammit," I muttered to myself, pulling the three inch spike out of my knee.

"My, my, Karus, how have you already managed to hurt yourself?"

My blood curdled, and I glanced up quickly to see the black robes of the Blightress billowing around her. White hair, pale complexion—she still wore bright red on her lips, her nails just as black as the day I met her.

"What the *fuck* are you doing here?" I rose, holding my wound.

"Such a way of speaking. Did he teach you that word?"

"Stop. You can't be here. *How* are you even here? This isn't real."

She shrugged. "It's true. I'm not really here, just as you are not really here. But that,"—she pointed at my bloody knee—"probably feels real."

I sighed and lifted my skirts, muttering, "*Sarchio.*"

Nothing. My wound stayed open, blood trickling down my leg into my laced boot.

"Spells don't work here, child."

I rolled my eyes. So that's what Revich couldn't tell me. I had to rely on my innate magic alone, not on spells I'd learned.

I pulled my trails of green forward, wrapping them around my knee in an attempt to stop the bleeding. It seemed to mostly work at least.

Letting my skirts fall, I looked around. I was standing in a massive room. Rough wood steps sloped gently upward and a curved ceiling was broken in places with beams of sunlight shining through to illuminate an enormous door ahead. Great branches of a tree wound along the door, spreading and tangling over the wood. Bits of grass and small, delicate flowers grew all over the wide stairs.

Without looking at her, I asked, "Why are you here?"

"I've not had the pleasure of seeing you perform much of your magic, Karus, as you were taken from me before you were born and insisted on leaving me when I brought you to my home."

"You're here to watch?" I scoffed.

She shook her head in that eerie, unnatural way. "I'm here to witness."

I squeezed my eyes shut, already irritated with her presence. "I don't want you to be here, just so we're clear."

"I can see that, Little Sprout."

I pursed my lips, biting on them. "Why did you try to stop Revich? In Viridis. Why did you erect that wall behind me?"

It was a question I'd been wondering ever since that day. I knew Revich did, too.

She tilted her head and narrowed her eyes. "Simply to see if I could. I myself am a curious sort of creature, Karus. I wanted to know just how much of my power he holds."

I turned away and looked up to the holes at the ceiling of the room, gathering my patience. It almost looked as if this trial was in a giant barn, and as I glanced behind me, the rest of the area was dark and difficult to see.

I took a cautious step forward, my knee more painful than I

cared to admit. I followed the steps all the way to the door. I could see its hinges rusted over, and I wondered where the animals were supposed to be. This was the iumenta trial, but it looked abandoned.

Ignoring the looming presence of the Blightress behind me, I listened. I reached out for heartbeats, searching for something living and hiding in the room.

I sensed three of them, weak and small, each one somewhere on the door before me. I stepped back, searching the branches for any sign of life—something tiny, maybe young.

The slightest mewling caught my ear, and I jerked my head up and to the right, catching the flicker of a scaled black tail, tiny and pointed.

"There you are," I muttered, looking for a foothold to climb the woven branches on the door.

I heaved myself up onto the one closest to the ground, grabbing ahold of another, beginning my climb, focused on that tiny, racing heartbeat.

My knee worked well enough, but ached already, and I wasn't even through the first trial. I cursed my clumsiness as I slipped, catching another branch with my foot and pulling myself back up.

I reached the creature, my head peeking over one last branch to see what looked like a cross between a kitten and a lizard. All black, it had sharp claws and long, pointed scales at its chest and down its back, its face blending scales and fur. Its eyes were wide and orange like a cat with pink, fleshy ears that were so thin, I could almost see through them.

"Hello, little one," I spoke softly, pulling myself to the branch with my arm for balance and holding my hand out for her to sniff. She did so and licked it eagerly, likely smelling bacon on my fingers.

"Should I take you down from here?" I asked, not expecting a reply and not getting one. She mewed again, this time sitting up and peering over the ledge. We were at least twenty feet up and the fall would be disastrous for us both.

She stood, her claws gripping the branch and mewed a third time, this one answered by her siblings. From that height, I could see them now, each having gotten themselves on a different part of this door, each far too small to be able to climb down.

"They are quite adorable, are they not?" The Blightress called up to me, standing at the base of the door.

I didn't reply, turning back to the lizardous cat creature, whispering, "If Rev would allow it, I think I'd just bring you home with me. I stroked her scaled nose, hearing a purring rumble loudly in return. "Can I take you down? Is that what you want?"

She replied with a short meow, and I scooped her into the crook of my arm, bringing my magic underneath to help hold her in case she slipped. I began my slow decent down to the ground, thankful the other two were not as far up.

I set her down near the Blightress's robes, glaring at her in a threat not to touch it before climbing to the left side, following the cries of the other two. Thinking I was clever, I reached the highest one first, letting her smell the grease on my fingers before snatching her into my arm and using my magic to lower her safely to the ground. I then climbed back down and stopped at the third on the way. By then, my fingers probably smelled more like her sister's tongues, but she happily lapped them anyway and let me take her into my arms.

Back on the ground, I lowered the last of the creatures, dusting my hands and grinning. All three were now batting at each other's tails, tumbling and biting.

"Aren't you forgetting something, Karus?" The Blightress grinned wide, turning to look over her shoulder.

A low growl shook the wooden slats at the ceiling, more of them breaking and falling fast, shattering on impact as a gigantic black form rose from the dark side of the room.

My blood ran cold as the Blightress warned, "Where there are kittens, there is a mother cat close by."

CHAPTER 67

REV

THE IUMENTA TRIAL

I counted the minutes as they ticked by because it was the only thing I could do.

I couldn't see her.

I couldn't help her.

I could only count time as it moved, squeezing my rhyzolm tightly, ensuring she still moved with time, too.

I would be able to feel when she was through the first trial. The portal to the next would open and draw power from me.

At least nothing could follow her through. Only one beating heart could enter my portals.

I reminded myself nothing could happen to her.

Nothing could actually hurt her in there.

But as it always seemed with Karus, what should be, often was not.

CHAPTER 68
KARUS
THE IUMENTA TRIAL

She looked exactly like her kittens, if her kittens had grown ten feet and sprouted razor-sharp spikes where whiskers should be and long pointy fangs where tiny baby teeth should be.

She crouched low, each careful step of her paw—the size of a lumen's head—jostled the ground, shaking more slats loose from the ceiling.

"She looks quite unhappy with you, Karus." The Blightress stood unafraid, with nothing to lose or gain if I tapped out of this trial.

"I don't need commentary from you," I snapped, my mind flying through every possible outcome.

I glimpsed a shining light of green behind the massive beast. The portal to the next trial had appeared. I just had to get through this creature without dying. I knew I couldn't really die here, but based on the throbbing in my knee, I knew one snap of her jaws around me would definitely hurt.

I just needed to get past her. I was agile and fast, two things I knew about myself and two things that could possibly save me.

I couldn't move her kittens. She'd most likely pounce if I even attempted to touch them at all. All three of them stilled, hunched close to the ground, watching their mother stalk her prey.

I kept my eyes on her coppery ones and thought of everything Figuerah had ever taught me about wild creatures. I knew hunters like this were more likely to sprout wings and fly than back down from protecting their young, and for all I knew, she had wings anyway.

I needed a distraction, something to take her focus off me just long enough that I could sprint past her and make it to the portal.

What did I know? What creature knowledge did I have that could get me out of here?

I knew lumens. And I knew quiphits. Both creatures were abundant in Felgren, and I had seen enough of Parvus chase a quiphit to know what their long ears and sleek, furry bodies looked like as they ran.

My decision made, I formed my green tendrils into the shape of a quiphit born in the summer, as green as my magic was. I formed tall ears, a narrow face and long green fur, its ears twitching in a patch of grass nearby.

I watched as one of the kittens perked up, raising its head to focus on my pretend quiphit that jumped from one patch of grass on the stairs to another.

The kitten bent low to the ground, stalking forward, just as I had hoped. My quiphit caught the eye of the mother cat but only for a split second as she returned her focus to me, taking another step.

A second kitten, then the third, caught sight of the seemingly unaware quiphit, all three of them stalking it as it jumped further away from me and closer to the other end of the room.

By the time the beast took one more step toward me, her kittens were out of her line of sight, chasing the green quiphit down the stairs and into the dark.

I stood very still, making sure not to lock eyes with the black beast as she bared her teeth and turned her head to see where her babies had gone.

I saw the opportunity and took it, racing off to her other side, headed to the portal just behind her gigantic spiked tail.

The long black plates lashed out my way as she returned her attention back to me, and I ducked, feeling the whoosh of air over my head, inches away from slamming me back and breaking bones.

Her roar was great in the disintegrating room, but I did not hear the end of it as I avoided her swinging tail once more and dove through Revich's second portal.

CHAPTER 69
KARUS
THE LAPIS TRIAL

I splashed into a stream, not unlike the one where I had left Revich. Its cool, clear water trickled over hundreds of green gems which cut into the palms of my hands.

I pulled myself up, seeing my skin indented and wiped my hands on my wet skirts.

I was in a glen, golden blossoms swaying in the breeze and the sound of the trickling water catching in my ear.

"Clever, Little Sprout, to distract her with her own litter."

I gritted my teeth and turned, finding the dark form of the Blightress hounding me here, too. "Please go away."

I turned back to the stream, bending down to inspect the gems.

As I sifted through the water, I realized they weren't just gems. They were replicas of my conduit ring which itself was missing from my forefinger.

I sighed and followed the path of the stream, brilliant emeralds shining under the shallow surface of the water as far as my eyes could see.

Now, I understood why hardly any channeler passed this trial. I was going to have to find my real conduit ring out of thousands.

I sat on the bank to rest a moment, pulling my skirt up over my knee, a dark crimson stain expanding across the fabric, my skin a broken mess of fresh and crusted blood. I tore a strip of my skirt and wrapped it around the wound, pulling the makeshift bandage tight and tying it off.

I stood and sighed again, glad to be out of danger, but not looking forward to going mad searching for my ring.

I wondered how channelers got out of this trial. If they tapped any of these rings three times, would it move them on to the next? I'd be careful when handling them, I supposed.

I scooped up a handful of sliver bands, each holding a single teardrop emerald, each the same size and length, each exactly like the last.

I let them fall through my fingers, then took another scoop.

I wasn't sure what exactly I was looking for. A feeling? A recognition of the ring I wore everyday?

I sifted through again, as the Blightress moved to sit across from me.

"Did you speak to Thalia?"

"Yes," I mumbled, inspecting my next handful.

"Did you get the truth you needed?"

"Yes," I spoke again, holding one ring up to the sun, looking for some sign I had found the real one quickly and with the greatest luck a channeler had ever known.

"Your answers are irritatingly short."

"I learned from the best." I grinned, standing and moving a few feet down.

She followed, watching as I scooped two handfuls of rings, letting them fall through my fingers, splashing back to the stream in light plops.

"How is my sister? Does she fair well?"

My gaze shot to her, taken aback. "You care?"

"Yes, Karus, I care about my sister. I have not seen her in some time."

"She confirmed you gave her magic. You gave Felgren magic and the first Baron magic, too."

"Just as I told you."

I took another scoop, this time inspecting each one for flaws I knew wouldn't be on my ring. "You can't blame me for not believing something so absurd."

"I can and I do. I hope you will believe me in the future when I tell you more of my story."

I scoffed. "You're not going to take this time to tell me now? That's surprising."

Each of these rings looked exactly the same. Each one a silver band that fit perfectly on my finger, each one holding a green stone with the same exact faucets as the others.

I tossed them into the stream and set my chin in my hand, elbow resting on my good knee.

"I wish you would believe I'd like to see you thrive. I do not wish to distract you so with my story when you are trying so hard to complete these trials."

I glared at her across the stream, again not believing a word she uttered from her red mouth. "Then stop talking and let me think."

I chewed my bottom lip and she fell silent for once.

What did I know about my conduit ring?

I knew Revich kept it safe for me while my mind had been lost. I knew he returned it to me the day he asked me to be his companion. I knew he cleaned it and slipped it on my finger during our ceremony.

But none of those things had to do with its origin.

I closed my eyes and went back to that day. The day I left Hyrithia, taken by Heimlen to Felgren Forest.

I relived it, step by step—Geyrand's kiss, the lumens across the little bridge, my handkerchief flowing in the breeze straight to them. I saw Heimlen's face before me as I declared the lumens broke at the slightest scent.

"My dear," he had replied, "you are hardly the slightest of anything."

I raged.

I didn't know who I hated more, Heimlen or the Blightress sitting before me.

That was a lie. I knew exactly who I'd happily kill if he wasn't already dead.

Breathing deep, I reset the scene, remembering how I took his gloved hand and my clothing had changed, forming into a gown that was the perfect replica of what I would have chosen out of hundreds.

My conduit ring had come last, the silver band forming over my finger, topped with that sparkling teardrop emerald.

I remembered Heimlen had commented on it, but I had never asked why.

"It really is a beautiful ring." She held a replica between her long, black nails, studying it closely.

"All of them are," I mumbled, swirling my fingers back in the water, feeling for any sign or pull in a certain direction.

"Yours is quite simple. Have you noticed, Little Sprout?"

I cocked my head and waited for her to continue.

She grinned, tossing the ring back into the water. "Of all the other channelers, yours holds a single, simple stone. Why is that, Karus of Felgren?"

"If you know, either tell me or stop talking."

She laughed in that chiming, eerie way and continued, "I believe I do know. You see, emeralds are the symbol of eternal life. Emerald is the color of your eyes and the trees of Felgren. And a single emerald stone was the first ring ever given by a Baron."

A chill swept through me. I knew who she was talking about, and I knew part of this story without needing to hear it.

She nodded, pulling at her sleeves, watching the glimmering rings in the water. "Yes, child, a single emerald was given to me by Adaynth on the day we bound our lives together."

I swallowed, bracing myself. "My conduit ring is the same one given to you by the first Baron?"

"I still hold a fondness for it, Karus." She picked up another replica, holding it up to the sun. "It never surprised me that the child I gave my power to would prove her bond to me in various ways."

The day was turning miserable.

Each time I spoke to this woman, I learned more about my past and hers without really asking to. I inhaled deeply and scooped another batch of rings, determined to pass this trial and leave.

She was silent, letting me concentrate. I was thankful for that much at least.

I studied my forefinger on my right hand.

I dropped the rings and held it up to the sunlight, turning it around.

I closed my eyes again, keeping my hand in the air, thinking of the ring that I wished was only mine. I imagined its exact weight, the exact press of the band across my skin, closing over my finger as a constant reminder of how much I belonged in Felgren.

I opened my eyes and grinned, seeing my conduit ring shine in the sun.

It had never left my finger. I just had to recognize that it was there.

The green portal opened behind the Blightress, and I stood, proud of accomplishing what many other channelers before me could not.

She stood with me, clasping her hands together with a snide remark, "How ironic that you passed the trial about needing to believe the truth that's right in front of you."

I ignored her again and moved past to step into the portal.

Two down, two to go.

CHAPTER 70
REV
THE LAPIS TRIAL

That was quick was my first thought, followed closely by a fierce sense of pride.

I wasn't surprised she got through the caygon and her kittens, but she was the first channeler I'd trained to pass the lapis trial. Hopefully, she wasn't the last.

Poor Clairannia had sat at that water's edge for ages, sifting through the thousands of ruby and diamond rings, looking for her exact one which she could not realize was still on her finger. She'd finally tapped one of them three times, sending her back to me where I assured her, she would pass the next trial. Figuerah had given in almost immediately, not caring about passing what she didn't want to follow anyway.

I wanted to see Karus, but then again, I didn't.

It would mean she had failed one of the trials, and I so badly wanted her to pass them all.

Two down.

Three to go.

CHAPTER 71
KARUS
THE MEDICUS TRIAL

My head smacked into a wooden surface at the same time I plopped ungraciously into a hard chair.

I rubbed my nose, running a finger under to check for blood.

I glanced around, finding myself in a small room, a single lantern lit on the desk where I sat, my right hand, palm down, pinned to the wood.

Pinned.

Not only that, my skin on the back of my hand was flayed wide, drawn back across my hand with precise cuts, each side also pinned to the table with tiny, sharp needles not unlike the ones from Lia's embroidery kit.

"You have got to be joking," I said in dismay as a pile of bones fell out of empty space onto the table. I assumed they were the exact ones missing from my flayed hand.

At least it didn't hurt. My knee was more painful than the absolute insanity of this trial.

The Blightress stood in front of the desk and gave an interested hum, tilting her head to study the white bones in front of me.

"I do hope you paid attention to those medicus books in Viridis, Karus."

"A hand puzzle? Really, Revich?" I muttered, picking up one of the bones with my free hand and studying it closely.

I tried to wiggle the fingers of my right hand, but of course, couldn't. The bones of them were not connected to the ones that should have been fit in the back of my hand because they were lying in a pile on the table.

My *bones*.

I blew air out of my lips, wanting to smack my head against the table again, this time of my own accord.

I stared down at my open skin, convinced I would never choose to be a medicus conduit.

I knew how Clairannia passed this trial. She'd probably gotten straight to work, fitting each of the thirteen bones on the desk perfectly the first time.

But what had Figuerah done?

She hated medicus magic, and honestly, was terrible at it.

I chewed my lip as the Blightress studied me.

There could only be so many different combinations of bones. I just needed to work at it to get them fitting correctly.

I began with the long ones. I had no idea of their names, but, recalling some of Clairannia's medicus books, I knew most of the bones in the hand were long and thin. I had no clue what to do with the pile of eight oddly curved pieces.

I found the shortest of the five longer bones, unsure if it was a part of my thumb or littlest finger. I set it down and looked for the longest instead, assuming it would fit below my forefinger…maybe my middle one?

I groaned, eyeing my conduit ring, actually contemplating tapping out of this one.

How had Figuerah passed this trial?

I tried to think like her. She was clever, observant, she held no fear either—quite the woman to behold, in my favorable opinion.

I flexed my left hand, hoping I could somehow catch a glimpse at the bone structure under my skin.

I frowned, looking up at the Blightress. "Can channeler magic cut through skin?"

She grinned wickedly, her iridescent eyes a rainbow of color in the lantern light. "Why don't you try, Little Sprout?"

I chewed on my lip again, my gaze flicking from my healthy left hand to my open right.

I summoned my power, thinking of a thin, sharp knife which formed in green above the only working hand I had.

If I cut into my left hand, I could see exactly which bone went where. But I wasn't sure how much it would hurt, or if it would stay that way for the last trial. Guessing by my knee wound, it would.

I couldn't just use a spell to mend my hand, either. And what if I needed both hands to complete the agricola trial next?

I huffed.

The other two trials had been more than they initially seemed. Maybe there was something similar to this one. Surely, not every channeler adept to medicus magic knew exactly the right positions of each of these bones.

There was more to this than a horrifying bone reconstruction, I was sure. Medicus conduits did more than heal wounds. They could *feel* their way through the body, finding the sources of pain and ailments that could not be seen on the outside.

When the Black Fever had ravaged through Hyrithia, the medicus conduits had been completely perplexed, finding no source of the sickness in the bodies of its victims.

I knew now that was because Heimlen was manipulating the disease through a channeler's magic, which was something innate and in the core of a magic wielder.

I straightened my shoulders and closed my eyes, imagining the inside of my left hand. I focused on each bone as I drummed my fingers. Each movement was precise, each flick was using at least one of them and if I was ever to do the same with my right, I needed to see each one's place.

I fell into my own body, seeking that pattern, that array of bones completed in my left hand, laying it flat on the table as I picked up the first of the oddly rounded bones with a wisp of my magic.

I placed it opposite of the one I could sense on my left, using my magic to set it gently in my right hand. I picked up the next, this one more like a round pebble, placing it snug against the last.

I continued with each of the eight smaller pieces, a bottom row of four, followed by a top row of another four. I kept my gaze bleary, no longer in that room, but inside my left hand instead, moving on to the longer bones, using my magic to pick up each one.

The shortest was my thumb, and I snapped it into place, picking up what I saw next—my second longest. I followed along with the other three, hearing a satisfying click with my littlest finger, opening my eyes to see the pins falling away and my skin reforming with sinew over each bone, closing without a scar to remember I had put my own hand back together.

"Impressive, Karus. I thought for sure you were going to cut into your other hand and bleed all over this table."

"Yes, I'm sure you would have loved to see that," I retorted, standing and walking around the desk to the portal that had appeared after my last bone was set.

"I would not," she replied.

I studied my hand again, flexing my fingers. Taking a deep breath and assuring myself that none of what I'd just done was real, I stepped through to the last trial.

CHAPTER 72

REV

THE MEDICUS TRIAL

I was going to get an earful for that one.

But she'd done it.

I just hoped she wasn't bleeding all over the place like Figuerah had been.

I continued to pace the bank of the stream, fiddling with the rhyzolm in my pocket.

The next trial would be trivial for Karus.

Then she'd step through the portal and think she was coming home to me.

She wouldn't.

And I'd wait here all day, promising myself I was doing the right thing.

Assuring myself that she'd make it through the last, just as I did. Just as all other Barons had before her.

She was meant to hold some of this power.

That truth needed no persuasion in my mind.

But it might in hers.

CHAPTER 73
KARUS
THE AGRICOLA TRIAL

I was more careful this time, catching myself and staying upright out of the portal.

I stood in a room of dark stone, a single ball of yellow light hovering at the ceiling. In the middle of the small room stood a short table. On the short table lay a small, square porcelain pot, its feet carved into a sprawl of flourishes.

I stepped closer, inspecting the contents. A single seed lay atop three inches of soil.

I picked it up, eyeing it closely.

"A cherry tree," I realized.

This was Revich's faith in me. It was a cherry tree I grew the first time I showed Heimlen what I could really do with my power.

Now, it seemed Rev wanted me to grow another, but a much smaller version.

"He didn't give you much to work with." I heard the Blightress somewhere behind me.

Tuning her out, I pressed the seed down into the fresh soil, sending tendrils of my magic up to the light to make it grow.

The room filled in brilliant sunlight, the *Simulair Solum* spell held somewhere by Revich, not by me.

I closed my eyes and wrapped my hands around the small pot, pouring growth, and beauty, and new life into my power.

A stem shot from the soil, soon forming wiry branches that grew into a trunk, withered as if it was a hundred years old and flaked in a curved shape. Next were the blooms, revealing themselves as tiny, pink blossoms.

I had to watch carefully and pull my power back as it grew, adjusting the strength I gave the tree, knowing if it grew too large, the pot would shatter.

This was a trial of precision. I needed to grow this cherry tree to just the right size for the porcelain pot given to me.

The blossoms opened wide in brilliant white and pink, scenting the air, and I pulled all of my power back, just as the tiny tree, a miniature version of the one I had grown in Felgren, unfurled its last bud and the last green portal opened in front of me.

That was the easiest trial yet.

I'd passed them all.

I'd done it, proving I was a conduit for the Baron of Felgren.

I gently touched the petals, wishing I could take the tree home with me when the Blightress moved in front of the portal, inspecting the flickering green light.

"I'm leaving now. You need to move." I stood in front of her as she faced me.

"Where do you think this leads?" she asked.

"Home. I'm going home. Now, move." I swiped at her arm, finding only air.

So she really wasn't there, somehow projecting herself instead.

"He lies," she declared, refusing to move out of my way.

"I'm leaving."

"This portal does not lead to Felgren, Karus."

I tilted my head back and groaned. "Why are you like this? You want to see me thrive? Then leave me alone with the man I love." I shook my head, my anger rising to the surface quickly. "You only want to tell me this, tell me that. What about what *I* want? You see me as yours? As a daughter? Fuck. You. I owe you nothing, and you owe me nothing. You will not take Revich's power, you will not take over Felgren, you will not take back what you gave to me. Go sit in your white palace with your creatures and leave me alone. Leave the *isle* alone. Your time is finished."

I stepped forward, ready to go through her if I had to.

Her hand shot out and grabbed my arm.

I looked down, confused. "How did you—"

"Do. Not. Go." Her eyes flashed in iridescence, anger pooling from her in black tendrils.

Her grip tightened, and I grabbed her hand, pulling at her fingers. "Let me go! I thought you weren't really here!"

Her face flickered for a moment like a flame about to extinguish. "That portal leads to the B—"

But I didn't stick around to listen. I was done listening to her. I rushed through the portal, yanking my arm from her grip, finding my way back to my love.

CHAPTER 74

REV

THE AGRICOLA TRIAL

Fastest one yet.

I laughed to myself, so fucking proud of her, when I felt another soul enter the trial.

What the fuck?

There were two people in there. I could feel an enormously powerful presence in that room with Karus.

It could only be one person.

This wasn't going to work. I was going to have to go in there.

I sought my power as Baron, starting my hands low to the ground, then slowly lifting, separating them while a viridescent green light shaped into an oval portal that would lead right to that room.

"Why would you do this, Baron Revich?"

At the same time I felt Karus leave through her portal to enter the Baron trial, I heard the voice of the woman who haunted her, coming from somewhere behind me.

It was a beautiful, smooth tone with massive power hiding just beneath its surface.

I gathered my own power, bundling it back into my body, it too sitting just beneath my surface, ready to use at any moment. I slid my hands into my pockets and turned.

The Blightress looked nothing like her sister.

Where Lia held a warmth and a round face, bright grey eyes and long black hair, this woman was tall and thin, her cheekbones sharp, her full lips red as fresh blood.

She wore black robes over a fitted black dress, the neckline reaching up below her chin, giving her a regal air. Her white hair fell in graceful curls down her shoulders and her nails were long and pointed.

"You are not welcome in this forest. Leave. Now."

She stepped forward, her eyes flashing in shades of pink, green, blue, and yellow. "This is my forest, Revich of the Hallow Marshes. Tell me, can you not handle this power? Do you wish to give it away, place your burden on the one you claim to love?"

My fury flared like a flame on dry wood. Blue tendrils smoked around my arms, and I clenched my jaw, replying, "This isn't your concern. Karus is not your concern. Now go, or I will force you from this place."

She laughed, stepping closer still.

Without any more warning, I called to the roots beneath her as they cracked through the surface, snaking over her legs, my power wrapping around her arms, forcing them her sides.

"Is this the best you can do with all that power, Revich?" She tsked her tongue. "No wonder you're giving it over to her."

Her arms flew wide, breaking my hold and she bent forward. In one graceful sweep, black spilled from her fingers, wrapping around the roots wound over her legs. With a single touch, a simple brush of her power, the darkness flowed like ink tipped on paper, spreading over the surface to corrupt the very life of Felgren. Jagged thorns rose from the withered surface of each root, never once piercing her void-black robes as she stepped out of the Blight, its growth rapid behind her.

"*Simulair Solum!*" I called forth the sun, holding the light to face her, the forming Blight at her feet withering and recessing back into the ground.

I closed the spell, calling branches from the nearby trees. They wrapped around each of her arms, pulling them out to the sides, preventing her touch on their surface.

She laughed again, tilting her head back in amusement as if this was a game, as if she was toying with me. She grinned in pure malice, opening her red lips to speak again when a giant oak leaf slapped across her mouth, wet and silencing her.

I walked toward her. "Leave or I will force you to go."

I knew she held more power than I did, but I could tell it was dampened. I felt her presence before me, but elsewhere as well when I squeezed the rhyzolm in my pocket.

Her voice was bodiless and echoed through the trees as she glared at me. "If she accepts the power of the Baron of Felgren, I will find you and kill you. You are weak, just as they all were weak, and you will be powerless, Revich of the Hallow Marshes. I look forward to watching you bleed."

I stepped closer, her eyes narrowing on me as I countered, "You think you have some claim on her. You don't. You never will. We will share the power of Baron and then we will come to stop you."

Her face fell into one of confusion, her voice sounding again through the trees. "The power of Baron cannot be shared. How have you done this?"

I opened a portal behind her that led as far north as I could manage. "Like I said, this isn't your concern."

I pulled my hands back to send a ball of blue light blasting toward her chest just as I unwound the branches from her arm. My magic burst through the air into nothing as she disappeared from Felgren and I was once again left alone.

CHAPTER 75
KARUS
THE FIFTH TRIAL

I plunged face-down into mud.

The slimy grit coated my tongue, and I spit from my mouth, wiping it with my sleeve.

I looked around, rubbing at my eyes and finding that I had not, in fact, returned home.

"Rev?" I called, my voice young and high-pitched, not one I recognized.

I looked down to my chest, finding it small and thin. I was wearing a ripped brown overcoat. Several of the buttons were missing up the front, and one of the pockets was patched with black thread.

My hands were little. I stared at short, stubby fingers caked in mud with dirt under wide fingernails. My emerald conduit ring was missing.

Revich hadn't been keeping secrets about the conduit trials. He'd been keeping a secret about this.

Whatever this was.

I pulled my short body up from the ground, surveying my surroundings.

I was at the edge of a small village. Wood houses lined muddy streets, smoke billowing from their chimneys. The sun was rising on the horizon to the east, and behind me was a vast wilderness of the strangest trees I had ever seen.

Each one was enormous at the root base, their trunks long and thinning out at the top to a small display of dark green leaves. The roots of each tree wove under and over the muck, a tangled maze of thick wood that spread across the silt, wet and bubbling.

"Rev!"

I turned back to the village, my eyes searching for him.

A woman stood on the doorstep of the nearest cabin, wiping her hands on her dirty apron. A sense of familiarity washed over me as I squinted at her. Her pitch-black hair was pulled up into a bun at the nape of her neck, bits escaping and hanging over her ears. Her skin was tanned against her brown, drab dress. Her eyes were a deep blue.

I knew those eyes.

Those were Rev's eyes. Even the shape was his, along with the straight black brows above them.

She smiled, and I found my feet walking forward, not of my own doing.

She put her hands on her hips, addressing me as I neared. "Revich Schayel, how have you managed to muck yourself up already? Don't you come in here with that all over your hands and face. Go wash before breakfast."

She pointed to the side of the door where a bucket sat on the mossy ground, its surface glassy with dark water.

"Yes, Mama," I spoke in that same little voice.

She went back inside, and again, my feet took me forward.

My mind raced with realization, confusion, and a threatening doom that settled into my stomach for who and where I was. I watched my small hands—*Revich's* small hands—rinse in the bucket, splashing water on his face—*our* face.

He glanced in the small, dingy mirror hung on the side of the wood house, and as his hands wiped at his cheeks, I saw Rev as a child. His face was thin, too thin, his eyes that deep blue of his mother's. Black hair in need of a wash had been cut short, falling in thick beginnings of waves across his forehead, curling around the nape of his neck.

He—*we*—sniffed the air and smiled, two front teeth missing, the new ones barely peeking through.

I laughed, the sound coming from his chest light and uninhibited.

"Do you know what I'm doing here?" I asked, watching our mouth move in the reflection.

He didn't respond, but splashed water on his face again, wiping away the last of the mud.

It seemed, however this had been done, I could speak through him, but he did not notice.

Why did Rev, *my Rev*, send me here to this memory of his? This must be the village of Mire in the Hallow Marshes. This must be a time when Revich was very young. I'd guess no older than six or seven.

What was he trying to show me, and why? Why would he put me here, and how was I supposed to return home?

Frustrated and curious, I said nothing more as he straightened and turned toward the house. I wondered if I could stop the movement. If I was able to use my own thoughts to speak, perhaps I could move his body as well.

Our short legs stopped, and we moved backward.

So, controlling his body was possible.

I decided to let this memory take place, carefully watching for any sign of what I was supposed to do here. At least my knee no longer throbbed.

If I was supposed to just observe, why was I able to speak and move?

He wiped his feet on the step up into the house and opened the door, the scent of bacon frying hitting his nose and he sniffed again.

"Did your father find anything this morning?" Rev's mother was at a small fire, flipping thin slices of fatty bacon over a black pan.

He moved to the small table in the room, standing behind a chair, holding his arms out in front of him. Bits of blue tendrils left his fingers, weak and broken, but he managed to use magic to pull the chair toward him, shakily with short, jerky movements.

He climbed into the seat and answered, "No. Father's talking with the warden about the order."

She stiffened, her back still turned, nursing the bacon and watching carefully as it cooked.

I had heard the words of his reply, but I did not know the meaning of them.

Revich eyed the stack of three metal plates across the table, lowered his head and opened his hands, pulling the top plate with his magic, lifting it high in the air and jerking it toward him.

He let go too soon and it clattered to the tabletop.

His mother turned and stood, hand over her heart. "Rev, don't dawdle. Your father will be back any minute."

She brought the pan to the table, setting a soiled rag underneath, forking two slices of bacon and setting them on Revich's plate. She then added a single piece to the other two.

She turned to the loaf of bread near the oven and Revich tore at one of his pieces, splitting it in half and giving the other to his mother.

I knew his little face held a wide grin, because I was also grinning. Even as a child, Rev loved with gifts.

Bringing three slices of bread to the table, his mother sat, eyeing the gifted piece of bacon and winking at her son, gobbling it up at the same time he did.

"I'm coming with you today to help fill the order as fast as we can. So, eat up." She sighed, looking out the dingy window. "It's going to be a long day, Little Love."

Rev scarfed down his food, filling his empty belly.

I decided to speak, trying to gain some knowledge of why *this* memory as I lived it with him. "How will you help fill the order?"

She cocked her head to the side. "I've mined before. You know that."

I nodded, thinking of what else I could ask to understand what was happening this day. "For rhyzolm? We're filling an order to...to the people of the isle?"

She bent forward and felt my head. "Are you feeling alright, Revich? Maybe you should stay home and rest. Though I'll have a difficult time convincing your father unless you start vomiting now."

Right on cue, the door burst open and a man strode in, pulling off his boots and tossing them by the door.

The weight in the room shifted suddenly. I could feel the tension in Rev's body and see it in his mother's.

I took the opportunity to look Rev's father over. He wore his hair short, cut almost to the very skin of his scalp, the color difficult to really discern, but somewhere lighter than black. His eyes were blue, but held an icy a coldness to them, none of the warmth of Rev's.

He was about Revich's height and build, strong arms and broad shouldered, likely from his work mining rhyzolm.

Revich had told me he didn't remember much about his parents. I knew they had both died when he was very young, and he became a ward of the village, families taking turns with each of the many orphans.

He had told me once it had kept him fed, but did not keep him loved, and I wondered now if he remembered he *had* been loved. Very much loved by his mother.

Revich eyed his father in silence, and I with him as he sat, picking up his single piece of bacon and frowning. "Just the one?" he gruffed, glancing at Revich's plate.

His mother spoke quickly, "If we can help fill part of the order today, you'll have more tomorrow. I'm coming with you."

He huffed in reply, chewing the fatty meat before diving into his meager bread.

"What did the warden have to say?" his mother asked, taking Revich's plate and hers, bringing them to a small basin to wash in water I was certain was not fresh.

"The usual," he rumbled, his voice eerily like Revich's. "Since the order is for the Spire, we need the biggest pieces we can find. Showy bastards," he finished. Revich watched him carefully as if looking for any sudden movements.

"Today's the day, son." His father's gaze turned from his empty plate to Revich. He pointed, saying, "I can feel it in my bones. You'll find your first today. We'll head back to that same tree. Something was there. I can feel it."

He sat back in his chair, poking around his teeth. "You need to use that magic of yours and help us find more rhyzolm. You want more bacon for your father, don't you?"

His mother continued to scrub, taking the pan from the table and beginning her work again. "Of course he does. But his power isn't developed, Byn. Give him time. He practices every day, don't you, Rev?"

He nodded, smiling at his mother before locking his gaze back on his father. Byn eyed his son as well, giving him a slight nod before rising from the table with his plate. He handed it to his companion and murmured low, "I missed you this morning, Heirah."

I didn't mistake it.

The clench of her jaw, the tension in her spine as he bent down and kissed her shoulder. She swallowed and shifted away from him. The movement was slight, but stiff, and Byn grabbed her chin, forcing her to look at him.

No, I knew exactly what was going on in this house, and it seemed Revich did too as he suddenly sprinted from his chair, almost shouting, "Should we go, father? Mama can meet us there soon, right?"

Heirah nodded, giving a weak smile. "Right, Little Love. I'll follow your trail."

Byn turned to his son with narrowed eyes.

Helping Revich along, I sprang for his father's boots by the door, picking them up and handing them over.

He sighed and took them, headed to the door, pulling them on as he went. It opened with unnecessary force and Rev smiled back at his mother, forming a ball of blue light in his hands, tiny as a pebble. He backed up toward the door after his father while a scattered trail of his magic followed him. She laughed, grinning beautifully, and I recognized Revich's unburdened smile on her face.

I knew it well. I knew it often.

∼

RHYZOLM MINING WAS DIFFICULT.

Not only was the labor hard on the body, it seemed to be on the soul as well. Little Revich surveyed the miners we passed, his trail of light breaking at points before forming again, staying lit and hovering to lead his mother our way.

He followed his father closely, his boots squelching through the mud that came up to his knees.

I kept turning Revich's head as he tried to follow his father. We passed at least two dozen miners in the marshes, each one using a variety of tools to wedge underneath the exposed roots of the trees covered in green moss.

I knew that in order to mine for rhyzolm, you had to dig underneath the tree, finding the rocks imbued with the magic of Felgren that washed this way from the forest.

Revich had explained to me the difficulty in getting underneath the root system, and I saw it here, in this memory, as miners worked to pull roots apart, gaining access underneath.

"Why can't we just cut down the trees and dig for rhyzolm underneath?" I asked.

The backhand came quick, sending me, *us*, to the mud.

"Don't ask questions when you already know the answer. You know the marsh trees have not grown in hundreds of years. And you know these are all we have." He gestured around, glaring at his son, who picked himself up out of the muck and wiped his hands on his overcoat.

I hated this man.

I hated him before, but now, now this was me, glad he was out of Revich's life at a young age. He deserved to rot here in these marshes where no one would find or mourn him.

I thought again about what I was really doing here, in this memory, on this day, as I felt the sting on Revich's cheek.

He had hit him after the question I had asked, but I knew by Rev's reaction, this was certainly not the first time.

It would be the *fucking last* if I could do anything about it.

Perhaps that's what Rev had meant when I left for the trials. He'd reminded me I held a darkness inside, and I saw it now, blooming before me in a display of his father's skull smashed among the roots of these trees.

I had no tolerance for this.

And I knew at least one thing; Byn Schayel was not going to make it out of this marsh alive.

But was that really what I was doing here? I was supposed to plot the murder of Revich's father?

I highly doubted it.

I must be missing something.

The conduit trials were four.

This was a fifth, something different entirely.

Rev sent me here to *do* something. To *prove* something.

Each trial had been proof of magic—iumenta, lapis, medicus, and agricola.

What other magic was there for me to prove?

The answer hit like lightning, striking me to the core. I stopped following Rev's father, stuck in place, my mind in the body of my companion when he was a child as I came to the only conclusion.

This was a trial for the only other magic a person could wield on this isle.

This was a trial for a Baron.

CHAPTER 76
REV
THE BARON TRIAL

I watched the space where the Blightress had disappeared.

The fact that she had been able to appear in Felgren at all had me on edge.

It meant that she really could come at any time and take Karus from me.

Not that Karus wouldn't fight back, but I knew the Blightress held more power than my love. Certainly more than me.

I'd felt it from the rhyzolm. I felt it now in how she left, leaving behind a wake of power that needed to settle back into the wind, the trees, and the roots she'd left broken and exposed.

Karus had still not returned, which meant she not yet passed or failed her final trial.

She probably had it figured it out by now.

Why I had put her there.

I wasn't sure she'd know what to do, but that's the Baron trial at its core. The path to success would remain unclear until it was almost too late.

CHAPTER 77
KARUS
THE BARON TRIAL

My focus was keen.

Revich had sent me here to prove I could wield the power of a Baron.

He'd never meant for me to become a conduit.

He'd meant to share his power all along.

Little snippets of our conversations, little implications he'd left, they all made sense now, like the key to a map I'd been given, unknowingly leading me here to prove myself a fifth time.

I was livid.

I was enthralled.

I was hurt that he hadn't shared this with me, but knowing Rev, he was likely following some rule that made him unable to.

And I understood that, but felt the jab of his omission all the same.

Could I become a Baron?

Would this power be something I wanted and had strength wield?

When he'd said he wanted to train conduits with me at his side, he'd meant this.

He'd meant two Barons instead of one, and I struggled to even fathom *how*.

One magical forest, one Baron to lead it.

For hundreds of years since the Blightress had given some of her power to Baron Adaynth, that's how it had been.

And a woman?

Never happened.

The Baronship always passed to a man.

What would it look like in me? What would change, if anything?

I wanted to prove this one badly.

More than any of the other four trials, I wanted to succeed here, to show Rev that he was right, that I could do this.

But what exactly was I supposed to do?

"Hand me that shovel, son." Byn pushed down on a long wedged piece of metal, forcing his whole weight on the end of it, prying one of the larger roots from the mud.

It made a sucking noise as the root separated from the sticky soil. Rev handed him the shovel to wedge underneath, holding the root upright.

Rhyzolm mining really was dangerous.

Byn pulled up his sleeves and went in, crawling under the massive root that, if the leverage did not hold, would snap over his body, breaking it and killing him instantly.

I wouldn't miss him.

When his boots had disappeared, Rev moved to the entrance of the exposed underbelly of the marsh tree, ducking under with a lantern to help light his father's way.

I could see him digging with a small spade, the sound of metal hitting wet soil striking my ears.

"Anything yet?" Heirah asked, coming around the massive tree and wiping her hands on her skirts.

She'd been working on the other side, digging under the smaller roots where smaller rhyzolms might be found.

Rev shook his head and bent low, watching his father dig further.

Byn shoveled thick slaps of sludge from under the tree, piling up beside Rev as his little hands dug through, searching for any stones.

We all heard it. The crack of wood.

Byn scrambled out from underneath, just as the wedged shovel gave way, the root crashing down into the silt, splattering the three of us, but leaving everyone unharmed.

"This tree needs rest. We've dug here enough today," Heirah said, motioning to others nearby.

"Something big is under here. I can feel it." Byn pulled the shovel from under the root, walking around the giant trunk, looking for another way in.

Heirah followed and I could hear their argument, hushed and angry.

Rev poked at the base of the tree, his small spade digging under two roots that wove around each other in tandem, each the same size and width, each holding the other in a spinning weave of the perfect balance.

He jabbed his spade under once more, prying the braided roots from the muck slightly, and peeking underneath.

I saw it, too.

The oddly shaped clump of mud.

He reached in and pulled it out, dropping his spade and dropping the roots, sweeping the silt from the irregularly shaped stone that I knew well.

Revich had found his first rhyzolm.

A yell came from behind the tree and Byn stormed off. Rev dropped the stone and stood, his heart pounding as he searched for his mother.

"Don't lose it, Little Love." She came around the other side of the tree, noticing the rhyzolm and cleaning it on her skirts. She held it out for Rev to take and he did, his hand shaking slightly as she bent down to meet his eyes. "This one is yours. Our little secret." She winked and smiled to the side. The expression was so familiar, my heart broke watching the woman who gave him life and loved him so deeply.

I wanted to know her. I wanted to spend more time here, learning about her life, learning about what kind of woman she was.

But I'd never get to.

She was dead and this was just a memory.

Revich pocketed the stone, saying, "What were you arguing about?"

She rose to her full height and sighed. "This tree. Your father insists there's something big here." She paused, her eyes following the trunk all the way to the dark leaves at the top. "If we did find a large piece, the warden would be off our back, and we could rest the next few days."

"Let's keep looking then. I can go under, too. I'm old enough now," he insisted, his voice a show of confidence.

She chuckled and tapped his nose. "Someday, Rev, but not yet. We need you holding the light to lead us back out when it gets too dark."

He nodded and picked up his father's shovel.

The looming conclusion to this day slid down my spine, solid enough to make Rev's body shiver.

I knew what day this was.

This was the day Revich lost both of his parents.

"Just there, see that one? Wedge it right between, and I'll push down this way." Byn led Heirah as they continued to pry roots from the expanse of silt under this damning tree.

Rev watched, often shoving his hand in his pocket to squeeze his rhyzolm, curious at how it tried to lead him back to the village.

I would have been chewing my lip if I'd had my own to chew.

I needed to save his parents.

Well, I needed to save his mother at least.

Should I feign an injury and lead them back home?

Should I reveal the rhyzolm he'd found and his father would be satisfied enough to leave?

Should I injure Byn himself? Surely that would be satisfying as well as productive.

The problem was, none of those courses of action had to do with being a Baron.

I had learned in my studies and from watching Revich—even Heimlen—that the Baronship was about power. It was about precise training, searching for those who held powerful magic and helping them become more useful on the isle.

A Baron was a guide, a pathway, taking something unshapen that held potential, and molding it into something great.

The squelch of mud was sickening as two of the roots separated from the ground they'd grown into, leaving a dark, open space underneath the tree. There was a similar opening at the other end so that his parents could crawl through the entirety of it while they searched for rhyzolm.

Byn and Heirah pushed their wedges deeper into the mud, securing the opening as Rev brought the lantern closer.

His father went first, grabbing his spade, crawling underneath the root as it dripped its layer of silt. "I'll search to the left, you to the right."

His mother bent as well, ducking her head to follow.

"Don't go," I whispered through Rev.

She grinned back at me murmuring, "I'll see you on the other side."

Fuck.

Her last words to Rev, my last words to him as well before I entered the trials, churned my stomach. I wanted to grab her skirts and pull her away from what I was convinced were her final moments.

Rev was never going to see her again.

This is where she'd die, buried underneath a marsh tree, searching for the very stone that he was so adept at using.

I didn't need to panic, I needed to save her.

I needed to save Rev from this memory.

Rev stayed bent, his lantern lit, guiding his parents to their deaths.

I saw the slip of the spade. I saw the way it slid ever so slightly to the left, beginning to fall away from the root it was tucked under.

I took control of Rev's body once again, his hands shooting out to catch it, pushing it back down.

A Baron was a shaper, someone who could see the potential, the power in others.

I searched for that piece in this little boy.

I found it, hidden in what I could only call a cavern, a damp, dark place in his mind, and I burst the cavern door open.

Pulling from what I knew he would become, I gathered his power from Felgren and it shot forth from his hands in a blazing blue light, trailing underneath the tree, lighting the way and holding the roots above his parents as the wedge holding the entrance finally snapped in two.

In Revich's memory, this had been the end.

This had been the moment he lost the woman who loved him, but I could save him from that.

His power held strong as his mother screamed at the sound of the break, the marsh tree groaning, swaying slightly while his parents rushed to the opening on the other side.

She emerged and rushed to him, squeezing his little body tightly and crying, her tears streaked with mud. Byn followed, catching his breath on his knees, eyeing his son with an awe I doubted Revich had ever seen.

"You are so powerful, Little Love. You saved us. You saved us from a sure death." She hugged him to her chest again, her hands sliding over his hair.

I watched the scene as I was pulled from Revich's little body, a brilliant flickering portal nearby, waiting for me to leave.

I stood there, taking one last look at the woman who gave him so many of his features, his mannerisms, and what I now knew was his heart.

I loved her.

I murmured a promise that I would take care of him and give him everything we both knew he deserved.

Filling my lungs one last time in her presence, I stepped into the portal that would take me to her son.

CHAPTER 78

KARUS

Green grass lay brilliantly through a grove as I stepped out of the portal. The dry seeds of the maple trees spun lazily to the ground in an elegant twirl.

A man leaned against the trunk of a tree, his arms crossed at his chest, his attire in the form of a Baron, but different than Revich's, a slightly more jaunty cut, the collar of his shirt flicked open at his tanned neck.

I circled around, looking for Revich, who, once again, was not there. My face fell into my hands, and I was ready to scream.

"I do not wish to cause you distress. I only wished to see you here, before you do or do not accept Revich's offer," the man spoke to me, but I didn't want to hear any more.

I wanted to go home to Revich.

The silence stayed as the light flutter of maple seeds cascaded down on my head, still buried in my hands.

I finally rose from them, masking my face in strength with a deep inhale of my lungs, pulling from some place where my sanity still held firm.

He was tall, with a square jaw, hazel, deep-set eyes, and a piercing stare. A shadow of a mustache grew above his lip. His hair was a dark brown, cut short, but longer on the top, one piece curving over his widow's peak and curling onto his forehead.

I lifted my hands, gesturing to my body. My channeler clothing was filthy, covered in soil, blood staining the space of my knee, the hem wet and layered in a dark film.

He raised a brow, and I shrugged.

"Do you know who I am?" He kept his arms folded and pushed off the maple tree, walking my way.

"Of course, I do. How could you be anyone but him?"

"Who?"

"Adaynth. First Baron of Felgren, First Trainer of Conduits, Lover of Visalia, Betrayer of Visalia, and apparent Person Who Should Be Long Since *Dead*, but isn't, and is standing in my way of getting home to the man I love."

He smirked, his eyes brightening. "You seem to know much about me, Karus of Hyrithia. Karus of Felgren? Or was it Karus of the Northern Steppes? I'm not entirely sure."

The maple tree he had been leaning against burst into flame. The crackle of wood lighting on fire echoed through the grove.

He turned slowly and shook his head. "You're good at that, aren't you? Growing trees,"—he pointed to the maple seeds falling —"setting them on fire."

I took the flames back. My rapid exposure of wrath extinguishing with the smoke that rose from the damage I had done. "What do you want with me?"

"Truthfully? Nothing. In fact, I'd prefer you weren't here at all."

"Then why *am* I here?"

"Unfortunately, you passed the Baron trial and now will have the choice to take exactly half of Baron Revich's power for your own." He paused, slowing, but stepping closer until we were a mere three feet apart. "I hoped to convince you to decline."

I scoffed, folding my own arms across my chest. "Why? Because I am a woman?"

"No,"—he shook his head, closing our gap—"because you are *hers*."

I swallowed. "I am not."

"You do not face it well, but it does not make it less true. I see in you the same power that once brought Felgren to its knees, breaking it almost beyond repair before I could heal it."

"Was that before or after you killed your child?"

He stilled. His eyes darkened, and his irises filled with black. "Is that what she told you? That I killed our child?"

"It is what she believes."

He nodded once, his gaze flickering above me, following another maple seed falling. "Revich is calling to you, and I do not have much time. If you take this power, you are taking more of her into you. She gave you the power you wield, and yes, Karus, you would have been a channeler regardless, but she gave you that." He pointed to the charred tree. "She gave you that darkness, that rage that burns under the surface, and if you accept this piece of her as well…" He shook his head. "I don't know how you could not be more hers."

"I'm not—"

"You will become *her*, Karus. She seeks to replace the child we lost. She will not give up on that pursuit. Everything she does is in that one desire."

I began to fade, my breath catching in my lungs, my eyes closed even though I could see him, mournful before me.

"Remember that, Karus. Never forget what she wants most."

My eyes flashed open, catching on the eyes of my love, a deep blue, brimmed in dark night, his hair falling into his face as he held my head in his hands. The moon rose high above us, almost a full, brilliant silver circle.

"*Karus*. Karus!" Rev shook me and I blinked, then filled my lungs completely with Felgren.

"Dammit, Karus, say something!"

I grinned. "That was five trials, not four."

"Fucking dam—"

I didn't get to hear the rest of his curse as he slammed his mouth to mine, pulling me up, pulling me to him, breathing all of me in.

I scrambled into his lap, wrapping my arms around his neck and my fingers through his hair.

I ignored the tugging on my mind as his hands pressed to my back. The insistent pull was no more in this moment than an irritant to be set aside until we were done.

I didn't need to breathe. I didn't need food, or water, or sleep.

I needed him. I needed this sustenance more than—

"Do you accept, Karus of the Blightress, the power of the Baron of Felgren?"

The question was more of a scream than a breezy whisper, but I recognized Adaynth's voice. I broke from our reuniting to cover my ears, pressing my head into Rev's chest.

"It will only get worse the longer you wait to reply," he whispered, pulling on my chin to meet his gaze. He shook his head. "It is your question to answer. I will love you and care for you either way, but I wanted to give you the choice. I wanted you to see that you are more than capable of wielding this power. I will give it to you. I will share it with you. This is your path to choose. I come with you regardless."

His eyes were so much like his mother's. So brilliant and loving.

"I saved her. I saved her for you."

"Ah, Karus," he said, kissing each of the hallows of my eyes, "that is the lesson of the Baron trial. You return to the current Baron's most painful day outside of Felgren and you save them from that sorrow. But here, after the trial, you are reminded that time is not ours to change, even as a Baron."

My lips trembled, and I held off another yank at my chest.

He pressed his forehead to mine. "Thank you. Thank you for saving her in there." He paused, a small grin crossing his face. "She was beautiful, wasn't she?"

I nodded, muttering, "Yes."

"DO YOU ACCEPT, KARUS OF—"

"I accept on one condition." I addressed the force, staring into the bluest eyes I had ever seen.

I smiled as tears fell down my cheeks. I traced his with my fingers, cupping his face. "I wish to be able to save this man from any more pain. Somehow, some way, I wish to be able to keep him happy, and safe, and loved."

The earth stilled. I swore time truly did stop for just a moment. One small moment, before we both heard the last three words on the wind. "*I will try.*"

The rush of power was great.

Revich's shoulders dropped. He leaned into me at the same time I felt I could move the stars, which shone brightly in the sky.

His breathing was heavy and mine was expansive, spreading over every treetop, every inch of the space between, through their core, down into the earth, through even the smallest droplet of water as it fell from the tip of a leaf thousands of acres away from where we sat on the ground below my first charred maple tree.

"Rev..." I breathed, the fulfillment of power through me too great in that moment.

"I know."

"I can..."

"I know."

I pressed my hands into his chest. "Are you alright?"

He nodded, looking back up at me. "I feel like I've been split in two, but otherwise fine."

My new power begged to be used, begged to be wielded in the forest which synchronized with my every sense of being.

"It needs a release," he continued. "Something to pull you back down from its force." He kissed my neck lightly, moving up to the base of my jaw.

"How did you release it before?" I rasped, knowing he was right. I couldn't keep it here like this inside of me.

"Tears. I kneeled on the steps of the Fortress and wept."

I closed my eyes and melted into the brush of his thumb across the bottom of my lip, the stroke of his fingers as they slid across my shoulder in a light graze. I sighed, falling onto his mouth, tugging on his lower lip, mumbling, "Let me find a different release, Rev. Let me find it with you."

I burned. I flew. I saw the entirety of the isle, spread over miles and miles of forest, and marsh, and plains, and mountain.

I held onto him with every ounce of strength I had left, for if I should let go for even one single moment, I would disperse into the wind, forever riding upon it, forever holding no place to land.

His mouth, his hands, the hard length of him inside me kept me grounded, a place in time I could stay and accept all of what I had now become.

The Blightress's given power and the power of the Baron of Felgren fused and mixed. As I slid my body over Rev's, each of these parts of me warred and loved, raged and embraced, like two lovers reuniting, forgetting all that had been said and done in what was the past they'd rather forget.

He wrapped an arm around my waist as I felt I could float into the night. He slid his other to the nape of my neck, convincing me to stay with him, keeping me from spreading into the sky as something entirely new, something entirely different than the woman I was.

My power sought more than release. It sought chaos and precision.

The earth underneath our merged bodies rumbled and my hips responded in ravenous pursuit of the one finality over my lover's body that could ground me, keep me solidified.

He watched my face with love and awe, vigilance and pride.

And as my eyes filled from emerald green to the abyssal black, I knew.

His face was pain, remorse, as if he knew that by my accepting what he offered, he'd lose a little part of me in return.

But I had made a condition. I'd have the power to make him happy, make him whole.

I slammed onto him again, taking it all, closing my eyes and shoving aside all the dark, all the black, my eyes flicking open once more to watch his face as they refilled with brilliant green.

He grinned and I kissed that grin, the roots of the charred maple tree coming to the surface to wind over the earth in a knotted headboard and four sturdy legs.

I grew the grass, I released my power to form a soft mossy pillow under his head. Our bed of the forest held us up off the cold ground, our bodies bare, our bond seeping over our hands, clasped in remembrance of the day we'd bound ourselves together until the day we no longer breathed.

His blue, my green, were there again in an enchanting symphony of power.

His magic roamed, a caress over my hips, pushing down on his, a brush of pleasure over my breasts and up my neck, reaching my mouth to touch my bottom lip.

I needed to come back down. I needed to expel some of this power as it built inside of me before I was lifted from his body into an expanse of time where he could not follow.

"Stay here," he whispered, bringing himself back up to catch me. "Stay here, with me."

His mouth met mine, another anchor to keep me from drifting, his hands winding around me once more.

"I...I'm trying." I saw the grove, the maple trees that spun from the earth around us in the same pattern of the place I had been before. Their seedlings fell, drifting in a dance to the ground, the tree I had burned years ago taking the same place as the one I had charred just minutes ago in another Baron's presence.

I knew this place. I *built* this place, and I wondered for a moment if I had somehow gone back to it. Not in space, but in time, the first Baron the only thing missing from where I had been.

"You will stay." He held me still and turned, laying me down on our bed of grass and roots and moss, one hand holding my leg to his waist, the other gripping mine above my head. "I need you to stay. Do not go where I cannot follow."

The twirling seeds fell into his hair, over our bodies, as he held me to the earth, using everything he had to keep me here with him.

His body was my salvation, my only hope at surviving this transfer of power whole and mortal, and as he slammed into me again and again, I cried out, my body solidifying, my power blooming into a maple tree in my mind, its roots strong, its trunk a solid char of black, leaves a verdant green.

I found my end in his arms, my peak in his mouth on mine, my essential release underneath his hard, warm body, which met with my own in the same moment and place of grounding ecstasy.

CHAPTER 79
REV

Five weeks.

It took five weeks for her to ground herself as Karus and as Baron.

During that time, she settled, slipping into her immense power slowly, each day another sure foot into control.

There were days I was sure she was gone. Not in memories like before, but in spirit as I held her body close in sleep, bringing her consciousness back to me from wherever it had gone. I'd tug on that bond between us and she'd float back down to me.

She broke our bed. Twice.

The fireplace mantle once and Lia's favorite slab of granite.

She used her new combined power in menial tasks as practice, often finding it too much, letting too much of herself into what she tried to accomplish.

When I held the rhyzolm, her power no longer hummed, it fucking *roared*, drowning out any other power in the vicinity.

I could no longer check to see if Philius's power was growing with his training. No longer could I tell if Ilyenna's power was drained by her growing child.

I only heard her. Only felt *her* when I held it.

When Clairannia and Figuerah arrived with Figuerah's companion, Nyeimah, the Fortress felt full and light. Laughter around every corner, the three friends reunited as I remembered them before, inviting Nyeimah and Moira to join them on their daily lumen rides and tours of Viridis.

During those weeks, I mostly saw Karus in the evenings, both of us adjusting to our power as we kept to our duties. She took over training Philius and Mychael, doing what she could to catch them up to the same level of Talon, Ilyenna, Rell, and Renn.

My power had been halved, just like my soul the day Karus had joined it. I felt it there inside of the woman I'd grow old with, like a physical piece of me I'd given over to her.

She bloomed and beamed, a radiant sun, as we spent our weeks busy, productive, working together for the goal we both shared.

This would work.

And it would work well.

Two Barons, building a course of life in Felgren to train even more channelers at once and bring more magic to benefit people's lives.

We were to leave by portal in one week for the north, stopping to spend time with Geyrand and Vivianna's family before heading to the Attatok Mountains to meet the channelers Madame Zoreyah had chosen. We'd give them their Offerings, then head to the Spire to do the same before coming back to Hyrithia to meet again with the Queen. There, we'd form a solid plan in our expedition to the Blightress's heart.

Karus hadn't heard from the Blightress since the transfer of power, and though she told me everything that had happened in the trials, I still waited for her to show when we least expected it. So I kept my guard up at all times, practicing my portal magic so that I could create two at once if I needed to get Karus out of her reach quickly. She'd never leave if there was danger and I could only produce one.

"When do I get to learn portal magic?" she asked, her bare feet propped up on our massive wood desk in our study, dropping her quill in her Baron journal and rubbing her eyes.

I glanced to her beside me, two black chairs shoved together on one side of the desk before the enormous window that led to Felgren. "When you can make the bed without splitting the footboard."

She pushed my arm in laughter, and then pulled me back toward her, reaching for a kiss.

I obliged as I always did and shut my own book, the task of writing the day's training suddenly seeming unimportant and droll when her mouth opened on mine, pulling me in deep.

"You know, Karus," I mumbled over her lips as she searched my pockets for our styris tea flask, "I used to be a much more productive Baron in this study."

She took a long swig and handed it to me, a wicked, fiercely beautiful smirk on her red lips as she hopped up on our desk, leaning back and swinging her legs. "Productivity has many forms, Baron Revich."

"Mmm." I stood and slid my hands up her legs, splitting them apart and bundling her skirts at her waist. I leaned toward her, between her legs, both of my hands on either side of her hips.

I'd imagined this exact moment so many times in the past, a burn that snaked underneath my skin, painful and damning, and here she was, her black eyes filling green, her crimson lips parting in her anticipation of my touch.

"You dropped this," she revealed, slipping the rhyzolm into my front pocket. I didn't even need to touch it for it to thrum. Every day its pull to Karus and her power grew stronger, and this day was no different as it buzzed softly against my ribs.

I watched her, waiting, her smirk growing into a joyous smile as she tilted her head back and laughed. "Well, Baron Revich? Aren't you going to kiss me?"

"Eventually."

She shrugged, her fingers toying with the buttons of my vest. "Then I'll wait, my love." She caught my stare, her face softening and she inhaled deeply, pushing herself into me. "I'll wait for you forever."

As it was and always would be, I knew I'd do the same.

CHAPTER 80
KARUS

"Do you think that when we die, somehow, some part of us will remain here?"

Figuerah's eyes met mine before we burst into a laugh matched in joy and mirth.

"Clairannia, where did that come from?" I chortled, weaving her crown of golden blooms in the same field of yellow we'd met in many times before.

I pulled another flower, lying on my stomach, elbows dug into the dirt. Figuerah already wore her crown, the light petals complimenting her dark skin and honey eyes.

"I just want there to be something, you know?" Clairannia turned her head to me, lying on her back, staring up at the brilliant blue sky. "Something of us like this that stays here forever, taking up space if our bodies no longer can."

"Goodness, girl, it's nine in the morning. Save the heavy talk for afternoon tea at least."

Clairannia threw some of my stock of long-stemmed flowers at Figuerah who laughed, pulling them off her chest.

"Hey!" I shouted. "I need those!"

She giggled, helping me pick them up, setting the flowers back into my pile.

"I know what you mean." I sighed, weaving another one through the stem of the chain I'd made. "I don't come here when you two aren't here. It's not right. It always feels off, like I don't belong in this space without you both."

Figuerah smiled down at me, leaning on her hand. "Let's do it then. Let's promise that when we die, many, many years from now, we send a part of ourselves here. We bask in the sun, lie in the fields, and our color will be yellow."

"Our sky will be clear." Clairannia sat up, her brown eyes agleam, her black hair sliding over her cheeks.

I rose as well, placing the completed golden flower crown on her head. "Our sun will be bright. Our love will live on together. Right here. Promise?"

I put my hand forward and they put their hands over my open palm.

"Promise," Figuerah said.

"Promise," Clairannia returned. "Now, about the party food…"

We'd spent more days than I could count since Clairannia and Figuerah's arrival planning this party. I was exhausted, falling into bed each night from full days of training, balancing my own power, and taking the few hours after dinner to help Clairannia plan every tiny detail for the celebration.

We were celebrating so many things—companion bonds, Ilyenna and Talon's growing baby, my own part in the Baronship—I was glad there would only be one grand night and Revich and I could leave immediately after to spend quiet time in the north visiting Geyrand and his family.

Revich promised an empty cottage was waiting for us near their home, providing us with a few days to just…be.

"When you say these Hyrithian's are missing,"—a yawn interrupted my question—"do you mean missing-missing, or missing, likely traveling and haven't been seen yet?"

Clairannia, Figuerah, Nyeimah, Moira, and I were sitting at the dining hall table, now unrecognizable as such with banners and ribbons, floral bouquets, and strings of magically woven lights littering its long surface.

"So far, missing-missing. The whole group of them just up and left." Figuerah was forcing a particularly stubborn red rose into a vase already full of the blooms. "The Queen has sent a command-ment of soldiers to search for them."

"And you say they all had survived,"—my next words came out mid-yawn—"the Black Fever?"

Moira piqued her head to the side, her violet eyes narrowing toward me as she licked her hand and then stuck another peony petal onto the lighted ribbon.

"Karus, we can finish up here," Nyeimah urged, her hazel eyes warm against her olive skin and resting on my tired face. She fit Figuerah so well. I smiled just in the knowledge that she'd waited for her all five years that Figuerah had been gone from their village.

"She's right. You're useless anyway." Figuerah jabbed another rose into the vase, eyeing my sparse one, the bundle of cream blooms still lying on the table.

I nodded, rising, so tired I didn't even want to walk back to bed. I'd happily lay my head down here and rest, just listening to my friends talk about the celebration tomorrow evening.

"I'll take you, Karus." Moira rose and stretched, fluttering to my face. "You don't look so good."

"Give her a break, Moira. She does too much. And then I come here and demand this extravagant party while she's still slipping into her new powers." Clairannia tsked her tongue. "Really, we can finish this tonight, go rest."

"I don't mean tired." Moira leaned in close, studying my black eyes. "I mean something's not quite right. You look…more."

I quirked a brow. "More?"

"More. Like *more* than you've ever looked."

"Moira," I said, rubbing my eyes, "please just make sure I make it to bed."

She scrunched her face and shrugged, pulling on my hand to follow her out of the dining hall.

When we reached my door, I told her goodnight, getting her promise she'd show up on time and dressed for the celebration tomorrow night.

I slipped into the room, finding Revich on his chair, whittling at something over a basket of wood shavings.

"I'm too tired to ask," I muttered as I fell into our bed, kicking off my shoes and burying my head into my pillow.

He followed me, also not bothering to undress, pulling my back to his chest, wrapping his arms around me and kissing my shoulder.

"Do you want me to help you into your nightgown?"

"No, I want to sleep."

He chuckled, snuggling his head to the back of my neck. "Alright, my love. Sleep."

CHAPTER 81

SAELYN

The risk feels worth it to me.

I was seventeen and empty.

The risk feels worth it to me.

I was seventeen and constantly on the verge of tears, my mother and Pah-Pah helping me into my dress, my dark locks woven into a thick band of intricate braids across the top of my head, half of my waves falling down my back in contrast to my pale skin.

The risk feels worth it to me.

I was seventeen at my own party, the lanterns aglow in a warm, muted heat, the colorful banners draped across the trees, somehow dull and out of place now that my chest ached and my throat weighed heavy with the fear that I had ruined everything.

That by refusing the risk he felt was worth it, refusing to hear any more of Thevin's sweet words which rang in my ears since he had spoken them in my room, I had broken us. I had set us unknowingly on a new path where we could not return to where we had been.

I had begged for things not to change.

Pah-Pah was wrong. I had taken no risk, but Thevin did. Even by standing still, things had changed and I could not return to the place where we had been the best of friends. Only friends.

I sipped a goblet of red wine handed to me by Pah-Pah with the most remorseful smile I'd ever seen on his sun-kissed face. He'd done his kohl in a dark blue, he'd said in honor of the shade of my eyes.

He nudged me, holding out a golden plate of miniature cinnamon buns, each dabbed with white icing. "Will you talk to him tonight?"

I shook my head at the plate, my stomach writhing anyway, let alone with eating the sweetest food here. "He doesn't want to talk to me."

"Oh?" He set the plate down, chewing one of the sweets. "If that's so, why has he been staring at you since he got here?"

I looked up, my gaze knowing exactly where he was, as if my heart had tracked his every move since he'd arrived at the party sixty-seven minutes ago.

He leaned against one of the trees in the clearing, party guests passing by, his eyes locked on me, regardless of who moved in front of him.

My breath stilled. My heart raged.

The risk feels worth it to me.

I was seventeen and ready to feel. Ready to love, ready to know what it meant to be wanted, to be touched. I was seventeen, and I didn't want to fear the future changed, knowing the past had slipped me by, my best days there in those moments where I had spent them with *him*.

I was seventeen, and I was ready to take a risk.

I set my goblet down and rose, my dress of cerulean velvet over cream silk slipping over my feet in a delicate ensemble that was chosen for me to wear, not something I would have picked myself.

Thevin uncrossed his arms, pushing off the tree, his movement in my direction matching my own in his, passing through the sea of people, some of them dancing to the music that lifted through the night air, eating, drinking, and laughing.

He'd told me he was falling, confessed what my smile did to him as if his own had not had a mark on my heart since I was ten years old, having no name for what I felt, only wanting him around forever.

He'd wanted to risk what we had—the friendship, the laughter, the bickering at the stupidest, smallest little things just to have something witty to say, to jolt both of our hearts in our chests.

We were young. We were new. We knew little of love or life or what it meant to really take risks at all, but as our bodies closed in, mere inches apart in the crowd, I understood what Pah-Pah had said.

This was the risk worth taking. This was the change that could ruin or save me. This was the path I wanted to choose. The one Thevin had laid out before me as the one he wanted to take, hand-in-hand, heart-in-heart.

He offered his hand, and I took it, wordlessly slipping into a dance, moving across the grass with the other couples to the same endearing tune.

The light blue eyes of the friend I loved stared into mine as we swayed, the music shifting soft and light on the warm breeze that filtered through the trees of Felgren.

"I'm sorry," I spoke, breaking the silence between us.

"No, Sae, I'm sorry. Your words were clear and precise, and I once again did not give them the credit they deserved." He took his eyes from me and glanced around. "It's a beautiful party. I think your mother invited everyone she's ever known." He smirked with a chuckle I knew he did not feel.

I swallowed, choosing my words with care. "I've thought about what you said."

"Don't. Just forget it. We're best friends. We always have been, and we always will be."

"I don't want to forget it."

We stopped in the middle of the dancers. He let go of my hand, my waist, and took a step back, shaking his head. "Don't, Sae. You don't need to feel like you have something to prove here. You don't need to find some way to make me happy. I am happy. I'm happy being here every summer with you. There's nothing more you need to do."

"Thevin, I—"

"It's okay," he interrupted, his voice breaking. "You're still my favorite person." He shrugged, sniffing slightly. "I'll continue to irritate you, and you'll continue to tell me where to go. Nothing changes, just like you said."

He moved forward, pulling me close, his chin resting on my head pressed to his chest.

I should have reversed time. I should have gone back, and my first words at us meeting on the dance floor would be, "Thevin, I love you. I have loved you all my life, and I want to risk all of what we've shared if it means I get to be with you."

But I didn't.

And then I couldn't.

Too much time had passed as he hugged me to his chest, and I pressed my cheek against what was solid, and warm, and home.

"Sae?" Pah-Pah tapped my shoulder. "I'm sorry to interrupt, but your mother is calling for you."

I broke from where I wanted to stay and nodded.

Thevin gave me a small grin, brushing a thumb on my cheek. "Meet me at the meat pies when you're done?"

I drew breath to speak, but Pah-Pah interrupted.

"I am sorry, dearest, but she is insistent."

His face was pained as if he could hear the words she spoke to him in command, loud as thunder across the darkening sky.

I looked up to the clouds billowing in, knowing the guests would soon be drenched by a summer rain.

My eyes locked back on Thevin.

"Go, Sae. I'll see you after at our fort in the grove." He leaned forward and whispered, "I'll grab a bottle of wine if you can manage the cheese."

There he was, as he always had been.

The same Thevin with his taunting mischief written across his face, no sign of his confessions to me the day before.

I lied with a grin, nodding and following Pah-Pah, wondering how my seventeenth birthday had gone so terribly wrong as my name lifted through the rumble of the incoming storm, traveling along the wind.

CHAPTER 82

KARUS

It really was a beautiful party.

The silk banners were strung across the trees in shades of red, gold, green, and blue. I knew Clairannia had chosen them all to represent each of the people she loved most here in Felgren, and I knew she'd never admit it.

The celebration was small, just for those of us who resided in the forest with the addition of Clairannia, Figuerah, and Nyeimah.

Pompeii and Mychael laughed together, dancing to music that played from a spell Clairannia had learned in the Spire.

Moira had shown up on time and had been dressed in a gown of crimson petals, newly green maple leaves fluttering at her waist every time she flew.

Ilyenna was finally able to keep food down and finally showing some growth, her pale cheeks now continually rosy with the glow of motherhood.

Revich pulled me around the dance floor, and I hung on for dear life as both of us had no talent for dancing, though I whispered in his ear how much talent our bodies had for other things.

"Are you trying to get me to throw you over my shoulder and leave this party?" He pushed my long, white-streaked hair behind my ear, leaning down to whisper there, "You look at me like that one more time and it's done."

I laughed, twirling around so he could catch me again. "Like what? This is just how I look."

His eyes glistened and his lips curled to one side as I lived for. "That's the problem, Karus. I'm always wanting to throw you over my shoulder."

I fell into his chest, stifling my chortles into him, my body shaking in laughter.

"It's about time to go anyway." He kissed my forehead. "Say goodbye and I'll work on the portals."

He left and I sighed.

The few weeks we'd had didn't feel like enough.

I wanted more of my friends, more laughter, more sneaking away for the thirty minutes I could spare to the field of yellow blossoms.

"Do not cry, Karus, I cannot keep myself together if you do." Clairannia already had a tear rolling down her round cheeks, her hands in mine as her lips trembled.

"It's the best party I've ever been to. You make everything you touch more beautiful than it could have been without you." I pulled her in, kissing her thick black hair. I squeezed her so tightly, I tried to hold that moment in time and keep it with me.

Figuerah's arms wrapped around us both as she rested her head of thick braids on mine. "We love you, we miss you, we'll see you in the Attatock Mountains in a few weeks."

I nodded, pulling away and wiping my tears, blowing them a kiss as I backed away to where two similar-sized portals glowed at the edge of the celebration clearing.

Revich was addressing the channelers, hugging each one, taking Philius's hand instead. We'd be gone for a few months, but to them, it would feel like only two weeks or so.

I waved goodbye and held out my hands to talk to Moira.

"I'll see you soon. No stealing bread, no forcing Lia to quit. We need her to keep making cinnamon buns because honestly, Moira, you aren't very good at it." I laughed as she narrowed her eyes.

"At least I didn't shatter Lia's favorite stone slab and *pretend* it slipped." She grabbed my face with her long green fingers. "Are you sure you should go, Karus?" She shook her head. "Something's not right. I don't know enough about humans and Baron magic to know exactly what."

"I'm fine, Moira. Revich and I have enough power between us to stay safe. We'll be back before you know it with more *humans* to train."

She grimaced, sticking out her tongue, and fluttered out of my hands.

I waved and headed over to Rev.

"Ready?" he asked, taking my hand and leading me to my portal. They'd both lead to Geyrand's farm, where they knew we'd arrive within the hour.

"Ready." I kissed him and let go, gathering my black skirts to step into the portal.

My head cracked against the hard, green surface, sending me sprawling to the ground in front of it.

"Karus!" Revich yelled, pulling me up. His fingers brushed my head and came away with a smear of red.

I rubbed my nose, following his hands to feel the gash at my brow. "That really hurt." I peered behind him. "That portal you made is defective."

"She's okay," he called out to the embarrassingly large number of people who had witnessed me falling on my backside.

He turned to the portal, refusing to let go of my hand, placing his over the surface. His palm fell through before he pulled it back out and cocked his head at me.

"That's strange." I stepped forward again, this time with more caution and placed my own hand at its surface. I pushed with no give, placing the other on the surface as well, all my weight going into the press of my palms against the solid shine of light.

"I don't understand. Try this one." Revich led me to his, and I pressed with the same result.

"Maybe something's wrong with my magic? But I've gone

through your portals before during the trials." I shook my head, biting my lip. "The power of the Baron and my other…"

I trailed off, the cold chill of realization coursing through me.

My heart hammered, pulsing in an ancient rhythm passed down through time, one it was my turn to feel.

Revich tried his portal, his hand falling through as he looked back to me in concern.

"Revich." I looked into his black eyes and muttered, "I know why the rhyzolm hums so loudly towards me now."

He shook his head, still not grasping what countless women before me had innately understood.

I beamed, taking his hand and pressing it to my belly. "It doesn't thrum for me, Rev." I laughed in disbelief and shook my head. "I carry two heartbeats and cannot enter your portals." The same understanding I had just felt dawned across his face, and I pressed my forehead to his, whispering, "The rhyzolm thrums for our child."

CHAPTER 83

SAELYN

I barely noticed how far we trekked up the long, winding staircase that I had loved to run up and down as a child. Pah-Pah led the way, passing all the alcoves, the portraits, including the one of my parents, both Barons, both very obviously in love when it was painted just months before my father's death.

I glanced as I always did at the portrait to meet his eyes, the same ocean blue as mine. His black, wavy hair was mine, his smile was mine. It had always been uncanny to me, looking at my own face in my father's features.

We reached the top, entering the first door on the right as my mother addressed Pah-Pah.

"Thank you, Pompeii. Please begin to pack. I will help Saelyn with her things. Inform Talon and Ilyenna, we leave in the morning. Sae will want to tell Thevin, I'm sure."

I watched Pah-Pah turn to leave me with my mother in the tallest tower, in the room she had told me she once occupied when she was first brought to Felgren, many years ago.

"Of course, Baron Karus." He glanced at my frown, then looked back to her. "Let me know if you need anything more."

My mother nodded without turning, knowing her Overseer left without needing to see him go.

She stood on the balcony that faced north, cut into the slanted wall of the room. She'd commissioned the balcony years ago, and it had become her usual place of dwelling, especially on moonless nights when she said she just wanted to see the stars.

I knew what she was really doing out here all those times. I knew my father had died in the northern forest and that she found comfort looking out over the spread of trees, seeing through the great shield of misty green power that protected us in Felgren.

Her stark white hair billowed in the storm's arrival, as rain drops began to pelt on the stone landing where she stood.

"Why does Pah-Pah pack? Where are we going?"

I reached her side, and she brushed a hand over my head as she still gazed north. She inhaled, filling her lungs fully before slowly exhaling and finally turning to face me.

Her eyes, typically black, filled with the most brilliant emerald green I'd ever seen, and I smiled in awe of her beauty. "I wish my father could have been here, Mama. I wish he had been here to celebrate with us tonight. I wish he had not died, and I wish…" My voice trailed as I imagined what it would have been like to have a father to run to on this night, my heart broken by the friend I loved.

She grinned and leaned toward me. I caught her scent on the wind. Earth, pine, lavender. Her hand tucked my black wayward hair behind my ear.

"Saelyn, my Little Love, your father *lives*." She lifted my chin as I frowned. "And our time has come to save him."

A BLIGHTRESS OF WRATH

THE CONCLUSION TO A CONDUIT OF LIGHT SERIES

Join my newsletter and social media to keep up-to-date with news and new releases!

Please consider leaving a review on Goodreads or other reviewing sites for A Baron of Bonds. Reviews help new readers find my books. Thank you, dears!

CONTENT WARNINGS
SEE AUTHOR'S NOTE

A Baron of Bonds contains the following details and themes:

Consenting sex between adults, alcoholism, birth control, pregnancy, pregnancy loss, loss of child, spousal abuse, sexual assault implication between two adults, the physical abuse of a child, potential drowning, and surgery.

ACKNOWLEDGMENTS

I love this story.

My hope is that you, dear reader, love it, too, but regardless, thank you so much for taking the time to read it. I've met some of the most amazing people through this series, and I hope you'll stay with me through every one of my releases. Thank you.

My twin sisters-in-law and mother-in-law came along with me again in those very first stages of this book coming together. They made it through the mystery, extremely long sentences, and spicy scenes with grace and insightful comments that helped shape this story into what it has become.

My dreamer friends, who I am blessed to have met after A Conduit of Light's release, have been so encouraging and helpful in understanding a reader's outlook on certain characters and events in this book. Thank you, Elaina, for loving the Blightress. Thank you, Rachel, for loving Rev.

Thank you to my friends for encouraging my writing and being so proud of what I've accomplished so far.

Thank you to my parents for buying me an endless supply of clean, historical romance books when I was a teenager. Those stories helped shape me as an author today, and thank you especially to my mom for selling A Conduit of Light in her shop and convincing people all over her little town to read her daughter's first book.

I'm so thankful for my two children who encourage me so sweetly in my writing and get so excited, that they sit down to write their own books. I hope I can continue to be an inspiration to you both as you watch me work hard and fight for my dreams. I hope you do, too.

It takes a special kind of person and love to have the patience my husband, Reed, has in watching and encouraging this budding writing career of mine. He has always been a fantastic father and that has never been more clear to me in writing this book. He takes our kids to parks, shopping malls, indoor bouncy houses—any place where they can move and play while I sit at my desk, hunched over too far, completely entranced in this world I created. He tucks them in eight nights in a row to ensure I get ARCs out on time, he makes a lot of their food, and he kicks them out of our room when they wander in to steal sticky notes from my desk. I'm not saying this is unexpected from a partner, but I am saying, I know I have an amazing one.

About the Author

Chelsey Ann Tompkins was born a storyteller, specializing in tales of love and soulful romance. Her adolescence was spent reading countless historical romance novels, along with the classics by Jane Austen. However, *Jane Eyre* will always remain her favorite. When she is not dreaming up heartbreaking romance stories, you can find her brewing yet another vanilla latte, taking her kids to the park, quilting, or indulging in the blissful silence a bubble bath provides. She resides near Seattle with her husband and two children.